Retribution
Book V

04/16/18

Follow us on

Facebook:
www.facebook.com/SuperiWorld

Twitter:
@Superi2015

www.superiworld.com

To order additional copies of this book, contact:
Superi LLC.
www.superillc.com

Superi

RETRIBUTION

Book V

CLINT THURMON;
CHRISTINA R. WILLIAMS

Chapters

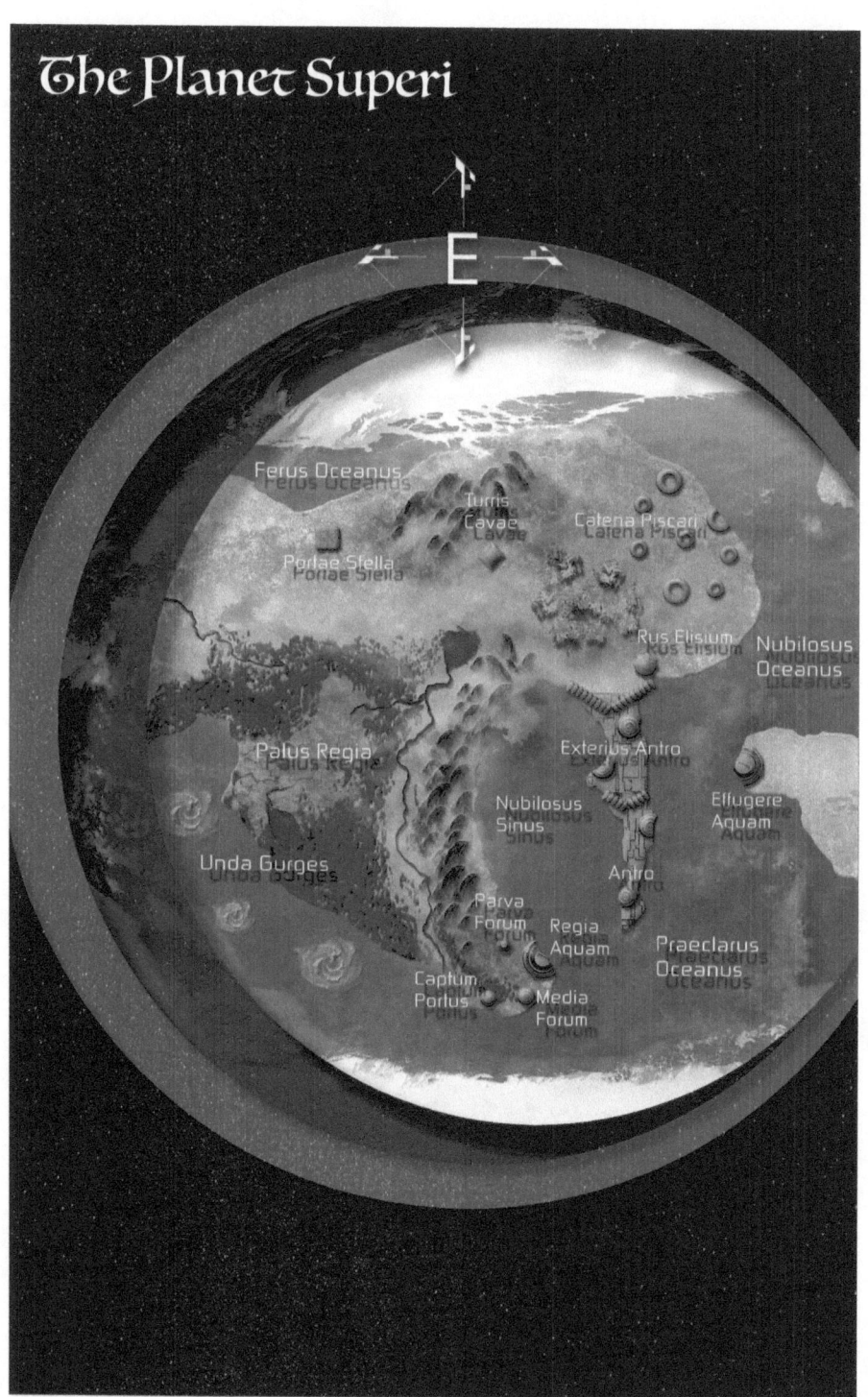

The Planet Superi

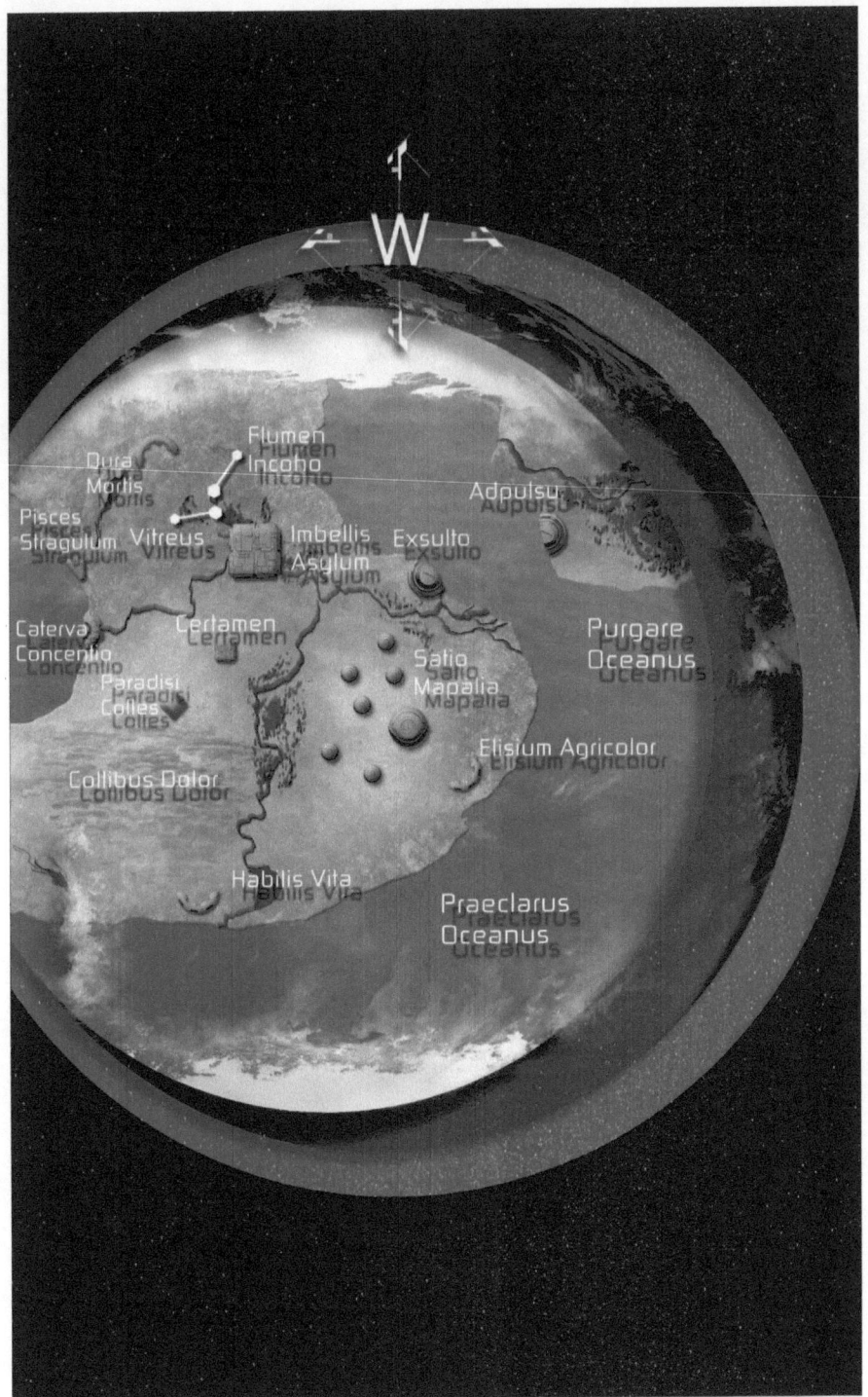

Reference/Dictionary

Tristan Matthewson..........(Tris-tan Matthew-son)

Anliac Aquam ....(An-li-ac A-quam)

Shashara Jacobs ....(Sha-sha-ra Jacobs)

Davad Jacobson ....(Da-vad Jacob-son)

Montilis Aquam ....(Monti-lis Aquam)

Triton..(Tri-ton)

Razoran ....(Ra-zor-an)

Socmoon ....(Soc-moon)

Inabeth Aquam ....(In-a-beth Aquam)

Superi ....(Sup-ery)

Imbellis Asylum ....(Im-bell-is Asi-lum)

Pisces Stragulum.................(Pi-sces Strag-u-lum)

Exterius Antro ....(Exter-ius Ant-ro)

Catena Piscari...........................(Cat-ena Pis-cary)

Caterva Concentio........... (Cat-er-va Con-cen-tio)

Certamen ....(Cert-a-men)

Exsulto Adpulsu .... (Ex-sulto Ad-pulsu)

Vitreus..................................(Vi-tre-us)

Antro ....(Ant-ro)

Paradisi Colles ....(Para-di-sy Col-les)

Palus Regia...................................(Pa-lus Re-gia)

I

Dance Partners

Thump, thump…Thump, thump…

"Ahh," Anliac groaned.

Cracking her eye lids, she slammed them closed again when the glaring light of the twin red suns sent shards of pain lancing through her skull. She turned her head, and her cheek landed against something solid and warm. Her breath quickened.

Thump, thump…Thump, thump…

She felt weightless, but she wasn't falling. There was no rushing of wind or sense of gravity's pull. There was only that heartbeat. The one that was not her own. Unable to find her voice, she opened her eyes again.

Cradled in Tristan's arms, the image of him was like a healer's touch to the mortally wounded. He was beautiful. His skin was like white marble, chiseled to physical perfection, gilded in gold and streaked with red.

"Welcome back, my love," he whispered. Her own heart

1

stuttered when his full lips turned up in a smile. "You had me worried."

While his words made little sense, the flare of his yellow eyes revealed the depth of his concern. Content to be held, she lifted a weak arm and traced her fingertips along the hard of edge of his jaw. Sliding her hand to the back of his neck, she said with a lopsided grin, "I miss your hair."

He chuckled once and then said, "Take her and keep her safe."

Her weight shifted as she was handed off to another, and the semi-conscious veil protecting her mind shattered at the prospect of separation. Panic struck, like a fire in the wheat fields of Turris, and consumed her. Launching herself out of his embrace, her wild eyes warded off the reaching arms of the Angeli Guard as she turned in a slow circle, gaping. Imbellis was burning. Its walls were shattered. Everywhere she looked was death.

"Easy, beautiful," Tristan said. "You're okay."

Her head snapped towards the sound of his voice, and she saw what her mind had masked before. Tristan's chest plate was gone. There was blood…and a lot of it. Nausea rolled over her, her world hanging in the balance, as she asked, "Are you hurt?"

"No," he said, reaching out to steady her, "but you are."

His words triggered the return of her memory, and fast on its heels came concern. "The gods…" She groaned and applied pressure to both temples when pain slammed behind her eyes. "Where are they?"

A solid impact struck the ground, reverberating through the terra beneath their feet. Together, they turned. A hundred feet away, Thor stood with Mjolnir in hand. His chest plate had been ripped away, and what remained of his armor was dented, embedded with grass, and dulled by dirt. His missing helm revealed a visage fueled by fury.

Lifting the war hammer, Thor pointed it towards Tristan and thundered, "You will tell me what magic you used, boy, to lay hand to my weapon."

"It's just a weapon," Tristan retorted. "Like its owner, there's nothing special about it."

Thor's eyes narrowed. "Only a handful across the universes have been able to wield what was forged for me. You," he snarled, "are unworthy."

"Be glad I did not turn it on you," Tristan told him as he stepped between Anliac and Thor.

Thor tracked the movement. "Tell me what I want to know," he demanded, "or she will pay the price."

Golden light exploded out of Tristan's marks, and he growled, "Leave her out of this."

In his peripheral vision, Thor caught sight of Qandisa, and his lips curled into a malevolent grin. "Or what?" he goaded as the goddess, a black mist in her demonic form, descended to stand at his side. "You can't fight us both."

"You're missing your wings, goddess." Tristan smirked. "I guess Anliac clipped them."

"Not on this planet, nor any other," she hissed, "would that happen." Enraged, she charged.

Tristan was much faster. He met her with a right hook that sent her flying towards the tree line to the West.

"My turn." Thor grinned and advanced.

A frozen staff appeared in Anliac's hand.

"No, Anliac!"

"He's right, Tristan," she said, moving to block the god's path. "You can't fight them both."

Glaring over Anliac's shoulder, Thor told him, "I'm not done with you, boy, but I don't mind putting an end to her first."

Anliac slammed the end of her staff into the ground, and the terra rose around the god like two colliding waves, trapping him. Before he could break free, she turned to Tristan. "I'm not fast enough to take her. You have to do it."

"You're hurt," he noticed as blood trickled from a head wound down her temple. "I can't leave you here."

"He'll never touch me," she vowed. "He has little defense against my elemental abilities, but they are useless against the goddess. Go!" she shouted when Thor broke free, showering them with chunks of terra. "I've got this."

With a deafening roar, Tristan vanished.

Thor tried to give chase, but Anliac became an obstacle. "Where do you think you're going, earthling?" she asked. His laughter sent chills down her spine.

"I'm not of Earth, little girl," he told her, "but I'll take your life just the same."

He flew straight towards her, his war hammer leading the way.

Anliac held her ground, waiting until the last moment to sidestep, then brought her staff upward to connect with the underside of his chin. As his head snapped backwards on his spine and his feet swung by the ground, she pivoted in a tight circle to gain momentum and shattered her weapon against the side of his head.

His shoulders hunched forward as he flew through the air and crashed, two hundred feet away, into the rubble of a crumbled section of wall. He rebounded quickly, gaining his feet, but not fast enough.

Conjuring a war hammer of solid ice, with adrenaline cloaking her pain, Anliac was on him. With the long-handled weapon gripped in her hand, she swung it in an upward strike and delivered a solid blow.

Thor crashed through a tall wall of unbroken stone and disappeared.

She tracked him by his bellowed scream until he exploded through from the other side. Refusing him time to recover, she charged again, swinging the ice-hammer in a high arc.

He blocked the blow with Mjolnir. Hammer to hammer, her weapon shattered, leaving only the handle of it in her grasp.

Taking advantage, Thor used his left foot to sweep her own from beneath her. As she fell, he slammed his fist into the underside of her chin, forcing her head to snap back and sending her into an awkward backwards roll across the cobblestoned street.

Landing on her stomach, she slammed both fists into ground, and the terra rolled. Using gravity, she gained her feet.

Finding Thor, her eyes went wide when she saw Mjolnir streaking towards her. Disoriented, her reaction time slowed. His weapon was her undoing. The pain was incredible as the front, lower section of her ribcage snapped like twigs, and the force of the blow slammed her into the wall at her back.

She wanted to scream, but she had no air with which to do so.

Two quads of Angeli Guards saw Anliac go down.

"Move in!" one quad leader shouted. "First quad! Cover the healer! Second quad! Let's show this earthling what we're made of!"

The sight of the three Superians in silver and black armor offered Anliac hope. When the healer dropped to her knees, Anliac grabbed her hand and placed it over her broken ribs. "Hurts..." she whimpered.

"I know," the healer said, laying her other hand beside the first. "This won't be pleasant, Angeli, but I've got you."

As the Fulgo healer wielded her ability, Anliac's back arched, her mouth opened in an agonized gasp, and then she began to scream.

Thor was closing in fast, but the second quad of Angeli Guards held their ground and waited on orders from their Mortalis commander.

"Aer wielders," he shouted, "vortex!" A spherical, swirling mass formed. "Ignis! Ignite!" The vortex became an inferno fed by the first element. "Loose!" came his third command.

Thor dodged, but the wielders countered. He leapt into the air, trying to go over it, but the commander issued his next command.

"Now!"

The vortex exploded. Thor's cries of pain echoed throughout the city as he was catapulted across it from the blast.

Her duty complete, the healer sagged and then toppled to

her side, drained.

Scanning the surrounding Angeli Guards for their marks, Anliac grabbed the arm of a level one terra wielder and said, "Get her to safety."

Squatting down, he lifted the healer into his arms. "I'm on it," he said as he started off in the direction of the tower.

To the remaining six wielders, Anliac said, "Well done."

"Where is Tristan?" the commander of the first quad asked.

"He's dealing with the shape-shifting monster," Anliac told them. "He trusts that we can take this god on our own."

"And we will not disappoint him," a female aer wielder replied, then she warned, "Here he comes."

Anliac thrusted out both arms. With her hands, she commanded two buildings, one to either side of the street Thor was charging down, to collapse on his head. Hoping to turn the mound into his tomb, she commanded, "Wielders, link yourselves."

Shoulder to shoulder, the wielders merged their abilities. With ignis and aer being the strongest elements to the quad, Anliac gave the command. "Chain fire!"

A fluid line of flames, two feet in diameter and white-hot, streaked towards the rubble.

"Aer wielders," she readied them. "Now."

Encased in a swirling vortex of aer, the ignis line's heat redoubled. When fire met stone, the toppled buildings began to melt.

"Don't let up until it's sealed," Anliac warned when, across a clear sky, dark, ominous clouds rolled in. Thunder rumbled like a caged beast. Head back, heart pounding, Anliac said, "We need to break up that storm."

Having heard the order, an aquis and aer wielder closed rank to do as commanded, but one asked, "The fires, Anliac... shouldn't we be glad for the rain?"

"No," Anliac replied as they watched coalescing energy claw at the aether. "The god wields lightning."

As if to prove her point, the sky loosed its first bolt. Jagged and great enough to cleave a mountain in two, it struck Thor's prison and shattered the stone. The Angeli Guards moved closer to Anliac, who used her elemental ability to shield them when chunks of terra exploded outward from the mound, raining death on those caught in the downpour.

Thor rose from the debris as rage made flesh. "For that," he bellowed, "the whole of Superi will pay!"

The Angeli Guards paired up; two sets to Anliac's right, one set to her left. She felt their presences but held the god's angry stare with her own.

"It looks like I'm back just in time," the terra wielder said, taking up his position after returning from the tower without the healer. "How are we going to kill this guy?"

"In one perfectly executed maneuver," she told him. Then she gave the order: "Vacuum!"

The aer wielders sent forth a whirlwind that held the god in place, then the ignis wielders used the aer as fuel for the boxed fire trap that, in turn, denied the god his ability to breathe. His blond hair shriveled into black wisps that disintegrated before the flames ever touched him. When it did, the armor on his forearms and legs became a furnace; his exposed skin blistered and peeled away from the bloody tissue beneath it.

Anliac saw his right shoulder flex and his grip tighten on Mjolnir. Before he could aim and loosen his grip, she cast forth a single stone that pierced his wrist and left a hole in its wake. The hammer fell.

Taking Anliac's lead, the terra wielders fashioned spears from rocks and hurled them at the god. Two punctured through Thor's leg armor and into his thighs. A third entered his open palm, dragging down the hand that would have conjured his weapon.

The ignis and aer wielders dropped their offense when Anliac charged the god. Her use of gravity assured her footing and carried her swiftly over the jagged, melded stone. With her left hand prepared to defend, she planted her feet and threw her weight behind her right-fisted swing.

Thor, taking the impact to his lower jaw, felt his feet leave the terra as his body took flight off towards the North, but it was lightning, conjured by his own hand, that brought him down.

Cheers erupted from the Angeli Guards, but her fear for Tristan sobered her. "The battle is not yet over."

***

Tristan tracked the goddess by the destruction left in her wake as she crashed through walls, toppling whole buildings on her forced flight out of the city. From twenty feet away, he witnessed Qandisa, battered and bloodied, roll to a stop before the tree line.

This should be fun, he thought when, a moment later, the goddess stood. Shifting into an eight-foot-tall, horned, shadowed form, she was without injury.

The goddess, dragging in ragged breaths, glared with

abject hatred and said, "I'm going to kill you, you stupid…
little…" Her eyes flared as the Angeli disappeared.

He wasn't there to listen to threats but to end one. At a
speed not even the goddess could track, he slammed a left
cross into Qandisa's stomach, folding her in half. Pivoting,
he avoided the horn she tried to skewer him with when she
unfurled, then stepped back and delivered a solid front kick
to the center of her chest.

The impact tossed the goddess into the trees, but after
hitting the ground, she came up fighting. Snapping a trunk at
its base, she hefted it as one would a staff and swung out as
the Angeli closed in.

To Tristan's heightened sight and agility, the goddess's
attack was slow and clumsy. A simple sideward jump and
the move was countered. His arms shot forward, and he
buried his claws deep into the hard wood. Ripping the trunk
from her weaker grasp, he returned the blow, but the goddess
ducked beneath his swing. The tree line took the hit, and a
dozen trees snapped, trunks exploding into deadly splinters
as limbs and leaves rained down on them.

Throwing back her head, the goddess roared, and her
form began to shift. Her height grew to rival that of Belua and Torren as her physique expanded with equal mass.
Bulging, rippling muscles exploded beneath the surface of
immortal flesh as the shadow fled. A golden rod appeared
in her hand. She pointed it at him and snarled, "Playtime is
over…"

She knew how fast he was and so she watched for it. The
moment his thighs and calves tensed to charge, she swung
the rod she held in her hand, intent on breaking him in half.

She underestimated him. She felt her head snap back on her spine as he came up beneath her swing with one of his own and clipped her chin. She stumbled but didn't fall as she brought her rod to bear again.

Tristan launched himself into a reverse roll to avoid the hit and then sprung towards her. Her crossways slash was wild, but she nailed him in his left shoulder, tossing him through the air.

As gravity pulled him down, he landed, knees bent, with both feet and one hand planted in a three-point position. He used his other hand to maintain balance until he'd slid to a stop.

Appearing every inch the predator she was, she stalked towards him. "I am a universal goddess," she hissed. "I cannot be killed."

A rush of energy flooded his body, raising goosebumps on his flesh as it brought the golden markings of an Angeli to life. Blood gorged his muscled frame as his strength intensified. Calm stoicism smoothed the stress lines around his eyes as light flooded forth from them. His visage changed to one of euphoria as the void claimed him, and when he spoke, his voice was like the sound of many waters: deafening and powerful.

"Then you have met your match," he said, meeting her halfway, "for nor can I."

Her eyes tracked nothing more than a blurred trail as he moved in swift circles around her. "AHH!" she cried out as a fist slammed into the back of her left knee and flipped her, feet over head, to land on her stomach in the grass.

With a curse on her lips, she rebounded, but her feet left

the ground again when Tristan used a felled tree like a battering ram to propel her, in a high arc, into the air. Refusing to eat more dirt, she turned gravity to slow her fall and landed just north of the city, on a path that led to an ancient grove.

Tristan was there to meet her, but he hesitated when he should have attacked, in awe of the beautiful creature the goddess had become.

Grasped in her hands were two golden maces that paled in comparison to the golden sheen of her perfected flesh. Obsidian eyes, lined in coal, peered back at him as her height and musculature diminished, yet her confidence grew. With one mace held high and the other low, she taunted him.

"One last dance, Angeli, and then I end this." She smiled and broke the entrapping trance of her new form by revealing the jagged, black teeth of a monster.

Tristan ran straight for her and dodged to the right for the first swing of her mace. He kicked out, only to fear that his shin bone had shattered when her second mace fell upon it. He loosed his fist, fueled by pain and fury, but Qandisa spun out of reach and countered with a punch of her own. He took it in his right shoulder but held his position as he brought up his left hand to capture the mace meant to crack his skull.

The goddess, a weapon raised high over her head, and Tristan, a fist reared back to be released, both froze as Thor fell from the sky. A trail of smoke marked his descent as he bounced twice off the unforgiving terra, then landed in a heap between them.

Retreating, Tristan heard the lightning god's growled, "Ow," as he gained his feet and loosed Mjolnir in one fluid movement.

Tristan ducked, sucking in air at the close call, and then cursed when Qandisa flanked him, forcing him to turn. He sidestepped the downward strike of her mace, but Mjolnir caught him in the solar plexus, stealing his breath. With a growl of his own, he turned to face Thor, but Qandisa introduced her mace to his kidney. Skidding across the grass-covered terra, he tumbled onto the road that led to Imbellis before coming to a stop. By the time he was on his feet, his enemies had converged.

Anliac was right. He could not defend against them both, so he bared his claws and bid them to do their worst. Then golden lightning set the orange sky ablaze, shaking the aether, and the fight came to a sudden stop.

To the West, in the center of a grassy field, appeared a black, gaping hole. The lightning struck out in a square pattern around it, as if trapped inside of an invisible box that increased its energy. It pulsed and thickened, a gateway forming at its center, but the image it revealed was not of Superi. The sky was far too blue, the grass much too green, and according to the growing grins on the deities' faces, whatever was to come through would be trouble.

II

New Threat?

"What is that?" an Angeli Guard asked Anliac as they all turned to face north.

From the direction of Bealson's Grove, a dark shadow coalesced. Violent bolts of lightning struck at the terra in a pattern that shook the entire city.

"I can't see," she fumed. Cursing, she added, "We're out of time," before giving her orders. "Rally the guards. Gather everyone who can hold a weapon and have them march on that location. And for Superi's sake, hurry."

"You heard her," the leader of the first quad barked. "Let's move."

As the quads broke into pairs and scattered, she called out, "Where is Jaccoo?"

Without slowing, a Fulgo with stark-white hair called out over his shoulder, "He's running the injured to the Tower," and then he was gone.

Anliac started off at a trot but increased her pace the

closer she came to the Asylum without finding the Mortalis. When she did, he was tying a strip of linen around a man's thigh to stem the steady flow of blood pouring from a jagged wound.

The injured Nox had his eyes closed, but Jaccoo looked up when her shadow fell over them. "What's happening?" he asked.

"You need to get to Pisces Stragulum," she said, cringing when the lightning struck again.

Finishing his task, Jaccoo stopped a Fulgo on his way past. "Hey, are you on your way to the Tower?"

"Yeah," the man replied, his eyes straying repeatedly to the bloodied Angeli. "Do you want me to take him off your hands?"

"Thank you," Anliac said as she lifted the Nox and draped him over the Fulgo's shoulder. "I need Jaccoo's help."

As the Fulgo turned to leave, Jaccoo asked her, "What's happening?"

Pointing to the shadowy gateway, she answered, "There are more gods coming, Jaccoo. We're going to need all the help we can get."

Her fear twisted his gut. "Tell me what to do."

"Gather our reinforcements," she told him, "and bring them through the gate at the Northwest side of the city."

"You shouldn't be alone, Anliac," he insisted. "You're too important."

"Tristan's alone!" she yelled, her voice pitched high in fear. When the percussion of Jaccoo's departing speed boomed, she ignored the burning city and the cries of those in it as she raced to find Tristan.

***

The blinding lightning strikes and opening gateway distracted the gods, but not Tristan. Lunging forward, he covered the space between them instantly and nailed Qandisa with a left-hooked body shot. It tossed her backwards and sent her sliding across the grass. Pivoting on his left foot, he planted a hard right-cross into Thor's jaw, who spun like a top and landed on his face before the gateway.

As the new arrival stepped through the opening, Tristan drew back his shoulders and loosed a battle shout. Arms held out to his side, his muscles engorged with blood and power, he taunted, "If you've come to do what they could not, then get on with it."

"It's been a great while since last I laid eyes on a true Angeli," spoke a god.

As tall as a Fulgo, with a golden headpiece covering his stark-white hair, the man wore the face of an animal the likes of which Tristan had never seen. His loins were girded in white linen, but the rest of his frame was left bare, exposing long, lean muscles beneath grey flesh.

"I am called Munsin," he continued, "and I assure you, we mean you no harm." At the arch of the Angeli's right brow, he said, "These two invaded Superi without the consent of the council."

"We did what the Earth gods were too afraid to do," Thor retorted from his knees, shaking with rage. "So either lay waste to this pathetic excuse for an Angeli or get out of my way."

"I am but a god that offers a way, Thor," he replied as

two goddesses emerged, "but today, it is not your path I'm concerned with."

"Stand quietly, son of Odin," a goddess with hair as black as raven's wings and skin the color of pearl said when Thor's mouth opened again, "whilst I endeavor to undo the damage you've wrought here."

In a blood-red gown, she moved to stand on Munsin's left side with grace and beauty. Yet, it was the extra arms that held Tristan's stare until she said, "I am called Parvati, and this—" she pointed to a second goddess— "is Kali."

With a grin, Kali bumped Thor's shoulder. "Tsk, tsk, Asgardian. Daddy's little boy is in trouble," she said in passing as she moved to stand at Munsin's right side.

Involuntarily, Tristan's gaze dropped to her ample bosom, straining against the green silk of her tabard-style dress. The splits in its sides and the peach-colored flesh it revealed stopped at a slender waist that captivated him. He gulped and subconsciously looked for Anliac, in case she'd caught his wandering thoughts. It was a testament to her beauty that the last thing he took note of was the weapons of war she held clasped in eight different hands.

Another god came through the gateway, a dark-haired, onyx-eyed male in light, black chainmail. He took advantage of Tristan's speechless state to say, "I am called Ares. I believe you've met my brother, Apollo."

Though Ares was impressive in size, it was the aggression that poured off him that focused Tristan's attention. Mention of the sun god's name filled him with renewed fury and sent a surge of adrenaline coursing through his blood. "You do yourself no favor by claiming kinship with the man who attacked our world unprovoked."

Taken aback, Ares asked, "Do you deny attempting to reopen the gateway between Earth and Superi?"

"Do you deny casting the curses upon my ancestors? The ones that live in our blood still," Tristan countered, "as punishment for a deed committed before our time?"

"I cannot deny knowledge of the event, but what was your hope, Angeli, when you reignited this conflict?" Ares queried. "Retribution?"

"Without a curse," Tristan said, "and yet, you reveal your ignorance." Ignoring the god's scowl, Tristan continued. "The Angeli had nothing to do with the reopening of that gateway. The decision was made by those who held the accounting of what transpired between our two worlds. Those of us called Angeli fought against it, but a greater number of denizens are tired of being hindered by the curses that Earth cast. They would see them lifted. They would see Superians made whole. This was not the will of the Angeli." Tristan's eyes flared. "But Apollo's transgressions against us made it so. In the fight at Bealson's Grove, he ensured we would fight."

"You are a weak, pathetic people," Thor sneered.

"Is that so?" Tristan retorted without a change of expression. "Then why did you summon aid? If I am weak, Thor, then what are you?" he asked. "We both know you can't beat me."

"I sent no summons," Thor growled, gathering his injured pride as he came to his feet. "I want the pleasure of killing you myself."

Tristan laughed, darkening the god's scowl and furrowing

the brows of others. "I'm not that easy to kill."

Munsin chuckled, lessening the tension. "So it would appear."

The eight-armed goddess smiled. "The Angeli have proven more than a match for the both of you, Thor, so perhaps you should hold your tongue." Her oval face tipped to the side. "Although, I rather enjoy watching you embarrass yourself."

All of Parvati's right arms rose as she exclaimed, "Enough! Kali, stop goading him, and you…" She turned her hard stare to Thor. "Be grateful that you failed, for if you had killed an Angeli, Odin's anger would have been the least of your troubles." With both deities silenced, she declared, "We are not here to incite violence, Superian, but to end it."

"Speak for yourself." A crooked half-smile appeared on Ares's face. "I'm all about bringing it."

"Ares…" Parvati rolled her eyes and missed Qandisa's attack.

A curse flew from Tristan's lips as the tip of a golden dagger met the bone of his left shoulder before ripping the flesh wide. His right arm shot out at an upward angle as he wrapped his fingers around her slender neck and dragged her from her elevated position above him. Rearing back his head, he slammed it into her own and watched her eyes roll back as she fought for consciousness. Dropping to her knees, her wings hung motionless from her back. He pulled her from the ground until they were eye-level.

"I'm going to kill you," he vowed.

"You are fast, Superian, and very strong," Kali said, advancing to aid the other goddess with equal measures of rage and pleasure, "but not even an Angeli can defend against me."

"Hold," Parvati said.

"I will not allow Qandisa's death," Kali warned, though her forward progress stopped when Parvati laid a hand upon her shoulder. "If his flesh can be parted," she said, "I can kill him."

"No one is to touch the Angeli," Parvati commanded. "Ares…stop. Thor…"

Lightning crackled overhead, accentuating his bellow. "I don't answer to you!" he snarled as he charged to cover the distance separating them.

Munsin snapped his fingers, and Thor entered and exited from a transparent egress that lead nowhere but back to itself. Angered, he threw Mjolnir into the transparent doorway, only to curse when he was knocked senseless from behind by his own weapon.

Forgetting herself, Kali chuckled, then glared at Tristan as if the slip of humor was his fault.

Positioned defensively before the goddesses, Ares heeded Parvati's words, but as he unsheathed his xiphos, his eyes revealed his displeasure.

To Tristan, Parvati said, "Release her."

"No," Tristan replied, tightening his grip.

"Now can I kill him?"

"No, Ares." Parvati sighed. "This is not what we want, Angeli, but we cannot leave her behind." When still Tristan did not relent, she shook her head, dismayed. "Do as you must, God of War."

The swordsman's speed was equal to Anliac's, but

Tristan's fist had shattered the goddess's face long before Ares reached him. His grip around her throat was all that kept her vertical.

Ares plunged his sword through the back of Tristan's left shoulder until half of the blade protruded from the front. "Let the goddess go, Angeli," he said. "You lose."

With a slow turn of his neck, Tristan looked over his shoulder at Ares. Maintaining eye contact, he said, "You... should be afraid." And then, with a left-footed front kick, he rolled Qandisa head over feet before pushing backward, until the hilt of Ares's sword met his flesh. As Ares's grin slipped, Tristan's grew.

The god moved to withdraw his weapon, but Tristan reached down with his left hand and grabbed the god's leg, preventing his retreat. Without releasing his hold, Tristan spun to face his enemy. Wrenching the hilt of the sword from Ares's grasp, costing the god his balance, he carried Ares's leg forward with him. With his right hand, he reined blow after blow down on the god, pummeling his face and chest.

From inside his black boot, Ares pulled free a double-edged dagger and buried it in Tristan's thigh.

Tristan let go, stumbling, as he pulled free the dagger and armed his left hand. Though the sword stabbed through his shoulder limited his mobility, he was right dominate, and he'd yet to find a blade that could equal the damage of his claws.

"Get up!" Thor shouted. "Munsin, let me out of this trap! Kill him!"

"Umm..." Ares said, translocating to stand beside the

gods, "we might have a problem. It would appear I've angered the boy."

A bright light forced them to cover their eyes and turn their heads to the side. In the wake of the sunburst, golden markings that seemed like living things spread just beneath the Angeli's pale flesh.

His arms were held down, with his wrist crossed in front of him. Eyes closed, his bald head and broad shoulders hunched, Tristan's muscles were rigid to the point of snapping. The blade, buried in his left shoulder, began a backward slide as he began to heal. No sooner had the blade hit the ground than the wound sealed closed.

"Well…" Ares scratched at the short whiskers on his chin. "That complicates things." When Tristan reached down and lifted the sword, Ares said with narrowed eyes, "I'll be wanting that back."

"Seven gods of earth have stood upon Superi," Tristan stated. The change in his voice and the power of it silenced even Thor when, like rolling thunder, he continued. "Of them, more than half have drawn weapons against us. Your words claim no harm, while your actions prove the lie."

"Did you know," Munsin asked Thor in a hushed voice, unaware of Tristan's heightened hearing, "what kind of monster you would face by coming here?"

"I was not born a monster," Tristan replied, causing Munsin to wince. "I am what both worlds have made me."

"Parvati!" Thor shouted. "We both know he cannot be allowed to live. Let me out. With Ares at my side, the Angeli will die."

Qandisa, fully awake, shifted into her shadow-demon

form and glided to the gathered gods. Pausing before Thor, she glared, but her voice was ominously low. "How dare you suggest that a Greek god is a greater ally than I? Your insult will not soon be forgotten." Standing in front of the gateway, she found Tristan's stare. "We will meet again, you and I," she said, then stepped through.

Ares tossed his hands in the air. "What just happened? After the beating she just took, she's just going to leave?"

From within Bealson's Grove, Anliac leapt the wall and raced for Tristan's side. The sight and scent of his blood enraged her, but her voice and hand were steady as she held out her open palm and said, "Give me the sword, Tristan." Once in hand, she flipped the blade sharp edge out in a reverse grip and demanded, "Now tell me who it belongs to."

Those who'd come with her through the wall were still at a distance, affording Ares the time to appreciate the glaring warrior Angeli. As his eyes slid over her with intimate interest, he said, "You are as beautiful as you are brave. Why do you waste your time on him? Come with me," he said, "and I will make you a queen."

"The way you look at me reminds me of someone." She took a step forward, as if summoned by his words, and then dashed his hopes. "I would love to introduce the two of you. It won't be hard." Snapping her fingers, she divided the terra beneath Ares's feet. He jumped and rolled to avoid falling into the crater. "I just need to kill you first."

Coming out of a forward roll, he dusted himself off and grinned. "If you think Thor and Qandisa were a handful, honey, then you're not equipped to take on me."

In the field, a black shadow opened into a gaping hole

that rivaled the one that stood open for the gods—ten feet tall and fifty feet wide. The lightning that flowed through the aether was a deep purple, shattered by a blue-white light that crackled around the portal's edges.

Ares's visage was not the only one to change as the image beyond the opening became clear. It was not the difference between the orange-hazed sky of Superi and the clear blue of the one beyond Earth's gateway, nor was it the difference in the landscapes that lay along the distant horizons in both. It was the Superians, emerging in force, that put the invaders on the defensive.

The animalistic Superians appeared feral, the epitome of predators who'd cornered their prey. The tall, pale-skinned warriors were like the undead who no longer feared the grave. The more musclebound, dark-skinned Superians held their weapons and shields with the confidence of skilled fighters.

As elemental wielders, those who'd come from the wall with the Angeli fell in at their backs in time to hear her reply. "I do not stand here as a god," she said, "for to do so would leave me weak. You stand for yourselves. You stand for nothing. But we," she declared as those at her back begun pounding their fists against their chest, their weapons against their shields, their feet into the ground, "stand as one, for Superi."

Munsin licked lips that had suddenly gone dry, his Adam's apple bobbing when he tried and failed to swallow. "I believe it is time that we go," he said. "Parvati?"

"What?" She shook her head, breaking the link that had formed between herself and the boy standing at the fore of those coming through the portal. Though younger and far inferior in size, he inspired in her a fear she didn't quite understand.

"I'm leaving," Munsin told her. "With or without you, the way will be closed." He turned on his heels and headed for the gateway.

When Munsin's trap fell, Thor hefted his hammer.

"Don't be stupid," Kali rebuked, tugging down his arm. She stood at his side and watched those from the portal converge on the Angelis' location. "They would slaughter you."

Locking glares with Tristan, Thor vowed, "We will finish this."

"But not today," Parvati said, urging both god and goddess through the gateway. "Ares, let us go."

"Be content with what has been reborn," Ares cautioned, "and leave the gateway between our worlds closed, or the gods of Earth will eradicate your kind. We will not make the same mistake twice."

As she and Ares took the step that would carry them far from Superi, Parvati found her eyes drawn to the boy one last time.

III

Aftermath

Set looked like an unmovable mountain as the onrush of Angeli Guards poured through the portal of Pisces Stragulum and diverted around him. The wind had picked up, plastering his black hair against the webbed, diamond-teardrops that marked his face and carrying the cheer of the wielders to the soldiers rushing to meet them on the field of victory.

Davad, breathless and flushed, slid to a stop beside him. "Where are they?" When Set only shook his head, he was forced to track his pinned, piercing blue stare to find them.

"The gods are gone," Set stated when Davimon joined them.

Davimon sneered. "Cowards."

"Idiots," Set mumbled and started forward.

Davimon scoffed as Davad's right brow shot towards his hairline.

Staring at Set's departing back, Davimon said, "I know he wasn't talking about us."

"He'd better not have been," Davad said, leaving Set to walk alone as he and Davimon kept their own company.

Tristan stood with his arm around Anliac's waist and watched his brother's measured approach. It was not Set's size nor stature that demanded notice. Though he was no longer the skinny kid from Exterius Antro, it was the energy that he exuded, the confidence of his stride, the dark visage he wore on his young face that forewarned of his deadly nature. Fixated on his brother, he was startled when Anliac spoke.

"The gods fear us," she said, "but..."

He squeezed her waist and finished her thought. "They haven't met an epoto."

"Exactly," she agreed.

"Then let's be glad that the last one is on our side," Tristan told her.

"Let's hope he is," she tensed, "because he really doesn't look happy."

"Six..." Set growled as he closed the remaining distance. "You faced six gods...ALONE!"

His brother's visage was colored with fury, but Tristan's heightened senses told a different story. The energy pouring off of Set was one of fear. "Set," he began.

"Shut up," Set warned, his body shaking with pent-up energy and rage. "You promised, Tristan. Two Angeli...two gods. Any more than that, and you were to call in reinforce-ments."

"I know, but Set..."

"NO! Six, Tristan. You could have been...I could have lost..." He broke into tears.

Tristan snatched him by the front of his shirt and dragged him into an embrace, holding him close for as long as Set would let him. "I'm okay," he assured him. "I heal, little brother."

Set stepped out of Tristan's reach, drying his eyes and spreading his glare to include Anliac. He shook his head at the blood and gore covering them. "She does not," Set stated, "and there are limits to healing, Tristan. Your bald head is testament to that."

Anliac's barked laugh caused the corner of Set's mouth to twitch.

"It's not funny," Set scowled, peeved that her warped humor had infected him.

"No." She smiled. "It isn't." After a quick hug and a ruffling of his hair, she said, "Anger rides hard on the heels of relief, Set."

Ignoring Anliac, he waited for Tristan to look at him. "I will not be left behind again. That was…brutal, brother. From now on, we will fight together or not at all."

"Understood," Tristan said as Davad and Davimon approached.

"So, um," Davad said, scratching the top of his head, "the portal is still open. Set, you have to be getting tired."

"The portal is anchored," Set told him. "I didn't want to worry about holding it open if we'd come through to a fight."

"You can do that?" Davimon asked.

Set's reply was ice-cold. "You'd be surprised at what I can do."

"Okay, then." Davad directed his next question to Tristan.

"What now?"

"Divide and conquer, I suppose," Tristan told him as he turned to stare at Imbellis. "Send in the wielders to put out the fires. Use the soldiers to gather the injured. Tell them to take them to the Tower. It held up better than the rest of the city."

"Send a messenger through the portal," Anliac interjected. "Tell Shashara we need her to gather the healers. They've got their work cut out for them."

"And the Angeli Guard?" Davimon asked. "They're waiting for orders."

"Tell them to sweep the city," Anliac said. "Make sure those lifeless monsters have all been beheaded and burned. It's the only way to kill them."

"Monsters?"

"They're warriors," Anliac explained, "brought back from the dead to fight on the side of the gods."

Davimon whistled low. "It makes a man glad to be a Superian," he said. "Nothing lies on the other side of the grave but death for us."

"Find our commanders," Davad told him, "and get them started. I'll get word to Shashara."

"Done," Davimon replied, pivoting towards the masses to give them directions and leaving Davad alone with the other three.

"So," Davad said, "do we think they'll be back?"

Curious himself, Set moved to Davad's side, where they both crossed their arms and waited on a reply.

Tristan and Anliac exchanged a pensive glance.

Clearing his throat, Tristan said, "We don't know. It

would appear even the gods are divided on the subject."

"What does that mean?" Set asked.

Anliac answered. "The four who came through the gateway, Set, they were here to collect the two we fought."

"But of the four," Tristan added, "one was willing to fight against us, and one spoiled for the fight, so… we don't know."

Set's shoulders sagged. "You just said you only fought two."

"Well…" Tristan's head tipped from side to side. "I never fought more than two at a time."

Rolling his eyes, Set threw his arms in the air, giving up, before collecting himself enough to say, "We should make our way to Imbellis. The people need to see you."

Starting that way, Anliac called out to a passing guard. "If you see Jaccoo, tell him we're looking for him."

"Yes, ma'am," the guard replied, pausing long enough to place his closed fist over his heart before moving on.

"Why are we looking for him?" Tristan asked.

"Our people may need to see us," she told him, "but the whole of Superi needs to know what happened here."

Davad sniffed pointedly.

"You disagree with her?" Set asked as they climbed over debris to enter the city.

Finding level ground, Davad stopped and stared. "'The white-stone city, ethereal in its beauty'; that is how my father once described Imbellis. Look at it now."

Streets were lost beneath the rubble. Buildings were toppled. Homes were ruined. The heat of raging fires thickened the stench of death that wafted with the smoke like a heavy fog.

"We warned that the war would land on Superi," Davad said, "and that there would be no neutral ground. Those who were not here have no right to the knowledge gained."

Walking off, Tristan swooped down and captured a fist-sized stone in his hand. Squeezing it in frustration, the stone disintegrated into dust. He heard Set and Davad's sharp intake of breath and felt their eyes boring into his back, so without turning, he said her name, "Anliac," and hoped she understood.

"Go on," she encouraged, knowing he'd reached his limit. "Gather your thoughts and meet me at the plaza when you're ready."

He nodded and disappeared around a corner.

Angling for a standing wall, Davad stuck his entire upper body through a hole and measured the twelve-inch thickness of the stone. Backing out, he said, "Considering the damage, it's a wonder either of you survived."

"That I survived, yes," Anliac conceded. "But not Tristan." At Set's queried look, she confessed, "When I transcended, my potential power hit an apex, but Tristan..." She hesitated. "With every fight, he grows stronger."

"How much stronger?" Davad asked, the lines around his eyes and mouth tightening.

She opened her mouth to speak, her head turning back and forth, but she had no answer. Glancing at Set before guilt turned her eyes to the ground, she finally said, "Let us be glad he fights on our side."

As they neared the plaza, Angeli Guards formed rank to escort them through the throng of people blocking access to the damaged stone steps that led to the Tower—and to Tristan.

He stood above them, watching the survivors of the first battle gather themselves together as they watched him in turn.

The double wooden doors at his back opened, and Shashara stepped from the egress. Taking Tristan's hand, she held on to it until Anliac ascended to take her place, and then she reached for Set.

"How did you beat us here?" Set asked her as they took their place to the right of the others.

"Are you kidding?" She grinned. "I forced the Alphas' gate-maker to get me and the healers here as soon as you popped that portal."

Having overheard, Davad leaned back to see around Tristan and Anliac. When Shashara did the same, he asked, "You forced him?"

Set, holding her hand, laughed when she giggled. "What did you do?"

"Later," she promised them both as Tristan stepped forward with Anliac to address the crowd. Silence spread along with his words.

"I've always preferred the shadows, leaving the suns to cast their light on those who sought it. I did not seek to lead. We," he said, stretching his arms out to his sides, "did not seek to lead, but I speak for us all when I say we are proud of those who follow us."

The crowd erupted into cheer.

"Apollo, the god of their single sun, was weakened by the might of ours. Thor, a god of lightning, was struck by his own element as Superi herself turned it against him." The roar of the people grew.

"Ares," Anliac shouted over the noise, "their god of war, was knocked flat on his back by the fist of an Angeli!"

"They sent their dead to war with us," Tristan stated, "and we gave them a death from which they will not wake again!"

Holding up her hands for quiet, she said, "Today, though the cost of it surrounds us, was a victory."

"We don't know if the gods will return," Tristan said, "nor the numbers we will face if they do, but I say…if they feared facing the Angeli, they will tremble at the might of Superians untied. So let them come!"

IV

Invitations

Anliac had forgotten about the two extra guards Tristan had sent with her until one of them called out, "Hold."

Lynette, the Fulgo who'd been her constant shadow since coming to Pisces Stragulum, placed herself between her charge and the man rushing up.

"It's okay," Anliac told them. "Jaccoo, what do you have for me?"

Handing her a scroll, he said, "All of the Angeli Guard commanders have given their preliminary reports. The damage is severe, but the East side took the brunt of it."

"What have we heard from Shashara?" she asked.

Jaccoo ducked his head. "The death count…" When he looked at her again, his eyes said it all. "We found a senes ad domum, full of the elderly, and a sanatorium, both burned to the ground. Shashara's report has been included."

"Thank you, Jaccoo," she said, clasping the scroll but letting her arm hang at her side. "Let me know when the transcriptionists are ready?"

"Yes, ma'am," he said, turning back towards Pisces Stragulum.

When Anliac veered from the path that would carry them to the Tower, Lynette asked, "Where are we going?"

"You heard Jaccoo," Anliac said. "I want to see the damage to the East side of the city for myself."

"Imbellis will never look the same. Will it?"

"When a thing is broken, Lynette," she told her, "life offers us two choices. We can cast the thing off as ruined, or we can take the pieces and create something new."

Lynette grinned. "Since when have you become an optimist?"

"We have eyes on us," the Nox guard said. "Do we know him?"

"No," the Mortalis guard replied. "Anliac?"

"I see him," she said, coming to a stop, "but I don't know him."

They watched as, in a rush, the Fulgo man scribbled onto the parchment perched in his left hand, then shoved it into a pocket sewn into the folds of his black robe. When he looked their way, he grinned and took off at a dead run towards the Southern gate.

"Catch him," Anliac ordered the two guards. "Lynette, come with me."

Knowing the Angeli was much faster, Lynette pumped her legs to keep pace until they were numb. "We're… running…the wrong…way," she gasped between strides. "Whoa!" Her feet outpaced her eyes when Anliac shoved off the terra and leapt into the air, leaving her flat on her back.

"Ugh," she grunted as the air whooshed from her lungs. Rolling onto her stomach, she slammed the sides of her closed fist into the ground in frustration and then scrambled to her feet to find Anliac.

The foot traffic was steady but slow, which made it easy for Anliac to separate them from the ones she was waiting for. Hidden just beyond the Eastern gate, she waited for the pounding of the interloper's footsteps to become parallel with her position, then used her superior speed to pivot around and clothesline the man.

On his side, with his hand wrapped around his throat, his pale face turning red, Anliac told him, "You have to breathe out if you ever hope to breathe in again." When he didn't listen, she delivered a sound kick to his ribs.

A great gasp accompanied his grunt.

"Running south to go east wasn't the smartest plan," she said. "Too obvious."

Slow to stand, he took a moment to reply. "It was not my plan to outrun you, Angeli, but to separate you from the others."

Her eyes flashed a fiery gold. "Again…not the smartest plan." His grin annoyed her.

"My name is Theo," he said, offering a bow that went too deep, showing the back of his head. "I am a messenger for Nutrine, who sends an invitation." He held out the expensive, folded parchment, sealed with his master's signet.

As she took it, she asked, "Did he tell you to spy on us as well?"

Clutching at the paper in his pocket, causing it to crinkle, he began backing away. "I am but a simple messenger," he said as he opened a portal behind himself and disappeared through it.

Lynette arrived in time to see it happen, her last steps dragging her to Anliac's side before she doubled over, her hands on her knees, and threw her guts up. Between heaves, she glared up at her charge and said, "I hate you right now."

Anliac chuckled. "Take a moment to catch your breath."

"If he was a gate-maker," Lynette said, holding the stitch in her side, "why did he run?"

"He said it was to get me alone," Anliac told her as the Nox and Mortalis found them.

"Do you believe him?"

"No," Anliac sighed, "but whatever his intent, it is done now."

The guards dipped their heads before the Nox spoke. "We're sorry, ma'am. The Fulgo gave us the slip."

"Well," Lynette said, "he didn't get past her."

"Don't worry about it," Anliac told them absently as she opened and read the invitation and then held it out for one of the men to take. "See that Tristan gets this, but make sure Davad and Set are informed as well."

"May we ask what it says?" the Mortalis queried.

"The Five have been invited to Certamen by Nutrine himself," she told him. "It would seem the appearance of the gods has the man suddenly interested in discussing terms for an alliance." She smirked. "And, of course, he offers strategic planning for future conflicts between the worlds."

"Do you think the gods will return?" Lynette asked.

"I do," she said. "Their hubris demands it. Go," she told the guards. "Tell Tristan that I will return in time to share last meal. Tell him…" Growing emotional, it took a moment before she tried again. "Tell him I am where I am needed most, but I will need him when I am done."

"Yes, ma'am," the guards said in unison. Their hearts were as heavy as their steps as they turned to go.

The East side of Imbellis was comprised mostly of homes, but not one had been spared. The lightning and the fires that had spread as a result left families to pull deceased loved ones from the destruction. They lined the dirt roads with their dead.

The sound of their wails threatened to break her. "Come, Lynette," she said, starting towards the nearest mound of rubble. "Let us see what help we can offer to those who've lost everything."

"Yes, ma'am," Lynette replied, steeling her resolve as she bent her back to the task.

***

The Mortalis guard called out to Tristan in advance of their approach. "Sir, we've a message from Anliac."

Gesturing them over, he reached for the parchment just as Set walked up.

"What does it say?" Set asked him, looking to the guards when Tristan opened the letter to find out.

"It's an invitation to come to Certamen," the Nox replied, "from Nutrine. He wishes to meet with the Five."

"I'm sorry, sir," the Mortalis said, "but that is all we know."

Tristan tucked the parchment into his back pocket. "He's right. Nutrine wants us there the day after tomorrow. Thank you," he said to the guards and then asked, "Where is Anliac now?"

"She said she would find you before last meal," the Nox told him, "but she feels she's needed on the East side of the city."

Set nodded his head. "The hardest hit. I'll see what I can do about sending more manpower in that direction. Starting with the two of you."

"Yes, sir," the guards said, taking their leave.

"What now?" Davad asked, changing course after glimpsing Tristan's expression.

"Read it," Tristan said, handing over the invitation.

"It has to be a trap," Davad speculated as he read it.

"Are we planning one, or preparing for one?" Triton asked as he set down a crate full of bolted cloth carried from the hull of his ship and destined for Shashara's hands.

"Nutrine's," Set told him.

Triton's coal-black eyes turned euphoric. "Oh, I bloody hope he's that stupid."

"What's your issue with the man?" Tristan asked, intrigued.

"Let's just say that he has a way of acquiring things I want." Triton grinned. "Like the garden."

"A garden?" Set's brow twitched.

"Don't judge what you haven't seen, boy," he retorted. "Its beauty is as rare as your ability."

Davad smirked. "You wouldn't survive a season that far inland."

"Sorry to interrupt," Lan said, coming up on the gathered men, but changed what he'd been going to say when Triton's shoulders slumped. "Are you okay? All…right then," he said after receiving a glare from the pirate for his show of concern. "Tristan, you're needed."

"What's happened?" Tristan asked, but he was not alone in coming to attention.

"There's been no new attack," Lan replied quickly, "but you need to come with me."

They followed him to the North side of the city, to a sight beyond imaging, where bodies lay in rows piled chest-high.

Tristan's blood ran cold. "Are those our dead?"

Lan's feathered neck sank into his shoulders. "Yeah."

Davad, ashen-faced, refused to look away from the carnage. Quietly, he asked, "How many?"

Slow to respond, Lan answered, "We're not sure. We've given the order to bring the dead here, but the extraction process is going to take time. You heard about the sanatorium and senes ad domum?"

"No," Set answered for him.

"Burned down," Lan informed him. "Add that body count to what's coming in from the East side of the city…" He shook his head. "We have a problem."

"Death sickness." Triton grimaced. When Davad and the brothers looked at him, he explained. "A healthy man spreads sickness after death. The healers don't know the cause, but we need these bodies buried before it spreads to the living."

"Superi could grow a forest with this many bodies returned to her soil, but…" He shook his head. "We don't have the time to dig so many graves." At Tristan's scowl, he added in self-defense, "I'm being realistic, brother."

"He's right," Triton said. "We don't have the time, nor

the man power, to plant these people as seeds the way they deserve. However, we do have a terra wielder capable of creating a common grave.

"No," Tristan objected. "You all treat her like she's made of stone, but her heart is bigger than all of ours. I'll not put her, or our people, through that. It's disrespectful, both to the dead and to those who love them."

Lan cleared his throat, hesitant to speak. "There's another option," he said.

"Name it," Davad told him, "because I agree with Tristan. A common grave is not one."

***

Anliac entered the tent that had been erected for their privacy and went straight for Tristan. The moment she was in his arms, she fell apart. "It's finished," she said, her silent tears coursing down the side of his neck. "There is so much death, Tristan. We may have pushed back the gods, but today was no victory." She turned in his embrace when Shashara entered, escorted by Set, but she didn't move away.

Pale and wide-eyed, Shashara let herself be led away from the opening. "There were too many," she said, just above a whisper. "We had to ask the families to wrap the bodies of their loved ones. It was all we could do to wrap the ones unclaimed or unidentifiable. Stop it," she snapped, jerking away from Set as if he'd struck her."

"Shashara…" he said.

"No." She sniffled and pointed outside of the tent. "Those people do not have an epoto to block their grief, their sorrow…their pain! We should all feel this," she cried. "We thought we knew what we were facing, but we did not, and now hundreds are dead." Turning woeful eyes on Tristan and Anliac, she said, "You are right. We did not ask to lead, but if we're going to continue to do so…we need to do better than this."

"We will," Tristan said as Davad came in.

"You don't have to do this," Set told him, feeling everything Davad did.

Grim, Davad said, "The herald gave the call for ignis wielders. Once they were told what would be asked of them, only a dozen remained." Taking a breath as he squared his shoulders, he continued. "I cannot throw my element, so the burden of this will be on them, but I can lead. I can light the first fire," he paused. "I can stand with them while they watch their people burn by their hands."

"How can I help you, my brother?" Shashara asked, reaching for him.

He backed away from the comfort. "We asked them to stand and fight. They did. This has to happen," he said, "and we all have our part to play."

"Which is why I'm going to need a moment alone with Triton," Tristan said. "Send him in on your way out." When Anliac tensed, he promised, "I'll be by your side before you reach the platform. Davad, can you walk everyone out?"

Stepping forward, Davad wrapped his arm around Anliac's shoulders. As they exited the tent, he said, "What you did for them today…it was heroic."

Set paused, holding Shashara back by their clasped hands, long enough to say, "The dead are not honored by their burial, Tristan. We honor them by ensuring that those responsible meet the same end. We finish what they started.

We break the curses and rain retribution down on the gods of Earth."

"I'm with the boy," Triton said, brushing passed the departing couple.

"Then we are all in agreement," Tristan said, widening his stance and crossing his arms over his chest. "I need you to stop being a ship merchant for a moment, Triton. I need you to be the pirate, or better yet…I need you to be the mercenary."

Triton's jaw clenched. "Explain."

"I need your friends," Tristan told him without hesitation. "All of them. I… *we*… need mercenaries."

Triton tensed as his eyes narrowed. "Be careful what you ask for, Tristan."

"You weren't there, Triton. You didn't see. We called it a victory because the gods retreated, and we were still standing, but…"

His golden marks flared so brightly that a guard ducked in to ask, "Is everything okay, sir?"

Reining in his emotions, Tristan's marks dimmed as he said, "Yeah. We're all good." To Triton, he said, "The gods possess abilities we've never seen. There is little more Anliac and I can do without becoming a risk to Superi ourselves. If they come at us in numbers, we're going to need more than an army of volunteers, more than soldiers."

"You want killers," Triton stated.

"Yes," came Tristan's stoic reply. "We need killers who are loyal to the Five and aimed at those like the Alphas, who would sit in Pisces Stragulum while those in Imbellis burned. And should the gods return, we'll need them for that too."

"Mercenaries do not work well with others," Triton told him. "Soldiers least of all."

"If they do their job," Tristan said, reaching for the tent flap, "the soldiers will never know they're here." Ducking out, he waited for Triton to do the same, and then said, "What the Alphas did today was treason, not to the five of us, but to Superi. They will answer for it." Keeping his promise, he left Triton behind and took Davad's place with Anliac just as she took her first step onto the platform erected at the start of the stone street that lead to Bealson's Grove.

A great mass of people, divided by their wrapped dead, stood to either side of it in rows five-deep. Resentments were high. The line between the Feras loyal to the Angeli and those loyal to the Alphas had been set, and a new chasm had opened between the people of Pisces Stragulum and those of Imbellis, who resented that it had been their city destroyed.

"There are no words that can ease the sorrow in your hearts," Shashara said, the first to speak, "but know that it is shared equally by those of us who stand before you."

"Their deaths will not be in vain," Set spoke, "and they will be avenged."

Anliac squeezed Tristan's hand before she let it go. Her voice, piercing in its beauty, revealed the depth of her sincerity. "We would have you know the weight of guilt we feel for each body that is to be returned to the cycle before its time. I say guilt because, at last, our youth has betrayed us. We were ill-prepared for what we would face, and that ignorance played a part in the pyre that will soon be set. For that, we ask forgiveness."

"Even as we offer you assurance," Tristan said, his voice reverberating and strong, "that no such ignorance remains. As your loved ones' bodies are turned to ash, know that the last of our youth burns with them."

As Tristan and Anliac took a step back, Davad moved forward. The ignis wielders standing at the edge of the platform came to attention when he spoke. "The Angeli have been reborn, revealing a blood right that belongs to us all, and now the gods have returned to keep us from reclaiming it. They have reignited an ancient war, but this revolution will bring about a retribution from which the gods will not recover."

Broken sobs intermixed with shouts of agreement.

"We are Superians," Davad said, "and so we shall send the spirits of our fallen into the aether, as our ancestors did. Not by laying their bodies into the terra with a seed, not by setting felled timbers to flame. No," he said. "In ancient times, the burden and honor of seeing the dead consummated with Superi fell to the finishers; ignis wielders who held the title of consummatorem."

Stepping from the front of the platform, the wielders fell in at his back, two by two, as they made their way to the dead. The sky was dark. The moons' light was dim, and so, when the wielders raised their arms, spheres of fire held in their palms, the flames banished all other sights.

The grieving did not see Davad hit his knees. They did not see the tears coursing down his cheeks. They would not know that it was his hand that touched first upon the linen cloth, wrapped around a girl who'd yet to see her first decade of life, but the wielders knew…and that was enough.

"Forgive me," he whispered, then set cloth to flame and rose to his feet.

One by one, the rolling spheres held by the wielders were released, each thrown farther than the one before, until the bodies were consumed.

From the platform, Tristan's voice boomed, "By the dead are the living untied!"

V

Betrayed

The old marketplace of Pisces Stragulum was crawling with people. Some were newly returned from the funeral site, some held out open arms to offer comfort, and others waited with anxious hearts for the Angeli to appear.

"Can you comprehend the position you've placed us in?" Lunam asked Sole as her pacing paws packed down the grass in her trek. "They will know that we received the call for reinforcements and ignored it. We've lost their trust."

"We never had it," Sole countered, but when her triangular ears laid back against her soft, orange fur, he moderated his tone. "If our loyalty comes into question," he said, "we will tell them that we did what they failed to do. We protected Pisces Stragulum when they left it all but defenseless."

"They won the first battle with the gods," she said. "A thing you swore they could not do."

"The gods of Earth are as varied in strength and abilities as Superians," he retorted. "Until we know the nature of the gods they fought, you should restrain from vaulting them so high."

"It is not their hubris that concerns me," she stated. "It is yours."

Sole's wings ruffled from shoulder to tip, his grey fur quivering along his spine as he angrily said, "The destruction of Imbellis and the hundreds who now lay burning does not seem a victory. The people of Superi will see today's event as I do: a sound defeat. And when they turn from the Angeli and seek a true leader, the Alphas will rise. I am the one who holds the knowledge of the past. There is no greater strategist that lives. And you, Lunam, with your ability, are the greatest General ever to be born on Superi. We do not need the Angeli."

Lunam waited for Sole to finish his overzealous speech, then she reminded him of who held the true power.

Striking at the pain center of his mind, she made him feel the agony of imaginary wounds. Starting at his paws, she crippled his heels, then moved on to his joints, making his mind believe that they were being ripped apart.

He howled. His head, tossing back and forth, dropped to the terra as he batted at his ears with his front paws. His body shook, trapped in a violent seizure.

Belua and Torren were beside themselves, uncertain of what to do or who to defend, and the loyal Feras were at an equal loss. The Angeli loyalists bore witness to their counterparts' Alphas as they turned on each other.

Forcing her voice to be all Sole heard, she flung her words into his mind and dared him to challenge them. *You overstep. It has been a great passing of time since your power was greater than mine. In the race of the aether, I'm faster, and as long as that remains so, you will always bow... to me.*

Releasing him from his torment, she allowed him to rise onto all fours and said, "For too long, we've done things your way. Now we will do them mine. The Angeli did not know what they would face with the gods, but we did. They defeated Superi's enemies without the knowledge you're so proud of, but the sharing of it could have changed the fate of Imbellis and its people."

Tensions grew within crowd upon hearing her words, but she was not finished. "I will speak with Angeli about the gods. I will share with them what we know..."

"That is a mistake," Sole told her, careful to lace respect through his retort, lest he end up on the ground again.

"It will be done, Sole," she told him. "And in addition, you will begin training the young epoto, as I've previously suggested."

His upper lip furled, baring his teeth.

"It's no longer a suggestion," Lunam said before he could speak. "You will do this." Finding Belua in the crowd, she said, "Find Truliam. His services are needed."

"The pyre still burns, and the epoto is with the Five," Sole said, then asked, "You would have me go to him now?"

As the Fulgo gate-maker, wearing the colors of the Alphas, stepped into the clearing, she replied, "I would have you see the death we've caused. Let it motivate you to teach Set well, because if the Angeli slit our throats for what we've done, he will be the last true epoto."

With her head hanging low, she turned for the far side

of Pisces Stragulum, where a padded bed before a banked fire awaited her. She did not acknowledge Torren's soothing touch upon her back as her loyal guard took her place at her side, but she was grateful for the transference of strength. Her own was currently waning thin.

"You heard her," Sole growled. "Open a portal to Imbellis. I have orders to follow."

It was the work of a moment to see it done, but the view beyond the opening would be branded upon the psyches of those who peered through it forever. They felt the heat of the fire that raged. They heard the cries of the grief-stricken people, their broken sobs and shattering wails. Shifting wind wafted rolling smoke into the city of Pisces Stragulum, and it carried with it the stench of burning flesh.

The Five stood upon the platform in white tunics that fell to mid-thigh over fitted black breeches. The flames of the pyre reflected off their stoned, silver, V-shaped signets as they bore the scene in stoic silence.

When Sole moved towards the opening, a moment of chaos ensued when a half-dozen Angeli Guards moved with him, to collide with Belua and the Feras that followed.

The confusion was clarified when Lishous said, "After what I just heard, Superi will be damned before I trust you with *my* Alphas."

"Hoorah!" the Angeli guards concurred, following Lishous to the portal.

"Will this night never end?" Sole asked the aether as he started his men forward.

VI

Lost and Found

King Normis had the guards on heightened alert. In heavy black armor, they paced back and forth atop the sloped walls of the turret, weapons in hand as they kept watch over the hundred-square-foot area that it incased. Made of stone and mortar, embedded with symbols etched in arcanite, the "killing room", as it had been dubbed by one of the Five from Pisces Stragulum, was their responsibility. They were the city's first line of defense, so when a portal opened, they were ready.

Stepping through, Davimon bellowed, "Hold your fire!" He shoved Lishous to the side, away from the loosed arrow that would have found its way into his friend's throat.

Lishous hit the ground hard. Shaking out his full, white fur, he regained his bearings and his feet. Slowly turning his head towards the arrow that had pitted the stone, he tracked its trajectory back to its source: an old, leather-faced Mortalis man, who stood next to a woman with braided red hair.

With a nod towards the guilty, she did as the other guards had done and stepped back, leaving the old man to fend for himself.

"Lishous…" Davimon warned as the Fera took off across the stony ground and leapt onto the wall. Latching hold with his claws, he climbed to the turret, where the guard dropped his crossbow and found his knees. "Lishous, do not kill him!" Davimon shouted, running his hand through his light brown hair, tugging at it in frustration as he shook his head.

As Lishous hauled the guard to his feet by the chainmail overlaying his dark blue uniform, the man swore, "It was an accident." Eyes darting to Davimon, he cried, "Please, don't let him kill me."

"Normis won't be happy if you eat a guard, Lishous," Davimon called out from below. "Besides, you've told me yourself how tough aged meat is. You won't like it."

The Mortalis guard paled as he nodded in emphatic agreement.

Dragging them nose to snout, lifting the man from his feet to do so, Lishous warned. "Go tell your commander you are no longer a guard for the wall, because if I see a bow in your hand again, I'll rip off your arms and use them to beat you to death." Expecting his command to be followed, he stepped to the edge of the turret and jumped. Landing lithely on the ground, he rejoined Davimon, who led them towards the heavily armored, double wooden doors that was the area's only egress.

"The world has become full of danger, my friend," Davimon told him. They crossed a plaza of sorts, cobblestoned and surrounded by merchant shops that curtailed to the needs of the wealthy and titled.

"What's your point?" Lishous asked as he watched the rich of Regia Aquam strut through the streets with their noses in the air.

"You shouldn't be so hard on the guards," Davimon told him. "With the Angeli building an army made up of all four races, it's become impossible to know friend from foe at a glance." Pausing for a moment, he asked, "Has ever such an army existed?"

"No," Lishous stated, "but friend or foe, I'll not have arrows flying at my head."

"I hear you," Davimon said, starting them forward again. "All I am saying," he continued, "is that the lines are no longer clear."

Coming to a stop before the King's massive stone fortress, Lishous nodded towards the adorned steel gates and said, "You should remember that in your dealings with Normis."

"He's our King, Lishous."

"I'm going to make a quick trip into Media Forum," Lishous informed him, ignoring the statement. "I told Michael I'd gather his things while we were here."

"I'll go with you to the King's stable," Davimon offered.

"No," Lishous declined. "I'm faster than the King's horses, and besides," he said, "I could use the run. I'll find you after."

"Lishous?"

"Later, Davimon," he said, dropping to all fours and finding his stride. As the lavishly dressed citizens of Regia Aquam, going in and out of their Angeli houses, blurred in his peripheral vision, his direction clarified.

Shoving aside his concern over Lishous's discontent, Davimon stared ahead at the fortress of grey stone and focused his thoughts on what he'd say to the King as he made his way inside.

Crossing the marble-tiled floor of the foyer to the winding staircases, he walked down the hall, passing the guards without a glance, to the elaborate metal door of Normis' chambers. There, he was stopped by an attendant.

"Master Davimon," the servant greeted and dipped his head, "welcome home."

"Thanks, Sean," he said. "Would you mind letting the King know I'm here?"

"Right away, sir." Rapping his knuckles twice to alert the King, Sean slipped inside. A moment later he returned. "The King is…occupied, but if you'd care to wait?" He gestured to the seating area.

As time stretched on, Davimon sat. He paced. He waited until his patience waned thin. Finally, it snapped. "Who is with the King?"

Sean blanched. "No one, sir."

Davimon's eyes narrowed. "Then what has him so occupied?"

Hesitating, Sean replied quietly, "The view, sir, and private musings."

Davimon stilled as anger suffused his face with heat to match that which flooded his veins. "Is that so?" he said, shoving Sean aside. Without Sean to prevent his entry, he busted through the door and into the King's chambers.

Normis sat behind his massive, square, stone desk with

his chair spun round to stare out of the two walls made of glass. "No one but you would dare to barge in on a King," he said and then turned to face Davimon. "You have information for me?"

"None that holds importance, apparently," Davimon retorted, glaring into the iron-grey eyes of his Mortalis king.

Rising from his seat, elongating his heavily muscled frame as he came from behind his desk to stand before his subject, he said, "Perhaps you've been absent for too long, Davimon. I fear that you've forgotten your place. I think it best that you're reminded before you deliver your report." He held out his hand and demanded, "Kneel."

Gritting his teeth, Davimon did as bidden, and though it grated, he waited for permission to rise.

"What news do you carry?" Normis asked, noting the undulating pupil of Davimon's left eye. The yellow and silver four- and five-pointed stars that ran from the oracle's left temple to his chin were reason enough for the King to pull back on his power play.

"The gods invaded Imbellis," Davimon stated. "The city has been devastated. The death count was high." Focusing his attention away from the horrific images in his mind, he continued with his report. "The Angeli were victorious in sending the enemy into retreat, but the gods called in reinforcements before the Angeli could discover how to kill them."

"What regions supported them?" Normis asked. "I know the Alphas have emerged from hiding and are reported to be in Pisces Stragulum with the Five."

"They are," Davimon told him, "but they offered no aid

during the battle, nor did any other region. The Angeli went in with only their Guard and those of the city itself to defend Superi."

"The Fera?"

"Have yet to send any significant numbers. However," Davimon said, "they will. And while the Alphas have yet to take their stand with or against the Angeli, you should know that the Feras are divided. More join the ranks of the Angeli Guard every day, and as to the Fulgo, Certamen has sent an invitation to the Five."

"Is that so?" Normis scoffed.

Surprised by the King's disregard, he added, "They say he is trying to secure an alliance. If he is successful, the Fulgo will have found favor with the Angeli by being the first to take a solid stand beside them. It is favor we need, my King."

"Nutrine," Normis stated, "is a pompous fool and of no concern to me." Aloud, but more to himself than to Davimon, he said, "The divided numbers of the Fera nullifies their threat. If the Nox have yet to make their move, then we will wait to make ours as well. Let the others die in these first battles. It will ensure our numbers dominate when we arrive to win the war."

"With all due respect, King, that is a mistake," Davimon insisted. "Do not let the Mortalis be the last to take their stand beside the Angeli."

Cocking his head in contemplation, Normis said, "Your loyalty to the Five grows apace with your absence from Regia Aquam. Tell me, how fares your loyalty to your King?"

"The gods are beings of great strength. They possess abilities beyond that which we are capable of, and yet, Superi is at war with them. We are at war, my King," Davimon said carefully. "And while you require that I kneel…the Angeli ask that I rise."

***

Lishous slowed when the quaint wooden homes of Media Forum rose up around him. White smoke trailed tranquilly from chimneys, and the scent of fresh-baked bread and pies added an aroma to the feeling.

He waved at a woman with an apron tied about her waist, who stood in her front yard, beating at dirty rugs with her broom. Her daughter, hair done up in pigtails and missing both front teeth, clucked at the yard birds as she cast seeds onto the patchy green grass for their breakfast.

A young man and his father, fishing poles resting on their shoulders, greeted him in passing, but as he continued at a measured pace, his thoughts raced. These people had so little. They bore no titles or wealth, nor did they possess the arrogance or prejudices that came with them.

Heavy of heart and with a conflicted animus, he entered the old section of Regia Aquam. The repaired or newly constructed buildings stood in contrast to those layered in paint after decades of standing. The monster sent by the gods had left its mark behind, but the people were resilient and, having no alternative, had placed the horrors of the day behind them.

From beside the communal well, the captain of Media Forum waved. His black fur shimmered blue beneath the light of the suns, dulling the dark blue of his decorated uniform as he stared over.

Though the man's speed markings, which ran from his thighs to his calves, were hidden, Lishous knew they were there. Nicolelas Nutruminson had first been trained by him and then had received a surname when his predecessor adopted him after he'd saved her life. Clasping forearms, their smiles were genuine as they greeted one another as brothers.

"You're a welcomed sight," Nicolelas said. "How long are you here?"

"If fortune favors me at all, not for long," Lishous replied. "I'm here to gather Michael's things."

One of Nicolelas' eyes was yellow and the other was green, but they both narrowed in question. "Michael was a servant of lesser rank than even you or me," he said. "You'll not find much in his apartment, but I'll take you there."

They hadn't gone far when, bewildered by the level of poverty infesting the inner section of Media Forum, Lishous said, "I wasn't aware things had grown so dire. Has it really been that long since I was here?"

Noting the clusters of homeless wretches gathered in shadowed corners and narrow alleys, he shook his head, but when they reached the apartments reserved for the servants of the fortress, he was appalled. The rotting wood of the buildings' outer walls bode ill of what was inside.

"In any other region, these buildings would be condemned," Lishous growled. "A stiff breeze could bring them down." A raucous barking erupted, and he turned towards a feral dog whose ribs promised very little meat. And yet, he watched the desperate spill from their holes to give it chase. "Has the King digressed so far in his leadership that he would let his people starve? How long before all of Media

Forum suffers the same?"

Nicolelas, taken aback by the treasonous remark, left it without reply. "Come," he said. "Michael's room is within."

The stairs creaked beneath their weight, and when they stepped into the hall leading to the closed wooden door of Michael's private space, the floor groaned as if about to give way. Turning the lever, it snapped in Lishous's hand. He tossed it aside and entered first. After, all he could do was stare.

A straw-stuffed mattress, made up with a faded, thread-bare quilt, lay in a corner on the warped, wooden floor. A scarred chest of drawers sat in the center of one wall, with a cracked water pitcher placed inside a basin that had long since lost its painted design on top of it. Beneath the wax-covered window that offered the room light without the benefit of a view was a round table and two chairs.

Crossing to the closest, he pulled back the hanging sheet. "Are you kidding?" he snarled as he yanked out the only items in it: three simple white robes.

"I do not understand your countenance or your words," Nicolelas said. "While it's true that poverty has plunged to a new degree in Media Forum, the reality of a servant's life should come as no great surprise." His lips pressed thin, he watched as Lishous move towards the chest of drawers with the robes clutched in his hand. "You and I are both from these streets," he continued. When Lishous's swiping arm knocked the pitcher and basin onto the floor, causing it to shatter, he shouted, "What are you doing?"

Prying up the loose board Michael said would be there, Lishous dipped his fingers into the slot revealed and fished out the scrap of green cloth. It was sewn around the edges and pulled taut into a makeshift coin pouch. He upended its contents onto the table. One by one, he counted the silver coins…the eighty silver coins that had taken Michael years to save…that he and Davimon would make in a month.

And in that moment, everything changed.

Dropping the servant robes, he turned to the captain of Media Forum and said, "I forsook my race. I ignored the call of the Alphas and the dreams they cast to bow to a king who desires only my death. And I've done this," he added, "out of the loyalty I have to Davimon, but that ends now."

"What are you saying?" Nicolelas asked, his hand falling without conscious thought to the hilt of his sword.

Though noting the action as conviction settled like a mantle and his shoulders squared, Lishous restrained from reacting. "Michael is no longer a slave," he said, "nor am I, for the Angeli live as an example of a better way. They serve their people, Nicolelas, and in return, their people follow them. I…follow them."

"They will mark you a traitor," Nicolelas stated.

"So be it."

"Davimon's loyalty will come into question," Nicolelas continued, "and it will take your head to clear his name of suspicion. You know too much. You've been too long among the Five." His eyes rounded. "Superi help us if Davimon feels the same," he said. "The King loves him as a son. The betrayal would pit Regia Aquam against Pisces Stragulum at a time when the gods…" His jaw snapped shut and then he said, "They are children playing at war, Lishous. They are ill-equipped, and they are going to set Superi on fire. You've not thought this through."

"Have you put the pieces together yet, old friend?" Lishous asked, taking Nicolelas off guard with the swift change of topic. "Do you know who the epoto of the Five is?"

"No," Nicolelas said, going along with it as his mind scrambled for ways to save his friend from whatever madness gripped him. "Should I?"

Like a floodgate opened, Lishous loosed his tongue, and the words would not be recalled. "He is the son of Beth Mathews. You do remember her, right?" Not waiting for a reply, he said, "He has her strength. Her will. Her heart. And should Normis turn on Pisces Stragulum, the Five will come. Your men will bare steel against your captain's son, against those he calls family, and by giving the order, your honor will count for nothing. So," he said as he gathered Michael's coins and moved for the door, "upon such a day, should you side with your king, I'll see you die there as well."

Heart racing, Nicolelas shook his head. "You can't mean that."

The deadly gleam in Lishous's eyes left no room for doubt. "Your view of events is shrouded in a shadow cast off by a king who cares only for his race. He and those like him are responsible for the fracturing of Superi, and I will not stand idly while the division grows. I choose the children, as you call them, for they seek unity. Normis rules a region, but the Angeli, they are destined to rule the world."

Without waiting on Nicolelas' reply, Lishous left the apartments alone. It took him twice as long to return to Regia Aquam as it had for him to reach Media Forum, but he entered the first establishment he came to with robes hanging on display. Purchasing four of them for Michael—three of differing, solid colors, and one made up of a multitude—he waited for the merchant to wrap them in a common cloth. Paying with his own coin, he left to find Davimon, hoping his business with the King was finished.

He pondered what he would say to his friend as he made his way towards the King's fortress. *Here you go, Michael. I'm afraid your robes were stolen, but these suit you better anyway.*

Aloud, he said, for his own comfort, "Better days are coming…"

VII

The Road Less Traveled

"You're leaving?" Shashara asked Set when he stood from their table, his breakfast left untouched.

"Sole is waiting for me," he told her.

"How can you trust him?" she asked. "Especially after what happened the night of the funeral."

"I don't," he said, "but with my father dead, I thought I'd never find anyone to train me. Sole has decades of experience, Shashara. I can't say no. If I'm going to fight…I need him."

Shashara's hands were shaking. "Anliac and Tristan talk about the strength of the Angeli being equal to that of the gods, but the healer that laid hands on Anliac said she could have died. And the fact that Tristan can heal is irrelevant. He can bleed. He can feel pain. Set…" Tears slipped from her eyes to spill down her honey-hued cheeks. "You are not an Angeli, and I don't want you to fight. I don't want you to die."

Cupping her cheeks in his palms, he kissed her and then pulled her into his embrace. "I don't want to die," he said. "That's why I'm taking lessons from a traitor, Shashara, because I have to fight. I'm an epoto, a member of the Five, and Tristan is my brother."

"You were with Sole all day yesterday," she said. "Your place is with us today. Come to Certamen. Please," she added when his expression darkened. "I don't trust the Alphas, especially Sole."

When a knock sounded at the door, he said, "Talk to Tristan," as he opened it to find Sole waiting.

"About what?"

"Just talk to him," Set said, stepping out into the light of the twin red suns. "I have to go."

Dressing in the black, fitted breeches, boots, and sleeveless shirt designed for the Five, she yanked her silver cloak from a peg on the wall and left the home she and Set had claimed to find Tristan. She found Davad first.

"Where's Tristan?" she asked.

Looking up from the scarred desk he sat behind, he said, "He had a late night," before bending back to the cloth receipt that lay waiting on his signature.

"The meeting," she sneered. "Yeah, I know, but where is he now?"

"Honestly, sis, I have no idea. I've had my hands full organizing the relief effort for Imbellis. Finding housing, clothing, and food for those who lost everything in the fires is all I can handle right now. This trip to Certamen is irritating. Nutrine should be coming to us. I don't have time to fool with fools."

"Set isn't coming," she told him. "He's training with Sole again. I told him I didn't like it, and he told me to talk to Tristan, who seems to have disappeared."

Anliac came up behind her, from the dirt road running parallel to the dock. "Set will be fine," she said, ushering over the man holding the reins to their horses. "And as for Tristan, he'll join us before we reach Certamen."

With a dozen mounted Angeli Guards as escort, they left Pisces Stragulum for their meeting with Nutrine, but Shashara's silent seething became too much.

"You're in a mood," Anliac stated, avoiding Shashara's glare by diverting her stare to a falcon flying overhead.

"She's not the only one," Davad grumped, tugging at the high-collared, grey shirt Anliac had shoved him into earlier in the morning. "I don't get why I have to go. Wasn't suffering through the trip to Regia Aquam enough?"

Shashara snorted.

"You have something to say?"

With a sideways glance at her brother, Shashara said, "Regia Aquam was no punishment, Davad. We've all heard the stories."

The guards at their back chuckled.

Davad swallowed hard, his Adam's apple pressing against the snug collar. "I don't know what you're talking about."

Looking straight ahead, not even trying to fight her grin, Anliac said, "Freckles. Wasn't that the name you gave her? Or perhaps," she teased, "there were just too many for you to remember any particular one?"

"I hate you both right now."

"I hate a lot of things," Shashara said.

"What's that supposed to mean?" Anliac asked.

"Nothing," Shashara sighed. "It's just... Am I the only one who feels like we left too soon?"

"We've done what we can," Anliac told her. "We've swept Imbellis for the dead, the undead, for monsters, and for gods. On our end, it was clear, so we went home."

"And repairs are underway," Davad said, "but if you feel like one of us should be there, I'll turn this horse around right now."

Anliac laughed. "You must really want out of that shirt."

"You have no idea."

Shashara shook her head. "The grey looks good with the black and silver, Davad. It makes you look...older. But I wasn't talking about the city itself. I'm worried about the people," she explained. "Imbellis is in turmoil, and after what happened between the Alphas the night of the funeral, I can't say that Pisces Stragulum is faring any better. We shouldn't have left either city to deal with so much alone."

After a moment, Anliac said, "When the gods attacked, we hit a learning curve, Shashara. We didn't know how many of them we would face, nor what their abilities would be. We had no plan to get the citizens out of the city, and as a result, we were ill-prepared to deal with the massive number of injuries."

"Fatalities," Shashara corrected, "not just injuries."

Anliac continued through her interruption. "The wielders were pulled from the fighting to deal with the fires and storms. The guards had their hands full dealing with the undead soldiers, and the Alphas..." Anliac's chin jutted forward as her visage hardened. "We had no way of knowing that they would turn their backs when they were needed."

"Is this supposed to make me feel better?" Shashara asked, her right brow arched. "Set's spending all of his time with one of them."

"It should," Anliac said, "because now we know. We know that the strength of an Angeli is equal to that of any gods'."

"I'm so sick of hearing you and Tristan say that," Shashara said, sighing. "You forget I saw your injuries, Anliac. I helped peel Tristan's bloodied armor off him. What little was left of it, anyway. So you can stop pretending like I don't have a reason to fear…like you can't die."

"The only Superians capable of defeating a god is an Angeli," Anliac stated, sitting stiffly in her saddle. "Neither Tristan nor I asked for that responsibility. However, we have no choice, and if we are to succeed, we cannot afford fear. We cannot dwell on our mortality."

"I know that," Shashara snapped, "but—"

Anliac spoke over her. "We knew to expect the unexpected when it came to their powers, but how were we to know that their weapons would have minds of their own, or that they could shift from one kind of monster to another on command? We couldn't," she said, "but we know now. We'll adapt and be better prepared next time."

"You still don't get it," Shashara told her.

"Then explain it to me," Anliac replied, her brows arching at Shashara's tone.

"An Angeli is an entity possessing abilities like those of the ancient Superians," she said, "but it won't be enough to save the world from Earth's gods. The two of you act like you're in this alone, but the truth is you choose it, and by doing so, you endanger us all."

"We choose it?" Anliac harrumphed. "If you know of another way, Shashara, share it."

"Razoran has strength. Triton has aquis ability. Jaccoo has speed. It takes three to make one, but collectively, are they not close to what an Angeli is?" Shashara asked. "And if so, why do you and Tristan insist on fighting a losing battle alone?"

"I understand your logic," Anliac admitted, "but we lack the numbers."

"Then I say it's time we start recruiting," Shashara stated with a lift of her chin.

"Lan and I were thinking the same," Davad said. "We're preparing a regiment of guards who will evacuate citizens, while another will evacuate the injured and bring them to you, but we're worried about thinning the ranks of fighters. Recruiting was our solution."

"Why would you bring them to me? I'm not a healer," she reminded him.

"Perhaps not," Anliac said, "but the healers answer to you nonetheless."

"And the Alphas," Shashara asked, "what about them? They answer only to themselves."

Anliac, dropping her voice so her words wouldn't carry, assured her, "We have eyes on them now. If they make a move, we'll know it."

Shashara scoffed. "Is that what Tristan told Set? That he had eyes on them? Who, Anliac, short of an Angeli, can take on an epoto as old as Sole?"

"Look," Anliac told her as her patience waned, "now is not the time to discuss details. You're going to have to trust us."

"You're right," Shashara retorted. "Now is not the time. The time would have been before a decision was made. Don't think that I'm not aware of the meeting between Tristan, Riker, Lan, and Triton; one that I wasn't invited to be a part of."

"No one was trying to leave you out, sis," Davad said, "but you were exhausted."

She turned on him, eyes narrowed. "Were you a part of that discussion?"

"No," he said, "but I get it. We each have our part to play, and we can't always stop to talk things over. Sometimes decisions simply must be made. I didn't wait to ask permission before issuing orders to start the rebuild. I took those I needed and put them to work."

"We are not of one mind," Shashara said, ignoring his statement. "We are a collection of individual thoughts, a rounded perspective that allows us to see the bigger picture. If too many decisions are made alone, we will be divided by them."

"Don't take this the wrong way, Shashara," Anliac said, "but since the battle, your attitude has been… trying. We won. What else do you want? I mean, really, what is your problem?"

"It's too much," Shashara admitted. "Set has refused to sit out another fight, but ever since Tristan told him about the battle, he won't talk to me. He won't talk about the gods, or the war. He won't talk about the insanity of trusting Sole to train him. He won't…" Her voice cracked. "He won't talk to me…and we talk about everything."

Nodding, Anliac said, "You're scared. We're all scared. None of us were prepared for this, but turning back is not an option. Like it or not, Set's right. We need him, and we need him trained. If we come up against a god with abilities we can't defend against, it will be up to Set to even the battle."

"And get him killed in the process." Shashara shook her head. "He has to touch them to drain them, or have you forgotten?"

"Shashara…"

"No, Davad," she said. "We were trained to fight, how to pick our battles, but it was never against entities like the gods. Set is not prepared for this kind of fight."

Anliac hit her limit and pulled up on the reins to turn her mount around. Furious, she snapped, "I could have died, Shashara, but I fought. Wielders fought, many of whom did die. Guards with no abilities at all fought…and died. Civilians without any kind of training fought…and died. This is war." She scowled. "Welcome to it."

"Shut up!" Davad barked, having had enough. "Both of you. You want to have a meltdown? Do it when we don't have an audience. These people are looking to us for strength, for direction, it won't serve anyone to be seen as children. And trust me," he said, arching a brow as he drove his point home, "you're both acting like one."

Gathering the reins, Anliac started to turn to him, but a dust cloud caught her attention. "We have company," she said. The guards were already turning. "And they're coming in fast."

Two archers brought string to cheek. At the last moment, just before they loosed their arrows, Anliac shouted, "Wait, that's too fast… It's Tristan."

Curses accompanied their lowered bows.

"What are you doing?" Davad asked as Tristan ran up… facing backwards.

"It's nice that you could find time to join us," Shashara snipped, "with all the meetings and decisions you have to make."

Tristan's smile slipped, but when he jogged up next to Anliac and saw her grinning down at him, it returned. "Triton and Razoran challenged me." He laughed. "They swore their horses could outrun anything or anyone, even if they had a speed ability. Here I am," he said, his grin growing. "They should be along shortly."

"Get up here," Anliac told him and scooted forward in the saddle to make room for him. Once he'd settled, his warm arm coming around her waist, she said, "They knew you were faster, dear. They just needed to get rid of you."

"What?" Tristan asked, sitting straighter. "Why would they want to get rid of me?"

"Maybe they held a meeting you weren't invited to," Shashara replied coldly. "Maybe they laid plans that don't include you. Maybe…"

"What's your deal?" Tristan asked, twisting to look back at her.

"She needs her attitude adjusted," Anliac retorted, "but she might be right."

Tristan leaned until he could see Anliac's profile. "Explain."

"He really wants Nutrine's garden," was her reply. "My guess? They're using the alone time to lay plans on how to get it."

"Trust a pirate to stay true to his nature," Davad said, quoting his father.

Nathin fell back from the advanced convoy of guards, leading a rider-less horse to Tristan. "Glad you could join us," he said, offering a nod of respect. "Your uniform is in the bag," he told him, gesturing to the pack hooked onto the saddle horn, "but there's a small pond coming up if you'd like to wash first?"

"Do you really think Triton tricked me?" Tristan asked Anliac before answering.

"Yes, dear. I do."

Chuckling, Tristan said, "Yeah, let's stop so they can catch up. But um, hold on to the reins for me, would you?" Tristan grinned, lifting Anliac to sit in his lap and delighting in her squeal.

Anliac smacked the back of his arm as all but Shashara laughed.

VIII

Decent in the Ranks

Busy clearing away the breakfast dishes, Egweene stopped to answer the knock at the front door. "General Riker," she said, "what a pleasant surprise." Taking a step back, she offered, "Please, come in."

"Thank you, ma'am," he said, eyeing the staircase in the corner as he entered. "I take it the boy is still asleep? Set," he added when her head tipped to the side.

"I'm sorry, General," she said, "but he left with Sole before the suns' rise."

Noting how she picked at her fingertips, he asked, "Do you know where they were going?" When she shook her head but failed to meet his hard, black stare, he tried again. "Ma'am, is there something I should know?"

She hesitated. "The Five have shown great trust in me. Serving the House of Angeli, one hears certain things not meant for their ears, and I'm not one to wag my tongue, General."

73

"Something has you concerned," he stated, "and it should, because Set was supposed to be with me today."

Hesitant, she said, "Shashara was upset that Set was leaving with Sole. She was crying over it, and though Set said it was something he had to do, he was worried."

Tensing, wrinkles appearing at the corners of his eyes, he asked, "How do you know?"

"He didn't touch his breakfast," she said, "and fresh sweet buns are his favorite."

Riker squeezed the outside of her shoulders. "You've been a great help. Thank you," he said as he turned for the door.

Egweene stopped him. "When Shashara told Set that she didn't understand, he told her to talk to Tristan. I was going to go find him myself once my chores were finished."

"I'm sure everything is fine," he told her, "but to make us both feel better, I'll track him down."

As soon as Egweene closed the door behind him, he took off at a run. He'd seen Truliam in the old marketplace, and as the Alphas' gate-maker, he would know where Sole had taken Set.

Finding him at the communal well, carrying a dipper of cool water to his lips, Riker stormed up and asked, "Where are they?"

Truliam paused, his brows skewed, and then he drank his fill despite the rude interruption before asking a question of his own. "Who?"

"Listen here, you pale-skinned…" Riker's muscled arm shot out to grab hold of the Fulgo but grabbed air instead when a portal opened and Truliam back-stepped into it.

"Sole," Truliam spoke from behind him, forcing Riker to pivot and fall into a defensive stance before his mind registered the non-threat, "and young Set are at the gateway site opened by the gods."

"Which one?" Riker demanded.

Truliam swallowed hard, his brows climbing towards his forehead. "There's more than one?"

"Tell me where they are!"

Unruffled by Riker's outburst, he replied, "I have."

As his instincts moved to match his mounting rage, Riker's hand fell to the hilt of his double-edged short sword. "Open a portal. Now."

"And if I refuse?"

"Either the aether or your gut will have a hole in it before I leave," Riker vowed. "Your choice."

Leading Riker away from the foot traffic, Truliam said, "For generations, my forefathers have produced progeny of like ability, and we have served the Alphas without fail or question." Finding a safe place to open the portal, he stopped and turned to face the other man. "Until now."

"Meaning?" Riker asked.

"I am ashamed of what transpired on the day of battle," Truliam confessed. "I was with them when the signal for reinforcement came in. There were no words spoken, but a conversation was had, and they did nothing. The confrontation between them during the funeral added to that shame." He paused to collect his thoughts and gather his courage, then said, "Loyalties have shifted."

"Why are you telling me this?"

"Because," Truliam replied, snapping his fingers and

conjuring a portal, "as trained with a sword, as I am in my ability, I've done as you've asked without fear of your blade. I would know, as you would know, that young Set is safe."

"You fear for the safety of the Five."

It wasn't a question, but Truliam's lack of reply hastened Riker's step through the opening.

Set and Sole were easy to spot in the open plain, and seeing that Set was unhurt, he sagged in relief. Starting towards them, Lan's white feathers drew his gaze to the Southern wall of Imbellis, where he worked with the terra wielders to rebuild it. It wasn't long, however, before the tree line obscured his view.

Focused on Set, he saw the boy lift his arm. When energy crackled, dancing on his fingertips, he picked up his pace. By the time a shadow had formed, he was in a full run. There was nothing unusual about the black and purple coloring, but the shape of the vortex was unlike any he'd seen. There was something about the way it swirled and twisted that was…wrong.

Sole spread his wings and lifted into the air.

Riker, unprepared for the shock, tripped over his own feet and scurried to keep moving forward, while maintaining his balance. That's when he saw it. Spreading outward in an expanding circle, starting beneath Set's feet, the emerald-green grass was dying. The death it carried rushed to meet him, blocking his path.

There was no explosion. The terra did not quake, but there came a loud *BOOM*, and then the gateway stood open. Inching forward, Riker touched the toe of his boot to the cursed ground. When he suffered no ill effect, he ran again.

Only, this time, his eyes were trained on a shimmering door that stood at the end of a long hallway, lined with pillars of white, and hoped it would not come open.

Fortune deemed him unworthy. A musclebound Mortalis, in a blue toga that hung from one shoulder, appeared in the hall with a golden trident in his hand. Pointing with the three-pronged spear as one would a finger, the man shoved forward with his shoulder expectantly and shook with rage when the resulting explosion failed to pass through the rift.

Slamming the end of his trident against the hallway floor, the gateway snapped closed against Set's will. The compressed energy became a wave that knocked all three men off their feet. Set was blown backwards into Riker, who'd almost made it to him, while Sole, wrapping his wings around himself like armor, rolled to a stop twenty feet away.

Set, flat of his back and laughing, pushed himself to his elbows. "Well," he said, "I wasn't expecting that." Riker stood, scowling, and brushed himself off.

Unfurling, Sole fumed. "I told you to stabilize that rift." Then he rolled his eyes as Lan and a handful of terra wielders ran up.

"Is everyone okay?" Lan asked, but that's as far as he got before his attention was drawn elsewhere.

"We had him," Sole continued to rant. "We needed to make him talk."

"What is that?" Lan asked, pointing.

Set, tucking the silver V that had fallen against his chest inside his white cotton shirt, glanced down at the black leather pant leg that had been shoved up to his knee in the tumble. It was the red diamond and swirling marks revealed on Set's calve that had piqued Lan's curiosity.

Standing of his own free will, Set addressed the gathered terra wielders. "Had events been dire, your quick arrival could have made the difference between victory and defeat. Thank you, but as you can see," he said, "all is well, and your skills are needed at the wall."

As the others departed, Lan stood his ground. "I'm not going anywhere," he said. Refusing to ask his question again, he cocked his head to the side, staring at Set's marks, and waited.

Set's reply came without hesitation. "I'm an epoto."

"A mark within a mark," Riker said, taking up Lan's cause. "The fine web shifts on your face, while the teardrops do not. Plus, they are different colors. Believe me, Set," he told him, "I've watched carefully. I've waited for the webbing to fade, but it hasn't, and now we discover this." Pointing to the red markings on Set's leg, he said, "That's a physical mark for speed or agility. Tell me I'm wrong."

Lan's arms fell to his sides as his jaw went slack. "How many abilities do you have? How long do you keep them?"

Set opened his mouth to answer, but Sole cut him off.

"You're both idiots," he said. "But you, Riker, are a general for Palus Regia." He sneered. "That you must ask is pathetic."

More interested in answers than being baited, Riker said, "An epoto can drain the energy of a wielder and, for a time, use that energy to wield the ability as if born with it. They are not supposed to be able to keep it." When Sole rolled his eyes, he and Lan turned to Set for explanation.

"I don't know what you want me to say," Set told them.

"The marks just show up. I don't know if it's theirs, or just another mark."

"But how do you keep it?" Lan pushed.

"By touching the one born with it," he said, "and then draining them until they are dead."

Without conscious thought, Lan and Riker backed away, their fear and rejection slamming like a battering ram against Set's emotions. It was Sole who stepped closer to stand at his side.

"And Lunam wonders why I prefer the solace of the caverns," he chortled. "Don't let them get to you, boy. All men fear what they don't understand. But for your knowledge… It's the dead's marks you carry."

"I was actually okay with not knowing," Set told him.

"What makes you an expert on epotos?" Lan asked.

"Being one," Set said, grinning, when Sole groaned at his secret exposed.

Riker, wide-eyed, asked Lan, "Did you know?"

"No," Lan squawked before their curses overlapped.

"You have a big mouth," Sole stated, stretching out his wings as he rolled his shoulders in irritation before settling them on his back.

Set shrugged. "When you put yourself in the middle of others' affairs, your affairs become others' business. Get used to it."

The bell from Pisces Stragulum tolled in the distance.

"Why don't you put those wings to use?" Riker suggested. "Fly up and tell us what's going on."

"First," Sole stated, "I don't take orders from you. Second, I don't want the whole of Superi knowing my wings work."

"Guaranteed, that knowledge will soon be common-place," Riker said, "whether you fly up or not."

"Looks like Set's not the only one with a big mouth."

"Shut up," Set ordered, and both men fell silent, though Sole's glare promised retribution. "Lan, what can you see?"

His hawk-like eyes gave him an advantage even over the Alpha. "They are either Nox or Mortalis," he said. "Collectively, they're too short to be Fulgo. Bobarnibus is with them, so they're friends."

Feeling the tension drain from him, Set chimed in. "They could be Fera."

"They're not," Lan assured him.

"How do you know?"

"They're wearing uniforms."

"So?"

"Describe them," Riker said, despite leaving Set's question unanswered.

"A blending of browns, greens, and tans," Lan started. "Tight-fitted caps on their heads. Brown boots." That's as far as he got before Riker took off to intercept the approaching regiment of men. "Well," he harrumphed, "that was rude."

"He recognized the description," Set said as they moved in the same direction at a more sedate pace. "I did as well. They're Nox. Now tell me how you knew they weren't Fera."

"Care to answer, Alpha?" Lan asked, dripping sarcasm.

"The Fera, those who live among the other races, have adapted to covering the parts of themselves that seem to cause offense. However, when battle is imminent, a Fera will most often shed such confinements. Therefore," he concluded, "there are no uniforms when we amass."

As the three of them joined Riker, talking with Montilis, the Nox General slid from his saddled horse in a uniform matching that of his men.

Clasping forearms with Set, Montilis said, "You change every time I see you, boy, but it looks like it's weight you've gained instead of marks this time." Taking an easy jab at Set's stomach, he teased, "You must have put on thirty pounds."

Set grinned. "Steady meals and a training yard has its upside."

Laughing, Montilis pulled him in for a brief embrace before asking, "Is my daughter around?"

Set shook his head. "No. She and the others are on their way to Certamen by Nutrine's invitation."

"That man is a snake," Montilis said, surveying his surrounds. Turning from the direction of Imbellis to that of Pisces Stragulum, he scratched his head and said, "From the looks of things, I should have brought laborers instead of soldiers."

"Sir," Lan pipped in, nodding to show respect for the man's station, "with your permission, Bob and I will see to it your men earn their supper."

"Call me Bob again, and I'll tar your feathers and laugh while you roast," Bobarnibus stated.

Draping his feathered arm around the other man's shoulders, Lan said, "Oh, come on, Bob. Don't be like that," as he started the soldiers towards the city.

Nostrils flaring, Montilis said, "The air reeks of death."

"The dead were consecrated by fire," Set told him, "and returned to the terra. I keep telling myself that by the time the scent of it fades, they will have found peace, yet I can't believe the lie. Only vengeance will see their spirits settled."

"How many did we lose?" Montilis asked.

"Somewhere between three hundred and fifty and four hundred," Riker admitted, "with at least a hundred more injured."

"And how many of them?"

"We don't know," Set said. "They disintegrated as soon as they were killed."

"We counted close to a hundred piles of ash," Riker told him, "but with the battle, there's no way of knowing how many were scattered."

"The Angeli are to face the gods," Montilis said. "It's our job to see that they are not distracted, so tell me everything you know about their soldiers."

Set couldn't hide his scorn before Sole took note of it.

Still, the Alpha answered, "You have not lived long enough to carry the memories of the first wars, but I have, and in those wars, conscience was abandoned. Those that came with the gods fought the same, killing without discrimination. Young or old, man, woman, child—they slaughtered them all. Death is the only way to stop them."

"Wait," Montilis said. "Of the hundreds that died, how many of them were soldiers?"

"A hundred, maybe," Riker told him. "They burned down a sanitarium and a senes ad domum."

"So, they targeted the old and the sick," Montilis said. "Tell me what we're doing about retribution." When Set dropped his stare, he asked, "We are striking back?"

"Oh, yes." Sole's grin grew until Set rolled his eyes at him. "We are."

"Not today," Set was quick to clarify. "Today was about seeing if I could open one of their gateways. I can. Now we wait for the others to return."

"Set…" Montilis cracked his knuckles. "Don't you see what this means? If you can get us to Earth, we can send in a team and capture one of the gods. We can force them to tell us how to break the curses." When Set just sighed, he added with fervor, "We could end the war before it begins."

"That's what I said," Sole concurred, "but the young epo-to here seems to need the Angeli to hold his hand before he can make a decision."

Montilis snapped his fingers and, shutting Set out of the conversation, said to Sole, "But you do not."

"No." Sole smiled. "I do not."

"The four of us make an excellent quad," Montilis continued. "There's no need to wait for a team."

"No," Riker said, joining in. "There's not."

"Riker, whoa," Set cautioned. "Sole is messing with your emotions. He's heightening your need for justice so that you'll go along with his plan. Don't be sucked in."

"He's not touching me," Riker countered, "and I would know if my mind were being played."

Remembering the battle between Montilis and Jacob, Set told him the truth. "Trust me, Riker, your training against a telepath is useless against an epoto." To Sole, he said, "I will not act without the council of the Five."

"Calm yourself," Sole soothed, "and let us talk of compromise. Walk with me?"

With Sole's focus turned elsewhere, the compulsion to do the Alphas' will waned, and Riker wasn't happy about the manipulation. Catching Montilis before he could move to follow them, he asked, "What are you doing, General?"

"Whatever I must," Montilis vowed, "to ensure my daughter never again faces a god, or in the very least, has the knowledge of how to defeat them."

"And if your actions get Set killed and she hates you for it?"

"That is tomorrow's problem," Montilis said, turning to catch up with the others.

IX

Earth's Hot...

"Why must you be so difficult?" Sole asked Set as Riker and Montilis joined them.

Frustrated, Set took a deep breath and then tried again. "Do you know what it means to create a gateway?"

Sitting back on his haunches, Sole replied, "I have the distinct impression you're going to tell me."

"The amount of energy it requires is directly correlated to the distance between the two points," Set said, including the other two men in the conversation. "Opening a gateway between Catena Piscari and Pisces Stragulum is easy, especially considering there's an oceanus to draw from, but a gateway between the Turris region and Pisces Stragulum? Ask Char the toll that took on her land. Look," he stressed, casting his hand out in the direction of the gateway, "more than the grass died, gentlemen. Every seed, every insect, every worm is dead, and all we did was open the cursed thing. The god on the other side was the one who held it open. It

---

was all I could do to destabilize it before what he cast got out."

"Okay," Montilis said. "You're right. No one here understands the risks in a way you do, but this is an opportunity we cannot miss."

"Superi might hold the energy," Set told him, "but I will be the conduit. What if I'm not strong enough? What happens if I fail?" When it became obvious that no answer was forthcoming, Set continued. "I'll tell you. I will go mad or die. The rift will slam closed. The gateway will explode, and those of you on the other side will be trapped."

"It's a risk I'm willing to take," Montilis said.

"I know you are," Set replied. "I can feel the vengeance you seek like acid on my skin."

"I think it kind of tickles," Sole said with a lopsided smirk.

Set closed his eyes and shook his head, his shoulders drooping under the strain, but he was sure to make his point. "I don't hold this against you, Montilis. In fact, I respect you for it. But the truth is, you are thinking of Anliac, and I have to think of Superi."

"If it was Shashara who was to face the gods, this gateway would already stand open," Montilis said, refusing to back down.

"No, sir," came Set's sure response. "It would not, because I know that on the other side of any gateway to Earth, there may be god. And if Sole is wrong…"

"I'm never wrong," Sole interjected. He was ignored.

"…And we can't defeat it, we've turned a god loose on Superi through a gateway no one knows exists."

"Perhaps Montilis has a vested self-interest," Sole said, "but you cannot dismiss my intentions as selfish. There is not one among us who does not understand the importance of knowledge. Ignorance loses every war."

Set chortled. "You don't give two dung piles about Superi. Your absence during the battle at Imbellis proved that. Your interest is in dissolving the curses at any cost, so that you may claim that title of Angeli. And don't act offended," Set sneered when Sole's chest puffed up in indignation. "You don't have to be an epoto to feel the jealous envy you have for Tristan and Anliac."

"Set," Riker said, speaking for the first time since rejoining them, "I outrank General Aquam. I was his teacher, his trainer, and yet when he was returned to Palus Regia, I was the one to hold him prisoner. I told him that he'd betrayed the whole by trying to save the one."

"I know," Set told him, "and there was a time I would have killed you to free him, but that was then. Now I know better. Do you believe this is the right thing, Riker? Do you believe it is worth the risk to Superi and to those we'll leave ignorant and blind if events go awry?"

Montilis visibly tensed and Sole came up on all fours, both eager to see which way Riker would sway the boy. Yet, the senior general was slow to give answer, and when he did, he was careful with his words.

"We know of seven gods," Riker said. "Superi holds but two Angeli. We cannot win with those odds, Set. We all will face the wrath of the gods to come, and to prepare the denizens of our world for such a day, we must first know how to defeat them. It's that's simple. Now," he said, "we can wait for the Five, but…I would have you answer one question before you choose that course."

Sole's curiosity was such that his head was near sideways. His brows were so furrowed that the wrinkles appeared deep and permanent. Montilis, on the other hand, planted his feet and crossed his arms. His chin was tucked, gauging Set from beneath lowered lids, as he clenched his jaw to keep silent.

"Ask," Set said.

"Who is the General of the Angeli Guard?"

Expression skewed, Set asked, "You think it's me?"

"During the battle at Imbellis," Riker asked, "where was Shashara?"

"She had a portal made that put her inside the Asylum," Set answered. "She did what she could to save those who couldn't make it out of the city. What's the relevance?"

"Where were you?"

"Outside of Pisces Stragulum, waiting on the signal for reinforcements."

"Then how did you know where Shashara was?" Riker asked.

"Reports."

"I see," Riker said. "And can you tell me why Davad was in Pisces Stragulum instead of Imbellis?"

"Davad's no coward," Set said, true anger coloring the words. "He had his hands full making sure everyone had what they needed. Without him, half our fighters would have gone in with sticks and stones. I still don't know where he came up with the weapons. And you can ask Shashara; without the supplies he gathered from nothing, the death toll would have been a lot higher."

"Who led the regiments inside Imbellis?"

Losing patience, Set's reply was terse. "Men chosen by Anliac, who reported to Lan, who sent updates through Jaccoo."

"And who received those updates? Who issued orders?" Riker asked.

"I did," Set said, sensing defeat.

"You are the mind that wields the fist of the Angeli," Riker told him. "You are their general. However, you are also Superi's last line of defense. That alone gives me pause."

"I don't know what you're talking about," Set denied, but he averted his eyes.

"If the Angeli face a god whose power they cannot defeat," Riker insisted, "you alone have the ability to save us. As you've said, Sole has different ambitions."

"So, what is it to be?" Montilis asked Set. "Will you save yourself on the off chance you will be the one to save Superi? Or will you take action to see that it doesn't come to that?"

"Two of you will go in," Set said, giving his answer. "One of you will stay with me."

"Why?" Montilis asked, eyeballing Riker as if entering competition.

"Because I want someone to survive, to spread word of our inflated hubris when the rest of us get ourselves killed."

"Riker can stay with you," Sole said. "I'll have more fun with Monti."

"We're not close enough for endearments, Sole." Montilis grinned. "But in this case, I'll let it slide."

"Where are we going to do this?" Riker asked.

"By successfully opening the gateway," Set told them, "I think I can find my way back to Earth without tampering with a rift controlled by the gods."

"That would limit our chances of encountering them," Riker concurred, "while giving us our best shot at taking one of their denizen captive."

Set snapped his fingers.

"If that's a gateway, I'm an epoto," Montilis said, perplexed by the speed and ease with which the rift had been made. As wide as two men and tall enough that a Fulgo wouldn't hit their head, the portal's creation and stabilization was instantaneous.

Fighting not to grin, Set said, "Just go. I'm right behind you."

Stepping through, onto the grass-covered fields north of the grove, Set was the last to enter before the portal closed. The men strained to see the gateway site of the gods, which now stood off in the distance.

Their proximity to the river made it necessary for Sole to speak up. "Practice run?" he suggested, his triangular ears twitching.

"I don't want to put more strain on land already drained," Set replied. "Riker, you're staying with me?"

A stiff nod and then Riker said, "I've got you."

"Walk twenty feet ahead and then turn and face me," Set told him. "I need a focal point. You two," he said to Sole and Montilis, who were discussing what they might find, "need to shut up."

"This good?" Riker asked.

"Yeah," Set told him, taking off his shoes and stockings to nestle his toes in the grass.

Standing barefoot, Set locked eyes with the older man, then opened himself up to the power he fought so hard to keep caged. He knew he stood on Superian soil. He felt the crisp blades of grass pressed against his soles. He saw the tree line blocking the view between Imbellis and Pisces Stragulum. He smelled the crisp, clean water flowing down the Vitreus River behind Riker. He could feel the heat of the twin red suns and the pull of the planet he loved so much, but those were common things seen through common eyes.

Viewed through his ability, the world changed. The terra became more than soil for his feet. It became a dais, and in this moment, he was king. Each blade of grass bowed to him. The treetops swayed at his whim to cool his heating flesh. The oceanus churned, its waves crashing upon the distant shoreline, anxiously hoping to be called upon. He was not alone. Superi had him.

Everything on Superi held its own light, an energy that would never dissipate, and all things seemed to move. Some, like the rocks and gems within the terra, moved slowly, while the lights of the waters were as lightning: swift and brilliant. They called to him, these lights, begging to be controlled, to be consumed, repurposed according to his will.

As an epoto, he grabbed hold of the light, the intangible aether, and used its power to send his mind soaring ever higher. The sweet voice of his mother was singing in his ear of a time when Superians flew among the stars. There were so many.

Beyond the suns, past the moons, his body remained

where it stood, but his mind traveled onward through the vastness of space. Planets with stories of their own to tell hung suspended there, awash in a myriad of swirling colors, but it was to a blue orb that he was drawn. Upon the seeing the single sun that hovered over it, Set did not need his ability to know that he'd found Earth.

Great land masses appeared, separated by grey waters that turned a brilliant blue the closer his psyche was drawn to them. Feeling the strain of exertion, he latched onto red terra and dropped the psychic anchor that the rift required.

"Set!"

Someone screamed his name and, suddenly, his eyes were his own again. They opened to a rift, a swirling vortex of massive proportion, rolling with angry streaks of white lightning. They held their breath, terrified, until at last, it stabilized and stood open.

"Thank Superi," Riker muttered when Set's blue stare met his. "You're alive…and you didn't kill us!" True, the general had run, as the others had, to escape the spread of death created by Set's unleashed ability, but he'd kept his promise. He'd stayed within the epoto's sight through it all.

Set shook his head to clear the beads of sweat rolling from his forehead to burn his eyes. "I'm good," he said, his voice unrecognizable under the strain. "It's stable…for now. GO!" he bellowed when Sole and Montilis stood frozen.

"Go where?" Sole growled. "We can't see beyond the opening."

"Go anyway," Riker shouted.

They took off at run, bellowing a battle shout, as they leapt through the gateway. Falling into a forward roll, Montilis came to his feet with his sword in hand. Sole's black lips were peeled from his dagger-like fangs, his fur a ridge running down his spine.

"Hot, hot, hot!" Sole yelped, stepping off the metal road they'd landed on. Once his paws touched the red soil running alongside it, he stood, raising one at a time. "Their sun scorches their land. Do you think they could be immune to ignis?"

"I don't know," Montilis said. "From what I was told, the dead soldiers turned to ash after beheading." He turned in a slow circle, shading his eyes with the side of his hand from the brilliance of their sun. "This land is barren. There's no life here."

"Plains of dirt, mountains of more dirt," Sole grumped, "Collibus Dolor has more to offer."

"But that blue sky, Sole," Montilis noted as he put away his sword. "Have you ever seen something so beautiful?"

"Once or twice," Sole replied in dry humor.

Curious, Montilis opened his hand, palm up, and closed his fist, but only beads of moisture formed on his darkened skin. Repeating the process, a bulbous, green plant with cruel needles as armor burst open and fell into jagged pieces. Held in the concaves was a milky-white substance, but no aquis to quench their thirst.

"According to the histories," Sole stated with growing concern, "our abilities work here."

"There's nothing wrong with my ability," Montilis told him. "The only water source here is deep underground. It would take time to pull it to the surface, unless, of course," he said, "you want to do the honors and rip a hole in this place."

"With pleasure." Sole grinned, but then it slipped and his head cocked. Ears turning like tuning forks, he asked, "Do you hear that?"

Montilis strained, closing his eyes to block out his other senses. "I don't hear anything."

"Open your eyes, idiot," Sole replied, "and look."

Traveling down the metal road at a speed that required great power, a beast in red barreled down on them with four black feet that did not step but rolled.

"Superi help us…" Montilis said, staring through the monster's single, translucent eye. "The beast has swallowed an earthling whole."

"Then let us split it wide and take what we came for," Sole replied.

With the enemy upon them, Montilis drew his sword and said, "We have to stop it first." Lunging, the tip of his blade pierced the monster's armor, but the speed at which it traveled yanked the hilt of his hand. Dragged forward, Montilis hit the road hard, splitting his scalp at the hairline and busting his nose and mouth until blood dripped from his chin.

Sole, not about to let his prey slip free, sent his terra ability running beneath the road. The beast was fast, but he was faster. Once ahead of him, the flat metal surged upward into a wall.

The beast let loose a screech to rival a dracon's and its backside slid back and forth like a fish's tail as its head dropped low. A loud *BOOM* accompanied the collision as its armor was crushed. It's eye, less durable, shattered like a pane of glass when the earthling was launched through it upon impact. Its dying breath issued forth as grey smoke, and its blood, seeping from its underbelly in rivulets that sought the terra at the edge of the road, was clear. The scent of it burned the nose.

On his feet and moving, Montilis paused to wrench free his blade before kicking the side of the hissing hunk of metal.

"I'm going to take a guess and say it's as good as dead," Sole stated, trotting by Montilis on his way to see if the earthling had survived.

"I'm not convinced it was ever living," Montilis retorted.

"He's in bad shape," Sole stated, "but still breathing."

Joining him, Montilis whistled at the twisted legs and bloodied flesh that had been skinned of clothes. One arm hung as if ripped from its socket, and thick, red blood pooled beneath the back his head.

The earthling coughed, coating his teeth in blood and staining the silver strands in his black goatee. Eyes, so deep a brown as to be ebony, were wide with stark terror.

"Porfavor… no me comas."

Sole growled, causing the earthling to squeeze shut his eyes and spew forth sound that made no sense.

"La luz de dios me circula. El amor de dios esta dentro de mi. El poder de dios me proteje. La presencia de Dios me cuida. Donde Dios esta, todo estara bien."

"I can't believe this," Montilis said, stringing curses. "After everything, we can't understand him."

"I will," Sole stated, pressing a paw to the center of the middle-aged earthling's forehead.

The man's chest rattled, his breath a ragged, fruitless

pull, and then mercy was granted to him through death. The knowledge he'd held was now possessed by another.

"They call themselves humans," Sole stated, thrown off keel by the influx of information. "His name was George." Looking up, chasing the horizon at the end of the black asphalt, he added, "Set put us in the middle of a desert. It could be days before another car comes through here."

"Car?"

"You were right," Sole told him. "That," he said, gesturing towards the crashed vehicle with his snout, "is called a Toyota Corolla, a car created in the year of nineteen ninety-four. George wasn't swallowed by it. He controlled it from the inside."

"What else did you pull from his mind?" Montilis pressed, eyes narrowing at the implication of the Alpha holding higher ground. "We were supposed to bring him back alive."

As Sole began the short walk towards the pulsating gateway, he said, "Don't worry, General. I'll share the knowledge gleaned with the epoto everyone seems to trust."

Exiting, they stumbled upon a scene more startling than the one they'd left behind. Armies in differing uniforms, Feras interlaced among them all, stood as a silent wall, enclosing the gateway.

"Run…" Set gasped, short on breath. "Run!"

Energy depleted and expecting to die, Set couldn't hold it, and the rift slammed closed. As predicted, the gateway exploded, and Set felt himself fly before all went black.

X

Worse Than Us

"Get a healer over here!"

Riker's shout brought him to a dazed consciousness.

"Move back. Move back," came a gruff, familiar voice. "Let me get to him."

"Swinney," Set gasped as the hunched old man struggled to kneel beside him. "What...what would I do...without you?" He winced at the healer's touch. "AHHH!" he screamed, remembering well the price of pain extracted for healing.

He continued to do so until Swinney was satisfied he would live. After taking a proffered wet towel and mopping the sweat from his eyes, he reached greedily for the water flask Riker shook in his face.

"I should kick all of your arses," Lan berated as Set worked himself into an upright position to take the next water flask offered to him.

Drinking deeply, Set wiped his mouth with the back

of hand and replied, "I agree." Scanning the gathering, he said, "Send these people away, Lan. The danger has passed. Not you." His command stopped Sole, who'd turned to slip away. "You have information to share."

Scratching at the wiry whiskers sprouting from his chin, Swinney protested, "I'll be sticking around, if you don't mind? I answer to your woman, and she would be none too pleased if I left you to die so soon after saving you."

Returning from disbanding the men, Lan demanded, "What were you thinking, boy? Every eye from here to Certamen could see that monstrous thing."

"I…" Set tried, but that's as far as he got.

"The alarms were given." Lan threw his feathered arms into the air. "By now, even the Mortalis king has heard of this. Not to mention the damage done to the river by those cyclones."

"Cyclones?" Set asked.

Disbelief spread in Lan's beady eyes, blinking repetitively.

"You do realize there are more important things going on here, right?" Riker asked.

"I hope so," Lan answered, "because the rest of the Five will be back soon."

Reaching a hand up to Riker, Set sought help to stand, but once on his feet, he took control. "Lan, summon runners and see what you can do about retracting the signal. Take Swinney with you." A sharp glance silenced any objection coming from the healer. "See that Jaccoo is sent to Certamen. If you're right, and the gateway was seen, I'll not have negotiations with Nutrine suspended over a misunderstanding."

"Are you going to tell me what you were doing?" Lan asked, peeved.

"You know what you need to know," Set told him.

"Huh," Lan grumbled. "I see. You know, that's the first thing you've said that made you sound like them."

Lan's disappointment was a physical blow that Set felt in his gut, but it didn't stop him from holding a steady stare until his friend was the first to look away.

As the gathering scattered, and the four were again alone, Set spread his glance between the two men who'd crossed over. "Where is our captive?"

"Dead," Sole told him, "but I retrieved what information he had before he expired."

"He?" Riker asked.

"A fifty-year-old man named George," Sole told him. "He lived in a region called Texas, in a place named Midland, but he had crossed a border into his homeland of Mexico, seeking a reunion with his mother."

Set caught himself leaning forward to study Sole's moving lips, as if to aid him in understanding the foreign words. "How did he die?"

Sole's chuckle could have been the giggle of a girl. "In a car accident."

"A what?" Riker scowled.

Set held out his hand and demanded of Sole, "Show me."

Sole positioned his head beneath Set's palm, and with contact made, the Alpha gave the young epoto a taste of what it meant to connect with another of his kind.

Set's hand took a moment to fall after Sole moved on.

"The curses have truly damned us," he said. "Their civilization is as much machine as it is human. And the things they've created…the weapons they possess… The earthlings are not the helpless beings our ancestors encountered."

"That doesn't sound good," Riker stated.

"No," Montilis concurred, "it does not. Was there anything hopeful in the human's mind?"

"They're divided," Set told him, "even more so than we are."

"The gods cursed them too?" Montilis asked, as surprised as Riker.

Set shook his head. "They've done it to themselves. While both worlds claim four main races, they have further divided themselves into thirty sub-races. Although, they've crossbred until it's impossible for most humans to know their true origin. Self-righteousness is the common thread between them, each seeking seclusion from the others as they proclaim their own race superior. And while we fight to end segregation, they fight to keep it."

"It's worse than that," Sole interjected. "They have continents, as we do, but where we have regions, they have states. These states make up countries, and the countries have armies the likes of which Superi has never seen. Their sole purpose is keep the denizens of other countries out."

"If I'm honest here," Riker said, "I don't understand any of that."

"Look at George," Sole explained. "He was born in one country, but longed for another, believing it of more value. And he is not alone in his thinking. There are others like him, who would give their last coin to gain entrance instead of investing that coin in their homeland."

"It's their history," Set said. "They are a warlike and greedy people, hungry to devour the land soaked in the sacrificed blood of their enemies. Even now," he told them, "they are building a wall to make sure that permission is granted before crossing the border between their two countries."

"And that is only two," Sole pointed out. "There are many more countries, countless states and providences, and war has ravaged them all at one time or another."

"And it's all over race?" Montilis asked.

"Race is but one dividing factor in their culture," Set replied. "Politics is another. We have the lawyers meddling in the Asylum; their job to ensure the peace accords are adhered to. There are so many politicians on Earth, they should be their own race, and the trouble they've caused throughout their history is irreparable. Our lawyers work for the good of Superi. They know that to do otherwise would get them killed, but their lawyers…" His nostrils flared as if catching a foul odor. "They first write laws to protect themselves, and then they do whatever they want."

"And then there is what George called religion," Sole continued. "It means the belief in and worship of a god. It's strange, though, he's never seen the one he serves, and the only other deity he knows of is one called Lucifer. Him, he hates, and denies him the title of god."

"He knows nothing of the others?" Riker questioned. "How can that be?"

"As far as he knows," Set answered, "the gods we've encountered are for children's tales and do not exist."

"That can't be," Montilis said, struggling to digest the new information and the implications of it.

Set's eyes darted hurriedly as he searched through the memories Sole had shared. "I don't know how it's possible," he said, "but it's true."

"Okay," Montilis said, pulling his thoughts into focus, "let's talk about what we know. We know we can open a rift, and we can keep it open long enough for an assault. We know the earthlings are divided, incapable of forming any real defense against us, so long as we deny them time. And," he concluded, "we know our abilities work there."

"The humans are weak," Sole added, "and fragile."

Taken aback, Riker asked, "Fragile?"

Nodding, Sole told him, "Without their gods to defend them, we will slaughter the humans, delivering a bloody insult before we turn our fury on those who cast the curses."

"They are truly that divided?" Riker asked.

"Yes." Set smiled darkly. "I believe they are."

XI

Tainted Soul

This could have gone better, Ares thought as his father caught hold of his right shoulder, crushing the armor to hold him steady. The solid front-kick delivered after sent him sliding on his belly, catching sight of his bloodied face in the high gloss of white marble, where he spilled into the ethereal, round room of the Grand Hallway.

Relieved that he'd stayed inside the towering pillars that lined the space, he peeked beyond them to the black void, pinpricked with starlight. "Whew, that was close."

"Imbecile!" Zeus bellowed, his white toga clinging to his muscular frame as he moved to attack his son again.

"Father, please!" Ares cried, holding out his left hand, as if that would be enough to ward off Zeus's rage. "I did not go to start this war," he said in a rush. "I went to collect Thor."

A vicious kick to his left ribs was Zeus's reply. "Do you know what you've done, boy?" he demanded, grabbing Ares by his armored chest plate and lifting him so that their noses were almost touching. "Do you?"

Spittle, accompanied by Zeus's hot breath, landed upon Ares's turned cheek, but he answered. "The Angeli are stronger than we remember. They are our equal."

On a thunderous growl, Zeus tossed him backwards, drawing pleasure from the resounding crack of Ares's skull as it connected with a pillar. "I care not about the fractured Superians, nor their guardian Angeli," he sneered as Ares landed on his hands and knees.

Arms buckling, Ares split the skin above his right brow when he face-planted the marble. He moaned through the throbbing pain, deciding it best to stay prostrated before his father rather than take more abuse. Besides, the block Zeus had placed on his ability to heal couldn't hold for much longer.

"You represented the Greeks," Zeus fumed as he paced, "and you made us look weak." Energy coalesced beyond the hall in blue-white streaks that offered flashes of light to the black abyss. "You do not instigate an attack unless you are certain of victory. You were trained better! We do not lose to mortals," he bellowed, "regardless of where they're from."

Pushing off the floor with his functioning arm, Ares struggled to rise. Swaying on his feet, he risked saying, "The one I faced could heal. I wasn't prepared for that," he said, "but I will be next time. I swear on the river Styx, I'll find a way to kill him."

Eyes narrowing, Zeus countered, "Do not make promises you cannot keep."

A loud *BOOM* cut off whatever else the king of gods had

to say as Nordic symbols burned into the white marble between the father and son. In the center of the circular pattern, without injury and in armor newly repaired, Thor appeared.

Taking a knee, Thor bowed his head before locking stares with Zeus and saying, "If it is a pound of flesh you seek, spare the innocent." Standing, he cast a glance over his shoulder at Ares and then added, "Take it from the guilty."

Lightning strikes accentuated his warning. "You, Asgardian, would not survive my wrath."

"I fear no Greek," Thor countered, then wished he could recall his words when Zeus's right foot collided with his chest. As his newly repaired armor concaved around Zeus's sandaled foot, his ribs snapped, and he braced against the pain that followed.

Already airborne, the bolt of energy that followed hurled him into Ares. When their combined weight was tested against a pillar, it snapped, and as it gave way, the two men spiraled off into the darkness.

Curling one bicep into a mountainous ball, Zeus stretched forth his other arm. His flat palm pointing his fingers in the direction they'd disappeared, he said, "*That* is how it is done by a Greek."

There was a shimmer in the aether, a precursor to Poseidon's appearance that Zeus missed. But the god, in the blue toga he'd favored for eons, made his presence known. "They tried to kidnap me. Me!" He bellowed in a murderous rage. "Curse those damned Angeli."

Misunderstanding, Zeus chuckled. "Who was it this time? Michael? Or did he enlist Raphael in his scheming? I tell you, brother," he said without waiting on a reply, "their god is a constant thorn in my side."

Confusion cocked Poseidon's head. "Not those angels, you idiot. The Superians. They opened a gateway and accessed the Great Hall."

Zeus stilled. "That's impossible. They would have no way to find it, as none of the Halls are connected to Earth."

Poseidon shook his head in slow wonder. "How is it you always manage to miss the point? How they found the Hall is irrelevant. They could have accessed it through the gateway Munsin left anchored. The point is…"

"MUNSIN!"

"Ugh," Poseidon groaned, covering his ears as his brother attempted to shake loose the stars.

Instead, between two pillars, a doorway of light appeared. Munsin entered through it. "We've been expecting your invitation."

"We?" Zeus queried, short of patience.

"Come, Qandisa," Parvati coaxed as she, too, joined the gathering, but Qandisa resisted.

From beyond the doorway, she said, "I'll not listen to that pompous Greek's insults." Upon hearing Zeus's laughter, she wailed, a high-pitched keening that made them cover their ears, and then she disappeared.

Zeus crossed his arms and glared at Parvati. She apologized on behalf of the goddess. "Qandisa has not suffered a defeat since the Egyptians were conquered. To lose to mere children…" She shook her head.

His arms fell to his sides as he turned to face the void and bellowed, "You were defeated by children?"

"Who are you screaming at?" Parvati asked with unease.

"It would appear Odin is as displeased with his son's failure as I am with mine," Zeus told her. "I've put them both in a time-out."

"Munsin," she asked, dropping her shoulders on a sigh and casting Zeus a disapproving stare, "would you summon them back here please?"

"If that is your wish," Munsin agreed, then closed his eyes to concentrate. Forthwith, two doors appeared, one on each side of the room between standing pillars, and from them toppled the men.

"Zeus," Parvati chastised upon seeing Ares's condition, "shame on you. Let him heal."

Snapping his fingers, Zeus conceded, and as Ares restored his flesh and armor, he made his demand. "If, in fact, your opponent was a child, how did you lose?"

"Forget the last battle, brother," Poseidon said, "and focus instead on what they thought to do with me!"

A burst of fire erupted suddenly. The six gods shielded their faces as they backed away.

"Why," Hades asked as he stepped from the center of the flames, dressed in black, light armor lined with blood-red adornments, "am I never invited to such gatherings?"

"Douse the heat, Hades," Zeus grumbled. "I have my wrath to keep me warm."

The flames were sucked into the egress of Hades' making, and as the marble repaired itself, he stated, "It's good that you're all here. We have a problem."

"No kidding," Poseidon grumbled. "Have they found a way to enter Tartarus? Did they attempt to capture you from there?"

"What are you talking about?" Hades asked, his black eyes narrowing on his brother's. "What is he talking about?"

"What are *you* talking about?" came a chorused reply from Zeus and Poseidon.

"Iblis and I were playing cards," Hades told them, "when he was told that a soul had been collected, but…" He paused for dramatic effect. "It's tainted."

"You play cards with Shaytan. Impressive," Munsin said. "I'd imagine he is quite the skilled cheater."

"On the contrary," Hades replied, "he's one of the honest ones. If you want to beat a cheater, try playing the Fates. Those harpies are—"

"FOCUS, people!" Poseidon shouted.

Hades went slack-jawed before snapping it closed. "Oh," he said, "I know you did not just take that tone with me." As the onlookers fell silent, he added, "And in front of company, no less. Tsk, tsk, brother."

Without giving an inch, Poseidon pressed. "Tainted with what?"

Ignoring the god, Hades directed his answer to Zeus. "A soul showing up with a Superian imprint is cause for panic in the underworld. A heads-up would have been appreciated."

Parvati, standing to Zeus's right, tensed. "How did the Superians get their hands on a human?"

"Were they not used in the last assault?" Hades answered with a question of his own.

"No," Thor jumped in. "We summoned only the dead to fight."

The air thickened into a wavering heat that blurred their

vision and made breathing difficult.

"Calm thyself," Zeus soothed. "We'll handle it."

It was the wrong thing to say.

Ebony spikes speared from Hades' black armor as flames erupted across the back of his shoulders like a cape of fire. His black hair was pushed from his face as if standing in a windstorm. As his onyx eyes became deep hollows, swallowing the whites of them whole, his voice went as deep as the pits he ruled. "I told you last time…kill them." In less time than a blink, he was across the room and in Zeus's face. "Kill them all! That is what I told you, but you did not listen. Now you will," he hissed, "or more than the Superians will be destroyed. I've warned you, brother. You know what aether does to souls, so end them, and do it without humans."

As white-hot flames encased Hades upon his departure, Zeus pulled back from the heat, throwing his hands up to protect his face.

Munsin, fearing Parvati stood too close, opened an egress directly behind her. Pulling her through with him, they exited again at a safer distance away.

"That wasn't creepy at all," Ares stated.

"Aye," Thor concurred. "What's his problem?"

"A lot, I would wager," Munsin piped in.

Zeus, stringing curses beneath his breath, turned and walked away.

Poseidon stepped up in his place. "This is not a joking matter," he said, "and Hades is right to be afraid. Of the Greeks, none hold a position of more importance. A sudden, great influx of souls into the underworld would break the gates of Tartarus, and Earth would be flooded with the souls of the dead. Worse, and you know this as well as I, brother," he said, "the Superians taint the souls of their kills. How many such souls did it take during the last war with Superi before Tartarus' gates threatened to fall?"

"That's not the half of it," Ares interjected on behalf of those who did not know. "Tartarus holds an entity of terrible power. We cannot risk his escaping. Even the universal gods, have reason to fear him."

"Apollo approaches," Munsin said, slamming his palms together and creating a two-doored entry point for the sun god's use.

As the doors parted and Apollo emerged, his visage was dire. "We have a problem."

"Another one?"

The question came from Zeus, who'd had about enough.

XII

A Lesson in Negotiation

"Circum vertere."

The Angeli Guard turned their backs as Tristan sloshed his way to the edge of the pond.

"Ugh," Davad said, turning as well. "Get dressed already, would you? No one wants to see all that."

"Speak for yourself," Anliac teased, wiggling her eyebrows at Shashara, who blushed and averted her eyes.

Chuckling, Tristan's massive thighs bunched and bulged as he climbed the sloped bank to reach his pack. Tugging on his fitted, black leather pants, the sculpted muscles of his back and shoulders playing beneath his pale white skin, he grinned up at Anliac. "You keep looking at me like that and Nutrine is going to be in for a wait."

"Like I care," Anliac replied to the snickers of the guards, laughing herself when Tristan's yellow eyes flared, caressing her with a burst of light.

Pulling on his boots, Tristan left the long-sleeved shirt in the pack and pulled the black leather tunic on over his head without it, cinching it at the waist with the silver belt Anliac had bought for him. From an inside pouch, he took a thin-linked chain and slipped it over his head, adjusting the silver V signet of the House of Angeli to lay center of his chest before gathering his things.

"Your horse, sir." A guard held out the reins for Tristan to take.

"Thanks, man," Tristan replied, his smile stretching into a grin as he gained his saddle. "Look who finally decided to join us." There was a moment of confusion as the guards searched for an approach and came up empty, but then he said, "There," and pointed.

Distant specks of dust became a cloud of it. Riding hard in front was Triton, with Razoran at his side. Heading towards the wide, white-stoned road that would take them into Certamen, they intercepted the pirate and his first mate.

"While I won the game," Tristan stated, "it would appear I'm also the one who got played."

Triton didn't waste time denying the charges, nor did he attempt to disguise the mischievous twinkle dancing in his onyx stare, but replied instead, "I thought you would have learned better by now, boy. Sometimes you have to lose a battle to win a war."

Shashara's soft words caught Triton off guard. "I take it your plans to usurp Nutrine's gardens went well then?"

Quick as that, a mask of stoicism turned Triton's humored visage to stone. The change was so abrupt that even Razoran threw back his head and howled.

"*Heeyah!*" Triton barked as he nipped the horse's flank

with the heel of his boot, surging out before the others. "Don't we have a meeting to get to?" he asked without looking back.

The high white walls surrounding Certamen were so pristine that the suns' light reflecting from them impeded sight. The four approaching Fulgo, dressed in white robes with golden seams, all but disappeared in front of it.

Golden piercings followed the straight outer lines of the men's ears to their pointed peaks. Delicate rods punched through their brows, cheeks, noses and lips, and were attached by fine-spun chains that splayed across their white skin. It was a measure of the city's wealth that its servants would be adorned so.

In a line, shoulder to shoulder, the Fulgo servants presented themselves to the Five and their company, but it was the man who held the right, center position that spoke as they bowed in unison.

"Welcome to Certamen," he said, straightening. "If it would please you to follow," he continued, "Master Nutrine awaits your company in the arena."

Triton stiffened in his saddle.

Razoran's ears twitched as his grey eyes peeked sideways at Davad.

"If rumor can be believed," Davad spoke up on their behalf, "Nutrine is known for entertaining his guests in his famed gardens. Perhaps they are not so grand as the stories suggest?"

"On the contrary, young master," the man told him, "Master Nutrine is quite fond of his gardens and enjoys sharing them with such honored guests as yourselves. You have but to ask."

"I'll keep that in mind," was Davad's reply as they entered through the city's painted wooden gates.

The stone buildings that peeked above the outer wall were revealed in their entirety, and they were enormous. The streets, paved with purposefully laid stone, slipped like spider webs from the first plaza, where marbled water features and polished stone benches beneath sprawling tree branches offered comforts to the citizens.

There seemed to be no distinguishing features between businesses and homes, beyond the storefront signs and well-kept yards, for everything mimicked the craftsmanship of the ancient Superians. The city was undeniably beautiful, with its high arches and ornamented stone, but there was no denying the hardness, the coldness, that thrived within its fortified walls.

Following apace with their escorts, they stayed mounted as they journeyed deeper into the city. Considering the amount of stone and marble surrounding them, the large, manicured field off to their right drew attention. A single pole, the circumference of Tristan's thigh, sat at the far end of each side.

"What purpose does that stretch of land hold?" Davad asked.

"The games, Master Jacobson," the escort on the far right answered. And then, with a quirk of a grin, added, "At least, those that do not require weapons and armor."

Approaching a hill with constructed tunnels running through it, they were directed to a street that would take them over it. From the top, they gained a vantage that allowed them to see the less impressive side of Certamen, where the streets became gravel and homes were built of wood.

The street veered, carrying them towards the center of a hill, where the ground dipped on the other side into a massive bowl-shaped amphitheater. At a downward angle, rows of empty benches encircled the whole of it, wrapping themselves around the hundred-square-foot stage of grey stone, where Nutrine and Maltris waited.

Narrow paths of hard-packed dirt split the seating around the area. Choosing one, they traveled downward, towards the awaiting stage, and passed one of four tunnels that offered the crowds of the amphitheater an exit without having to climb the hill.

With no more than a cursory glance within the pitch-black openings, the Angeli Guards moved onward, but as an Angeli, Tristan's heightened sight saw more. Whispering a warning to Anliac, she made note of the eyes peering out at them from the tunnel's dark depth. She wondered how many more were waiting within the others, but she and Tristan both held their tongues to see how the situation would play out

"Welcome," Nutrine greeted, spreading wide his slender arms. His royal blue robes shimmered as he stepped forward on long legs. With a flourishing wave of one hand, his long, black-lacquered nails following, he bowed overly low and peered up at them with yellow eyes lined in coal. The golden hoops dangling from his pointed ears jangled as he straightened. "It pleases me that you have come." Scanning their group, he said, "Though I'm disappointed your youngest member could not also join us." A quick upturning, a flick of his head, and the escorts were dismissed.

"Set is of no concern to you," Anliac replied.

Tristan asked, "Why are we here?" as they took their cue and dismounted.

Leaving the Angeli Guards at the base of the stage with the remaining members of the Pero, who were dressed in their red silk uniforms overlaid in light, black chainmail, they took the stone steps that would put them on level with Nutrine and his guard. Maltris, marked by the golden rope running the length of his left arm, watched their every move as the six of them gathered before his master.

It was Triton who summoned Nutrine's stare before he could reply to Tristan's question and brought about one of his own. "How is my ship, pirate?"

"You well know," Triton replied with a tight-lipped grin. "Your ship lies on the bottom of the oceanus, Nutrine, while the beauty of mine continues to inspire envy."

Clearing his soured expression, Nutrine clasped his hands together and turned his attention to the others. "I had thought to throw a party in your honor, but…" He shrugged then dropped his arms to his sides. "I've heard the tactic did not serve King Normis well."

"So you thought instead to bring us here?" Shashara asked. "What is this place?"

"The Five prefer to negotiate in the open, yes?" Nutrine answered. "Besides, this place holds special meaning to you."

He wasn't looking at Shashara, but at Tristan, and so Tristan was the one to ask, "How so?"

"In the days of old," Nutrine said, "this was the arena where warriors, wielders and non-wielders alike, could prove their worth in games of combat to gain glory and honor. Later, it became the stage upon which auditions were held for positions among the most elite units of Superi."

"Like your Pero guards," Tristan stated.

"Indeed."

"Interesting," Anliac quipped, "but what does that have to do with Tristan?"

Nutrine continued without acknowledging that she had spoken. "The stone upon which you stand has tasted the blood of both your mother and your father."

Tristan could not hide his curiosity. "They competed here?"

"They more than competed," Nutrine divulged. "They thrived. Despite her Mortalis blood, Beth Mathews was the perfect woman: cunning, swift and agile, smooth with a sword and deadly with her ability. She laid waste to her challengers time and again, gaining her a position in the Tacita." He chuckled at a private joke. "Though, for truth, they should have renamed the quad Excidium, especially after Matthew took his place beside her. Beth was a ruthless, meticulous, killer, but your father took his time. He enjoyed playing with his prey. He gloried in the hot spray of their blood as it landed upon his flesh. It enlivened him."

Davad and Shashara found their stares colliding, a single unasked question connecting them. *Had their father fought here too?*

"However," Nutrine continued, "Beth was crowned champion after defeating him."

The corner of Tristan's mouth twitched. "That doesn't surprise me," he said.

"Talk of the past leads us to the present," Davad interjected. "Why are we here, Nutrine?"

As was his way, Nutrine answered with a question. "What is it the Five want?"

It was Anliac who replied. "What we want," she said, "is the end of the needless segregation of the races. What we want is an end to the segmentation of classes that results in the discrimination and servitude of so many. What we want is equality." She caught and held his stare. "What we *demand* is the release of your slaves and the unity of Superi in facing the gods."

Skipping over Shashara, with confusion clouding his visage, Nutrine made eye contact with Triton and Davad before settling on Tristan. "It's not my desire to offend your woman," he said, "but surely those cannot be your true demands."

"*His* woman?" Anliac squawked. The ground revealed her outrage with a foreboding tremble.

"Ah." Nutrine snapped his fingers. "My apologies," he said. "I am yet unaccustomed to women holding equal rank with men. In my defense," he added, "old habits die hard and will not be broken in a day." As his stare collected those of the men, he stated, "I thought perhaps one of you would share more reasonable demands."

"What do you mean," Davad asked, "by more reasonable?"

Lifting his voice, turning in a half-circle that, for a moment, placed his back to them, he spoke as if to a crowd.

"Alas," he said, "why not ask that I lay the whole Superi at your feet?" Sweeping his hands back, away from his body, his bow was mocking before he stood upright. "You ask for what I cannot give."

"How," Shashara asked, "is it not within your power, at least as far as the Fulgo are concerned?"

"What slaves we have in Certamen," Nutrine told her, "are criminals. What you call slaves, we call servants. Richly adorned, well cared-for servants, whose families have served for generations. We do not steal the children of others, nor subjugate any Fulgo child to the insanity of alchemy. We do not trade them as slaves nor as servants. Can your race claim the same? In truth, Miss Shashara, as a young woman of budding beauty, you would find life in Certamen quite pleasing."

Shashara's back went ramrod-straight, but she didn't speak. Her pressed lips and narrowed eyes said it all for her.

"Contrary to rumored belief," Nutrine continued, "women here, in Certamen, are not seen as less than men. They are a delicate, precious thing to be cossetted and cherished."

With a smirk, Anliac asked, "How, then, do you explain Shorlynn and her unwanted betrothal to your man here, Maltris?"

Nutrine sighed. "My dear lady," he said, "the alchemist, Malstar, sought that betrothal on behalf of his niece with fervor. Before the rise of the Angeli, she was most eager for the advantages of such a union."

"Perhaps the wedded women are considered of greater worth, but what of the unwedded?" Shashara called him out. "What of those too low to wed up? What is their worth?"

"Worth, like beauty, is measured by the one who seeks to claim it," Nutrine replied, "but none here are abused." Pausing to collect his thoughts, he sought to redirect the conversation. "I speak only for Certamen. As for the Fulgo race," he said, "you are asking them to discard thousands of years of tradition. And for what? A world in which the races of Superi live as one? A world where gender plays no part? Your world of a happily evermore will never exist. Not on this planet," he added with a chortle. "Here, there are those meant to rule and those meant to *be* ruled."

Anliac scowled. "Meaning women."

Without flinching, Nutrine told her, "It would be easier for a sheep to slay a wolf than to force the Fulgo Nation to follow a woman." When the ground quaked again, a smile stretched to his ears. "My dear," he said, "you make my point for me. Women are far too emotional to rule.

Tristan caught Anliac's hand when she would have raised it against Nutrine and spoke before more damage was wrought between them. "You stir coal to flame with your words, Nutrine. Was that your intent when sending the invitation?"

"No," he said with such sincerity that it could not be denied. "Your women speak of equality. In theory, it is a grand idea, and yet impractical. Consider a parable. Two sons are born, one to a farmer and one to an innkeeper. The farmer's son works day and night beside his father. His back grows strong, and he learns to wield a sword to protect his father's farm. Such was his skill and reputation that he was offered a position among the guards of Certamen.

"Now," he continued, "the innkeeper's son lazed in his

father's establishment, drinking his rum, playing with his women, and barking orders to the servants. Upon a day, the guard enters the inn, his coin purse full of silver earned from harvests reaped and protection given. The innkeeper's son, seeing all that the man has, grows angry with jealous envy and demands an audience with the Master of Certamen.

"Here is his claim. They are of the same gender and age. They are of the same race and were born of the same station. Therefore, what one has, so should the other have. He demands equality. What says the Five?"

Tristan, brows furrowed, shook his head. "You mistake our meaning."

With a tilt of his chin, Nutrine replied, "Then explain it to me."

"We do not believe that every man and woman are to be treated as equals," Tristan clarified. "We believe that all men and women deserve the right to reach for more than they were born to. We believe that a farmer can become a king if they can capture the hearts of the people. We believe a king can lose his crown if he forgets that to lead, he must first serve. We believe that, should one work to hone their skills, they deserve the gains – to their station and to their purse – despite race or gender. So you see—"

Interrupting him, Nutrine said, "Then the Five are more dangerous than the gods, for they reside in a world of fiction and would make Superi a slave of their delusion. In the world you describe, Tristan, the innkeeper's son kills the farmer-turned-guard. He steals his silver and turns his father's inn into a brothel for higher profits. With the guard rotting in a shallow grave, the man's father is left unprotected and made a slave to work land he no longer owns. He has a new master, one who honed the skill of thievery and, with it, reached for more than he was born to."

"That is why there are laws," Davad retorted.

"No, young master," Nutrine countered, "that is why there are kings. We see to it that those who are deserving receive reward, and those who seek undeserved reward find shackles instead."

"And what of women?" Shashara asked. "Cunning, swift and agile, smooth with a sword and deadly with her ability. With those words, you praised Beth Mathews for her skill in the arena. 'A ruthless, meticulous killer'. Is that not what you said?"

"It was."

"Was she, then, as a woman, unworthy to rule?"

"If Beth had been born a Fulgo," Nutrine answered, "she would have been a queen of invaluable worth. She, like all women of our kind, would have been pampered, adored, and given her heart's desire, so long as she served her king. It is obedience that we demand, and in return, we give them everything else."

Speechless, Shashara's jaw dropped, but catching the approving nods of Triton and Davad, she punched the latter and glared at the former. Prepared to turn her ire loose on Nutrine, Tristan stole the moment.

"What you are describing," he said, "is just another form of slavery."

"These subservient wives," Anliac asked, "what happens to them should they forget their place? Do you simply send them to bed without supper, or do you beat them back into submission? Remember," she cautioned, "a fair number of Fulgo women now serve the House of Angeli, as members of our guard."

"As I have said," Nutrine huffed, "I speak only for the Fulgo of Certamen, and you would be hard-pressed to find a woman among us, wife or servant, who would speak against us."

In a move that surprised Nutrine and his guard, it was Davad who stepped forward. "Then it is up to you, King of Certamen, to do your part in changing the ways of the Fulgo."

Looking over Davad's head to Tristan, he asked, "I thought I was to negotiate with the Angeli?"

"We each serve a purpose," Davad stated, forcing the return of Nutrine's attention. "It is mine to negotiate with kings. Here are our demands. All the unwed women of Certamen will be given the choice to leave its walls in search of a different life."

"Are we to leave the wedded ones to suffer?" Anliac spewed.

Glancing over his shoulder, Davad said, "Not even the Angeli have the right to cleave in two what has already been united. Marriage is sacred, Anliac, and the vows are forever." Turning to Nutrine, he stated, "You will show just cause for each slave's shackles, and the length of time decreed as punishment for their crimes. Those found to be unjustly enslaved, or who have served an undue amount of time, will be set free."

"Is the whole of Superi to answer to the Angeli?"

Davad spoke over him. "You will prepare your men. You

will answer the call of the Angeli when it comes, and you will fight in the war with the Earth, as a united Superi."

"Perhaps I should just give you my city." Nutrine chuckled, but his humor shriveled when Davad spoke again.

"Lead Certamen, as we lead Pisces Stragulum, and you can keep it," Davad said. "Hold your current course, and we might see our first farmer crowned a king."

"You arrogant pup…" Maltris' right hand reached for Davad's throat, but his eyes widened as his expression changed to one of pain. His fingertips turned blue with cold until he feared they'd shatter if he moved them.

"There's no need for that," Nutrine said, pulling down on Maltris' arm as Tristan pivoted to face Anliac.

He did not chastise her defense of Davad. He did not speak at all, but held her gaze with a steady one of his own. However, when Nutrine asked, "What do I get in return?" he found himself pivoting again.

"Are you serious?" he scoffed.

"Deadly," was Nutrine's reply. "You are all but taking my crown and naming me Regent to city I have ruled for decades. You are taking our heritage and our culture and demanding that we live as you see fit. You would sit in judgment of our judges. You would release criminals whose crimes were not against you, but against Certamen. You would take command of my generals, of my warriors, to fight for your purpose. Is this you, Davad Jacobson, reaching for more than you were born to? Tristan, does might make right in the House of Angeli? Is that your definition of equality? Maltris…"

Given his cue, the Pero leader spoke. "Here is the truth

as we all know it. The Alphas have proven that they will not follow children into war. Peace," he stated, warding off their reprisal for his word choice. "Say what you will, but the oldest of you has yet to see the turning of their second decade. In years, you are children, and the Alphas will not concede to your command. Normis has made his demands clear. He wants Fulgo blood in exchange for his men." Maltris' visage darkened. "That will not happen."

"I tore that contract in half before setting it on fire," Davad stated. "There can be no conditions when it comes to the earthlings. We will face them as one."

"I would have paid good coin," Nutrine said, laughing, "to see the look on Normis' face at that meeting, but the act changes nothing. You want to free our criminals? Fine. Pay their debt in coin and see their shackles removed. You want to offer our women a different life? Fine. Do so. It will be but a temporary inconvenience. Once they see what trials and hardships await them outside of Certamen, they will return, and all will be well with them. As to our heritage and culture, it will be lost, but as with all pages of history, the future carries on. Therefore, the only vow I can make in good conscience is this: when the Mortalis and Fera join the Nox and Angeli, the Fulgo will follow the Five into war...but not before."

"That's it then?" Tristan scoffed. "You offer nothing and vow only to wait."

"Untrue," Nutrine countered. "I've agreed to every demand, save one. And in relation to the war with Earth, I've given the same vow as the King of Regia Aquam." With a crooked grin, he added, "For the sake of equality."

"Come," Tristan said to the others. "This has been a colossal waste of time."

Nutrine's control slipped. "You come into my city with your ludicrous demands, and speak to me of equality, as you spare not a moment to ask what I would have in return." Loudly, his voice booming within the amphitheater, he bellowed, "All hail the tyrannical king," and then he bowed not to Tristan, but to Anliac.

"We've asked only that you do right by your people," Anliac said, "and that you fight with us to protect our world. We ask less of you than we demand from ourselves, but you have our attention. We will hear your request."

"I have but one…request," Nutrine said, "but first, I would offer you a gift of knowledge that begins with a question." When silent stares met his announcement, he asked, "What is the significance to our marks?"

"They identify a person's ability and the strength of it," Anliac told him, annoyance written across her face.

"It's more than that," Nutrine said. "Who else?"

When his eyes fell on Tristan, he said, "Well, don't look at me. I had no markings until after my transcendence."

"Exactly," Nutrine said, snapping his fingers as his yellow eyes brightened. "And yet, you are an Angeli. Do you know when the Superians began being born with marks?"

"I've held my tongue till now," Triton stated, "but you'll not confuse the Five with whispered rumors that cannot be confirmed."

Nutrine countered, "But you know of what I speak."

"If you do," Shashara said, "tell us."

"The Mortalis race is known for coveting knowledge

of the past," Triton said. "Your parents were no exception. During our…travels," he grumbled, "they encountered a tidbit of a rumor that Beth became determined to chase down. According to the information gleaned from that little side trip, Superians were not born with markings. Upon coming of age, Superians suffered a rite of passage, and those that passed transcended and markings appeared."

"You've been holding out on us, pirate," Anliac said. "We did not know there was an Angeli expert among us."

"It is naught but lore, Anliac. You two are the first angeli to walk the planet in thousands of years. How could anyone know these things?"

"Shall I fetch the stones, Master?" Maltris asked.

"If the sea urchin is determined to contradict a man of learning," Nutrine said, "then I suppose it is necessary."

Razoran, a deep rumble stirring in his throat, peeled his black upper lip from his pointed teeth in a warning growl. Standing close to the fera, Shashara was surprised by the ferocity and, without thought, she smacked the end of Razoran's snout, right on the tip of his nose.

"Oh," she gasped, wide-eyed. "I'm sorry. You scared me."

Everyone, including Anliac, stared at her in disbelief. Razoran, blowing through his nostrils like an ox ready to charge, his snout wrinkling in inconsistent jerks…sneezed. What began as a quiet shaking of shoulders erupted into full on laugher, and that is how the Pero, who'd left to bring back the artifact, found them.

"Women," Maltris sneered as he approached the steps of the stage to retrieve the stone tablets. They were bound together with three finger-thick cords of metal wire.

"Men," Shashara snipped loud enough for Maltris to hear on his return trip to Nutrine's side.

"Look upon the past," Nutrine said, gesturing for Maltris to turn the tablets towards them, "and I will share my knowledge with you."

"The tablets are stone," Davad said, "yet I cannot place their type."

Maltris stepped back when Anliac moved forward.

"I do not aim to take it," she said, "but I would feel the grain."

Maltris looked to Nutrine, who gave his permission.

"The images are small, but the detail…" She shook her head. "The artistry is masterful."

"Tristan," Anliac said, "it's arcanite, and it's been manipulated."

"You think it's spelled?" Nutrine asked.

"For one who claims superior knowledge," Tristan said, moving in for a closer look, "you know very little. There is no such thing as spell work, but through alchemy and transmutation, metals can be manipulated to serve a purpose. The ancient Superians were known for it."

Tristan touched the top tablet and traced the words above the first pictures.

Peering over his shoulder, Davad asked, "What does it say?

Tristan shook his head. "I recognize a few of the words, but…" Tristan shook his head. "I don't know."

Nutrine spoke. "Qui sepuuntur." His words were clear and precise. "To those who follow." When curiosity brightened their youthful gazes, he smiled. "The language of the Angeli has not been completely forgotten. The knowledge is there for those who seek to find it. If you'd like," he said, "I can read the script to you."

Tristan looked to Triton, who nodded and said, "The chiseled words are old, but I can read enough to keep him honest."

Maltris rolled his eyes as he placed the tablets on the ground at Nutrine's feet. Squatting, Nutrine placed the point of his finger beneath the first word and followed along as he spoke.

"Let my words stand as a testament of truth. What once was one was torn asunder, and though we suffer the loss, hope lies in the markings of those born after. All are incomplete, but a measure of comfort can be found in the gathering of pieces. The glow of flesh stands as a reminder of what we were, of what we will be again, and of the revenge we will take on the gods of Earth."

The colorful images etched into the stones told the story. The first was of Superian man, black of hair and pale of skin with golden marks emphasizing his sculpted form. His right hand was encased in fire, while above his other hovered a stone the size of a man's head. With his fierce green eyes, he stared at them as if they were enemies. His anger was explained by the next image, one of a tiny bolt of lightning that slithered from the edge of the first tablet to strike and cleave the Superian in half.

Born of the first and second image, emerging from the gore, were two new beings. A fera, black of fur with fierce green eyes, stood with incomplete, silver markings running in dashed lines from hip to ankle. Beside him stood a fulgo, stretched lean and pale of flesh. His yellow eyes shone like gold through the markings of a gate-maker.

"Where can I find a woman that looks like that?" Davad asked, pointing to the image that followed. She was beautiful. Short blonde hair framed her sun-kissed cheeks and turned her grey stare into hardened steel. Every muscle spoke of her strength, but her full curves and slender waist was wholly female.

With a twitch of a grin, Maltris replied, "Not sure, but if you find her, ask if she has a sister."

"Well, that's too bad," Davad said when Nutrine, using two hands and extreme care, flipped to the next tablet. The woman, having fallen victim to the lightning, appeared hidden beneath spilled ink that had pulled itself into two blots before drying.

One of the stains became a man with double-pointed ears, obviously Nox, but it was the woman that drew their attention. She was Mortalis, a broken wretch, and she was in agony. Upon her left hand were pieces of red markings, the promise of an aether ability, and yet she reached out, imploring them to save her from the pain of the curse.

"It is one thing to know that the curse divided us," Anliac said, "but another to see it so vividly depicted." After a brief pause, she added, "I never thought of the pain involved."

"But there is hope of more than vengeance, Anliac, in the war brewing between Superi and Earth," Nutrine said, turning to the last tablet. There were only two stories were left to tell.

The first was the four; the Fera, with his hand laid upon

the Fulgo's shoulder, and the Nox, his eyes turned to the Mortalis, where they stood in pairs on opposite sides of the page. Their markings were aglow with the promise of power.

With more questions than answers, Davad was the first to address the words written beneath the images' feet, in the center of the stone. "What does that say?"

"What has been broken can be repaired through the balance of power and energy," Nutrine read aloud.

Shashara, finding it difficult to breathe, held a hand at her throat as her eyes went against her will to the last image.

Mouths agape in perpetual screams, their bodies contorted in an unnatural way, the two pairs remained together. Together, they suffered, their eternal pain etched in stone.

"Who would willingly seek out the power capable of causing this kind of hurt?" Shashara asked. "What good would come from wielding the power towards this purpose? Where is the hope in this kind of outcome?"

Nutrine's trembling hands were not missed as he turned over the last tablet. Upon its back stood the two Superians, whole and wholly furious.

In the stunned silence that followed, Nutrine said, "If the Angeli should call upon Certamen, I will lead them to war with the earthlings at your command. Should the Mortalis attack in our absence, I trust that after the war is won, the Angeli will, in turn, aid us in delivering retribution. There is a condition to my vow, one separate from my request."

"Give voice to it then," Anliac stated.

"We will make such an example of the gods," he said, "that no world will ever challenge us again. And the humans that serve them..." His yellow eyes became hardened gems.

"They will be made to suffer, as we have suffered. They will be shackled as slaves, and their sentence will be paid at the end of their pathetically short lives. It is all or nothing, Angeli." He held out his hand for Tristan to take and asked, "Are we agreed?"

Tristan took Nutrine's forearm in a vise grip. "We do," he said before letting go. "Now name your request."

"It is a simple thing," Nutrine assured him. "I believe," he said, "that once the curses are lifted, should we find the other pieces of ourselves, that we will merge and be made whole. I ask that you help me find those pieces belonging to me."

"You would be made an Angeli," Anliac said, biting down on her bottom lip to keep her opinion off her tongue.

"No," he corrected. "I would become a Superian. Don't you see, Anliac? The world you are fighting for, one free of prejudices against, race, gender, and station, can only exist when only Superians exist. The Five speak of reform and attempt to sway the minds of men. It is impossible." He shook his head. "But remove the problem," he said, "and the impossible can be done."

Davad asked, "What makes you so certain merging is possible?"

"Many things," Nutrine said. "Tidbits of knowledge, I suppose, gained here and there, accumulated over time into hope."

"This is not the first we've heard of the possibility," Davad told him. "When the war is won, the House of Angeli will lend aid to all who seek to be whole, including you."

Nutrine's smile reached his eyes. "This news pleases me

greatly," he said, clasping his hands together as if sealing a pack. "Maltris, see the tablets secured."

"Yes, sir," Maltris answered. He crossed the stage to the top of the stone steps, where his comrade waited to take them off his hands.

During the exchange, Triton shouted. "Hold!"

"What?" The unified question spilled forth as they searched for the cause of Triton's outburst.

"I am sick," Triton growled, "of you entitled scoundrels hoarding truths that affect us all."

"Triton, calm down," Shashara coaxed. "Tell us what's upset you."

"Ask him!"

Though Triton's arm went nowhere near his sword, his tone set events in motion. Maltris handed off the tablets to the Pero gate-maker, who passed it off to another. By the time the four members joined their leader, Maltris had Nutrine at his back and was squaring off with Triton. Razoran, snarling like a rabid beast and staring at the wielder's throat, waited on the command to kill.

Davad, the dracon sword in hand, backed his sister towards a cleared edge and barked orders for the Angeli Guards, still on the ground, to take her. And then, twirling the blade as a master, he moved towards the nearest Pero, with a quad of his guards jumping onto the stage to back him up.

Refusing to drop from the stage, yet teetering on the edge of it, the terra wielder found himself trapped. Spotting the gate-maker, he had hope of aid, but it was short-lived.

Two Angeli Guards pinned the gate-maker's position

with swords, one to his throat and one to his heart. Trained, he could have escaped had it not been for the girl, Shashara. The little twit was good with threats.

"Can a gate be made without markings or eyes?" she asked him. "As I am prepared to turn both to ash."

Anliac had yet to move, but when a dagger flew from an Angeli Guard's sheath into the hand of an awaiting Pero, she favored her swords of ice. She conjured them from gathered moisture in the air and trapped his head between her blades. "Move," she dared him.

Enraged, the Pero with aquis markings peeking above the collar of his fine red uniform charged Anliac from behind. Tristan, moving before the Pero ever noticed him, slammed an opened palm into the man's chest and sent him careening into the empty stone benches.

With the Angeli Guards surrounding the stage and those with the Five having a clear upper hand, there was a pause in the fighting, during which Nutrine said, "Well, that was…" He cleared his throat and straightened his robes. "Dramatic. You," he said to Tristan as he pointed in the direction of his aquis wielder, "should hope he rises." Turning his attention to the others, he demanded, "Be rid of your swords, or the arena will taste of your blood."

"You are surrounded once again, Nutrine." Triton grinned. "And once again, you're in no position to issue threats."

Nutrine's response was a hiss of heated breath between clenched teeth. "We are not on a ship this time." As he spoke, in single file, the guards of Certamen spilled from the mouths of the tunnels and lined the arena floor. "Two paths present themselves," he said, shifting his stare between Anliac and Tristan. "Down one path, I will likely die, but so will most of you."

"And the other?" Davad asked, pulling at his shirt collar, which had grown suddenly tight.

"You can control your pirate," he shouted, "and explain yourselves. Why would attack a new ally? I did nothing! Now remove your blades! And girl," he directed at Shashara, "get your hands off him!"

Parting her swords, Anliac delivered a swift kick to the telekinetic's arse, which sent him stumbling back to his king, releasing both sides to regroup.

Tristan, eyes closed and pinching the bridge of his nose, shook his head before dropping his arms and addressing Triton. "Well," he said, "tell us why we attacked a new ally?"

"You." Triton pointed to the Certamen guard who'd taken the tablet from the gate-maker. "And you." He pointed to the gate-maker himself. "Come here."

"Ah, I see," Nutrine said. "Do as he says." Once the two men were in place, he gave the order before Triton could. "Show them."

They stood, side by side, and revealed their markings. Though of different elements and of different strengths, the markings produced a slight glow.

"But," Shashara began, confused, "the Pero is a level three. His markings are complete."

"None are complete, Shashara," Nutrine told her. "That is what the tablets tells us."

Maltris surprised them by saying, "Shorlynn is a piece of me. I would have cherished her, protected her...loved her. I would have coated the aether between here and Earth in the blue blood of those vile humans. I would have broken the gods and their curses, and then she and I would have merged as one. The Five took a piece of me, and now you would do the same to others."

"Okay, wait," Davad interrupted. "What?"

"Would you know why the entirety of Superi, even the great Imbellis, respects the might of Certamen?" Nutrine tempted him.

"Sweet Superi," Anliac said, a true grin brightening her face, giving a willing bow to the King of the Fulgo. "Your wives are precious."

"They are."

"Your slaves have committed crimes against Certamen."

"They have."

"You do not have true slaves," she continued. "You have willing, endeared servants."

"True," Nutrine said, waiting for her to say it.

"Certamen is a collection of matching people."

"And on that note," Nutrine asked, "does our arrangement stand? Good," he said, leaving them with bobbing heads in silent contemplation. "I'd say this has been as close to a flawless negotiation as one could ask for."

Davad's eyebrow shoots up. "Close?"

Glancing over his shoulder, up into the seating areas, where his aquis wielder was being aided to his feet by the hand of a soldier, he turned back to Davad.

"Ah," Davad said, averting his stare and hoping Nutrine left it at that.

"Come, pirate," Nutrine said, doing just that. "True beauty lies on land, not on sea, and you'll find no greater perfection than within my gardens. You know, the ones you covet but shall never claim?"

"The day is still young," came Triton's reply as the King and most of his Pero exited the stage in search of horses.

Shivering, Shashara asked, "What just happened?"

Davad chuckled. "Welcome to negotiations with a king, sister of mine, where a show of strength often results in a pointless skirmish." Lifting his chin, he closed his eyes as a brisk breeze cooled his flesh and emotions. "It's all part of the game."

"It looks like the aquis wielder is going to live," Anliac stated as the man moved on his own legs towards the nearest path back to the stage. A soldier flanked him on both sides, hovering in case he went down again, but he appeared steady. "For diplomacy's sake, I suppose that's good."

"It is good, Anliac," Tristan said, grinning as he captured her cheeks between his palms, delivering a swift kiss to her pouting lips. "Today is a good day."

"We did it," Davad said, a smile stealing across face.

For a moment, they stood in silence, allowing the weight of what had just transpired to sink in. Davad was right. They'd done it. Their negotiations to unite Superi, at last, had its first success.

Shashara looked around. "Are you guys ready to go home? I don't want to leave Set alone with Sole any longer than I have to."

"Yeah, let's get out of here." Tristan's grin held a mischievous turn. "Triton and Razoran can play capture the gardens with Nutrine on their own."

XIII

There Can Be Only One Alpha

"**Y**ou should have seen it, Davad," Razoran said for the tenth time, his eyes still big and the sharp-toothed grin still on his face.

It hadn't taken Triton and Razoran long to catch up to them, and Davad hadn't stopped smiling since. "You're fortunate Nutrine only had you tossed out of the city. You know how he feels about his gardens."

"It was a seed pod," Triton grumped.

"From a flowering plant that supposedly comes from Earth," Razoran elaborated, explaining Nutrine's outrage and their quick departure.

"I would have stayed with the two of you, but…" He gestured towards Anliac and Tristan, who rode side-by-side on their horses, yet still held hands. "Leaving Shashara alone with those two would have been cruel."

Razoran threw back his head and laughed. "There's nothing wrong with a little necking now and again." He scratched the tip of his nose with a curved claw. "Perhaps it's time you find a woman of your own to claim and cuddle up to?"

"I prefer the catch and release variety," Davad said with a sly wink.

"I blame Lishous's influence," Shashara piped in, "though Davimon is little better."

The easy banter brought lighthearted laughter that dried up as the East fields of Pisces Stragulum came into view. They were deserted.

Pulling from Anliac, Tristan tilted his head. Angling his right ear towards the city, he cupped his hand around it to better hear.

"What is it?" Anliac urged the others to be quiet as they all drew rein.

Without the talking, laughter, and thumping of hoofbeats, he heard what the others could not. "Yelling, I think," he replied. Then his head jerked up and his eyes flared. "Fighting."

Snapping the reins, he leaned low over the horse's back and buried his heels in its flanks, leaving the others in a scramble to do the same. A Fera at the Southeast stables spotted their approach and then three Angeli Guards ran out to meet them.

As they dismounted, two of the guards took their leads to see the animals stabled. The third guard said, "Thank Superi you've returned."

"Where is everyone?" Shashara asked. The way his expression twisted soured her stomach. Before he could answer her question, she bombarded him with more. "Have the gods returned? Is Set okay?"

"There have been no battles fought today. At least," he amended, "not yet."

"What's happened?" Tristan asked.

"It's the Alphas," the guard explained. "They're stirring trouble."

"Of course, they are," Anliac sneered. "Where are they now?"

"A crowd has gathered between the outskirts of the old market square and the dock," he answered, but then said, "Miss, forgive me, but there is someone waiting for the Five in Set's office."

"They can wait," Anliac replied. "This makes twice the Alphas have waited for our backs to be turned to deliver betrayal."

"Apologies, Miss." The guard gave a slight bow. "But an oracle is not someone you keep waiting."

Shashara whispered Socmoon's name, knowing the others would follow, and took off to find him.

"Mistress, please, wait!" The guard cried out. "It's not safe!"

"Sweet Superi," Shashara whispered, her steps faltering as the mob came into view. From the area surrounding the dock to the mess hall in the market square, there was standing room only. "He wasn't kidding. It looks as if the whole of the city has gathered."

"Yeah," Anliac said, "like tinder readied to fire."

The Fera loyal to the Alphas had squared off with those loyal to the Angeli. The Alphas, protected by the giants Belua and Torren, nonetheless had their backs pressed to the oceanus, where Triton's men stood ready. The remaining Angeli Guard, those not Fera, had formed a perimeter wall around the chaos in hopes of containing it.

They failed.

An Alpha loyalist threw the punch that ignited the violence, and the two sides collided.

"Enough!" Tristan bellowed, knocking aside all those in his path as he pushed to gain center ground.

To counter Tristan's order, the Alphas released Belua to enter the fray. A broad, backward swipe of his long, eight-foot arm sent men and women crashing into those behind them. When he pivoted to do it again, the back of his hand collided with Tristan's chest, shattering the bones and snapping his forearm.

Belua's screams, coupled with Torren's fierce roar as she bounded to her brother's side, brought the fighting to a standstill.

"What is going on here?" Anliac's beautiful but piercing pitch made hands fly to cover ears.

The mob parted as Socmoon clamored towards Tristan, his Fulgo height placing him above the heads of the crowd. "Resentment runs high, as does greed, among those who seek your demise, so they might lead."

With eyes gone wide and cheeks pale as death, Shashara glared at Sole. "What have you done with Set?"

Sole's silver fur revealed its white undercoat when it rose along the ridge of his spine between his great wings.

Shashara's hands became two orbs of white light. "So help me, Sole…" She started towards him. "I'll kill you myself."

"Be easy, child," Socmoon said, "and let not your fear run wild. Set is safe, as soon you'll see, when he returns from the white-stoned city."

Her relief made her knees weak, so when he held out his arms to her, she took the comfort he offered. Unable to stem her flow of tears, she clung to the patchworked cloak he always wore and let the bushy white beard that hung to his chest dry them for her.

"Davad," Anliac asked, "what is it?"

Though his words were hushed, they carried great weight. "We should kill them. Now," he said, casting his eyes over the crowd, "while we have them trapped and out-numbered."

Chilled by her brother's words, Shashara said, "You can't mean that." She took measure of the crowd's reaction, afraid that he'd been overheard. "You sound like Father."

"Did you not just threaten to do the same?" When she averted her eyes, he said, "I am what he made me, Shasha-ra, as are you." Positioning himself at the heart of the mob, he turned in a slow circle, seeking eye contact with both sides. "This is over. The attempts to intimidate us, the threats meant to scare us are finished."

"Why?" an Alpha loyalist shouted. "Because you say so?"

"Yes," Davad stated, gaining the Fera's full attention, "because despite our youth, there is a reason we stand be-fore you now. We," he said, gesturing to Shashara, "are the offspring of one of the deadliest assassins in recent Superian history, and though we are wielders, we are first our father's children. From those skills, none of you are safe, but that is not why this nonsense will end.

"Set's parentage holds an even greater legacy, and with it comes a power that no one fully understands, yet he is not the reason this infighting will cease. Anliac, second in power only to one on this planet, controls the might of the Nox military, yet she is not the reason we are here. He is," Davad said, following the direction he pointed, into the wake left from his approach, towards Tristan.

Reaching his side, he continued, "Tristan was not only born. He was reborn. He is a man spoken of in prophesy. A prophesy that clearly defines our path to victory. There is no one on this planet who is stronger, faster, more agile, or more equipped to lead and defend Superi than him. Yet, even knowing that he could crush each one of you, he offers you kindness. A kindness," he continued, "that this display proves you do not deserve." As his hand fell to the hilt of his sword, he declared, "And that is why you will follow…or you will die."

When Sole growled, Lunam spoke words of caution into his mind. *Careful, Sole. There are more here that agree with the boy than those who agree with us. Wait until war has weakened them to grasp at the power you crave. Now is not the time.*

"Bold claim for one yet to taste of battle," Sole challenged, ignoring Lunam as he jumped down from the docks to the packed dirt road.

"Humorous words coming from one who hid in a tent during the last fight," Davad retorted, pulling free his blade with less than forty feet separating him from the life he longed to claim.

When Tristan failed to act, Anliac asked, "Are you really going to let this happen? Davad doesn't stand a chance."

"I…" Tristan shrugged his shoulders, at a loss for words, as his head continued to turn from side to side.

Socmoon, unwilling to watch the boy die because Tristan was locked in an emotional cage, pitched his voice to carry, and said, "May you find peace in your return to the terra, Sole, for tonight, victory will be Davad's to hold."

Twirling his sword, Davad adjusted his grip. "That's what I'm talking about," he said with a crooked grin as he advanced.

Conflicted by the oracle's prophesy, Sole shoved off the terra with his hind legs and pumped his great wings until he hovered over the gasping crowd.

On the descent, the suns had found their path towards the oceanus' distant horizon when, beside the docks, on a patch of land designated for portals, a flash of purple warned of one coming open. Slightly larger than two men, Set came through first, followed by Montilis and a dozen of his Nox soldiers.

As the sudden onslaught of fear and fury funneled through Set's ability, it became his own, but his was equally shared for both sides. "You," he said, his piercing blue gaze freezing Davad in place, "sheath your sword and do it now."

Such was his shock at Set's tone that Davad did as he was told, but said in defense, "We did not start this," as he backed out of the middle, towards Tristan.

"No," Set said, "you did not." Walking through the crowd, Set narrowed his stare and demanded, "Find solid ground, Sole."

As he descended, the Alpha spoke. "From the first of our encounters, we've been transparent in our agenda. We gave fair warning of what would transpire should the Angeli become a threat."

"The threat to you now is of your own making," Set countered coming to a stop midway between the remaining Five and the Alphas.

"Tristan's rule threatens every ruler, every race, and I will not see the Fera fall victim!"

"Back down," Set shouted, fueled by the hatred rolling off Sole, "or I will back you down."

Sole growled. "You are the second to threaten me tonight."

"I do not make threats," Set countered, but the strength of his words was diminished when Shashara's guilt reached him. He grinned.

"They've demanded our loyalty," called out a Fera woman wearing the colors of the Angeli. "They shall not have it!"

"Hoorah! Hoorah!" one side shouted.

"The Alphas are our true leaders," retorted a man from the other side. "They have guided us and kept us safe. The collective dream has kept us united. Without them, what are we?"

"They've used that dream to control us long enough," one of the Angeli Fera fired back.

"They are us," came a bold reply from behind where the Five stood, causing them to turn. "We've waited a long time for the Alphas to rise. It is the Feras' time to rule."

"To the last child," Montilis stated, "every Nox would die before kneeling to the Fera."

Angry words exploded as the two sides closed in again.

"Protect the Five," were the words bellowed that found them incased by a square wall of flesh. "What are our orders?" a commander of the Angeli Guard asked.

"Tristan," Anliac repeated when Tristan's gaze became trapped on the terra at his feet, "what are our orders?"

"Despite all our efforts," Tristan said, "we cannot make them unite, and without unity, Superi will fall. Perhaps another can inspire them to become one, but," he stated, looking up, "I do not believe it is me."

Davad's expression went lax before anger tightened the lines of it. "After the speech I just gave, are you kidding me?" Davad chuckled in disdain. "If you're this weak, then perhaps you're right. But know this, Tristan; we've come too far to go back now. If you hand over leadership to someone else, every single one of us will be killed. Not by the Alphas, nor by the Fera loyal to them, but by those who've sacrificed and bled to make you King."

"I never asked to be King!" Tristan growled. "I never asked to rule anyone."

"That doesn't change what you are, brother. Lead them," Set told him.

"Besides," Anliac asked, "who would you trust to lead in your place? Normis? Sole?" Taking a gentle hold on Tristan's arms, she squeezed. "I'd sooner follow Nutrine than one of them."

"Your father," Tristan suggested, "or you?" Cupping her cheek, he said, "Superi knows you're strong enough."

"The people may know that they need me, Tristan, but they fear me," she told him. "They would never follow me.

They trust you. They love you." Though her eyes said it for her, she voiced aloud, "As we all do."

"I can't believe we're even having this discussion," Set argued. "When they tire of trading fists and draw weapons instead, it will be too late. People will die."

"The boy is right," Montilis said after talking his way passed a reluctant wall of guards. "Before Superi falls to chaos, show them who is King, even if you must shove your reign down their throats to do it."

Though less than a moment passed, events in Tristan's life collided in his mind to bring the present into sharp focus. The crooks and pirates, the killers, the monsters and gods he'd faced since leaving Exterius Antro... Jacob and his parents. Those called ruthless mercenaries and heartless assassins had sacrificed everything to protect against this eventuality. Yet prophesy had other plans, and history had unfolded according to its will, until here he stood. From the time of his rebirth, from the moment Malstar's needles had pierced his veins, this was destined.

Anliac knew the moment Tristan had made peace with what had to be done, and so she said, "Good. Now take control before I kick your arse."

Cupping her cheeks between his palms, he said, "Superi help me, woman, but I love you."

Expecting to be obeyed, Tristan ordered the wall to break and moved deeper into the angry mob of shoving hands and shouting voices. The golden lines that marked him for what he was began to pulse. Slowly at first, but as the violence surrounding him firmed his resolve, the pulsing quickened until it appeared to burn from his flesh, as if it would set his dark clothes aflame.

"Quiet," he said upon reaching center ground, but his command was lost to the roar of the mob. People pushed and threw punches until, inevitably, steel was drawn.

"I said *quiet!*" His voice, deep and powerful, brought their eyes to him just as the energy coursing through his veins solidified. His image was cloaked within an orb of light that burned as a golden sun.

"How easy you would make the gods' victory over us," he shouted. "I will not allow it." Like an explosion, heat and energy surged from him, reaching to the far edges of the people and wreaking havoc on its journey.

Those closest paid the price for their proximity. Blisters and burns appeared on their skin, while some caught in the middle were left with broken bones and contusions when bodies crashed together. The last of the mob, farthest from the blast, still found themselves on the ground and grunting from the pain.

Whether from rage or raw power, when he spoke again, his words were carried to them with a vibration that shook their ribcages. Terror filled their eyes.

"I DID NOT ASK FOR THIS!" Moderating his volume, if not his tone, he continued. "Nor did you. We know where the fault lies, and it is not on any denizen of Superi. That said…" He stood straighter, pulling his shoulders back, as he lifted his golden-eyed stare. "I will lead, and you will follow, because I do not fight for a race. I fight for my world, for all of its people." Even without the resounding bass of his Angeli voice, there was no denying the passionate commitment in his words. "I fight so that we may once again be called

Superians."

After pausing to see if he would be challenged, Tristan told them, "I wanted to be a different kind of leader. One that had earned the right, and whose people called him brother, but by your actions here tonight, you've forged a King. So, if you are more interested in dividing yourselves by petty differences than in defending the very planet that gives us life, then you are the problem. One that, as your King, I will destroy swiftly and utterly, and it begins now. Kneel," he ordered, "or stand and mark yourself my enemy."

Slipping through a portal no one had noticed, Davimon and Lishous approached from the direction of the docks.

"All hail the King," Davimon said with a good-natured grin. "May your reign survive passed the twenty-odd years given to dictators before they are deposed."

With Lunam focused on reading the internal thoughts of key entities, Sole, salivating to obtain the power Tristan had revealed, inched closer.

Lishous nudged Davimon's shoulder for his facetious remark as he passed him by to face Tristan from the edge of the dock. "True leaders," he said, "true kings, are not created through birthright. They are made. I believe you speak the truth when you claim you did not ask for the position you now hold, but I say you have earned the title." Turning, raising his voice to those gathered, he stated, "We could not ask for leader with greater strength, nor for a King with purer intentions." Facing Tristan again, he placed hand to heart and vowed, "I will follow you not because I fear your wrath, but because you give me hope." Then he bowed.

With his men forcing a path, Triton, who had made his

way to the dock, moved to Lishous's side. "I would have followed your parents anywhere." He nodded. "Now I offer that same loyalty to you." With their history flowing between them, Triton followed Lishous's example and covered his heart before bowing to his King. When his men went as far as to take a knee, Triton's right brow arched into a near point, but he wore a crooked grin when he again met Tristan's eyes.

The Angeli Guard dropped to a knee along with the pirates, followed by the Fera loyal to the Five. The townspeople, who'd stood on the sidelines as events had unfolded, took joy in doing the same.

That's when Set saw him. Sole crept towards Tristan's back, his claws extended as he reached for power.

NO! Lunam's telepathic voice slammed into their minds, but it was too late.

Sole leapt and buried his claws in Tristan's shoulder. Set, using every ounce of speed his stolen ability offered, crashed into the Alpha's side, yanking free the claws and breaking the connection.

Had he known what would happen, perhaps he would have chosen a different course, but the moment the two of them collided, before they ever hit the ground, pain made them scream. An equal battle between mind and body, they held onto each other with death grips, fighting the circulating power that threatened to destroy both.

Lunam, growing hysterical, screeched at Tristan, "Do something!"

People fell to chaos. Davimon and Socmoon groaned, dropping, as they caught their temples between the heels of their hands. Such was the sound of their sudden screams that no one knew what to do. Should they fight? Or should they run from whatever could drop an oracle to their knees?

The sound escaping Set was that of an animus being wrenched from the mind, threatening Tristan's sanity as well. "What do I do?"

Shashara's eyes were peeled wide, a torrent of tears coursing from them. She burst from the crowd to grab hold of Set's arm, intent on setting him free. As if struck by lightning, her body convulsed. Unable to let go, her mouth opened to scream, but no sound escaped.

I'm going to die, she thought, *and so is Set.*

The ground trembled as Anliac ripped a boulder from the terra and sent it hurling into Shashara. She winced as it struck, and then again as Shashara flew ten feet and landed in a writhing heap on the dirt road.

Davad rushed to her side. Knowing the answer, he asked anyway, "Are you okay?"

She was pale as death, but the pain abated as her fear for Set returned. "Oh, please," she cried, attempting to stand, "help him." She reached for Set, but then she screamed, clawing at the cloak hanging from her shoulders. "I'm on fire!"

"What?" Davad asked, seeing no flame. Unfastening her cloak, he tossed it aside before she really hurt herself, then watched as she peeled the black shirt she wore from her left shoulder.

Purple sunbursts covered her flesh from collarbone to elbow, with yellow, wavering lines running between them. "What is that?" she asked, her blue eyes in a panic. Her head spun to check her other shoulder for the long slivers of red and black, given depth by tiny swirls, that she'd been born with.

Davad said it before she could. "Your mark is complete? How did it finish? Watch out!" he yelled as he grabbed the front of his sister's shirt and yanked her forward.

Glancing back, she saw the tip of Sole's left wing slice in front of her face, after which Davad was no longer pulling. It was she that pushed, avoiding the path of the epotos rolling across the ground, even as the sounds they made burned themselves into her psyche and broke her heart.

"Break them apart," Socmoon gritted out from between clench teeth, "and do it now, before by their power, we are all devoured."

Sole's agony reached an apex, his eyes rolling back in his head, as Set's screams grew weaker.

"What's happening to him?" Shashara cried. From inside of Set, a brilliant, white light appeared to envelope and consume him.

Placing herself in front of Tristan and Anliac, it was Skylar who acted. Her wild red hair lifted, as if caught in a current, and when she spread wide her slender arms, the air abandoned even their lungs as it surged forward for her embrace. Veins appeared at her pale throat and throbbed at her temples as she released a growl even the Fera approved and slammed her palms together.

The percussion kicked up a storm of dust and debris, tossing people about to leave them in crumpled piles upon the terra, and leaving even the Angeli blind to Set's fate.

"Set!" Tristan shouted.

Anliac caught his arm when he would have stumbled into the storm to search for his brother. "Skylar," she asked, "can you clear this?"

Hysteria tinging his words, Tristan said, "Hurry. The light around Set has gone out."

Skylar closed her eyes, and with a few calming breaths, she also calmed the storm. Heavy objects dropped first, some landing upon unprepared victims, before she pursed her lips. With a gentle blow, she created a breeze that pushed the dust away from their location.

Most picked themselves off the ground and called out to those they hoped to find in one piece. All thoughts of rebellion were suspended in the aftermath.

"Set!" Tristan called out.

"Tristan," Shashara shouted, "help me with him."

"I'm fine," Davad told them, pressing his wadded shirt to his left eye. "Find Set."

"NO!" Lunam wailed, rushing to Sole. She nudged at his neck with her nose, licking his face to rouse him. "No, no, no. Oh, please...don't be dead."

"Set!"

"Set!"

"Set, where are you?"

As if submerged in water, Set heard his name being called as if from a great distance, and he fought his way to the surface of consciousness to answer them. "Here," he said, though his voice did not carry far. There was a burst of wind and then Tristan ripped the dead weight of two men off his chest.

Abject fear held Tristan frozen as he stared down at his

brother's face. Set's flesh had become a covered canvas of designs marked with varying colors.

Shashara fell to her knees at his side. Covering her mouth with her hand, she asked through her tears, "Does it hurt?"

"I feel like I've been thrown in a lava pit, and I can barely breathe," he said, attempting a smile and failing miserably. "But I think I'll survive."

Davad rested a hand on his sister's shoulder. When he and Set made eye contact, what he felt went beyond words.

Set nodded to let Davad know that words weren't needed.

"Oh, wow," Anliac exclaimed, having taken the time to thank Skylar before joining them. "Look at you."

"I look that bad, huh?"

She cocked her head to the side. "I'm not sure if bad is the word I would use… but your eyes are beautiful…"

Rolling them, he said, "Great. That makes me feel so much better. Wait… What?" Needing help to his feet, he stretched out his hand. "What's wrong with my eyes? Oh, what the…" It was on fire, and the markings that spread from there were none that he'd seen before. With huge eyes and a racing heart, he asked, "What's happening to me?"

Lunam, flanked on both sides by Torren and Belua, gave him his answer. "Our history and the knowledge of it is gone. You stole that which was not yours to take!" She nuzzled Sole's lifeless body again. "You are damned by them, as he was," she said. "Now you will know the cost of carrying those marks on your flesh, to have your mind burdened by a thousand others, and to carry the weight of their psyches as he did. You wretched child!" she cried out. "Sole is dead!"

XIV

Changes

Even with his eyelids too heavy to open, Set knew where he was. The sweet aroma of gardenia and jasmine that permeated the air put him in the Angeli dwelling shared by Tristan and Anliac. Once Tristan had discovered her fondness for the flowering plants, he'd used them to build a border around their home.

The cold stone pressed against his bare back caused a moment of confusion. He was none too pleased about having his legs shoved into pants that felt like they were made of a blacksmith's apron—itchy and rough—but he knew he was downstairs, in the living room. He could hear people hovering around him, more coming from the direction of the kitchen, and still more milling about outside.

For all the voices he heard, the one that he craved was silent, but he caught the familiar rhythm of her breathing coming from an upstairs bedroom. The sound of her heart beating, slow and steady, said she was asleep. The image of her curled up on her side, her skirts tucked demurely, her long, chestnut waves spilling over her cheek and splaying out behind her in wild disarray made him smile.

A solid thud followed, then Tristan said, "He's waking up."

Though Set's mind was mostly awake, his body was slow to respond to its commands. He managed to peel open his eyes a crack, caught Tristan's stare, and closed them again.

"What happened?" he groaned. Anliac and Davad left Triton and Davimon standing in the doorway to the kitchen and moved closer.

"What do you remember?" Anliac asked him.

He thought back to the night before and his eyes popped wide. "My hand…it was on fire, and…" He swallowed hard. "You said something was wrong with my eyes?"

"You, um…" Davad scratched at the new sprout of whiskers on his chin. "You passed out when the fire spread, and your eyes, well, they're sort of hard to explain."

It grew so quiet inside the house that those outside seemed to be shouting, but the silence was filled with fear. Choking on it, Set forced his torso off the stone and swung his legs off the side. The world went topsy-turvy and his stomach rebelled. Leaning forward with the first heave, Set started to topple.

Tristan darted forward, pressing a flattened palm against his brother's chest to push him upright, and then everything went wrong. His angeli marks flared as if responding to a threat. It spread from his hand, an invisible heat that crept up his forearm as if the limb had been shoved into a furnace. It was the sickening pull, that familiar drain on his abilities, that sparked his temper and gave him the strength to break the connection between them.

"Son of a…" Tristan pivoted away from Set to avoid the temptation to break his jaws. He shook his hand in hopes of cooling it off.

"Oh, thank you," Set gushed.

"What was that?" Anliac snapped, rearing back her fist to slug his shoulder.

Tristan caught her wrist to spare her the pain. "That's probably not the best idea," he said, letting her go. "Besides," he lied, "it scared me more than it hurt."

When the two of them turned to look at Set, Tristan's first instinct was to go to him, but Anliac said, "Give him a moment."

Set heard her and was grateful. No, he hadn't meant to drain from Tristan, but once done, his head had cleared. Now he only wished he could return to the fogged reality of a moment ago.

Purple-hued spheres of varying sizes covered his feet and ankles before disappearing beneath the cuffs of his pants. Tightening his abdomen, blue diamonds moved along with yellow crescent moons across the expanse of his stomach. In a seamless transition, long, red, twirling slivers, like the golden marks of the Angeli, trailed up his ribcage to line his chest. Over his shoulders, encasing his arms to the elbows, were more designs and vivid colors than his mind could detail in one glance. Though his forearms and hands remained free of markings, his fingers touched upon his face as his eyes sought answers.

Anliac understood the expression Set wore better than

anyone there. It wasn't that long ago that she had woken on another slab of stone. She remembered the freezing terror of feeling like a prisoner trapped in a body not her own.

"The red markings continue up your neck, Set." She hesitated. "The left side of your face is unchanged, but the right side now carries Sole's aether mark, and your eyes…" Trapping her bottom lip between her teeth, she bit down and shook her head.

"It's nothing bad, little brother," Tristan hurried to explain. "Your eyes are like star fire. That's all."

Set scoffed. "That's all, huh?" He shook his head.

"They're still predominately blue," Tristan told him. "There's just a lot of other colors sharing the space now, like gems that sparkle."

"I see." Set nodded once as a strange calm settled over him. "And all these markings," Set asked, "did I kill Sole?" When the fear in the room spiked and no one answered, he said, "I'll take that as a yes." Checking over the marks again, he added, "Not even I could have guessed how much power Sole's fur kept hidden. No wonder he stayed underground." Taking a deep breath, he let it out slowly and asked, "So what does this mean? What does it change?"

"I think we should start with what Lunam said," Davad piped in.

"Davad, shut up," Anliac snapped.

"No," Set stopped her. He focused on Davad. "Refresh my memory. What did she say?"

"She told you that Sole suffered under the psyches of thousands of minds," Davad told him with a tad too much enthusiasm, "and that now you would do the same. So…"

He could hardly contain his curiosity. "Can you hear them? Is it even Set we're talking to? How would we know?"

"Nice, Davad," Tristan stated. "That's real nice."

"Sorry, man, but we were all thinking it," Davad replied.

"Honestly?" Set lifted his shoulders and then let them fall. "I feel more alone in my head right now than I have since I drained Calstar. I don't hear anyone. I mean..." His head bobbed back and forth as he considered his words. "I know the other psyches are there, like a low buzz in the background, but they seem to have managed to shut Calstar up and are keeping themselves entertained. Besides," he said, closing his eyes to focus, "their voices aren't important. Their knowledge, however, is."

"What kind of knowledge?" Anliac asked. "What do you know?"

"I know that Pisces Stragulum used to be a trading village. Fish and cloth," he told her, "that's what they were known for."

Triton shivered and then growled, "What?" at Davimon when the man had the audacity to chuckle. "The boy talking about thousands of voices bouncing around in his skull doesn't make you wish for a bottle of rum?"

"Why didn't you tell us that you took the marks of those you kill?" Anliac asked. When Set's star-fired eyes went doe-eyed and innocent, she grinned. "The fire last night took your clothes... All of them. You are covered in markings."

He didn't give her the answer she sought, but said instead, "So much for my modesty."

"Set..."

He held up his hand. "I can feel your fear, Anliac, as I

can feel all of theirs." He scanned the room and watched eyes drop like flies to the floor. "The answers you seek would only serve to make it grow."

Davad forced a laugh and said, "Please. It will be a cold day in Collibus Dolor before I'm afraid of you. I'd just stand behind Shashara if you really freaked out." Turning serious, he added, "I'm afraid *for* you. The whole of Superi is going to panic when they discover what it really means to be an epoto, and let's be honest, there's no hiding…" With a floppy wrist, he gestured up and down in Set's direction, "all of this."

Scowling, Tristan said, "Enough, Davad."

"Seriously, Set," Davad continued anyway, "you can kill with a touch and take any ability you want and keep it. That makes you as dangerous as the Angeli."

"I've heard the stories," Anliac said, "but seeing it with my own eyes, I understand."

"Understand what?" Set and Tristan asked in unison.

"Why the epotos were hunted down and killed," she answered. The looks they shot her made her wince, but she said what needed to be said. "Your ability is a threat, and in a world such as ours, people will work to see that threat removed. Look at what they've done to us," she said, reaching for Tristan's hand. "I fear it will be worse for you."

"I agree," Davimon stated. "In truth, it amazes me that you've lived as long as you have. The fear of those with your ability has not abated with time."

"Jacob," the three boys said at once, but Davad was the one to elaborate.

"My dad was a telepath, one of the strongest of his kind,

and he could do much more than hear thoughts. He used his skills to look out for Set as much as for Tristan. Given time, he could push his will on others. That's how he made Exterius Antro safe for them, and why we hated leaving the city behind. Most people there were told that Set was a gate-maker. He started pushing those thoughts on people as soon as we entered the city."

"That's why Palus Regia doesn't allow telepaths to be a part of our court systems or councils," Anliac confessed. "They can't be trusted not to act on their own agendas."

"The same for Regia Aquam," Davimon said. "Normis doesn't trust them."

"That's enough talk of untrustworthy telepaths," Triton stated, his crossed arms a measure of his irritation. "Jacob was as good a man as any one of us, and in most cases, a better one."

A rap on the front door spared them from the awkward tension left in the wake of Triton's defense of Jacob. But it was replaced by an entirely different type of awkwardness when Skylar came inside, only to stop and stare.

"Well, hello," she chirped, her yellow eyes brightening as they traveled leisurely over the expanse of Set's exposed flesh.

Blushing under her scrutiny, Set chuckled a bit and warned, "You'd better look your fill before Shashara finds her way down. We don't want to see her jealous."

Snapping out of it, she said as quickly, "Sorry. It's just… wow. I've never seen so many marks on one person. The interplay between the differing abilities," she concluded, "they're beautiful."

"Thanks." Set grinned. "I think."

"Do you know what they all are yet?"

Cocking his head, he asked, "What do you mean?"

"We haven't gotten that far," Anliac answered.

"Well," Skylar offered, "after last night, we can assume ignis is one of them."

"What about an aquis ability, Set?" Anliac asked, her curiosity piqued.

"How would I know?"

"This close to the oceanus, you would know." Her shoulders drooped in unexpected disappointment. "I can feel the pull of the element." When her remark was followed by silence, she peeked around the room at the other wielders, but none seemed aware of what she was talking about. She shrugged. "Or maybe I'm just weird."

"We all know you're weird." Davad smiled at Anliac. "What about you, Triton? You're an aquis wielder. What do you feel?"

The crooked grin on Davad's face earned him a pointed look from Triton, but he answered. "Considering the number of marks on you, boy," he said to Set, "I wouldn't rule out any possibility. The only pull I feel from the oceanus is that on my heart." When the women in the room began to smile at such a sweet sentiment from so harsh a man, he glared at them in response.

Letting the pirate off the hook, Skylar said, "I'm with Triton. I don't feel aer any more than others do until I conjure how much I want to control."

"What about aether, Set?" Davimon asked. "I doubt you're an oracle. Both of your eyes remain the same." He hesitated. "Well, they look the same as each other, I mean, but…"

"The only thoughts I hear are those bouncing around in my head," Set told him. "Granted, those thoughts are not all my own." He grinned when Triton blanched. "I'm sorry, guys," he said. "I would tell you if you I could, but I think the only way to know is to wait for an ability to manifest."

Suddenly, they felt a small concussion, followed by the sound of splintering wood. It was Shashara's screams, however, coupled with breaking glass, that sent Tristan, Anliac, and Set racing for the stairs. It would have been a close one had it not been for their fear of bumping into Set on their way up. His sudden stop at the top of the stairs almost made it happen anyway. The door to Shashara's borrowed room had exploded out into the hallway.

"Shashara!" Set shouted as he stepped over the pieces to reach the threshold. "Aww…" He rubbed at his sternum as his heart broke right along with hers.

She sat on the edge of her bed. Drenched from head to toe, with hot steam rolling off her, she stared out of a broken window, ignoring the scorch marks that marred its frame.

Turning sideways to slide past Set, Anliac picked her way through the shards of a shattered ceramic water pitcher and basin. She sat beside Shashara and reached for her hand.

Slowly, with sadness and fear gripping her so fiercely that Set felt strangled by it, Shashara looked up at Anliac and asked, "What happened to me?"

XV

Releasing Chaos

An aura of pale white surrounded him, guiding him down the dark tunnel. Its walls were made of jagged rock, and the scent it held defined its age; musty, earthy, old. Yet the entity that walked the hardpacked path was older still. Black of skin with a jackal's head, a light dusting of ebony fur covered his lean, muscular frame. He feared nothing the passageway might hold beyond the stalactites hanging from the ceiling; a hazard of topping seven-foot.

As he came to a stop before a recessed wooden door, his cloak, made of fine-spun gold, settled on his broad shoulders to touch upon the ground. Adjusting the golden armlets encircling his biceps, he did the same with the belt that held his golden breechclout in place. He tugged at the gold we-sekh collar suspended around his thick neck. Heavy though it was, its pull was nothing compared to the gravity of what he must do. Still, there was no help for it.

Waving his hand in front of himself, the door creaked in

complaint before it vanished. He quickly crossed the threshold into the cavernous room of black stone. Torches, set every ten feet, ignited to reveal a vaulted ceiling that created echoes from their voices.

"Mother," Anubis greeted as his fathomless black eyes met a matching pair.

Nephthys stood across the room, before the massive, black iron doors, which had been cut from the cavern itself, as if she'd been waiting. Her honeyed skin took on a darker hue beneath the pristine white of her sleeveless robe, which slipped like scented oil over rounded curves. As deep a black as a raven's wings, her silken hair spilled over her slender shoulders, framing the startling beauty of her angular face.

With her hands clasped before her, her smile never touching her eyes, she replied, "My son. You should not be here."

Anubis growled, low and menacing. "You will not get in my way. Not again," he said. "The taint upon the Ba and Ka are proof that the Superians have returned."

She softened her expression. "You cannot know that," she said. "It was one human, and he was found in Mexico. So many of the Natives worship animal spirits, Anubis." She shrugged. "Is it so hard to consider the possibility that one of those spirits was angry with him, and in taking his life, tainted his soul?"

"There is only truth in death," Anubis answered, "and we are both gods in its name, so save your lies for those who fall victim to them. I will not allow history to repeat itself. I will save what I can, preserve what balance I can, even if it means releasing him."

One step was all Nephthys allowed, then she was standing before her son, laying her hand atop his forearm in the vain hope of deterring his action. "Have you forgotten, Anubis? You say you will stop history from repeating, and yet, if you do this, you will be the catalyst of history's rebirth. Even with the help of others, do you remember what it took to lock him away?" When Anubis's black eyes shifted to an angry red, she changed tactics. "You know what he is. You know he can't be controlled. How many humans will he slaughter before his bloodlust is quenched? And how will the Duat hold up under the influx? More than just tainted souls can split it wide."

His red stare became orbs of white as her words triggered the memory of betrayal. "I remember everything, Mother. How you aided the Christians in deceiving me. How you tricked me into trapping him in a cage that has stood for two thousand years." He yanked his arm free of her touch. "How well I remember…"

"It had to be done," Nephthys stated. "He was killing humans by the thousands. And let's face it," she said, frowning, "dimwitted as humans can be, plagues can only be blamed for so long before other explanations come to light. That period of history was complicated, as our present and future will be if you continue on this course."

"I've heard enough," he said, then vanished, only to reappear at the massive doors.

Pivoting, she turned towards the black egress. As he lifted his hands to press upon the doors, she warned him, "Let your memory hold this thought, son. This time, I was the voice of reason."

"I'll share your reason with Father presently," he threatened as he shoved open the doors.

XVI

Loyalty Lines

Set inched his way into the room, envious of Anliac's position beside Shashara on the bed. "I think I know what happened."

"You think?" Shashara snapped, fury igniting her bright blue eyes. But she couldn't sustain her ire through her fear, invoked by what covered Set's skin. As silent tears spilled down her pale cheeks, she captured her trembling bottom lip between her teeth and shook her head.

"Don't, Shashara," he said, taking two strides to close the distance between them. Going to his knees, he reached for her hand. "Don't shut me out. Don't fear me, please. I can't take it."

"I gave you my word," she whispered, trembling, "along with my heart, but your eyes have become as your mind." She caressed his cheek with her fingertips before letting her hand fall. "The piercing blue that I cherish is still in there, but it's surrounded by fragments I do not know at all. How can I trust that you are you? How much of the one I love is still in there? Set," she whimpered, "what have you done?"

Her question, coupled with her emotion, strangled him. Rising slowly, he paced as he collected his thoughts and began to speak. "I did what I had to," he answered. "I felt Sole's hatred, his drive to kill my brother and take his power for himself, and…" As memory renewed his fear, his breathing grew erratic. His nostrils flared as his lungs sought air grown suddenly thin. "I searched for him, but I couldn't find him in the chaos. Then, as the people knelt, I found him. Sole's claws were going for Tristan's back…"

"And you wouldn't want to live if you lost Tristan." Shashara's eyes flickered to the stoic Angeli who stood propped up in the doorway, and then she whispered, "Not even for me."

"I would not lose you for him, either," Set told her. "I panicked, Shashara, and even still, I was almost too late. Sole had his claws buried in Tristan's shoulder by the time I intercepted them. Once it was done…" His hands shook with anger awakened. "Sole thought he was the only one left. The last epoto. The last whose touch could kill." He saw them cringe, but he continued. "Sole craved power, and there are none on Superi with more than the Angeli."

Tristan made a noise in the back of his throat that drew the attention of the others. "I'm not certain that's true anymore, little brother."

"You think because I'm marked this way, because of the abilities I now control, that I'm somehow more powerful than you are?" Set asked, a tad harsher than intended. "I told you, Tristan, you are a power source unlike any other, and

Anliac isn't too far behind you." Crossing to the far side of the room, he turned his back on them all and peered from the damaged pane. "If I didn't understand that before," he admitted, "I certainly do now."

Relinquishing her spot on the bed, Anliac moved to stand beside Tristan. He wrapped his arm around her waist and pulled her to his side.

"How is it you managed to win?" she asked and then felt Tristan's sigh. Without looking up, she knew he was rolling his eyes at her. She also didn't care.

Set was slow to answer. "With their help." Shashara's sharp inhale stiffened his spine, but he did not turn. "There are so many of them. He held them captive. He used them until they hated him. I suffered a thousand deaths, and so did he. And a thousand times, I stole his life to replace mine, but you're right. He should have been the victor."

Pivoting, Set focused on Anliac. It was too painful to look at Shashara's tear-streaked face with the emotions pouring from her. "When the world disappeared outside of the pain, they were there, cheering me on and chanting, crying out that I not give up. They are the reason I survived the gurges..."

Shutting out the room, he leaned back his head and took a moment before he confessed, "They will be with me always. But," he said, finding and holding Shashara's eyes so she could see the truth reflected in his own, "they do not control me."

"But they do talk to you?" Anliac asked, her golden eyes aglow with possibilities.

"They are thankful to me," Set told her, "for breaking the

cycle."

Crossing her arms beneath her ample breasts, Anliac scowled. "That's no answer at all."

"It's answer enough for now," Tristan intervened. "As far as I'm concerned, if they helped keep you alive, I'm grateful they got in your head."

Shashara fell back on her palm, as if she'd been struck, dipping the mattress behind her. Covering her mouth, she swallowed hard, her stomach turned by Tristan's statement. "You've no idea what you're talking about."

Taken aback, Tristan's eyes went wide. "What?" He looked to Anliac, who shared Shashara's horrified expression. "What did I say?"

"You've said nothing wrong," Set told him. "I'm grateful to them as well. Otherwise," he said to Shashara, "I wouldn't be here with you now."

"Wait," Tristan said with sudden focus, "what is a gurges?"

"It's a fight between epotos," Set replied, his head tipping.

Tristan chuckled at Set's confusion. "I guess we'd better get used to you knowing more than the rest of us, little brother."

"Gurges are dangerous," Set said, "and not only to the combatants. The repeated draining of each person, and the subsequent refilling...the continuous back and forth...It creates a current..." He gestured in slow, gathering movements with his hands as he searched for a better word. "A vortex of abilities, knowledge, and memories. Shashara," he said, "when you tried to help me, you had to reach through

170

the vortex to reach me. Be glad, babe, that you walked away
with an added ability. It's better than never walking away at
all. You could have just as easily been one more voice in my
head."

"I am grateful!" Shashara bolted off the bed, causing
them all to stumble back. Collecting herself, she began
again. "I'm grateful for every advantage that will help me
keep the lot of you alive, despite the idiocy of your choices,
but you…" Her voice broke. "I made you a promise, Set,
that I wouldn't let you lose yourself to Calstar's psyche. And
yet, so many times, I've feared I'd failed." Moving towards
him until mere inches kept them apart, she whispered, "How
many must I protect you from now, and how long before my
failure destroys us both?"

She did not run to other side of the room. She did not
scream for him to get away from her. When he raised his
hands to cup her cheeks, she dropped her gaze and backed
from his touch. That single-stepped retreat was far worse.

The skin around his eyes and mouth tightened to hide
the pain that otherwise would have been revealed. "This is
different, Shashara. They are not a mass of voices speaking
over each other in my head. They do not give voice to their
opinions or grapple for control." He took a deep breath and
held it for a moment before releasing it. "I wish I could explain it in a way that you all could understand, but here is the
truth. I know their beginnings, their lives, and their deaths.
Their memories are mine, and I feel them as deeply as they
do. From loss to victory, from reward to cost, they are as
much mine as theirs. And as for Calstar," he said, "he's quiet
and content in his new company. In truth," he assured, "it

feels as if he is all but faded away."

"It could have been worse," Skylar said, peeking head and shoulders around the doorframe. When all eyes turned to her, she said with a shrug, "I mean, I didn't know Calstar all that well, but he seemed like a nice guy." Fully entering the opening without crossing the threshold, she gawked at their incredulity. "What?"

"Nothing," they said simultaneously, then grinned at the return of their solidarity.

"Well," Skylar said, cocking her head and her right eyebrow, "what's going on in town is definitely not nothing. So…" Waving her fingers around on limp wrists, she said, "I know you guys have stuff going on in here, but we've got epic problems brewing out there."

As weariness settled on his shoulders, heavier than any mantle he'd ever worn, Set said, "Okay. Let's go."

"No." Anliac shook her head. "The two of you need to stay here and talk. Lead the way," she said to Skylar. "We'll follow you."

Set and Shashara stood in awkward silence and waited for the sound of boots to find the bottom of the stairs.

"Is Shashara okay? Where are we going?" they heard Davad ask.

"Does it ma—" The remainder of Skylar's answer was cut off by the closing of the front door.

Set fought a grin.

"What?" Shashara asked, her curiosity heavier than the strain between them.

He regretted his words the moment they left his lips. "I wasn't certain if he trusted me enough to leave you alone with me."

She hid her eyes upon the floor. Her long, wavy tresses fell like a curtain, hiding her face from him.

"There is something I would have you know," he whispered. "One indisputable and unchanging truth." He tracked the tears that dropped at her feet and counted each as diamonds, because they were shed for him, and he didn't deserve her. "My mind is shared, Shashara, but you alone possess my heart."

"I love you too, Set..."

"But?" He could hear the last word hanging.

"I'm afraid." She shrugged, at lasting forcing her eyes from the floor to settle on the starburst within his. "I'm afraid to let you touch me. To touch you..."

Confusion and nausea rolled together. He was adrift in an oceanus of fear. "Don't leave me."

"Oh, Set..." She shook her head as her tears were renewed. "I would never leave you, but I will not leave a lie to build a bridge between us either. You terrify me."

"I just held your hand," he said, breathing hard. "You touched my cheek."

"And each time," she told him, "I was afraid. Touching you is touching death, Set. Superi help me." She took a ragged breath. "I can see how much I'm hurting you, and I hate it. I know you did not do it on purpose..." She paused. "But you hurt me."

"I know what it felt like inside the gurges," Set rushed to tell her. "Wrapped in that vortex, I felt like fire was stripping away my flesh, burning it from my bones. I'm sorry you shared that pain by trying to save me. I'm so sorry."

"No." Shashara chuckled without mirth. "I know fire. I know the lick of flames on my flesh. That is what you took. You drained the heat from my very blood and left ice in my veins. I felt it travel, inch by frozen inch, through each of my organs. One by one, they succumbed to the cold. My flesh, covered over in pinpricks of agony, succumbed to the cold. When it entered my heart, I thought, 'I'm going to die and so is Set,' but in truth, my love, I was grateful for the promise of death if it offered respite from the pain."

Split wide by her confession, Set begged, "Tell me what to do."

The span of silence that stretched between them was an eternity of counted heartbeats. He stood on the precipice of damnation, waiting for her to tell him to go away. When, at last, she spoke, her words were his salvation.

"Take my fear of you, Set," she said, "as only an epoto can. Take it and feel it as your own. That way, you offer me the chance to move beyond the way I feel now."

The knowledge required had been provided a long time ago by an oracle who'd been captured by his fear. "Sit back on the bed," he commanded, "and show me your mark."

Later, he would wonder where the nerve to lay out such a bold order had come from, but as she moved with timid steps to follow his instructions, his only thought was to obey... and she wanted to forget. He'd do anything to keep her.

When he sat beside her, Shashara fought the urge to flee from the hand he laid on her bared shoulder. Slowly, as if he could sense the fragile hold she had on herself, he shifted her hair to spill down her back, sending shivers up her spine.

With gentle care, he tugged aside the remains of her tattered black shirt.

Overwhelmed with sudden dizziness, her quiet, "Oh," brought an endearing smile to Set's lips. "Breathe," he reminded her.

With the tip of a single finger, Set traced the purple sunbursts that covered the expanse of her smooth flesh, from her left collarbone to elbow, before turning his attention to the wavering, yellow lines that ran between them. His touch seemed to distract her from what he was doing in her mind, but to be sure, he said, "Your aquis marks are beautiful."

The smile she gave him, the shy smile that had been his alone since finding her beneath the tree in Effugere Aquam, released the vice around his heart.

Joy leapt in his chest, but not for himself…for her. The ability she'd so longed for was now one she could wield. He felt it, but he'd let her discover the treasure on her own and then, together, they'd find someone who could train her.

He took his time, searching through every nook and cranny of her mind and animus. Only once he was sure he'd siphoned every seed of fear and doubt tied to him did he ask, "Does my touch bother you?"

Shashara gave a moment to introspection. "No." She smiled. "I had not realized we'd even begun. There was no pain. Only…"

"Save your words, my love." He grinned. "Prove how little you fear the epoto." With a mischievous turn of his lips, he challenged. "Bare your ignis marks to my touch."

Following his command, her eyelids grew heavy as his lips, not his hands, found her right shoulder and the long slivers of red and black that rested there. Between planting kisses on each of the tiny swirls between the slivers, she grinned.

"Just to be on the safe side," she whispered, breathless for a whole other reason, "perhaps we should make sure there are no other marks to be found."

"I couldn't agree more," Set said, and he began a thorough search.

***

Exiting the house before Davad and the two women, Tristan called for his new guard's attention. "Daniel."

"Sir." The eager young Nox bowed nearly in half.

"You do not have to call me 'sir'," Tristan told him. "For Superi's sake, you're the one guarding my back. Perhaps I should be calling you 'sir'."

"Oh." Daniel paled, swallowing hard. "Please don't."

Anliac laughed. "Well, Daniel, I'll be the one guarding our King's back today," she said. "You and…" She held up her hand at Lynette's displeasure. "And you as well, Lynette, are to stay here."

"No one," Tristan interjected, "and I mean no one, is to go into that house until Set and Shashara have come out."

"If those are my orders…" Daniel's nod was stiff as he fell back into position beside the door.

Lynette, far more comfortable around the Angeli than the newcomer, had a more scathing remark to deliver before taking up her position. "You know we're going to talk about this later."

Tristan chuckled when Anliac winced and started them forward.

They'd gone no more than a dozen paces when Anliac and Tristan froze, causing Davad and Skylar to pause.

"Did you hear that?" Tristan asked Anliac, knowing his hearing was superior.

"That crash," Anliac confirmed. "Yeah, I heard it."

"Seriously!"

It was Davad's turn to laugh as Tristan and Anliac disappeared and Skylar fumed.

"It's not funny." Skylar huffed, stomping a dainty foot. "They could have carried.... EEK!" Her piercing screams wrenched a roar from Tristan that made her clamp both hands over her mouth. The Angeli had literally swept her off her feet, and now the world raced by in a blur.

A moment later, Tristan let her feet drop before steadying her and stepping away.

"Thank you," she said, wide-eyed and grinning. Her red hair was a fluffball of craziness framing pale, wind-pinked cheeks.

Anliac, who had Davad draped over her right shoulder, dropped her arm and shrugged him off.

Scrambling to find his feet before he landed on his butt, he glared. "Did you have to jump that log?"

"I could have let you walk," Anliac pointed out.

"Yeah." Davad nodded, wrapping an arm around his battered ribs. "Next time, do that."

Jumping onto a wagon occupied by Davimon and Lishous to gain a broader view, Tristan heard them say, "Glad you could join us."

He responded, "This is really bad."

Open fields spilled out behind a red, wooden barn with a

wood-shingled roof and double doors that stood closed. The dirt road that led from it was wide, maintaining its definition only by the grass that marked its boundaries on both sides.

And it was filled with Feras.

The townspeople were gathered along Pisces Stragulum's stone exterior wall. Some sat atop it, others pressed their backs against it, as still more inched their way closer to the conflict itself.

Davimon smirked. "True," he said. "Torren and Belua are being worked into a frenzy by this crowd. I tried to quiet them down, but Lunam isn't helping."

"What?" Anliac asked. "The Alpha is responsible for all of this?" Her gesture encompassed the growing number of people.

"Without Sole, the common dream is dead," Lishous volunteered. "She's no stronger than any other telepath now." He sneered. "She's lost her control over us, and she's not happy about it."

"Who are you?" Davimon asked his nearest and dearest companion with a quirked brow. "You told me you had dreams, but you never said you heard voices. You know that's weird, right?"

Lishous looked over and wiggled his bushy brows. "The only dreams I have are of you, big boy."

"Aw, shucks, you big flirt," Davimon said, slugging Lishous's shoulder. "You dream about me?"

Tristan rolled his eyes and started to smile but noticed a grey-skinned, barrel-chested, snout-nosed Fera had gotten too close to the Alpha. Torren reacted, coming up on her back paws, prepared to deliver a backhand that would've sent him over the wall to his death, but Tristan appeared between them.

"Enough!" he shouted, releasing his hold on the power his flesh caged. The brilliance revealed created a much larger space between the opposing sides.

Anliac moved to the middle of the conflict and placed herself between those loyal and those not. She managed to put a good number of the Fera at her back, while facing those with less honor. She spoke through them, to Lunam, as Tristan came to her side. "No harm will come to you if you bring no harm with you," she said. "Step forward and let us converse as equals."

With Torren and Belua ever present at her side, Lunam stepped beyond her guards to face her enemies. "What would you know of equality?"

"I cannot imagine the pain you must be suffering." Anliac's eyes drifted to Tristan, her heart clenching in her chest. It took will to turn away, but when she did, she was quick to regain her focus. "That stated, the hostility and discord you are attempting to sow here will not be tolerated. You will attack the people of Pisces Stragulum no more, neither their bodies nor their minds. Grieve as you must, and take what time you will before returning to the fold, but nothing has changed. The Fera will stand with us, or they will stand and face us when the war with the gods has been won." Doing her best to soften the hard edges of her words, she thought to take another approach. "Let us, together, wash him clean of the sweat and blood of battle and turn his flesh to ash, where it can become a part of Superi. Perhaps you'll find comfort in that."

"Comfort?" Lunam's eyes filled with more than tears. They filled with fear. They filled with fury. "What comfort is left to me now? What comfort is there for any of us? I CANNOT REACH MY PEOPLE," she screamed. "They are lost to me, as our history is lost to them, and it your fault."

"Oh, for Superi's sake, shut up." Lishous rolled his head across his shoulders to loosen the tension there as he said, "There is a reason you created the common dream, and it was to manipulate the masses." He gestured over his shoulder, towards Anliac and the non-Fera who stood beside her. "These people do not know the depth of your duplicity, but we—" he opened his arms wide, gesturing to the Fera on both side— "know well. Hundreds of times, you've planted your will in my mind while I slumbered, defenseless against your influence. Hundreds of times, you told me to kill my best friend, to shed the weight of him and escape to the wilds, where I belonged. You say that Superi has shut us out, but it was the Alphas that segregated our kind. It was you who told us we were different."

Sensing that his friend's temper was soon to ignite, Davimon drew attention away from him. "The search for differences that leads to naught but more division must cease." As he gained the crowd's focus, he continued, "Each race is different. The House of Angeli would not argue otherwise, but we are all Superians. Look at them," he said, pointing to Tristan and Anliac. "They could not be more different. One, a general's daughter and highborn; the other, the son of assassins. One, born a Nox, the other born…uh…"

"Mortalis," Tristan offered, the right corner of his mouth twitching. The man flushed scarlet but pressed forward.

"Thank you," Davimon said. "Mortalis. They are the only examples we have of what was once a perfect race, and yet, they are different in both power and ability. My point is this. With Tristan as our King, he eliminates every wall that has ever separated us, and I am grateful for it."

Davimon chuckled at his emotional vomit, but figured he'd gone too far to turn back now. So he continued, "For the first time in my life, I can put voice to a truth my heart has long known. Although I am Mortalis, my brother is Fera, and I could not care less what either of the two races think about it. That is the freedom, the unity, that the House of Angeli offers. The freedom to live as we choose." Distracted by Shorlynn's sashaying hips as she joined Skylar in the crowd, he added, "With the person of our choice. If you wish to live in the wilds, then do so. If you wish to live in a city, then do so. That is the freedom that the House of Angeli offers you. Stop fighting battles that have already been won by our King."

"Tristan is unbiased," Anliac stated, her pitch naturally rising as she used her Angeli power to emphasize her words. "He is honest to a fault, loyal to a fault, but he is not our King." A hush settled over the crowd. "He is our Alpha, and we, Superians, are his pack."

"How dare you." Lunam's triangular ears laid flat against her head. Her fur, the orange-red of fire, stood up along the ridge of her spine as she crouched, snarling, before Anliac.

"Calm yourself, Lunam," Anliac warned, "before you do something stupid. Lishous is right. You would call these people traitors and betrayers because you've lost control of them, when in truth, they are still very much loyal. Only now their loyalty lies with Tristan. Sole was a liar, and the secrets you keep make you little better. They will not follow you."

Scanning the crowd for those who might join the precious few who still stood with her, Lunam came up empty, yet she refused to back down. "You speak of loyalty yet give none. You speak of tolerance yet show none. You speak of secrets marking liars…" Her black lips peeled back from her sharp teeth in a grin to rival Lishous's in terror. "Ironic then, is it not, that you are surrounded by them?"

"If you have something to say," Tristan snapped, "say it."

"I have much to say," she snarled, her bushy tail swinging wide as she turned to Montilis. "Have you told your Alpha about the rift you convinced Set to open to Earth?" When he stiffened but did not reply, she pushed. "You remember, don't you? The rift you and Sole entered together? The one in which you and he killed a human?"

Montilis's visage never changed. When she turned on Davimon, the seer was less able to control his temper.

"And what of you, Davimon? You speak as though you and Lishous were issued from the same womb, but how many times have you abandoned him? Betrayed him? Let him suffer the cruel hand of your Mortalis king for the sake of your lofty position?"

"I know my crimes against my brother," Davimon seethed, "and yet I would die for him as he would for me, and that makes us family despite our disputes."

"Agreed," Lishous shouted to ensure there was no doubt.

"Will they still call you family, Shorlynn," Lunam challenged, "when they discover what you are? What you have

been from the beginning? What you've continued to be…
even now? In one fell swoop, you have betrayed Superi, the
House of Angeli, the people of Pisces Stragulum…" Her
laugh was cruel. "You've even betrayed the one you claim to
love."

Skylar, backing away from Shorlynn, asked, "What is she
talking about?"

"Forgive me," was the whispered reply that only she and
Tristan heard.

"She's the niece of Calstar and Malstar Luxson," Lunam
shouted, "two of the most conniving Fulgos on the planet.
Think, children. She's a mole for Certamen. How can you
call yourself leaders and not know this?"

"Is there truth in what she says?" Skylar asked, her words
carried forward by a foreboding breeze.

Approaching with an army, Set held up the back of his
hand to halt the Angeli Guards. They'd filed in behind him
as he'd crossed the town, uncertain, at first, of their purpose.
Some had thought to protect the town from him, and others
had thought to protect him from the town, but they'd all fall-
en in to follow as he made his march to the conflict.

With Shashara's hand clasped firmly in his own, he stood
in his breeches, barefoot and shirtless. The silence of the
people amplified every other sound: the rush of the wind
through the grain fields, the squeal of the barn's old doors,
the creak of leather as fighters shuffled their feet.

"Conniving, yes." Set nodded as those gathered around
the confrontation parted to make room for him. "The brothers were that, but their skill in manipulation paled in comparison to the master that was Sole. And Lunam," he said

with an icy smile, "before you try and deny it, remember that Sole's psyche now belongs to me. His treachery is revealed in the marks I now carry, each standing as a symbol for an ability stolen."

Lunam sneered. "A crime you're innocent of, I'm sure."

When Set gestured for him, Davad left his place beside the wagon where Anliac had dumped him and made the awkward crossing to reach him. With every eye on them and every ear attuned to them, he saw no point in whispering.

"I'm glad to see you both up and about, but, um…" He rubbed the tip of his nose with a crooked finger. "Couldn't you have found some clothes first?"

"See?" Shashara leaned in to say. "I told you." To Davad, she said, "With all the emotion on this end of town, there was no keeping him in the house, and apparently, there was no time to get decently dressed."

Feeling the eyes at his back as blades poised to strike, Davad asked, "Set, do you know something we don't?"

"Take her," Set ordered. He released Shashara into her brother's care, then took his place beside Anliac and Tristan. Giving Lunam his full attention, he responded to her accusation. "I take from those who would seek to take my life."

As he spoke, he closed the distance between himself and the one who sought vengeance against him. Stopping just shy of Belua and Torren intervening, he pitched his voice not to carry and poked the badger. "Careful, kitten, before your temper gets the best of you."

Lunam took three steps back before she realized she'd retreated. "How dare you call me that?" Her wideset eyes became like polished onyx gems when tears filled them to overflowing. "You have no right to speak those words. Those are not your words," she said, her voice rising in pitch. "I hope his presence destroys you, epoto. I hope they rip your mind apart." She slung the words as if they were a curse. "There are things worse than death, and I wish them all for you."

He felt it. She was going to run, but before she did, he wanted Belua and Torren for their side. So he raised his hands in mock defeat and backed off, but that didn't slow his tongue.

"Your words hold hatred, Lunam," Set told her, "but no weight. I'm done speaking to you. Instead, I'm going to give the Fera something they've never received from their Alphas. I'm going to give them the truth."

This truth, Lunam spoke into Set's mind, knowing full well the story he intended to tell, *could easily become your undoing.*

I'll risk it, Set thought back, loud and clear.

"Upon a time in Superi's history," Set began, "following the casting of the twin curses, four kings emerged. Together, they worked towards the recreation of all that had been destroyed. They created the four Nations. Yes," he said, "there were wars that lasted centuries. Yes, the cost in blood and lives was great, but then came the peacekeepers. The kings commanded the lawyers to create and establish laws that should have ushered in an age of peace, but in truth, peace had never stood a chance. Would you know why?"

Set waited for the crowd, especially the Feras, to express their desire before he gave them what they wanted. "One of the four was a traitor. You see," he said, "once the other kings were assured of peace, they tasked the Imbellis Asylum to recreate an Angeli. One that would reopen the rift to Earth, kill the gods responsible for the curses, and make whole the Superian race. The traitor, however, had other plans. These plans had been immortalized," he told them, "passed down through the generations until…the knowledge came to Lunam."

"What was the knowledge?" someone shouted from the back of the crowd.

"What was the plan?" shouted another.

Set held up a hand to quiet the questions. "Lunam, a powerful telepath and newly-made Alpha, discovered a secret denied her predecessors: the use of an epoto to amplify her ability. But," he explained, "Sole came with conditions. He believed the Fera were too dimwitted to function on their own, and so he offered Lunam a way to lead her people, a way to control them. She was your Alpha, but it was Sole's ability that allowed them to project the common dream that made you all pawns in their game."

He felt the anger and confusion welling up in the people, Fera and non-Fera alike, but it was not enough. Locking eyes with Lunam, they both knew what was coming. He watched the muscles in her back thighs bunch and release as she fought the urge to bolt.

"And what was that game?"

It was Torren who'd asked, and Set directed his reply to her. "Step one," he said, "hide Sole in the deserts of Collibus Dolor, so it was not discovered that the Fera had an epoto. Step two: convince the other kings that epotos were too dangerous to be allowed to live. Many of you are old enough to remember when the hunting for epotos started; the unprovoked slaughter of adults and children alike. Step three: wait for Malstar to recreate an Angeli. Their plan," he told them, "was for Sole to drain Tristan's power, so that they could, in turn, create the world they desired most. A world with only one perfect race. A Fera world."

"Yes, Sole and I maneuvered our people to where they were needed for the good of the whole," Lunam spoke out. "Is that not what a leader does? Yes, we've worked towards the rise of our kind. We've sacrificed so that we, the Fera, could claim this planet for our own... for our people. Is that not what an Alpha does?"

Not a single voice was raised to encourage her, and Set took advantage of the silence. "Events did not go according to their plan," he continued. "Tristan proved harder to kill than they thought. I am the epoto they did not think existed. And then there is Travis, your Alpha's true mate."

At this, the Feras stilled, their expressions darkened. While Lunam and Sole were their Alphas, Travis was the most respected and beloved Fera of his generation. Kind and just, many thought he should have been one to lead them.

"Travis is the reason your Alphas began to turn on each other," Set told them, "because Lunam discovered a truth that marked Sole a traitor of traitors. He intended to use the war with the gods to see Travis dead so that he could claim Lunam for his own."

Casting back her black stare to those that stared at her, she defended herself. "I cannot help if Set's words harden your hearts towards your dead Alpha, but do not let them harden your hearts against me. I did not know of Sole's plans for my husband, and once I'd discovered his intended betrayal, he was punished."

Torren turned to Lunam. With tears darkening the fur beneath purple, wide-set eyes, she demanded to know. "Did you betray Travis with Sole? Did you give him cause to believe that you would come to him in Travis' absence?" When Lunam held her tongue, Torren said, "Shame on you…and shame to you."

The words were severing. The crowd became a cacophony of curses and growls as the Feras came forward to cast Lunam out.

"Belua! Protect me," Lunam shouted as she turned towards the fields and ran.

A quick glance over her shoulder, and she knew she'd been forsaken. Torren and Belua stood before the Five, and the Feras who followed her were not interested in her protection. They wanted her dead. Without Sole, she was so much weaker, but she was still a telepath. The power she laced through the aether, shoving it into their minds, brought them pain and bought her a little time.

Davad, with Shashara trailing him, joined the others. "What now, Alpha?" he asked with a crooked, half-hearted grin. "Do we bring her back?"

Set, reaching for Shashara's hand, pulled her in tight. Needing to feel her against him, he wrapped his arms around her and laid her cheek against his shoulder. He peered at Tristan over her head and said, "Prophecy had Lunam plotting your death, brother, long before you were born." Shifting his eyes to Anliac, he told her, "From the moment we entered Collibus Dolor, they knew what you would become.

They let us leave so that you could be turned; two angeli to drain, instead of one, and all it cost them was patience.

"Someone or another," Davad interjected, "has been trying to kill us since we left Exterius Antro. What aren't you saying, Set?"

Running his hand down Shashara's spine, over the flowing waves of chestnut hair, Set spoke the words that had his gut in a twist. "She was going to kill you and Shashara, slowly," he said, "to punish us, and to make sure no one ever challenged them again."

There was a convergence of a sort that became the foundation upon which the Alpha of Superi would rise. Davimon and Lishous, Montilis, Triton and Razoran, Skylar, Lan, Torren and Belua, Shashara and Set, Davad, and Anliac, all gathered around him.

He seemed to grow in stature as his pounding heart gorged his thick, shredded muscles with blood. Furious, it showed in the illumination of the lines that marked him for what he was, but it was his voice, deep and ominous, that made the crowd avoid his golden stare.

"Lunam plotted to rip my family a part," Tristan stated. "She made it personal. If she wished to make an example of us, I want one made of her. I want her brought back…in pieces." Between the dropping jaws of his comrades and the covered gasps of surprised people, he asked, "Volunteers?"

XVII

No Use Arguing

Leaving Davimon and Lishous, with Lan's help, to organize the hunt for the disgraced Alpha, the rest of them headed towards the old marketplace, towards Set's office, seeking refuge from pressing eyes.

Razoran saw their approach from the docks and ran up to join them. "Hey, Set," he greeted. "I'm glad to see you're still in your skin. Man, your whole body went up in flames. Singed your clothes right off. It's a wonder you're not as bald as your brother."

Set blanched.

Triton chuckled as he passed them to walk beside Tristan and Anliac. "Don't worry, son. Only the wielders that carried you saw anything…important."

Shashara giggled.

"What?" Set asked, grinning as her laughter caught him up.

"Leave it to a man to worry more about his exposed parts

than the fire that exposed him in the first place," she said.

"Ha! Right," Anliac agreed.

Self-consciously, Tristan's hand rubbed the top of his head, running over the soft black fuzz growing in there.

"Stop touching it," Anliac said tugging down his arm and fighting a grin of her own. "I don't care if grows back or not."

As Davad moved ahead to open the door for Skylar, Tristan turned to Torren and Belua. "This is as far as you go."

Their confusion was shared. "We have protected the Alphas our entire lives," Torren protested.

Belua asked, "Who better is there to guard the House of Angeli?"

"We are guardians," they said together.

The interplay between the siblings was not missed on the others, but it served only to reaffirm what they already knew.

"Loyalty is proven and trust is earned," Tristan told them.

"We are grateful to count you among us," Anliac said, "but we have personal guards, and they have served us well."

Daniel and Lynette, always in the peripheral, glared daggers at their would-be usurpers, but Lynette, the more vocal of the two, found it impossible to hold her tongue. "Strong backs are better suited in the fields," she said.

Anliac turned on her guard with such disappointment that Lynette shrank from it. "If the two of you truly wish to be of aid, find Shorlynn and bring her to me."

Davad saw Skylar flinch. He saw her golden eyes fall to the ground, lost behind a veil of brilliant red hair until she looked up again. Her visage broke his heart. It hadn't been a conscious thought to offer her comfort, and even as his arms came open, he expected her glare, but they were both surprised when she went readily into them. Soothing her with small circles along her spine, her firm body pressed against his own, he had to admit she felt good there.

Disregarding the girl's pain, Torren answered for them both. "We'll find her." They pivoted with stiff spines and stormed off.

"Are we going in now?" Montilis asked.

Tristan's tone changed as quickly as his stare shifted to the General. "No one is entering that building unless we know they can be trusted."

Montilis crossed his arms over his chest and scowled. "Are you suggesting that I can't be trusted?"

"Why didn't you tell me about the trip to Earth?"

Silence.

"I never spoke to Sole," Tristan told him, "and Set, well, he's been a bit occupied. You and I, however, spent half the night talking about the defense of the Pisces Stragulum, about rations for the patrols, about starting a training school for the children. But not once did a rift to Earth or the killing of a human become the topic of our conversation."

"I..." Montilis started and stumbled. "I didn't think it was my place to..."

Anliac found herself caught between the two men she loved most in the world, but even she could not defend her father's weak excuse.

"You didn't think," Tristan interrupted him. "That much is truth, but there is a reason you hid your actions from me, and I would know it."

"It was as much my choice as his," Set stated.

Jaw clenched, Tristan replied, "Don't I know it."

Set shrugged. "Sole played me. He wanted to see if I could be convinced to act without your knowledge. He hoped it would drive a wedge between us."

"That will never happen."

"I know, brother." Set nodded as he leaned down to kiss the top of Shashara's head.

Montilis, hands held up in truce, said, "We wanted to end the conflict without involving everyone else."

"Shut up," Tristan snapped. "You are not my brother. My tolerance towards him and his actions does not extend to you. Hide something like this from me again," he warned, "and there will be trouble between us. Understood?"

A glance at his daughter and he knew he would find no ally there, so he conceded. "I understand. In the future, I will be more transparent in my intent. My apologies."

Tristan closed the space between him and the older man, his forward progress stopped by Anliac's pull on his wrist and forearm, and snarled, "Your intent could have gotten someone killed."

"I wanted to spare my daughter," was Montilis's honest reply.

"At the expense of my brother," Tristan stated, backing off. "It's not enough."

"Set," Shashara asked into the tangible silence, "who killed the human?"

"Sole," Set answered, "but its knowledge was limited."

"How so?" Anliac asked.

"Of all the gods that rule Earth," Set said, "it believed in the existence of only one."

"Odd," Anliac replied. "What of the others?"

"It believed the other gods were stories, myths," he said. "Nothing more."

"That doesn't make sense," Tristan stated.

"Very little about Earth does," Set told him. "It would take a great deal of time to explain the lengths humans have gone to segregate themselves. They are of one race, and yet they are divided by country, region, station, wealth, and rank. Wars have torn apart their lands for no more than varying colors of skin. Worse," he said, dragging in breath to continue, "they have something called religion, and the complexities of it become insanity."

"Still," Shashara said, "we've faced some of the gods. How is it the humans are blind to them?"

"Most humans believe that a person is better or worse depending on the land of their birth," Set explained. "It could be that the humans feel the same about the gods. Maybe it's not that there is only one, but that there is only one god for each faction of humans. Perhaps that's how they dismiss the others as fictitious or invalid. At this point, Shashara, all we have is speculation and supposition."

Montilis scratched his cheek, his nails bumping over the ridged scar that cut through it. Finally, he cursed and said, "We went for answers and came back with nothing but more questions."

"Dad…" Anliac sighed. "Your mistake was not in opening a rift to Earth. Your instinct to gain knowledge before acting was not in error. We know you are a general, but here, you are a soldier, and you failed to follow the chain of command. You went in without proper support, and as a result…" She let the rest play out. "What's done is done," she said. "We move forward."

"No," Tristan said. "We go back."

"Agreed," Set said and snapped his fingers.

Squawks of startled surprise broke out. The bunch of them peeked around the building, towards the docks. Dead center of the portal site was a shadow that seemed to unfold in a widening sphere that reached for the gateway's edges. They watched as it grew, crackling with purple lightning, until a clear rift was a revealed.

"Someone find Set some clothes," Shashara stated. Ignoring the guard that chuckled and took off to do her bidding, she stared in awe through the rift. "I've never seen a sky so blue."

Making their way towards it, Triton asked, "Do I want to know how you're doing all this?"

"All of what?" Set asked, though he knew.

Tristan made an exaggerated show of surveying the land. "The grass and bugs are still living. No one's dropped from being drained. How did you open it so easily, Set, and how are you keeping it that way?"

"Everything that is Superi, from the land to the animals to the denizens of it, is made up of energy. It is the one constant," Set explained. His shoulders tensed as his words were measured and weighed by those around him. "It will not be controlled, but it can be manipulated. It's about balance. I'm using the vast energy of the oceanus to maintain the rift, but," he clarified, "I'm not pulling from the deep.

There's too much power there. I'm pulling the energy from the waves, and the roll of the oceanus keeps the waves renewed and the rift stable. If there's a surge from either side, the oceanus is there to combat it."

Razoran rubbed sweating palms down the outside of his pants and said, "You make it sound like the aether is a person you have to say 'please' to."

The statement drew Set up short. "Actually, yeah," he said, "at least where the big things are concerned. The aether doesn't like to be disturbed, so it's best to appease it with balance when you're left with no choice but to stir it. What?" he asked, catching a glimpse of Anliac's contorted expression.

She smirked. "The boy who thought he knew everything is becoming a man who might, actually, know everything. It's disturbing," she said with a grin, but then wished she could take it all back when Set spoke.

"Lunam was wrong, you know," he said, bringing them to a stop before the rift. "There are not a thousand voices in my head. There are a hundred and seven. It's disturbing for me as well." Set missed the reactions on their faces when he was handed a shirt to pull over his head.

Hating herself for it, Anliac heard the question spill out of her mouth. "Tristan, are you sure this is a good idea?" She winced. "I'm sorry, Set, but we don't really know how—"

"Stable I am?" Set finished for her, dropping to his backside to pull on stockings before tugging on his boots. "How trustworthy I am? Am I even the one doing the talking? It's okay, Anliac," he reassured, standing. "What I've become is as complicated as what you were made, but I am myself, and

I will keep Tristan safe."

"As will I," she stated. "I go where he goes."

"Ah, babe," Tristan started, "you know we can't both go. What if the gods return? Thor, or Qandisa? Who here can face them if we're both gone?"

"What if you do not return?" Anliac countered. "No," she objected, "you're not leaving me."

"The threat of a god returning is real enough," Montilis stated, "but an attack from Lunam is more likely. She is without Sole, but that makes her more dangerous, not less. Either way," he said, "Tristan is right. Your place is here."

Slowly, a fierce scowl in place, she spread her glare between the two men and said, "Oh, I don't like this at all. The two of you will not conspire against me."

Tristan laughed as Montilis covered his grin behind a closed fist.

"No one is conspiring against you," Tristan said, "but I do need you to stay here."

She looked around at the crowd for an ally, but most avoided her eyes. "Fine," she conceded, "but only if you take Triton with you."

"Me?" Triton asked. "Why?"

"Because," Anliac swore, "if he doesn't come back in one piece, I'll need someone to kill, and my father and Set are not options."

Undaunted, Triton grinned. "You have a way of inspiring hatred and respect in equal measures, Angeli. Razoran, you keep an eye on my ship and crew."

"Aye, Captain. Always."

Turning in Set's embrace, Shashara cupped his cheeks

before letting her palms fall to his shoulders. "I'd ask you not to go, but we both know you wouldn't listen."

Clasping his hands at the small of her back, he nodded. "If, for any reason, the rift was to close, I'm not certain I could find them again. I need to be there to open a rift home."

"For me," Shashara asked, "take wielders with you?"

Daniel, Tristan's guard, made his position very clear. "I will be going, ma'am. I'm not a level three terra wielder," he said, "but next to Anliac, I'm the strongest we've got."

"Well, if Razoran has Triton's ship," Skylar said, "then I will have Triton's back. Not even the Angeli are as strong me in matters of aer."

"With your permission, General," a Nox in Palus Regia gear stated, "my name is Jophery. My comrade's name is Weston. We're both ranked level threes, trained as aquis wielders under Senior General Riker. Let us serve, sir, and we will not let you down."

"You're welcome to join us," Montilis agreed, making the soldiers' day.

After kissing Shashara soundly, Set promised, "See you soon," before letting her go.

"Later, babe." Tristan winked, laughing when Anliac stuck her tongue out at him, and then he asked, "Hey, Davad, are you coming?"

Davad shook his head. "Though I believe you should find an ignis wielder to take, Tristan, I also know they need to be stronger than I am."

"What are you going to do, then?" Shashara asked.

"Has anyone seen Socmoon?" Davad answered with a

question of his own.

"Yeah." Tristan nodded, walking backwards. "You should find out what the old—"

"Whoa there, boss," a Fulgo with ignis markings interrupted, grabbing hold of Tristan's arm to stop the step that would have cut him off at the ankles on the edge of the rift. "Getting a little close."

Tristan gulped, his eyes bulging at just how close he'd gotten. "What's your name?"

The man grinned. "My friends call me Shady."

"Shady or not," Tristan chortled, "you're coming with me."

"Absolutely," Shady agreed. "Where are we going?"

"Earth," several voices said at once as, one by one, they entered the gateway.

"This is what I get for eavesdropping," Shady lamented.

Tristan laughed, but he made sure Shady went in before he did.

XVIII

Unexpected

Exiting the rift, the nine companions stepped into a furnace, where the air shimmered with heat and the land had baked into cracked red mud and brittle, brown grass. Trees were sparse and set in clusters that offered little shade to the large, lazy beasts that ambled within the leaning fence posts, strung with rusted barbed-wire. In the distance, taking on the wavering image of a mirage, sat an unstirred surface of a lake that dried their mouths and thickened their tongues with want for water themselves.

"Whew," Skylar said, twisting her red hair into a knot atop her head. "If this is Earth, the humans can have it."

Set closed the rift, giving them a view of what lay behind them. It was only more of the same: a scorched and thirsty land.

Triton nodded. "Agreed."

"Not to complain…" Jophery winced. "But I feel, um… lightheaded, and I don't think it's from the heat."

"It's not," Montilis told him. "It's the pull of this planet. Superi's hold on its denizens is much greater. We felt it last time. In fact," he said, shielding his eyes against the glaring yellow sun as he peered into a sky so blue, it was a wonder their world needed a sun at all, "I wouldn't be surprised if the humans can fly."

Eight necks snapped backwards as if an assault from the sky was imminent.

"What is it?" Set asked Tristan, feeling the spike of anxiety that put worry lines in his brother's brow.

"If we encounter conflict," Tristan stated, "we might have a problem." At their angled expressions, he explained. "Daniel, if the pull here is different, how will it affect your ability? And," he continued without waiting on a reply, "we have four aquis wielders—nearly half our number—and no water." Shaking his head, he gestured at Shady, "Not to mention, we have an ignis wielder we dare not use, unless, of course, we're willing to set their whole world on fire."

"There is no moisture in their air," Triton corrected, "but there is plenty of water. It runs in rivers, hot and cold, beneath the surface."

"And I'm offended, boss," Shady said, hand to heart as if injured, but smiling. "I can push or pull any flame. On my honor, I'll only scorch the parts of Earth you permit."

"What about you, Daniel?" Tristan asked.

"Let us find out," was the terra guard's reply.

Flinging his right arm out to the side, a closed fist angled downward, he focused on the unfamiliar terra. Like an arrow through a fresh kill, a crack opened and rushed forth towards the others.

Set was directly in its path. His muscles bunched as he prepared to throw himself out of its way, but the tear was too swift and growing too wide. Just as calamity would have trapped them on Earth by killing their epoto, Tristan dove into the crack and caught him up by one arm. Jumping from one side of the chasm to the other, he carried them upward, launching them, on the last step, out of death's maw.

The ambitious leap carried them high enough that Set had time to say, "Show off," before Tristan replied with, "Tuck and roll, little brother," as the ground rushed up to meet them.

Tristan hit it at a run and came to a slow, round-about stop, where Set had bounced and rolled.

"Superi help me," Daniel gasped, pale of cheek and wide of eye. "I am so sorry."

"It's okay," Set assured him with a groaning, winded, moan. He took a moment to catch his breath before gaining his feet.

Tristan slapped Daniel on his back with a smile, and said, "A tad overkill, but all and all, I'll take it."

"Eh…" was all Daniel could manage beyond a sickly smile, for he'd rather die a thousand deaths than face the wrath of Shashara and Anliac…together…at one time. He wiped the sweat from his brow, beaded there by the image of his death.

In the wake of the tear, water had pooled at the bottom, and the wielders of it were eager to see their own strength after Daniel's display.

Weston, using both hands as if swinging a club, slung out a string of it that sliced the ground like a sword through flesh. So smooth was the cut that had the aquis not bubbled to the surface, they'd have thought his maneuver had failed.

Jophery, gathering a sphere of aquis that hovered between his palms, hurled it as hard as he could.

The aquis disappeared and then they heard the shattering of glass.

"No…" Tristan said in awed disbelief.

"What?" more than one man asked.

"The land lies here," Tristan told them. "It appears flat, but in truth, it rolls. I uh, saw a house…" He bent his elbow before sending his arm and pointed finger in an arc towards where he'd seen it. "It's a distance away, but there's nothing else out here that would hold glass." Dipping his head in due respect, Tristan said, "Well done, Jophery."

Montilis, who'd remained silent until now, stated, "If there are humans in that house, we've just lost the element of surprise."

"Not to mention, we could have hurt an innocent." At Jophery's fallen visage, Set hurried to say, "It wouldn't be your fault, but we should go and check it out."

"We should go now," Montilis told them. "Whatever those animals are, they're coming to the water."

"Oh," Skylar said, fanning before her nose with her hand, "I'm all about avoiding those things. I can smell their stench from here." As they followed behind her, she remarked, "I feel so…" her quick breaths conveyed her rush— "powerful here. Does anyone else feel it?" She glanced over her shoulder to check their expressions and found Tristan grinning.

"Every day," he said with such hubris that Skylar felt inclined to tell him, "Your bald head is burning."

"I self-heal," Tristan said, matching her tone, "but um…I think your freckles are spreading."

Skylar stopped in her tracks as both hands flew up to cover her nose. "No…" she cried, stamping her foot, much to the men's amusement as they took the lead.

They encountered first a white, picketed fence that offered no security whatsoever but added a picturesque boarder around the quaint homestead. There was a small silo, a two-stalled barn, and a small vegetable garden, which suggested the humans lived much as the Superians did. However, the faded blue, metal carriage that sat upon four black and bulbous wheels punctuated their differences.

The foundation of the house was red brick before grey, wooden slates took over to travel upward two stories. On the second story, on the front left side of the house, was the broken window.

"There's no one here," Set said, relieved, but he wore a scowl. It meant they were no closer to obtaining the information they'd come for.

"Are you sure?" Montilis asked, "Because we are all kinds of vulnerable, standing in the open like this."

Set nodded. "I'm sure. I would feel their fear." A heartbeat later, he said, "Wait…" Turning in a swift circle, he searched for the source of an immense anger. He shouted in warning, "We are not alone!"

"Blast it all!" Skylar exclaimed. "They do fly. Look up!"

"That is not a human," Set said with rising panic. They scattered around the fenced-in yard and waited for the thing to fall.

The size of a dracon without feet or fins, a dark green

snake fell to the earth, creating a vibration that seeped into their soles, a hundred feet from them. Its head, as high as the second story of the house, swayed back and forth as, with a forked tongue, it began to speak.

"*A dv nv i s do di – na s gi na l – a yo hu hi s di.*" *(Prepare to die!)* The words of the monster were lost on them, but the cluster of priceless gems embedded between the monster's reptilian eyes had their attention. "*Ni hi na s gi ni ge sv na – u li he li s di a di ha – Unetlanvhi – a da nv s di – a le – a yo hu hi s di!*" *(You are not welcome says Unetlanvhi, leave or die)*

"Does anyone happen to speak snake?" Montilis asked, his blood running cold.

"Nope," Tristan said, but seeing the odd tilt of his brother's head and the glazed stare with which he studied the snake, felt prompted to ask, "Set, can you get a feel for its mood?"

"*A DA NV S DI!*" *(Leave!)*

"I'm not an epoto," Skylar said when Set failed to respond, "but I think it's mad."

"Ah..." Weston choked on a chuckle. "You think?"

"We need to kill it," Montilis stated, goosebumps raising the hair on his arms.

"We need to know if we can kill it," Set said, correcting their course of action. "Tristan... sorry, brother, but you're the only one that heals."

Triton, keeping an eye on the reptile, hedged his way to where Montilis stood with Jophery and Weston. "You're eyeing those gems hard there, General," he said.

"They would make an extraordinary trophy, would they

not?" Montilis replied.

"Indeed, but you should know," Triton told him, "that when we've killed the beast, those jewels are mine."

"Put your greed away, Captain," Skylar chastised, "and pay attention."

"Woman..." Triton glared, gearing up for a tirade, but was distracted when Tristan disappeared.

No sooner had he done so than the Angeli tripped over his own feet and went into a headlong tumble that threatened to roll him right into the snake's path. Scurrying out of striking distance, Tristan found his feet and shook his head to clear.

"What was that?" Set asked.

"It might be poisonous, boy," Triton warned. "Take more care."

Tristan scowled. "Shut your traps. I've got this."

"Not all snakes are poisonous," Skylar said with a lift of her chin, "but leave it to you to clump everything together."

"If it's sassy like a woman and nagging like a woman, then it's usually a..."

Tristan was off and going again, but to worse results than first time. Before Triton could finish his sentence, Tristan's left foot landed upon a tiny bump in the ground, and his speed veered him off course.

Tripping over a wooden fence meant to keep vermin out of the flowerbeds, he tumbled into a wheelbarrow that launched him towards a small wooden well house, which he narrowly avoided crashing face-first into.

Not only his companions, but the snake as well, had become statues that portrayed humor. With his complexion unable to hide his embarrassment, he said, "I'm okay. I'm good. I've got this." But under his breath, he admitted, "I *think* I've got this."

This time, he took off at would have been a jog on Superi, and he found the speed he was looking for. Tracking the snake's eyes as it tracked him, he was ready for the reptile's strike and easily maneuvered around it. Then he closed in for a strike of his own.

Throwing speed, as well as his shoulder, behind a solitary punch, Tristan's fist ripped through the snake's raised underbelly like an axe to a tree. Its screeching wail followed him like crashing waves upon his nerves as he slid to a stop a safe distance away.

Wasting no time, he issued his orders before the snake retaliated. "Daniel, Skylar," Tristan called out, "see if you can get to the side of this thing and cause a little damage. Just don't forget we're over here," he said with them already on the move. "Keep your attacks aimed away from us. Montilis, get your wielders the water they need, and do it now."

"On it," Montilis stated. "Let's go, men," he said, running for the well house.

"Shady, come with me."

"Yes, boss," was the Fulgo's quick reply.

"What about me?" Triton asked, his barrel chest puffing.

"Guard my brother."

A full-bellied laugh came before Montilis shouted, "Those jewels are mine, pirate."

"Son of a…" Triton grabbed hold of the aqua source within the well and yanked a flood of it forth.

"Thanks!" Montilis called. He took control of the water

flow and leveled it, mid-air, before his wielders. "Slice that meat into steaks, men, and we'll eat it well when the battle is done."

The snake rose higher on its sinuous frame, rearing back its head to strike. Jophery and Weston turned water to blades and began their attack.

Skylar, scooping dirt into her hand for focus, blew the grains towards the snake. A mini-sandstorm whirled to life and flew into the monster's face at her bidding. Before their enemy could take a blind strike at the aquis wielders, Daniel discovered how fast he could pull chunks of rock and earth from the ground, and then he volleyed the beast.

Bloodied and beaten, with a hole in its belly, still the snake showed no signs of weakening. It was then Shady asked, "My turn, boss?"

"Have at it."

To the aquis wielders, Shady shouted, "Thicken your blades, gentlemen. They'll be going in hot." Planting his left foot back, he pushed his weight forward and onto his right foot, then shoved out his palms as if against a stone wall he would see tumble. The flames that issued forth were incredible, larger than anything he'd ever conjured on Superi. In pride, he shouted, "Yeah!" as the fire rolled forth.

The flow of water came to a boil. The wielders began to sweat, but they did not slack off. The snake hissed as its scaled skin blackened and shrank from the raw meat beneath it, only to be flayed by the onslaught of slashing blades.

Tristan, standing back, saw the forward fall of the snake's upper body as its jaws unhinged. "Watch out!" It was going for the aquis wielders.

Montilis, knowing any conjured sword from the heated liquid would burn his flesh, unsheathed the steel blade at his hip and held his ground.

Jophery and Weston panicked. They broke position and ran, terror on their faces as, against their will, their feet carried them not away, but towards the striking snake.

Tristan saw what was happening, but as he rushed to save them, his speed became an obstacle that tripped him up and slowed his progress. He managed to yank Jophery clear of the snake's attack, but when he turned to grab Weston, he was too late. The snake had swallowed him whole.

"Regroup," Tristan shouted, shoving Montilis ahead of him when the stubborn Nox tried to go for snake's throat with his bare hands.

"Sweet Superi," Skylar gasped once they'd gathered. "Do you see it?"

Jophery shook his head in denial even as he said, "There's not a mark on it."

"Steady your nerves, son," Montilis told him.

"Uh-uh," Jophery grunted. "I'm done. I'll meet you all back at the rift… If any of you survive." Feeling every bit the coward, he ran. He was pulled back by Tristan's hold on the scruff of his neck as the Angeli saved him from a forward path that would have made him a second course for the snake.

"You're a coward," Montilis sneered.

Triton concurred, "You're a traitor."

"But he's no fool," Set interjected. "What happened, Jophery?"

"My mind would not let me run," the trembling man replied, "and apparently, my feet are tied to my mind."

"So," Tristan nodded, "the snake has an ability after all."

Reaching around his waist, Tristan lifted the armored gauntlets from where they rode on his lower back; they were a gift from Triton in exchange for giving Davad the dracon sword and were always with him. One at a time, he slid his hands into the leather gloves, altered to accommodate his claws, and then adjusted the three straight blades that stood out as daggers over his knuckles.

As if the monster knew Tristan was coming for it, it slithered closer and hissed, *"Ni hi – ye li ni ge sv na – a da hi s di – a yv – a yo li."* *(You cannot kill me child!)*

Fastening the buckles on the underside of his forearm, securing the gauntlets in place, Tristan said, "I've already told you…I don't speak snake."

"Hold," Set ordered when Tristan's attack prompted the others to aid him. "You'd only get in his way."

They tracked Tristan by the damage he caused. They knew he'd passed the snake because three claw marks had ripped open its belly as before, but its girth protected the vital organs.

"The beast has no guts to spill, boy," Triton shouted. "Go for its heart."

They watched as the pirate's advice was taken. First came the sliding of rocks, as if Tristan had slid to a stop, and the snake shifted to face away from them…tracking its prey by more than sight.

None of them were prepared when the top half of the snake crashed to the ground, falling backwards from three deep stab wounds. They didn't see Tristan until he slid to a stop in front of them.

With blood up to his right elbow and dripping from both hands, Tristan held them up in confusion and asked, "How do you kill something without a heart?"

"I don't know, brother," Set said, "but if you can't kill it, I'm going to have to."

"No one here wants the snake's abilities added to your brother's, son," Montilis said. "Figure it out."

"Right," Tristan stated, taking a few deep breaths before going at it with the snake again.

"Thanks a lot, Montilis," Set said with a cock-eyed turn of his mouth and stare.

"Oh, puh-lease," Skylar teased. "You already have too many slimy psyches crawling around in your head. Why would you want to add another?"

"Good point." Set grinned, nodding his agreement.

"We have company," Triton stated over Tristan's battle shouts and the snake's wailing responses. "It, at least, looks human."

"Where?" Skylar asked.

It was a Mortalis-looking man, stout of build, dressed in black. His boots were heavy, his pants snug, and the sleeveless vest was left open. They watched him turn from the striped, paved path with a predator's grace, then onto the narrow, gravel way that led to the strange carriage before the front of the house.

"Well, now," Skylar muttered. A breeze lifted the man's black waves of hair, as if the wind desired to touch him too. "*That* is a beautiful man." She gifted them with a grin that showed her even, white teeth and the full bottom lip that was trapped between them.

As Triton, Jophery, and yes…even Set, lost their focus to the possibilities of those luscious lips, Montilis was drooling over something else.

"So are his weapons," the General said. The man drew near enough to give detail to the broadsword hanging down his back and the shortsword strapped to his thick hips. "Are such fine blades common on Earth?" he asked.

"No," Set said, a bit confused at the human's choice in weaponry. "They are not. Humans have found more effective ways of slaughtering each other."

"Then what kind of human is that?" Skylar asked. "Because I want one."

A gurgled roar was its death knell. They turned as one to see the snake's fall as, standing atop its massive head, a golden, glowing Tristan plunged his fist into its skull, shattering the precious gems to reach its controlling mind.

"NO!" There was no distinguishing between Triton and Montilis's devastated cries.

Tristan didn't care about the jewels as he rode the dead creature to the ground. Without missing a step, his eyes glowing and his marks burning as hot as Earth's sun, he bared his claws and stalked towards the man in black.

"That is no human, Skylar," Set told her as Tristan passed. "It is a god."

In the deep voice that foreshadowed chaos, Tristan growled, "Ares!"

XIX

Depths of Strength

Ares clapped his hands, though the smirk turning up the corners of his mouth negated the praise. "Well done, Angeli," he said with dripping sarcasm. "The Uktena is a valiant opponent. Although, your victory over the Cherokee spirit should not vault your confidence too high; they are only water spirits after all. And that one," he said, pointing behind Tristan, "came only because it was summoned. If you had the ability to understand, you would know that the Uktena was telling you to leave. It had no interest in fighting you, but it had no other choice than to follow the orders of the Unelanvhi."

Tristan sensed his companions falling into formation at his back, but Ares had his focus. "The snake is dead, and I care not at all about who its god is."

A chill swept up Skylar's spine and the hair rose on her arms. Standing closest to Set, she turned wide eyes to the epoto and warned, "Something is coming."

213

A moment later, the temperature dropped. Dark, ominous clouds rolled in that threatened to blot out the sun. An unnatural breeze wafted across their flesh, carrying with it a foreboding that chilled them all.

"You continue to show your ignorance concerning your enemies, boy," Ares told him with an arch of his brow, "for the Unelanvhi is like Zeus in the eyes of the Cherokee, and you've caused offense. Listen, Angeli, and tell me what you hear."

Though he resented the order, Tristan's sensitive ears tuned to the moans issued by the wind and discovered a voice within it; one that resembled the hissing of the Uktena. "I do not fear the wind," Tristan snarled, "nor the monsters conjured by it."

A bolt of lightning struck the ground as the Unelanvhi gave its response.

As the earth quaked and trembled in an outward ripple, like the surface of pond after a stone has been thrown, Daniel pointed towards the center of the scorched ground and said, "We have company."

As if Daniel's words had conjured it, a huge, pale-white and hairless fist punched its way free. A second fist exploded from the ground and then a creature clawed its way to the surface to stand as living clay clout in the skin of an animal.

Though small when compared to the Uktena, it nonetheless stood fourteen feet tall, with heavy muscles carved into every inch. Three long, fat fingers made up its hands, and it perched upon three toes, its heels sitting high like many of the Fera. A singular horn sat in the center of its wide forehead, above muddy, brown eyes that sought them out.

"Interesting," Ares quipped. He nodded in approval at the Unetlanvhi's choice. "It would appear the Cherokee spirit has called the Caddaja, of the Caddo, as its champion. Are you to be your companions' champion, Angeli? Or shall I have to slaughter my way through them to finish what you and I began?"

Montilis stood, stone-faced and eager, counting on the others to keep track of the Caddaja as he maintained his readiness to fight at Tristan's side.

It was Triton who said, "The Uktena was nothing more than a dracon with an ability, and this Caddaja is just another horned beast. We've defeated plenty. Go," he sneered in Ares's direction, "play with the little god, and when this thing is good and dead, we'll help you finish up with him."

"Brother," Set's voice was carried up from behind, "do not kill him. He has all the information we need."

There was no denying the malice that saturated Ares's laughter. "You Superians are fools. A true god cannot die."

"You are the fool," Set said in a flat monotone that raised the hairs at the nape of Ares's neck. "My brother will make you wish for death, and after I've taken all of the knowledge in your head – along with every drop of power you possess – I will grant your wish."

His head cocked to the side and his eyes filled with piqued curiosity, Ares asked, "Does Superi, at last, have a god?"

It was Tristan's turn to smirk. "You continue to show ignorance concerning your enemies, boy. He is far more than a god. He is an epoto." Without turning to look upon Montilis, Tristan commanded, "As I protect your blood, protect mine."

Then he became a streaking blur aimed at Ares.

The god's feet shifted towards a defensive, anchored stance, but before he could balance his weight, the Angeli's shoulder connected with his gut. The crash sent them rolling into a violent tangle of arms, legs, and weapons…farther away from the secondary battle that had commenced the moment Tristan had moved.

Hitting the paved road that ran before the Oklahoma farmhouse, Ares found himself fighting only air as Tristan disengaged. Unused to disorientation, the god translocated from his back to his feet, twenty feet away.

"You're fast," Ares stated, giving credit where it was due, "but here, on Earth, so am I." Raising his hand, palm up, he curled his fingers and beckoned Tristan to come. So fast came the Angeli's advance that the backhanded swipe of his armored gauntlets could not be parried; each of its blades carried the promise of pain.

To avoid them, Ares blocked the attack with the iron bracers encircling his wrists. Embracing the blow, rather than trying to thwart it, he rolled his weight with its momentum and onto his bent left leg. With his right, he put his power behind a vicious side-kick.

To Tristan, the god's movements were slow and allowed for ample time to counter, to seek openings of opportunity. His vulnerable left leg was a good start, so he swept out his foot to trip up his enemy, only Ares had been counting on it.

Going into an easy backflip, the God of war pulled his sword and used the tip to maintain his bearings. Once his feet found purchase, he lunged, blade first, for Tristan's heart, but the blade met with no resistance when the Angeli stepped to the side. With a quick turning of his feet, he attacked again, a horizontal slash meant to take Tristan's head.

Crossing his wrists, Tristan caught and captured the blade between his armored gauntlets. With a great heave, he tossed both god and weapon into the ditch that ran alongside the black road.

Reveling in the contest against a worthy opponent, Ares came up smiling. To prove his speed equal to that of the Angeli's, he rushed forward.

Three heartbeats it took for the god to cross the ground. One heartbeat, and the god threw his fist in an up-swing. Tristan dodged the blow and came around behind him.

Angling the three daggers that protruded past his gauntleted fist towards Ares's ribs, Tristan threw his weight behind the blow. Before the tips could find purchase, Ares conjured and covered himself with heavy, black battle armor.

With a wild, backhanded slash of his blade, Ares forced the Angeli into retreat.

Without his speed, Tristan never would have ducked in time, but the desperate maneuver had left the god vulnerable.

Tristan, his left fist clenched until his claws punctured the leather and sank into the palm of his hand, punched the blades protruding from his gauntleted fist towards the center of Ares's chest. The daggers shattered upon impact, no match for the god's armor. The force that followed them left a dent behind as Ares found wind and flew fifty feet before landing in a momentary heap.

Gathering his wits, Ares gained his feet. He took quick note of the other battle, where the wielders had moved into offensive positions and the Caddaja was advancing, before focusing on the Angeli. He stood in the center of the paved road, taunting him.

Discarding the gladius, Ares reached over his shoulder for the broadsword at his back and said with excitement, "Round one goes to you, boy, but round two…"

With a roar to rival thunder, he shoved off the ground, leaving a crater at his feet. He launched himself at his enemy in a split, over-head attack. When his sword struck dirt instead of flesh, Ares began to lose patience.

Ripping the blade from the earth, Ares slashed up and forward again and again, forcing Tristan to take to his heels. Strike and advance, strike and advance, backing the Angeli up one step at a time, until the ditch at Tristan's back caused his step to falter. Ares saw it and took advantage in an over-handed swing that should have seen the Angeli cleaved in two, but Tristan blocked with the clawed blades of his gauntlets, thwarting the attack.

The force, coupled with the sloping terrain, made Tristan do a backward roll into the ditch. He came up sitting on his backside.

"You lack experience, boy," Ares told him from his superior position upon the road, all signs of humor gone. "And here, I am not hindered by Superi's gravity. Here, you will discover the meaning of god."

Feeding Ares's misconception that he'd been defeated, Tristan asked, "Why did the gods come to Superi?"

"To finish what we started," Ares replied with a superior tone. "We should have slaughtered the lot of you the first time." With a growl of determination, he attacked, sword-tip down and thrusting hard.

The sword's blade was buried inches into the ground, and Tristan was gone.

Ares spun to protect his flank and folded in on himself when a solid front kick was delivered by the Angeli, driving him away from his weapon.

"I was told not to kill you," Tristan said, "but I made no promises." The two collided again, this time going hand-to-hand.

***

"Hold its attention," Montilis barked when the Caddaja's focus remained on Ares and Tristan. "That boy has his hands full as it is."

"We're over-balanced on the aquis side," Triton stated as they fell into a formation that blocked the Caddaja's path, "and this place doesn't give us a lot to work with."

"The aquis in the well-house has to come from some-where," Montilis said.

"It does," Daniel answered. "There's an underground current coming from…" His eyes ran over the dry ground, using his ability to follow the void inside the earth, until they came to ring made of a porous stone that held the surplus of aquis. "General…"

"I see it," Montilis told him. "Keep this formation tight until the monster charges, then we break and run for the aquis source."

"How do we make it charge?" Jophery asked. "It's not even looking at us."

"Like this." Shady grinned, and then a stream of red fire issued from his outward palm that hit the Caddaja square in its gut.

Clay flesh cracked and powdered, but the earth rushed up through the Caddaja's feet to renew it.

"It's not working," Shady said. "What now?"

The Caddaja roared.

"Oh, it's working," Skylar contradicted, "and it's coming."

"Break!" Montilis ordered, shouting new orders as they ran. "Diamond formation! Terra, take point. Ignis, fall to the rear. Protect Set."

"What about me?" Skylar asked, her yellow eyes growing wide as the lumbering beast dropped forward, running on hands and feet towards the source of his pain. She did not wait for orders but turned to face the beast. Gathering red dirt from the road before the house, she caught it up in a swirling vortex and blinded the Caddaja with it.

Unable to see, the horned beast slid on loose rocks and tripped over the dead Uktena, going down hard and buying the wielders time to take up position. When it rounded the side of the house, towards the well spring of aquis, it did not run but stalked forward, ugly and angry.

Daniel cracked wide the ground within the porous-stone ring, and a pool of aquis filled its belly. Jophery prepared a steady flow for the two master aquis wielders to use. Shady, launching one fire ball after another, kept the Caddaja moving forward and into range.

"Now!" Montilis shouted, and the three wielders conjured aquis weapons and volleyed their enemy.

Frozen spears, barrages of spikes, thin, round blades with curved teeth—and yet, there was no damage done.

As Jophery fell back, Triton and Montilis drew swords of steel. Triton went high, aiming for the Caddaja's neck, while Montilis swept low to severe the beast's hamstring, but their blades were useless against the Caddaja's stone-like skin. They were left to duck and dodge their way out of range of the Caddaja's retaliatory fists.

"Try thinner blades," Montilis suggested into the fray, and the chaos worsened as spinning blades whirled to find purchase.

The monster was hit; a slice to his left arm, one to his knee, one to the side of its face, and the Caddaja grew still... And then it frenzied.

It grabbed for Triton, who attempted to jump out of reach. Falling short, it was the surge of aquis sent by the General that carried him out of harm's way. In turn, after forming hundreds of projectiles out of it, Triton reversed the aquis' flow, shouting, "Duck!" for Montilis's benefit.

Trapping the Caddaja's feet in ice, Montilis lurched to the side and, reaching for more water, conjured a stave to shatter the casing.

A forward step by the monster saw the trap broken before Montilis could bring the weapon to bear.

"Aquis is no good," Set said, taking control. "Daniel, trap its feet. Now!"

The earth rose to swallow the Caddaja to its knees, and then there was a collective pause as they waited to see if it would hold.

"This is not easy," Daniel said through gritted teeth. "It's like pouring aquis into the oceanus and expecting it to drown."

"Oh…oh, oh, oh!" Skylar shouted. "Let him go! Let him go!"

"What?" Daniel was not the only one to ask.

"He's absorbing the terra," she hurried to say. "He's growing."

"Shady, you're up," Set told him. "Ignis seems the only thing to hurt it."

"But not kill it," Shady pointed out as he moved from Set's side to square off with the beast again. Planting his feet, he positioned his hands, rolled his shoulders, and said, "Here we go," but paused when Skylar fell in beside him.

"Let me see if I can help you up your heat," she offered.

"Woman," Shady said with a crooked grin, "your presence alone does that."

"Are you ready?" Daniel asked, but the question was irrelevant. His strength failed, and the monster was released.

So much faster than it'd revealed itself to be thus far, the Caddaja bolted forward and delivered a front kick that caught Skylar in the shoulder and spun her like a top to careen into the water pool.

Shady was swept from the ground and squeezed in a vice grip of three fat digits. Knowing he took the risk of burning himself out, he pulled as much heat as he could stand into his own body and then set it on fire, becoming a burning orb.

The scent of scorched earth reached the Caddaja's nostrils around the same time as the pain registered in its eyes. Releasing a high-pitched scream, the monster tried to unfurl its fingers and fling the wielder aside, but Shady was fully invested.

With both hands, the ignis wielder latched onto the Caddaja's wrist, reveling in the triumphant feel of crumbling clay. He left himself wide open to the monster's other fist, a blow that sailed him into the air.

Set knew the moment he became the center of the Caddaja's interest. He saw Montilis and Triton as they united in his defense, and he bore witness as the Caddaja, shaking its stubbed wrist in fury, opened his mouth. What came out of it was fist-sized stones, conjured to crack their skulls. Taking too many hits, the seasoned warriors were forced to seek cover, leaving nothing between it and Set.

Skylar, groaning as she dragged herself over the retention wall to dry ground, rolled to her back to see Shady in a wind-milling free-fall. With her arm—the one that she could still move—she directed her wrist in a circle, creating a vortex that would guide Shady to the ground without him being flattened by it.

As soon as his feet found purchase, he ran to her side. Her collarbone was broken, a piece protruding through her pale, ivory flesh, and the sight of her blood invoked his, "Sweet Superi, how can I help?" His eyes skimmed her body for further injury.

Wrenching her head and screaming from the pain of doing so, she tried to see what was going on.

"Montilis is down," Shady hurried to tell her. "Jophery is with him. I don't see Triton."

"Set?"

Their stares found the answer at the same time, but there was none left to offer aid to the epoto. Not that he'd needed it.

Despite its bulking weight, the Caddaja moved like a

wolf stalking a lamb. But Set was no easy meat, and the Caddaja was about to find itself the prey.

For a singular heartbeat, Set's body went rigid. His star-fire eyes slid closed as an internal bargain was struck, and when they opened again, they were as cold as an endless, frozen tundra. His words were even colder.

"My turn," he said with a voice not his own.

His arms lifted from his sides. One hand became en-gulfed in red flame, and the other held the leash to a destructive wind. As the Caddaja approached, Set brought the two elements together. They fed from each other, turning into a white, incinerating fire that had a life of its own.

Throwing its ruined limb across its face to protect its eyes from the heat, the Caddaja turned to flee.

Set, in an odd display, balanced his weight upon his left foot and, bending his other knee, held his right foot aloft. Holding his breath, he waited for the Caddaja's heavy step to fall, and then allowed his to do the same.

The ground beneath Set remained steady, but the land betrayed the Caddaja. It split between sucking mud that groped for one foot and hard-packed earth that rejected the other, wrenching the monster in such a way that his leg was ripped from its socket.

The Caddaja bellowed in agony, it's eyes glazed by pain and confusion.

A white sphere, an aura of power, radiated around Set as his image blurred in ever-tightening circles around the horned beast. Between one breath and the next, Set came up behind the Caddaja. Wrapping burning hands around to its face, Set dug his fingers into its eyes-sockets and yanked back its head. He wrapped his legs around the top of its bulging neck to maintain his grip.

The others had rallied to Skylar and stood in fearful awe of the epoto's victory. They were chilled by Set's monotonous voice when he ordered, "Someone take its head."

Montilis and Triton where the first to act. Together, they moved to the left side of the monster. Conjuring from ice a thin blade, they dropped it in an arching cut that separated the Caddaja's head from its shoulders; careful not to dismember Set in the process.

Set fell with the monster's head, but as it hit the ground, shattering into a thousand pieces, a small vortex spared him the rough landing and settled him onto his feet instead.

Set nodded to Skylar and, sounding more like himself, said, "Thanks."

Swallowing hard and fighting a very real fear of the epoto, she shook her head and told him, "I didn't do that. You did."

XX

More?

The block saved Ares's nose from the flatting Tristan's fist promised, but it afforded the Angeli the opportunity to disappear. He didn't see the kidney shot that dented his armor, bending the metal and impeding his maneuverability, but as the blow spun him around, he caught glimpses of Tristan's location.

Tristan ducked Ares's fist as the god came full circle, countering with a left-handed uppercut to Ares stomach, then with a right hook to the weakened armor covering Ares's kidney.

Wincing but refusing to cry out, Ares jumped out of Tristan's range.

"Tell me how to end the curses," Tristan demanded.

"I should offer you my sword, Angeli," Ares said only half in jest. "Your skill is greater in hand-to-hand combat."

"Save your praise for someone who would find value in it." Tristan glared. "Tell me how to end this."

"Die," Ares taunted, "and see the curses lifted."

Tristan attacked with a right hook to the head, which Ares ducked.

Dropping to his knees, the god attempted to take out Tristan's but missed. The Angeli side-stepped before delivering a vicious front kick that forced him to roll out of the way or lose his teeth.

Gaining his feet, Ares said, "You wouldn't know what to do with the freedom you seek. Look at the humans. They have what you desire, yet arrogance was born from it. They were divided by it."

Tristan attacked again with jabs and cross-punches that came without pause as he raged, "Do not mistake us for humans. We've suffered the division caused by the gods long enough. We seek unity, and we'll have it, or the gods will answer for it."

Ares landed a solid blow to Tristan's jaw, effectively ending his tirade, but he put in a few gut punches just to be sure. "Perhaps, Angeli, but even if my father were willing…"

"Your father?"

"Yes, well…"

Whatever else the god might have said was cut short when Tristan appeared before him, wrapping his hands around Ares's head, squeezing in the hope of shattering his skull, before flinging him off to the right.

Ares landed on the balls of feet, amused by the outburst.

In the lull of battle, it was the silence of Tristan's companions that broke his focus. The time of a glance, a moment to ensure they were safe and the monster dead, and Ares gained the upper hand.

When Tristan turned again to his enemy, it was to find an armored knee slamming into his nose, breaking it clean. Blood gushed forth apace the tears that streamed from his blinded eyes.

Grabbing the Angeli by the throat, Ares put him on the ground, pummeling his face with his fists until his pale flesh was masked with dark and swelling bruises. When an elbow cracked his cheekbone, the pain gave Tristan the strength to bring up his arms to protect his battered face and to give his ability time to heal him. In the next moment, he felt the short-blade enter between his ribs.

The agony of the wound summoned forth the void that protected his mind from pain, but the onslaught of panic overwhelmed the lessons that Jacob had taught. The void shattered and with it, his self-control.

With his strength unleashed, Tristan shoved, and Ares went flying; a hundred feet he flew before beginning his descent.

Tristan rolled to his side. Grabbing hold of the hilt, he pulled free the blade and dropped it on the ground as he gained his feet. Taking short bursts of breath, he waited for his body to repair itself, but he did not feel the pain.

What he felt terrified him far more than the god he faced. He feared the power the pain had awoken, because he had no idea how to put it back. Tracking Ares's progress, Tristan grinned as he thought, *At least I know where to aim it.*

Ares took control of the fall, and though he could have translocated, he chose to make a show of it and landed one knee down, one up. His forward weight rested on the one hand that he permitted to touch the ground. Locking stares

228

with the Angeli, he said, "Do not look so pleased, boy." As he stood, his armor repaired, and a new gladius appeared in his hand. "You have limits," he added as he started forward. "Allow me to show them to you."

Clarity struck Tristan like lightning. "I think you already have," he said. "I am my own limitation."

With a twisted grin, Ares scoffed, "It is the ego of youth that most often brings death before his time. That you believe yourself stronger than a god will make your death all the sweeter, and I will savor the light as it leaves your eyes. And when you quicken again," he growled, with less than thirty feet separating them, "I will be your god. Don't worry, Angeli. You will enjoy being one of my soldiers."

Then he attacked.

Tristan's marks burned hotter, deepening to a dark, golden glow as the blade of the gladius drew near his neck in a horizontal slash. He could not tell if he sped up, or if Earth slowed down, but the sword was no threat to him.

He caught the swinging blade in his left hand, closing his fist around it despite the metal that cut into his flesh. His blood seeped from between his fingers and slid down his upturned wrist, yet it was the god that paled.

The voice that issued from the Angeli was not of the boy, Tristan, but was the gods' nightmare realized. The power of its expulsion vibrated through the sword that kept them connected, up Ares's arm to shake his body, to rattle his teeth, to steal the very breath from his lungs. But it was the Angeli's words that introduced him to fear.

"Call your father, little god," Tristan commanded. "It's time for the grown-ups to talk."

***

Cautious of the calm trance Set seemed trapped in, Montilis made his way around the crumbled pieces of the Caddaja's remains. The epoto knelt to lay hands on the beast's head.

"What are you doing?" Montilis asked.

"The body dies before the mind," Set answered, aware that he did not sound like himself. "Sometimes, thoughts can be removed even after death."

Triton, either fearless or crazy, walked over and slapped Set on the back of his shoulder. With a grin that cracked the mercenary's stone face into rippling wrinkles, he said, "That was fighting at its finest, boy. I worried you wouldn't be able to wield your new abilities without training, but..." He nudged Set again. "You did it."

"You were amazing," Skylar said.

Standing, Set turned to look at her and found the others nodding emphatically in agreement, but he was not interested in accolades.

"Unelanvhi, show yourself," Set demanded.

"Whoa, now." Montilis stepped in front of Set to grab his attention. "Hold on."

"I want to fight you," Set shouted. "I want your death. I want your knowledge for my own."

"What are doing, son?" Triton asked, a little concerned himself.

The sky churned with angry clouds as a growl of thunder gave voice to the Unetlanvhi's fury. Rain pelted them, punished them, before the spirit god unleashed its fury by way of a violent bolt of lightning.

As they leapt in all directions, diving head-long to avoid the strike, Skylar scurried to her feet to stare, bug-eyed, at Montilis. Her head kicked off to the side, in Set's direction, as she mouthed the words, *Do something.*

"What?" the seasoned general asked aloud, shrugging his shoulders and opening his hands in a plea for suggestions.

"Anything," Skylar said, her desperation showing, "before he gets us killed."

"Set," Montilis stated in a no-nonsense tone, "she's right. You need to calm yourself and think, boy, before you start a fight with a monster we can't even see."

Accentuating his point, a series of lightning strikes piggybacked each other, gaining strength as they crossed through the aether to slam into the road.

Triton planted his fists on his hips and smirked. "For a god, even a spirit one, its aim is awful." Taking advantage of the rain, he conjured the longest whip in aquis wielder history and lashed at the lightning's point of origin.

"Curse you, Triton," Montilis snarled. "Do not encourage him, or so help me…" When he could think of no worse a threat, he added, "I'll tell Shashara."

"I've got your back, Triton," Set said. "Now do it again."

The aquis whip cracked as loud as any lightning, creating a brief rift in the clouds that revealed…something. Set saw it. Raising his arms over his head, he rotated his hands until a vortex formed, which grew as Set fed it power.

Skylar felt the charge before the god unleashed the bolt. The aim was meant for Set, but the epoto refused to release the pull he had on the god's energy, so she wrapped him in air and yanked him out of the way.

"Sweet Superi!" she gasped at the close call. Wiping a sheen of sweat from her brow, she groaned when a shooting pain lanced its way through her collarbone, but she braced herself against it in case Set needed her again.

"Again!" Set bellowed, and Triton went back to work, conjuring a second whip and using them in quick succession.

Thunder roared, and Daniel, anticipating the next lightning strike, countered preemptively. A thick wall of terra flew up before Set, causing the epoto to step and turn towards him, though he maintained the vortex that he hoped would drag the god from its lofty perch.

Fearing Set's wrath, Daniel was quick to say, "I'm sorry," with both his hands reaching for air.

"Don't be," Set said. He fell into a crouch, as if to jump.

"For Superi's sake, will the both of you stop?" Montilis shouted. "We don't know what's up there." Completely ignored, he pinched the bridge of his nose and, sighing at the onset of a headache, said, "Your arrogance is going to be our end."

"Daniel," Set stated, sealing their fate, "prepare yourself. My ability may not be enough."

"For what?"

The terra groaned, it quaked, and then it shot upward, carrying Set with it. Using a gust of hard wind, he ensured that he alone stood at the apex, knocking Triton and the others down the mounding terra.

Terrified, scrambling to find or keep their footing, the others experienced the creation of a mountain. Its base widened until the farmhouse was knocked over and brushed away as debris before Set found his limit.

Sensing urgency, Daniel said, "My turn," as he set about finding his own limitations. The result elevated Set into the clouds.

"What are you doing?" Skylar screamed as she clawed her way across the unstable ground to strangle the wielder. She'd do it with one arm if she had to. "Get him down from there," she demanded.

"And risk him turning those powers of his on me?" Daniel shook his head. "Yeah, that's not happening."

Angling back her head to peer up the mountain, as far as sight would allow before the tip disappeared beyond the dark veil of clouds, she found she couldn't fault Daniel's caution.

Streaks of fire and swirling vortexes accosted the sky as Set sought his target. His target found him instead. The god was, itself, the clouds, and it formed a hand that closed around him. It wasn't until the nebula began to squeeze him in a vice grip that threatened to break him that he discovered he could not retaliate, for the god became mist when he tried.

Lifted from the mountain, Set was then shaken like dice before a gambler's toss. When an old, familiar nausea rolled his gut into his throat, he half-shouted, half-groaned, "Enough!" He stretched wide his arms to spin a vortex of air around himself, pushing back the hold of the god…and then he began to fall.

Montilis conjured a slick of ice, concaved to keep them on track. After yanking Skylar's back against his chest, he leapt, arse-first, for the scariest ride of his life.

Forced to sit on the Nox's lap, Skylar clung to the forearms holding her in place and screamed. When they didn't immediately die as she'd feared, she used her ability to press air against them, effectively controlling their speed and safety.

Triton, riding a monstrous wave of his own making, passed them, shouting, "Hurry! We have to catch him!"

"Oh, no…" Montilis said, feeling the ice slick as it began to crack. As much with his ability as with his arse, ice splinters were the worst kind.

"Don't! Oh, no," Skylar said. "Oh… no…" She twisted her torso to check Montilis's face for confirmation. In his haste to reach Set, Daniel was bringing down the mountain.

Shady held the back of Daniel's shirt. "I will not be buried alone. I will not be buried alone."

"You will if you don't shut up," Daniel vowed.

Shady's voice disappeared, but his lips kept right on moving.

Separated from the others, stuck on the far side of the mountain, where Set's descent was accelerated by a malicious downdraft, Jophery saw what the others could not. They would be too late. Lacking Montilis and Triton's skill, he did what he could and called upon the waters of Earth to gather and pool, to cushion the epoto's crash. Instead, he created mud.

There was a sickening splat as Set hit the surface, then it appeared the ground simply swallowed him whole.

Triton's wave let him down as Montilis and Skylar met the end of the disintegrating slick and took a hard tumble to a harder stop. Daniel and Shady, finding no relief on level ground, took off at a dead-run for Set, though the others were not far behind.

Reaching the edge of the mud hole, Daniel shoved forth his arm. His fingers curled as he mentally took hold of the epoto and pulled him out.

Once Set's head emerged, Skylar took over, lifting him with air to lay him out on the ground.

Covered in brownish-black sludge, Set sat upright, looked at them, and then burst out laughing. Coming awkwardly to his feet, encumbered by the extra weight, flames encased him from head to toe.

Panic made Shady pull the flames. Knowing better than to take in another wielder's ignis, he diverted the heat into the mudhole and watched while it baked.

"Thanks," Set said, shaking himself to dislodge his own dry layer of terra.

"I hope you learned something worth knowing, boy," Triton said, "because *that* was a fool's move." To make sure his words penetrated Set's thick skull, he gave the back of it a smack.

"Hey," Skylar growled at Triton as Set was sent flying, arms and legs flailing, to land in a slide over graveled ground. "Easss-y."

Triton rolled his eyes. "I didn't do that."

"Then what did?" Shady asked.

His question made them move to form a shield around Set against the next attack.

"I warned you," Montilis stated with a shake of his head. "You don't pick a fight with an enemy you cannot see."

"I don't know what you're talking about," Triton countered as the rain stopped and the sun reappeared, perched high in a sky of perfect blue. "It looks to me like Set scared it off."

"I didn't," Set told them as he broke free of their circle.

A voice, ancient and cold, wafted in the wind, but the words were not meant for them. "I leave them to you then."

"To who?" Jophery asked. "What does that mean?"

"Why are you asking me?" Set asked in reply, relieved that he recognized the sound of his own voice.

"Well…" Shady scratched at the side of his neck. "If the rumors are true, there's bound to be a voice or two rattling around in your head that knows something."

Set chuckled. "The voices have grown quiet since Omini took control."

"Took control," Skylar asked with rising concern, "as in, you're not you?"

"No," Set was quick to correct her assumption. "He doesn't control me, but he does control the others. It was their influence that had me challenging Unelanvhi. It was Omini's influence that told me to retreat."

"Has, um, Omini told you who he is?"

Reading emotions came second nature to Set, and Montilis was feeling nothing good. "I know he is the protector of the knowledge we carry, a guardian that steps up when circumstances grow dire. His psyche is not a threat," Set assured him, but when Montilis's anxiety spiked again, he asked, "Unless…is there something you know that I don't?"

"Yeah," Montilis answered. "Too much for comfort, actually."

Set felt Omini's psyche shift in his mind from calm control to leashed violence. "I would know it all."

"Omini Swuxson was alive during the first water war," Montilis began. "He was mad, an infamous murderer who held no distinction between warriors and civilians, between men, women, and children. He slaughtered indiscriminately, and the Fulgo praised him for his butchery. They made him the highest-ranking major in their fighting forces and would have vaulted him higher, but they feared what he would do with more men under his command. Set, he killed hundreds. He could manipulate the water inside of his enemies' bodies, slowing them until they stood no chance to defend themselves. His skill remains unparalleled."

Set corrected without pleasure, "Your daughter accomplished as much."

"She's an Angeli."

"She wasn't," Set told him, "not the first time. Not when she shriveled a man's eyes in his sockets."

"My daughter is not a monster," Montilis countered, "but the Fulgo were right to fear him, because in the end, he betrayed them."

"How do you know?" Set asked, seeking the source for validation of truth.

"The history of his carnage is required study for those in officer training," Montilis told him. "It was assumed that the Fulgo got rid of him."

Sighing, Set said, "I guess Sole got to him first."

Triton grinned. "On the bright side, he's on our side now."

Sickened by the guilt brought on by the knowledge of Omini's deeds and his complete lack of remorse for them, Set's attempt to smile back failed.

"Get down!"

Jophery's warning came too late.

The arrow was too close.

Set's eyes widened in disbelief, and he stared down the shaft that would pierce his chest. He recoiled, but it wasn't him that took the hit. Jophery's heart had taken it for him, and as his body thudded to the ground, Set's eyes remained fixed on the golden arrowhead that protruded from his savior's back.

"Who did it?" Set asked, but he found his answer when he raised his stare and found the two men standing across the black road.

With a sword clutched in one hand, and the other made of a spiked sphere, the grey-skinned man, wearing leather beneath his silver armor, stood with a bored visage and allowed the blond one to do the talking.

"Go home, Superians," the honey-skinned man, draped in a white toga, demanded. He pulled a second golden arrow from the quiver at his back and, notching it, brought string to cheek. "Or die where you stand."

***

Tristan reached out with his free hand and wrapped it around Ares's throat, who released his grip on the gladius to wrap both hands around the Angeli's wrist. Sensing the arrival of new gods and unable to break Tristan's hold, unable to breathe, he did the unthinkable to save face. He disappeared.

"Coward," Tristan cursed just as his ears picked up on a threat delivered. He moved as fast as his anger rose and placed himself between Set and a familiar archer.

Apollo witnessed Ares vanish, then found himself the center of the Angeli's focus.

"What's the matter with you?" Tyr asked as Apollo closed his eyes and began to pray.

XXI

Mercy

With his prayer cast, Apollo shouted, "It is finished, Angeli. This quarrel between our worlds is ended. Leave," he said, notching an arrow and aiming it at Tristan, "and be left in peace."

What began as chortle grew to a laugh. Tristan's countenance changed midstream, and in the hollow, booming voice of an Angeli, he issued forth a growled roar of rage. "What do any of you know of peace?"

"The boy has a point," Tyr quipped, though only Apollo heard.

Grabbing a tenuous hold on his temper, Tristan made his demand. "I wish to speak with the father of Ares."

The two gods turned their necks to look at each other. Apollo's brows furrowed and Tyr's arched in surprise before the sun god replied, "He is called Zeus. Speak the words you would share to me, and he will hear, for nothing that transpires on Earth is hidden from him. His presence is everywhere."

"Great," Montilis scoffed. "Another god that's afraid to show his face."

Skylar groaned and said, "Tell me about it."

"Let us test your words," Tristan told Apollo, and then looked skyward and said, "I know it was you who gave the order to curse my planet. Now you will reverse them both, or I will kill Apollo. I will kill the god who stands with him. And when I find Ares," he vowed, "I'm going to take my time in killing your coward of a son."

Across the clear, blue sky shot a streak of lightning that rattled the aether.

"A father tends to take offense when his children are insulted," Apollo said, "especially when one of those children happens to be his favorite."

"Then he should reverse the curses," Tristan retorted, "before insult turns to action. You'll die first."

As if in a coliseum, instead of an Oklahoma prairie, a roar that came from everywhere made them—the gods included—reach to cover their ears.

With a smirk, Apollo said, "It seems my father has given you his answer."

"And his answer marks you a liar," Tristan told him. "It also makes you dead."

Without warning, the ground behind the two gods opened, and a thirty-feet-tall red serpent with four legs, a tail with lashing tendrils at its tip, and three heads crawled its way from the chasm.

Seeing the hydra, Apollo and Tyr translocated across the blacktopped road to the open field, but on the opposite side of the graveled driveway from where the Superians stood. Apollo, seeing a clear shot at the slender boy, brought up his bow and fired.

With a flick of her wrist, Skylar changed the projectile's course. Speeding its progress with a current of air, she sent it for the serpent instead.

Angered, the monster started forward.

"Sorry," she squeaked when Tristan glanced at her from over his shoulder rolling his eyes.

"Set…" Tristan warned as he advanced on the creature, "watch your back."

Shady, who'd squatted beside Jophery's body to close his eyes, said, "We've got your boy," as he stood to join the others who'd closed rank around Set.

To Tyr, Apollo asked, "What do you see?"

"I see five warriors willing to die to protect the youngest boy," Tyr told him. "The two dark-skinned men who stand slightly forward from the three at their backs, they are the most seasoned. The tall, yellow-eyed man and the human-looking one, they are true soldiers. We'll have to go through them, because they will not give ground."

"And the girl?" Apollo asked.

Tyr licked his lips and groaned. "Do you see the way she favors her arm? She's wounded, but she's also wild; her pale flesh is barely enough to keep her spirit inside." Bending his elbow, he brought the back of his hand up to smack the center of Apollo's chest. "Do not kill her," he said. "She'll be my trophy."

"Focus," Apollo snapped. "What makes the boy special?"

"Does it matter?" Tyr asked. "If we kill him, the others

will scatter. That's why you came to me, to do what Ares could not, yes?"

"I will follow your lead." Apollo grinned and added, "War god."

Tyr grunted. "What a funny, funny little god, you are." His sneer remained as he said, "I will go left and flank their position. You'll have a better shot at the boy if they are forced to guard two fronts."

As Tyr took off at trackable pace, Apollo conjured an arrow to his bow, but waited to make his move.

"Here he comes," Shady announced, though they all had eyes to see.

"Set," Triton tried again, "are you sure you want to do this?"

"We know Apollo," Set replied. "The gods are trying to split our focus. The helmeted one will not be prepared to face you all. Besides, Tristan and Anliac have faced the sun god before. We know what he can do. I can take him."

"Fine, but whoever kills their target first will help to kill the other, and do not," Montilis stressed, "run straight towards that archer. You have to…"

"Duck and roll, dodge and evade, be unpredictable," Set finished for him. Tapping his right temple, he grinned and said, "Trust me, I've plenty of council."

He nodded. "When you're ready, Montilis said.

As Set stepped forward, they broke rank to do their part.

Tyr saw the boy start towards Apollo, alone and unprotected, as the Superians' priorities changed. The two seasoned warriors were running from the battle, while the others took up positions to protected them, so he sped his pace to intercept.

"Not going to happen," Shady said, then he launched a fireball for the god's bearded face.

Centering the blade of his sword before himself, Tyr held his course. The sphere of flames were split in half to explode somewhere behind him.

The fireball had failed to hit its target, but it offered a moment of blindness that Daniel took advantage of. Slicing through the top layer of the Earth's terra, he tugged, as if yanking a rug out from under him.

Tyr leapt to the side, off the Superian-controlled ground, and kept coming.

"How can a man that size have that much agility?" Skylar wanted to know just as Montilis shouted the command.

"Slant formation!"

"Show us what you're made of, beautiful," Shady stated.

As the three of them fell back to join Montilis and Triton, while angling themselves towards Set in case the bearded god changed course, Skylar conjured a wind that forced their enemy to fight for every step gained. His leathered skin was stretched smooth, and his lips were forced back from his yellowed teeth in a skeletal snarl.

When the summoned wind died without warning, Tyr found himself on his stomach with a mouthful of dirt. Slamming his fist into the ground, he came up angry.

***

Set chose his pace carefully, ever watchful of Apollo's stare, but the god's focus never wavered from him. "So," he said aloud, though the god was too far away to hear, "I'm the one you want."

Sensing that the others were beyond the archer's range, he fell into a deceiving sprint as Apollo drew his bow. Once loosed, Set tracked its course; distance allowed for ample time. Just when the god thought he'd gained an easy victory, Set allowed his measured pace to falter long enough to take a step to the side, grinning when the arrow flew by.

In a burst of speed that threw Apollo off balance and reaching in desperation for another arrow to notch, Set began to eat up the ground between them.

When the arrow was released, its aim on point, Set waited for as long as he dared. Then he veered to the right only to regain his path so fast that, to the god, he appeared never to have wavered at all.

A third arrow was notched, and Apollo held the taunt bowstring to his cheek, but he did not release. He watched the translucent blur that was the boy, counting the ticks of times it took him to gain given ground, and once he'd found the pattern, he let the arrow fly.

Set had been waiting for it. A small jump, a slight twist of his torso, and the arrow was history. Before another could be drawn, Set put everything he had into his speed. But when a mere fifty feet separated his hands from the god, something went terribly wrong.

It was as if Earth's sun had joined the side of its gods and focused its heat to cook him in his skin. Shelter from its rays became Set's sole purpose as he raced passed Apollo for the only tree in sight capable of offering it.

"What's the matter, Superian?" Apollo taunted. "Did you think you were the only one with tricks?"

He pivoted around, searching, until he found the boy using the trunk of a tree as a shield from the sun. Then Apollo fired again.

Left with no choice, Set darted to the other side of the tree and screamed. His skin darkened into an angry red, whelping into liquid-filled blisters that burst. Then the arrow thudded into the oak's trunk, allowing him to come back around.

The moment he did, he cursed and dodged, but an arrow finally found its mark. Checking the graze on his left shoulder, he shouted, "Wait until I get my hands on you, you sorry sack of dung…"

***

When the center serpent head struck, Tristan assumed they were finished sizing each other up. A wide step to the side avoided its maw. A leap forward put him under its thick, red-scaled, neck, where he buried his claws and leapt to the other side, ripping flesh.

The left head darted down, but he launched himself beyond its reach, only to turn and do it again when the serpent didn't give up. Finding himself up close to its torso, the breadth of it chest was enormous, the plate like tempered steel. Tristan slammed his fist into the center of it.

The dagger-like fangs that sank into his left shoulder and thigh belonged to the right head. The neck attached to it undulated like a whip. Tristan was thrown to the ground, rolling and skidding to a violent stop.

The monster didn't attack, but instead turned to watch him through three sets of eyes. Tristan rolled to his back and breathed through the pain of his body healing. Facing these creatures, sent by others, he could not maintain an anger towards them, and the lack of it effected his abilities. Still, realizing that he'd been the one holding back his true potential, he felt more powerful than ever.

"Okay," he said to the serpent as he stood, waving it forward, "let's do this."

As if it understood, the serpent's center head shot forward to grab him. Prepared for it, Tristan used his speed to get him going and then rolled under the attack to come up at the base of its neck. With a vertical jump, he wrapped his arms around the previous wound, narrowly able to latch one hand around his other wrist, and then squeezed. At first, the heavy muscle resisted, but at the first sign of softening, Tristan twisted, its neck snapped, and the head went down.

Enraged, the two remaining heads attacked.

Tristan dropped.

The left head's fangs sank into the neck of the center head and severed it clean. The right head swept him off to the side, where he landed flat of his back and without air in his lungs.

"Ow," he groaned, sitting upright and taking a moment before finding his feet again.

The two remaining heads turned to him in unison and roared.

"Don't growl at me." Tristan grinned. "I might have broken your neck, but you're the one who bit it off."

They hissed as their heads bobbed up and down.

Tristan's right eyebrow made a slow crawl into a defined arch. "Are you laughing at me?"

From the jagged edges of meat and scales, hanging from what was left of the mutilated neck, new tissue began to grow. When it split, becoming two necks that grew two heads, adding to the eyes that grinned at him, Tristan said, "Don't think you're special. I have a girlfriend back home that grows two heads all the time."

Four very large maws opened to roar their reply.

"Yeah, yeah," Tristan said, taking a solitary step towards reengaging when a thought stopped his progress. A quick peek at the dead Uktena, and Tristan told the serpent, "I'm really glad I didn't cut that things head off. Unless…Did you do that on purpose?"

The two heads on the end positions swung wide, setting up a perimeter, while the two in the center slivered back and forth, covering the middle as the serpent made an aggressive move forward.

"Avoid damaging heads, check," Tristan muttered, then bolted to the right before circling back around. At the serpent's back, left leg, he landed a solid punch to its knee, buckling the body and causing it to lean to the side.

As its tail swung to counterbalance its teetering weight, Tristan bared his claws and ripped a path with his left hand for his right fist to follow. Though his arm was buried to his elbow, he felt nothing but meat and grizzle.

Darting out of the way of its crazed circling, he waited for the heads to rise in search of him. Then, running at full speed for its right, back leg, he sank his claws past the bone and wrapped his fist around it. The crack of its breaking was sickening; the creature's wail was even more so. Disturbed, Tristan disengaged.

Supporting its weight on three legs, its tail limply dragging behind it, the serpent rose to face him. With a roar, two heads snapped forward. Tristan back-stepped and delivered a solid right hook that careened the center head into the other one, knocking them both to the side. Tristan took the opening and raced to position himself beneath the front part of its body.

Again and again, he slammed his fist into its chest plate, shattering scales, before digging deeper with his claws. The beast roared, entangled in its own necks as they fought each other for the right to kill him.

Before it got its heads together, he rolled towards its right foreleg. Finding the smallest joint, he used his claws and severed it clean. As the lower appendage hit the ground, Tristan found the closest exit as the serpent lost its fight with balance and fell.

Its struggle to rise and the agony of its screams when its weight touched upon the nub he'd left behind dropped Tristan's guard. He closed his eyes but for a moment, and when he opened them, all he saw was teeth.

Instinct and speed forced his hands to reach for its top and bottom jaws, prying them apart as if he could feel its fangs sinking in to him again. "Not...going...to happen," he growled, stepping forward as the jaws spread.

The skin at the corners of its mouth ripped, the bottom jaw gave way, and the head retreated as its cries renewed.

Tristan, maddened by his carelessness and irrationally angry at the serpent, rushed a direct attack against its vulnerable right side. Punching through its ribcage, he found a handful of spongy lung and ripped it out.

With the wounded head dragging like a second tail and precious breath escaping from the hole in its side, its back legs injured and a front one ruined, it attempted to flee.

Tristan witnessed its fall, wincing at the hard impact. Rubbing at the center of his chest with the heel of his palm, he realized his heart hurt. The pleading search for mercy that peered from those agonized eyes made him feel the villain.

Suffocated by the emotion, Tristan spoke to the serpent as he would have a felled enemy at the end of honorable combat. "You fought well, brother."

It whimpered, growing too weak to lift its head.

"I would end your pain if only I knew how," Tristan answered, knowing it would be the question on his mind, "but your body confounds me. I'm not sure you have a heart to stop."

Growing angry, he turned his attention skyward and bellowed. "This fight is over. Call your servant back, or kill him, but end his suffering." After a long pause and still no answer, Tristan cursed Zeus for a mongrel, then shouted, "You sent this creature, knowing it could not win. If you will not do what is right, send me the means and I'll end his agony myself."

When his pacing carried him close to the serpent, it whimpered. Using its necks more than its body, it attempted to drag itself farther away.

Stopping cold, so the serpent would settle, he said, "I'll get Set. He'll know what to do." Turning to do just that, a twelve-foot golden scepter fell and stuck within the ground two feet in front of him. Refusing to give thanks, he pulled it free, taking note of the inverted teardrop at its head.

As he positioned himself, the serpent did its part and moved its heads out of the way, offering him a clean throw.

"You were not my enemy," he lamented. Taking aim, he threw the spear and watched as it passed clean through the serpent to disappear upon its exit.

Tristan, fists clenched and shaking at the sky, roared, "ZEUS! SHOW YOURSELF, COWARD!"

Set's screams ripped the air and grabbed Tristan's attention. There was a rift opening in the graveled road where the house had stood, and from both directions, Superians raced towards it. Apollo, perched on a moving cloud, rained arrows down on Set's head, deflected by an aer shield.

Step by step, Montilis walked backwards towards the gateway, taking the brunt of the helmed god's wrath. He hoped his ice shield held up against the spiked sphere the man used as a right hand.

"Move, children," Triton shouted at Daniel and Shady. "Get your arses through that gate." Encircled by water whips, he lashed out at the god, making sure he suffered for each blow landed against Montilis's shield.

"What about Skylar?" Shady asked on the move.

"I'm here," she shouted from over by the gate. When Shady reached her, she said, "I can't go. Set's in trouble. Apollo is burning him."

"What?" Shady turned to look and gagged at what he saw.

"I'm the only protection he's got from those arrows," she told him. "He's too weak to form his own."

Montilis and Triton were coming in fast. The helmed god was too, as was Apollo, and the closer the archer came, the greater risk he posed to them all.

Set saw the blur that was his brother and braced himself

for more pain. The moment Tristan's hand closed around his forearm to swing him onto his back, the skin peeled from the meat like a glove removed.

Tristan stumbled.

"No!" Set shouted. "Run!"

"Go! Go! Go!" Triton bellowed.

Daniel was the first through the gate. Shady followed.

"Guys," Skylar said, "I'm getting tired."

Montilis's heels were precariously close to the edge of the rift. "I can't hold him," he said, just as Set, clinging to consciences by will, slid from Tristan's back to be caught in Triton's arms.

The ice shield shattered.

Montilis, thrown off balance, had just enough time to spin on the balls of his feet, towards the gate, before he stumbled through it.

Triton felt the boy stiffen as the spiked mace made its swing. Protecting Set, Triton turned and took the blow to his right side.

"I've got him," Tristan snarled. He grabbed hold of the wrist wielding the mace and used the weapon to wrench the god around.

Tristan felt the blade, held in the man's left hand, slide through his shoulder, but paid the injury no mind. He could do what needed doing with one arm. Pivoting to gain force, he launched the god at Apollo, causing him and his cloud to shoot higher, leaving his companion to find his own way down.

Grabbing hold of the hilt, Tristan pulled the sword free and tossed it to the ground. "Let's go home," he said, the last to leave Earth.

XXII

Gift and Curse

Daniel and Shady jump through the rift to hear Sha-shara shouting, "Is everyone okay?" She wasn't talking to them, but the dozens of people who'd narrowly escaped the opening of the rift. The light pouring through it from Earth was blinding, and had it not been night in Pisces Stragulum, deaths would have been unavoidable.

As it was, those still in the marketplace were huddled before storefronts and tucked between buildings, peeking from behind the central well or from behind the trees that stood to offer shade. They waited in anticipation of what would come through it.

"Thank Superi," Anliac whispered. She rushed forward to steady her stumbling father and exhaled a breath she hadn't been aware of holding. "Where's Tristan?"

"He's okay, but…"

"But what?"

Lifting his feet over the bottom edge of the gate took the

last of Triton's strength. Hitting his knees, Set rolled out of his arms. Dirt and a debris stuck to the raw and blooded tissue before he came to a stop, face-up.

Shashara screamed. "Someone get Swiney!" she cried as she scrambled to get to him. Crumbling beside him, she was afraid to touch him. His clothes were fine, and yet, nothing but fire could cause the kind of damage she was looking at. "Tell me what to do."

"Triton…" Set asked, "where…is he? He's hurt."

"Yeah, well," she said, her voice breaking, "so are you."

When Tristan stepped through, Anliac was waiting for him with fury shooting from her golden eyes, but when she saw his expression, her own visage changed. Stepping forward, she wrapped her hand around the back of his neck, pulling them forehead to forehead, and asked, "Are you okay?"

"No," Tristan replied honestly. "I'm really not." Then, turning from her, he found his brother.

Before joining him, Anliac ordered, "Guard that gate. Nothing," she said, "and I mean *nothing* that isn't Superian escapes this ground."

Four Angeli Guards unsheathed their weapons and positioned themselves before the golden window to Earth.

"What happened?" Shashara demanded.

Hitting his knees, Tristan ignored Shashara's question to say, "Curse their gods." Anliac laid supportive hands atop his shoulders.

"I…couldn't agree…more," Set stuttered through the cold chills that wracked his body.

"I'm so sorry, little brother. Here," he told him, offering

his hand, "pull from me and heal yourself."

"Hold on, Captain," Razoran said. "Don't you die on me. Help! Someone, help!"

Set's neck turned, his head lulling to the side, to find... "Triton..." Set gasped again. "He's hurt."

"Let's just worry about you right now, okay?" Tristan suggested with tears unabashedly coursing down his cheeks.

"Should...have been...me," Set groaned, refusing his brother's offer.

"What does that mean?" Shashara asked. "What is he talking about?" When no one answered, she said, "Set, let him help you."

Triton tried to stand, but Razoran was having no part of it. "You need to worry about yourself right now, Captain. Set has people..."

"Either help me," Triton stated through short, panting breaths, "or get out of my way. Razoran," he said, too weak to continue fighting a man with strength abilities, "her son needs me."

Knowing there was no arguing that comment, Razoran scooped Triton from the ground and carried him towards the boy.

Perched in his first mate's arms, the pirate scowled. "If I weren't busy bleeding out," he said, "I'd skin you for this."

"I'm just following your orders, Captain."

"How about we *not* talk about skinning people right now?" Shashara snapped. Tristan shuffled to make room for Razoran to lay Triton out beside Set.

"Brother, I'm..."

"We know, Tristan," Shashara snarled. "You're sorry."

"Watch it," Anliac warned. "This is not his fault, Shasha-ra."

"Triton," Set said through chattering teeth. "S-s-sorry…"

"Just promise me, boy," Triton told him, his voice growing weaker, "that you'll tell all of Superi… it took a god to bring me down."

Set started to laugh, but his face contorted in pain as the shaking in his body grew worse.

"Set," Anliac said after he'd gotten control of the pain, "I know you're hurting, but the gateway is a security breach. We need that thing closed."

Set tried to focus his vision and failed. Anliac's image refused to stand still. "It's a lot…of…power," he said between short breaths. "I'm…weak. If it…closes too…fast… If I can't… disperse…the energy…"

"The rift will explode," Anliac finished for him. "Then we need to get you healed."

Tristan offered his hand again.

"Triton…" Set started to object.

"No, son," Triton told him, "do your thing. I'm sure old Swinny is on his way right now to take care of me."

"This is ridiculous," Shashara said. In her frustration, she laid her open palm against Set's ruined check to force him to look at her. "You have…to heal…" Using his empathy against him, she poured her love and fear into her words, into her touch, and then watched in a stunned stupor as Set began to improve.

"Oh, wow," was all Tristan could manage.

"It looks like we have a new healer," Anliac said.

Wave after wave of energy pulsed across Set's marked

skin as small bursts of light. Under Shashara's touch, her ability magnified by her love for him, his flesh began to knit itself whole. As the burns healed, his body slowly stilled, until at last, the trembling stopped and he found rest.

What energy her mental exhaustion had left to her was used up by the strain of healing him, so when Shashara slumped forward, Set was there to catch her. "Rest," he said, handing her off to Anliac. "You did well."

Hammy stooped to check on his Captain. Triton's face fell at the news he carried before he nodded his acceptance.

"What's going on?" Tristan demanded.

"Swinny's not coming," Hammy said. "He's down sick himself."

Gritting his teeth, Tristan looked away. Noting Skylar's hold on Davad while a guard checked her collarbone, he turned to Shashara. "That leaves you."

With one shin braced flat on the ground and his other knee bent, Set leaned over Triton as he searched for the source of the blood. It wasn't hard to find. His right side had been crushed, punctured in a dozen places. "She's exhausted, Tristan. Leave her alone." To Triton, he said, "I saw the god swing and thought that was it. You saved my life."

Chagrined, Triton replied, "He was a mite faster with the swinging of his mace than I gave him credit for." Then he fell into a coughing fit that left his pale lips red and his grey-cast chin splattered with blood.

"Easy," Set cautioned, lifting the ruined side of his leather vest up over the wound. "At least the bleeding is slow."

"Not slow, boy," Triton corrected, "just running low on supply." Grabbing hold of Set's hand, his stare became intense. "You may wield your father's ability," he said, wheezing, "but you fight with the spirit of your mother. Both, my boy, would be proud. I am."

"Shut up, old man," Set scolded around the lump of emotion stuck in his throat. "You're not dying today. Tristan, get over here."

"What's the plan?" Tristan asked, preferring action over the sense of helplessness this night had been full of.

"Take my hand," Set told him, keeping a firm hold on Triton's. "He's the closest thing to a father we have left, Tristan. I will not let him die. We're going to see if I can pull some of your healing ability, and I'm going to give to him."

"Whoa," Tristan said once Set had begun. He swayed on his feet, like his blood had drained there, leaving his brain empty.

"Hold on," Set said, gagging. "It's working."

"Don't you do it, boy," Triton threatened, well enough to try and break Set's hold when he turned green.

Set yanked his hands free, grabbed his stomach, heaved, and vomited all over Triton's chest.

"Son of a…" Rolling in the opposite direction of the epoto, forcing Razoran to scramble out of the way, Triton came to his knees, bent at the waist, and puked- violently. With his gut empty, he yanked off the offending vest as he cursed. "It's a good thing you've got your skin back, son, because I'm about to tan your hide."

"You've been too long on land, Captain." Razoran smirked. "Your threats are getting soft."

Set, sitting back on his haunches, said, "My hide isn't doing anything else until I get some food in it. I am starving."

"Aye," Triton agreed, "I could eat a whole dracon about now."

Shashara shook her head. "They're barely back from the brink of death, and all they can think about it food."

"It's not their fault." Tristan grinned. "I think they just got a little bit more of being me than they bargained for."

Storming up, Montilis was in a fury. "If you had the ability to do this, why is Weston dead? Why didn't you try to heal Jophery? There was time, but you two didn't even try."

"None of us could have saved Weston," Set countered with a pointed look. "And Jophery was dead before he hit the ground. Anyway, it would have taken me and Tristan both. How long do you think the rest of you would have stood against the two gods while we tried?"

"We never should have gone through that gateway," Montilis said with his hands on his hips, shaking his head. "It was a mistake."

"One you pushed for," Set reminded him.

"Yeah, and it was a fool's move," Montilis told him. "We have no idea what your abilities are now, nor their limitations. What we do know is that you have a psycho in your head giving you orders."

Their raised voices had drawn attention, and more than a few eyebrows came up at Montilis's remark.

Knowing this was not the time for such discussions, Shashara, wiping away leftover tears, stated, "You're all idiots." When she had their attention, she said, "Over my dead body will something like this happen again. We are reforming a Council, and so help you all, it will be adhered to."

"Agreed," Anliac said, stepping to Shashara's side.

"There will be changes."

"Guards! Formation!"

"Sound the alarm!"

"Form a perimeter! Get these civilians out of the way!"

Turning towards the Northeast, towards the sound of the outcries, they saw a purple lightning storm that crackled too close to the ground.

"Close that blasted gate, Set," Anliac growled, pointing to the one he'd left open. She headed for the new threat forming just outside of town, gathering forces along the way.

"On it," he said, stopping, along with Shashara, to see it done. Montilis caught up with the others, cursing as he passed.

"You sure you're up for this, Triton?" Montilis asked, joining them. "Healing takes nearly as much out of man as it gives him back." Rapping his knuckles against the iron in his chest, he said, "Trust me, I know."

"I agree with the Nox," Razoran said. "Captain, why don't we sit this one out?"

Triton ignored them. Seeing Davad smoothing a salve over Skylar's chest before pressing a folded cloth to it, he called out with a grin that showed far too many teeth, "Skylar, it might be that I'm looking for a new first mate. What do you say to that, girl?"

Razoran growled.

Skylar laughed, but in a protective move that did not go unnoticed, Davad put himself between them—just in case—when Triton and Razoran left the line to walk over.

"That's my girl," Triton said, more winded that he was willing to let on. "Why don't we leave that," he said, tilting his head in the direction of the enlarging gateway, "to the others, and get us a hot meal?"

"Aye, Captain," she agreed. "That works for me. I think the fight is over for this collarbone until a healer can set it."

Despite their flippant words, worry was carried with their last glimpse, towards the defenders marching for the East gate, as they turned for the docks.

"Catch your breath," Anliac said as Char and Donnin came up at a full run.

"Lan is close," Char told them. "It looks like a portal is opening, but everything is black. The edges, the lightning, the center…it's all black."

"And it's massive," Donnin added. "There's a white crescent moon, but beyond that, there is nothing. We've ordered the packs to support the Angeli Guard, but Lan thinks it best to use the Fulgo and Nox defenders to set up a perimeter outside of Pisces Stragulum. With one, he wants to block access to Imbellis, and with the other, he wants to cut off the path to Certamen. He's waiting on your orders."

"Tell them all to back up," Set said. "That's not a portal. It's a gateway."

The eerie quality of Set's voice, coupled with what he looked like when they turned around, broke the line. His closest friends all but bolted. His body had taken on a translucent cast, his starburst-blue eyes the only solid thing about him.

When Donnin, holding Char behind his back, merely stood there, gawking, Set's monotone was worse than if had he roared. "Run. I can't hold this much power for long."

"Jaccoo," Anliac called to the speed wielder that had

become like her shadow after the battle of Imbellis; he was never far. As soon as she saw him, she said, "Hurry. Tell Lan to give the order to fall back."

"Do you feel like filling us in on what you're doing?" Tristan asked, looking at his brother.

"It's Omini's idea."

"Superi help us," Montilis groaned, wishing he hadn't heard that, considering the state Set was in. His concern redoubled when Set said, "I'm trying."

"Yeah, that's a little creepy," Anliac told him.

"The rest of you will have to catch up," was Set's response.

Shashara fumed, "Don't you dare run off and leave me again." Then he became a blur of multifaceted light racing towards a black hole.

Tristan and Anliac came to a stop at the same time he did. The Feras had not exaggerated the size of the gateway; fifty feet tall and a hundred feet wide.

"That's a monster," Anliac said.

"No," Set told her, "but there will be one coming through it. Stay behind me."

Anliac's spine went ramrod-straight. She slowly turned her neck to look cock-eyed at Tristan. "Is he our protector now?"

Tristan rolled his eyes instead of replying.

Murmurs among the gathered forces grew louder when two glowing blue eyes, positioned in the high-center of the rift, appeared.

As if the gateway were exploding in slow motion, an expanding of its belly that would eventually burst, a huge ball of black, leathered skin, rolled out of it. As the monster unfurled to stand thirty feet tall, spreading wings with a span of eighty feet, Apollo's laughter wafted from the side of darkness.

"Set," Tristan asked, "can you throw the extra energy your holding?" When Set nodded, he said, "Good. Blow it up."

"No," Set said, "I made a promise." As if throwing a giant sphere from over his head, Set sent the energy through the center of the gateway.

The god-made rift imploded, but not before Set was rewarded with Apollo's screams. "I did my part," Set said. "The monster is yours." Then he crumpled to his knees.

"Set!" At his side before he hit the ground, Tristan asked, "You good? You okay?" as he patted him down to see for himself.

"A little shaky," Set said, swaying. He was stable but pale.

"Stay with him," Anliac told Tristan.

"What? No. I can't let you face that beast alone," Tristan objected.

Anliac's narrowed eyes and the firm way she held her jaw said she'd had enough. "You're going to protect him." Her eyes dared him to speak. "I'm going to show you I'm more than a girlfriend who sits at home, waiting on her man to show up. Stay," she snapped, then engaged.

"Hey. You." She broke into a run and reappeared behind the monster on safe ground, away from the Angeli Guard and Fera packs, away from Tristan and Set. She sauntered up to the threat and snapped her fingers. "I don't know why you're looking at them. I'm the one that's going to kick your..."

On feet like a man's, the beast approached, its loins girded in black cloth but its torso bare. Spreading its wings, revealing webbed pits beneath its arms, its thick neck punched forward and then it screamed.

Covering her ears, cries of pain surrounded her as the soundwaves threatened the denizens' eardrums, causing them to bleed and some to burst.

Anliac, peeved by how much that hurt, returned the favor by introducing the pointed-eared beast to the voice of an Angeli.

The colliding soundwaves became a visible force, resulting in an explosion that had both beast and beauty launching themselves backwards into the air.

Shaking its horned head to clear it, the beast studied Anliac and her wingless flight, but then brought the fight to her.

She hadn't noticed the three-pronged, claw-like hooks on its wings until one came slashing for her chest. With Superi's moons giving her the light to see, she yanked moisture from a nearby cloud. Conjuring an aquis whip, she slashed back.

The beast dropped but regained height to bat at her with his uninjured wing. Grabbing hold of it with her free hand, she turned the whip into a short sword and sliced through the leathery tissue running between a set of long, delicate bones.

Its neck was too thick to turn. Its wings could not stop its inevitable crash, but she could. Pulling the moisture needed, she conjured an aquis whip even Triton would have approved. Swinging out as if to take its head, she wrapped it around its neck and yanked.

She heard the beast's strangled gag as she dropped below him. Gaining the ground as fast as she could, a heartbeat before the monster made impact, she drew upon the terra and raised a bed of long, viscous spikes to slow its landing.

The defenders' voices rose in praise, "Hoorah! Hoorah!" Tristan, supporting a grinning but weak Set, crossed to her.

As the beast's blood drained from multiple puncture wounds to pool on the ground beneath his suspended body, convulsing in the throes of death, Anliac asked, "This is what kept you away for so long?"

Tristan, stepping in close to her back, pulled her against him and kissed the top of her head. "It was a mistake to leave you behind."

She gave in to his embrace to let him know he was forgiven, then broke free and tossed her hands into the air to say, "That's all I wanted." She sashayed her way towards town, grumbling, "For Superi's sake, save me from foolish men."

"She's very bossy," Set pointed out as they traveled a safe distance behind.

Tristan laughed. "I like it when she bosses me around. Besides, just wait until Shashara gets a hold of you."

"Oh…god…" Set winced. Seeing his brother taken aback, he said, "What? Can you think of a worse curse to swear?"

XXIII

To Lead is To Follow

"You don't understand," Tristan told Anliac as they made their way to the mess hall. "I let myself get so wrapped up in battling all the monsters they sent that I almost got Set killed. We should have fought together, stayed together."

"There's no way you could have known that Apollo had control of their sun," Anliac pointed out, "nor that their sun could burn an ignis wielder. Does Set know how it happened?"

"He said something last night about humans polluting their planet's aether," Tristan replied, "preventing it from protecting them from the sun's rays. Apollo tapped into that and increased the energy of the most harmful rays; that's how he pinned Set down."

"Tell me about the other god," Anliac said. "Not Ares, the coward, but the one that got the drop on Triton."

Draping his arm across the back of her shoulders, wiggling his fingers until she reached up and took his hand, he replied, "I told you everything I know last night."

"Including," she said, "how you felt bad for the multi-headed serpent."

"You weren't there, Anliac. You didn't see it."

"Dad," Anliac called for him, gesturing that he should join them. Then she asked Tristan, "What do you think is going on now?"

Acknowledging the summons with an upward tilt of his chin, Montilis gave hasty orders to the forty-plus men he'd brought into town with him. Tristan replied, "I've no idea, but maybe he does."

After clasping forearms with Tristan in greeting, Montilis hugged his daughter. She asked, "Are we expecting more trouble?"

"No," Montilis assured her. "Davad's ordered added security to the town while the dignitaries are here."

Tristan's eyes brightened. "Has the Mortalis King finally decided to join us?"

"You'd have to ask Davimon," Montilis told him, "but Char and Donnin are here for the Fera, Riker…" Montilis cleared his throat and checked the ground before continuing, "…is here for the Nox, and a new man has arrived. Vincent, I think his name is," Montilis said. "He's here to represent the Fulgo."

Tristan's stomach growled.

Anliac grinned and smacked his gut with the back of her hand. "How would you like a side of politics to go with your eggs?"

"It's enough to make me want to skip breakfast," he replied with a soured expression. When his stomached growled again, he added, "Almost."

"What is he doing?"

"Who?" Tristan asked. Montilis pointed.

Triton was chewing on a turkey leg, its juices dribbling off his fingers and chin, as Razoran struggled under the weight of a heavy load.

Forcing Montilis into a jog and leaving Anliac to catch up, Tristan sped forward to see if he could help. "If your legs bow any more, Razoran, they'll snap. What do you have under that thing anyway?" The white cloth shimmied with the shaking in the Fera's arms.

Triton turned loose of the turkey leg long enough to say, "Take a look," before nibbling the last of the meat from the bone and discarding it.

"Or better yet," Razoran suggested, sweat dampening his fur, "just take it."

"Hey," Davad waved, spotting them as he exited the mess hall. Jogging over, he said, "I was just coming to look for you guys. What's that?" he asked, becoming distracted. Grabbing hold of the cloth, he looked to Triton for permission before removing it. "Oh…wow." Davad licked his lips and checked the corners in case he'd started drooling as he gawked at the longsword.

The handle was red and two feet long. Bands of silver encircled it at evenly-spaced intervals towards a round hook at the end. Its defensive guard was silver, inlaid with red designs that resembled the creeper vines that had been taking over Pisces Stragulum before they'd moved in. The defensive outer-guard was a vicious, fourteen-inch flowing blade that would have made a gorgeous weapon all on its own. But the sword blade… It was unlike anything he'd ever seen.

"It's as thick as an axe head," Davad stated, "and its sides have the same edge. It's what, four feet long? Six feet, if you count the handle. I bet it's a beast to hold up."

"Want to find out?" Razoran asked, his pointed ears laying back as the strain touched on his temper.

"Can I…?" Tristan asked at the opening, his fingers itching to hold it.

"Please, for Superi's sake…please." Razoran tried to lift it for Tristan to take, but his arms simply had no strength left.

"It's yours," Triton stated, drawing stares all around. "It's called a Zweihander, or two-hander," he explained as Tristan relieved Razoran of his burden.

Holding it out horizontally, in line with his sight, he admired the blade. "The craftmanship is incredible. Look at that arched tip… and the way those angles shoot out past the width of the blade into those beautiful points."

"Could you at least pretend it's heavy?" Razoran scowled. "Leave a man with a little pride."

"Oh…too heavy, too heavy." Tristan's shredded muscles strained against his skin as he feigned his arm giving out and the sword dropping. Of course, he never allowed the blade to touch the ground, but he grinned and said, "Razoran, your strength is truly legendary. I can't believe you carried this beast from as far away as your ship."

The others, already laughing at Razoran's wounded ego, turned their chortles on Triton when he corrected, "*My* ship."

"The antiquing around the three hollow moons and between the ridges on the flat of the blade is stunning," Shashara gave her two coins worth as she and Set found them after being sent from the mess hall to gather the stragglers.

"I thought we were having a meeting over breakfast," Set said. Then, his eyes falling on the weapon, he nodded in approval. "Nice polearm, and she's right. Those etchings are old, done even before your time, old man," he teased.

"It's a longsword," Triton told him, his smirk promising retribution for the age crack, "not a polearm. And that goes along with what the sword master in Antro told me."

"Were you thinking to sell it?" Knowing what kind of collection Triton had displayed in his cabin, Davad couldn't image the pirate parting with such a treasure.

"A man doesn't know what he has if he doesn't know the value of it," Triton quipped. "And girl, those pretty little lines between the ridges, and the empty innards of those moons, keeps the blood of the one you're killing from sliding up your arm and cheating you of your grip."

"Oh," Shashara said, pulling back as her upper lip furled. "Well, now it doesn't look so pretty."

Tristan, having stepped aside to give it a few practice swings, said, "Are you kidding me? I've never held such perfection."

"Oh, really?"

Tristan winced at Anliac's tone, but he had on his most charming smile when he pivoted to correct his mistake. "Ah, come on now," he teased, slowly circling to press against her back. He whispered, ticking the side of her neck, "I know how much you appreciate hard steel." When she giggled, he asked, "Do you want to play with?"

Montilis cleared his throat. "I hardly think now is an appropriate time."

"Probably not." Tristan grinned, then on a more serious note, turned to Triton and said, "The last time you gave me a sword, you'd nearly been killed by a dracon. This time, you were nearly killed by a god. In both cases, if I would have used my head more and my muscles less…"

"The body does what the mind orders," Triton told him, "and the mind learns to think by first taking action." Without pause for the change in topic, he said, "I'm going to tell you a story, boy, about how that sword came into my possession. You see, I used to run with a trio of mercs, and the female in the threesome had a knack for biting off more than the rest of us wanted to chew."

Set and Tristan shared a grin.

"You're talking about our mom," Set said.

"Yes, I'm talking about your mom," Triton replied, bobbing his head around as if it should have been obvious. "The Fera's name was Rinto. He had a level three strength ability and a cruel streak that surpassed it. Trust me, he's the last man you wanted to meet in a dark alley. He was a mercenary known for getting his mark, but he was butcher. As rumors of it spread, he couldn't find work, so he started hunting down his competition."

"He started killing other mercenaries?" Anliac asked, appalled.

Nodding, Triton replied, "And dozens died—by that blade," he added, gesturing towards the sword. "Mercenaries are not known for making friends. They're a security risk, but Beth had more than most," Triton continued. "When she received news that one of them had fallen to Rinto, she vowed vengeance, and then and there went to get it."

"Yeah." Set chuckled. "That sounds like Mom."

"We tracked him to Adpulsu. It wasn't hard," Triton told them. "It wasn't like the arrogant cur was hiding. He was gambling in the shadiest tavern at port. However, while your fathers and I were discussing the best way to go in," he said, including Davad more directly into the conversation, "Beth chose to make a decision of her own. That crazy woman started pulling in a monstrous wave, barking orders for me to get my arse into gear and help her. She flooded the whole tavern."

Through their laughter, and fighting his own, he gave them details. "Men and tarnished ladies, trying to escape through the front doors, were washed out on their backs. People were pouring through opened windows like litters being born."

"What?" Anliac asked.

"Yuck," Shashara said.

Triton chuckled. "Just when I thought no more were coming out, it started up again. Your mother—" he pointed a finger at Tristan and shook it like he was responsible for what would come next— "floated a frozen block of Rinto to our feet before allowing the oceanus to reclaim its wave. I remember it like it was yesterday. She flung that thick, blonde braid over her shoulder, turned her back on us and said, 'I'm sure you boys can handle it from here.'"

"The sword didn't break when the ice was shattered?" Anliac asked. "Or did you thaw him out before you made sure he was dead?"

"I changed the ice to water," Triton answered, "but only

so far as to get the sword, and then Jacob and Matthew flipped a coin over who'd do the rest. Matthew won, but Jacob swore he was cheating somehow. My point is this," he said to Tristan, "your mother's actions were often rash, but she always finished what she started. That sword will help you do the same."

"I'm surprised she let you keep it," Set said.

At that, Triton did laugh, full-bellied and shoulders shaking at the memory conjured. "I wouldn't go as far as to say that," he said after bringing his mirth under control, "but when she tried to take it from me, it dropped her like a stone."

After first seeing Skylar, then Donnin, and finally Riker sticking their heads out of the mess hall door, looking more agitated in turn, Shashara suggested they move things along. "I think Vincent might be ruffling a few feathers, guys. We should go. Besides, I'm starving."

"It's Victor," Davad corrected, "and he's a pompous, intelligent fool who's going to give me headaches."

At the mention of food, Tristan's stomach gave its vote. Headed that way, Tristan asked, "Well, who is he?"

"Don't worry," Shashara said, rolling her eyes. "He'll tell you all about himself."

Tristan paused in the doorway, the last to enter, and smiled at the collection of faces, with the exception of one. Tristan made his point by refusing to make eye contact with the six-foot-four Fulgo, who stood with his mouth perched to interrupt, and spoke over him, "It would appear the House of Angeli has grown from the Five to many, and we are glad you are here."

Char was radiant as she crossed the floor from the table she shared with Donnin, Lan, Belua, and Torren to the new arrivals. "There was no time last night for proper greetings," she said, cupping cheeks, patting arms, and squeezing necks. "It is good to see you all well." Holding onto Shashara a mite longer than the others, Char whispered, "We'll talk soon," before scurrying back to her mate.

Montilis and Riker took seats off to the side, and Triton and Razoran found places beside Skylar. Davad joined Davimon and Lishous at a table closer to the food line, while Set and Shashara tucked themselves away in a corner, content to let Tristan and Anliac deal with Victor.

"We're sorry to have kept everyone waiting," Anliac announced as she prompted Tristan to leave his sword by the door. "We've been informed that, as our councilors, there's something you wish addressed before we eat. We open the floor for that now."

"As one of those councilors," Victor stated, flashing teeth a perfect match to his pale skin, "allow me to introduce myself."

As he stood, his blood-red robes told Tristan all he need to know. "You are not one of our council," he corrected. "You are an unknown ambassador sent from the Fulgo after Nutrine's treachery and Shorlynn's betrayal. That is all."

"My father was one of the highest-ranking and longest standing war consultants Imbellis and Certamen have ever—"

"A man is not a man that must stand upon his father's deeds to prove his worth," Skylar popped off.

"Who are you?" Victor asked, whirling in his outrage.

Upon seeing her identity, his temper flared. "I'll have you know," he sneered at her, ensuring the hatred of everyone gathered, "Shorlynn is safe. She's married and beyond your reach."

"And yet," Tristan interjected, his tone a clear warning, "she is not beyond mine. Say something like that to her again, and I'll personally deliver Shorlynn to meet her end at Skylar's hand."

Tugging at the collar of his robe, Victor revealed his level two aer marks to the room. Black squares, captured inside and out by incomplete blue circles, ran from his neck down his right shoulder, disappearing again beneath the cloth.

"Look," he said, "you do not have to like me. Superi knows I have not the faith that others seem to have in you, but I am the voice of the Fulgo Nation. Nutrine has lost favor in his obsession over what comes after the curses have been lifted, while those he was meant to lead wish only to see it done. I was second to Calstar. This position belongs to me."

"And who do you answer to?" was Anliac's question.

Victor appeared confused. "The Council of Imbellis. We have no head, but we are the body that tends to the will of the Fulgo."

Her head shaking, Anliac said, "Imbellis was built to represent the best interest for all races. How, then, did it become a Council of Fulgo?"

"It was always Calstar's intent for the Fulgo to take over Imbellis," Set informed them, hating it, but backing up Victor's story. "He had designs on controlling Certamen as well. Shorlynn was his way in."

"And they have," Victor preened, "with my guidance. You will find victory over the gods if you show wisdom and heed my council."

"Yeah," Set chuckled from his corner, "you can leave now. When we decide to hold a meeting, you'll get your invite."

"I am a hair's breadth from being a king," Victor hissed, "and you would treat me like this? It's outrageous!"

"We're not much on titles around here," Shashara said ever-so-sweetly. Belua stood to show him to the door.

He found it himself rather quickly.

"Now," Tristan said, dragging Anliac with him to seats of their own, "what needs to be said?"

"Twice now, I've put members of the Five at risk," Montilis started them off. "That's two times when wisdom should have invoked better judgement on my part. Yesterday, we lost two brothers and came very close to losing two more. People die in war. There isn't a person here who doesn't know that, but before we forfeit anymore lives, we should all consider our actions before taking them."

"It lightens the burden of my guilt to know I'm not alone in feeling it," Tristan said when the room braced for conflict. "As I've told Anliac, I let myself become distracted by the minor battles and left my companions to fight the major ones alone. Worse," he said, "I led you all through that gateway. I took you in, uninformed and undermanned, for what we faced. Set, Triton, I can't promise that you'll never get hurt, but I can vow that it will never again happen as a result of my absence."

"What happened to me was the result of my inflated

hubris," Set replied, "not your inability to be in two places at once. Montilis, you were right when you said I know nothing about the abilities I've obtained, and an ill-trained fighter is dangerous to both enemy and ally, so help me to learn."

"The first lesson on what needs learning here," Davimon spoke up, "is the purpose of this council. This—" he waved his hand around as if trying to catch the words— "rift-jumping, monster-fighting, god-confronting nonsense must stop."

"Would you rather us know nothing when we face them?" Tristan asked, irked but not angry. "Would you, on a much larger scale, have me send defenders through to be slaughtered?" Slamming the side of his fist down on the table, emotion overwhelmed him as he argued, "I would know what monsters we face before I send you to face it."

It was Char who consoled him by saying, "I understand. As leaders of people, we all do. The terrible pull between protecting them from what would harm them by putting ourselves in its way, and the need to survive if we are to lead… it can drive one mad."

"Then what is a leader to do?" Tristan asked, his visage pleading. "Am I to hide from the fight? Am I to be a last defense instead of a first defender? I can't do that."

"And no one is asking you to," Lan said. "However, the way the Five are running things now, we can't prepare for the backlash of your actions. Fortune will only ride with us for so long."

"He's right," Lishous backed him up. "Lan deserves credit he's not getting. The defensive measures taken last night to protect Superi from what your actions stirred were his. Had the gods chosen to invade in that moment, his actions would have been all that saved us."

"However," Riker spoke out, "the fact that you are listening to us now, instead of fighting us, shows just how much you've all grown. No longer children," he said, "but rulers of Nations."

Into the awkward silence that followed, Shashara said, "We will not always agree with this council, and in the end, we will do as we must. But you have my word that we will seek the council's advice before anymore major decisions are made."

When none of the House of Angeli objected to Shashara's vow on their behalf, Shady stepped from a shadow, where no one had seen him. He smacked his hands before rubbing them greedily together and said, "I'm glad that's all settled. Now can we eat?"

"That's what I'm talking about," Tristan said, and the boys in the room made a dash for the food line. Noting Razoran, whose shoulder should have been shoving him out of the way to take his place, was absent, he found his miserable friend slouched in his seat. Asking for a second plate, he slid the extra in front of his friend before joining Char and the others. He overheard Triton's chuckle when Razoran attempted to raise his arms.

Belua and Torren were too big to fit in the seats, but Belua sat with his ankles crossed and knees bent, with his arms wrapped around them on the floor. Torren sat on her haunches in the space between the table and the wall.

"So," Tristan said, piling high the perfect bite atop a piece of flatbread, "what happened with Shorlynn?"

Torren answered, "We were told she's from Imbellis and

thought that's where she'd go. We were wrong. By time we realized our mistake, she was in Certamen. We can go in and kill her, if that is your order, but we will die in the process."

Char and Donnin stiffened as they awaited Tristan's reply.

"No," Tristan decided. "Shorlynn can cause us no further harm." He met Skylar's eyes across the room and saw the sadness in them. "But should she ever return, she'll answer for her betrayal. Now," he continued, focusing on Donnin, "I know Sole was your father, and considering their history, Lunam might as well have been your mom…"

"And then your brother killed my father, and you gave the order for Lunam to be hunted down and slaughtered."

"He did," Tristan replied without hesitation, "and I did."

Donnin stretched his hand out across the table. As they clasped forearms, he said, "I'm in debt to both Mattewson men, who allowed my hands to stay clean, because… They both really needed to die."

"It is done then?" Tristan asked.

"She found us," Belua answered, "and attempted to regain our loyalty by manipulating our thoughts. We'd disappointed you with Shorlynn and thought to redeem ourselves by completing your other task."

"Then there will be no further questioning of your loyalty," Tristan stated with a firm nod. "Nor of yours," he said to Donnin before catching Char's contagious grin. "Married life agrees with you, Char," he told her. He stood to go sit with Anliac, who, offended by Tristan's abandonment of her for the good line, had moved to sit across from Set and Shashara.

When she shifted her shoulder to block him out as he sat down, he said, "I've got news," to tempt her back around.

"As do I," Set said. He grinned and Shashara giggled.

Anliac groaned and rolled her eyes. "Go ahead," she prompted. "Tell him."

"Tell me what?" Tristan asked, intrigued.

"There's another reason the council wants you and Anliac to be more careful about not getting yourselves killed."

"Okay?"

"They need you both alive to... you know..." Shashara blushed. "...Make little Angeli babies, if we fail to lift the curses."

Tristan fell out of his seat as the laughter started.

XXIV

Service to the Five

"This is nice," Anliac said as she and Tristan walked the docks towards the blacksmith's shop.

Tristan chuckled and squeezed her hand. "Which part?" he asked. "The view of dirty old men scrambling the docks? The sound of pirates' curses wafting on the brine- and fish-scented breeze?"

"Yes, actually," she said, "because it's all so very normal. The suns are shining, no gods or monsters are attacking, and I get to spend a precious, peaceful morning with the man I love. It is going to be great day." She smiled.

"Hey!"

They heard Davad's shout and turned towards it. He was on his toes and waving like a crazed person, with a yawning Davimon walking with him.

Meeting them halfway, Davad stressed, "I'm not too late, am I?"

"For what?" Tristan asked.

281

"To change your mind," Davad replied, appearing in pain. "Davimon told me about the simple shoulder harness you want, with a hook in the center to hold the weapon." He shook his head. "Tristan, you can't do it. That sword deserves better."

"And you know what it deserves?"

"No," Davad said, slugging Tristan's shoulder. He grinned and added, "But Davimon does. He's seen it."

"So," Tristan teased, "this is your fault."

Davimon shrugged. "A weapon like that shows strength." With a stare that said as much as his words, he added, "Kings would fear its meaning."

"I admit it's an impressive sword, but um," Anliac said, "Beth didn't seem to fear it, nor the man who once wielded it."

"Who's Beth?" Davimon asked.

"My mother, Beth Matthews," Tristan supplied the answer. "She's how Triton came by the sword, after she…. washed out a rogue mercenary and took it."

"Ah," Davimon said, nodding his head. "I've heard the stories of Beth Matthews, and trust me, most men are not so brave as that."

"In other words," Davad stated, "that sword, properly displayed and hanging from the back of an Angeli, would have Normis shaking in his boots."

"Normis would pee his pants if Tristan or I showed up at all," Anliac pointed out. "Hey, um, why is Lishous standing over there?"

Glancing over his shoulder, Davimon hesitated before he said, "When we went back to Regia Aquam, it was, for

Lishous, the last time. Without ties to a King, a region or city, without purpose, I'm afraid my friend feels lost. They both do," Davimon added when Michael joined Lishous to wait on the sidelines for the conclusion of their conversation.

"They used to tease me about my arrogance, you know," Anliac said to Davimon. "Spoilt and selfish, they would say." She shook her head. "I didn't understand. Now I do." Taking a deep breath, her previous smile returning, she said, "Go to the blacksmith. I'm sure Davimon, with his vision, and Davad, with his enthusiasm, will be happy to escort you."

"You know I don't like fancy," Tristan groaned.

"Yes, you do, dear," she countered. "You just don't like to admit it."

Davad snickered, while Davimon lowered his head to hide his own.

"Fine," Tristan said. He snatched her around the waist and pulled her in to ask, "And what will you be doing?"

"I'm going to go give my attention to another man," she teased. "Two, actually." Then she gave him a quick kiss goodbye before heading towards Lishous and Michael.

"So," Tristan said, drawing their eyes away from Anliac's swaying hips before they couldn't be friends anymore. "What do you guys have in mind?"

***

Lishous folded his hands behind his back and watched her approach with a steady gaze, but Michael, his fear growing with every step she took, looked ready to be sick.

"Ma'am," Michael greeted, bowing at the waist. Even when he stood upright, he kept his head down.

"Michael," she said, "Lishous. It's a gorgeous morning, isn't it? Tell me," she prompted, "what have you planed for the day?"

"Davimon and I…" His head jerked as he shook off the disappointment. "We had plans, but—"

To save the other man from having to finish, Michael blurted, "I've been learning to farm." His eyes widening, he dropped into another bow and said, "Please, forgive my oversharing."

"Nonsense," Anliac told him. "I, too, enjoy growing things. Come," she said, "and I'll show you the garden Tristan started for me."

"Really? Yes, ma'am," Michael replied, glowing under her attention, "I would like that very much."

"I'll just leave you two to it then," Lishous said.

"Um…" Anliac stopped him. "If you wouldn't mind walking with us, I have a favor to ask of you both."

"Glad to help," Lishous told her.

"Me too," Michael chimed.

"What do you need?" Lishous asked for them both as they fell into step on either side of her. Together, they headed towards the old part of Pisces Stragulum and the Angeli houses built there.

"I didn't like the way Victor spoke to Skylar yesterday. I don't trust him, Lishous. I don't trust Nutrine. I don't trust Shorlynn, and they are all a threat to Skylar. She saved Set from Apollo's arrows when Set could not defend himself. Her actions made her one of us. Not just a part of this town, but a part of our family. I know it's a lot to ask," she said, "but I want you to look after her."

"You want me to guard her?" he clarified.

"Yes," Anliac stated. "I want to make you a guard to the House of Angeli. It comes with perks." She grinned. "A home of your own, coin to spare, and your loyalty and service returned by the house you represent."

"I'll not leave on a ship," Lishous told her, "and I mean that. I'm no pirate."

Anliac laughed. "Understood. Oh, and Lishous," she said, "I think Davad is smitten with her. They make a good pair... don't you think?"

"Is meddling a part of my job description?" Lishous asked, already scheming.

"Of course not," Anliac replied, feigning insult. "I prefer to think of it as a sign-on bonus."

It was Lishous's turn to laugh. Approaching their destination, the floral fragrance thickening as they neared Anliac and Tristan's home, he said, "I'm not much on flowers myself. If the two of you will excuse me, I have a little redhead to find, and we all know she's not going to like what I have to say."

"See?" Anliac grinned. "I knew you were the right man for the job." She chuckled at his rumbled response. After wishing him luck, she turned to Michael. "What do you think?"

The dark, night-blooming roses mingled with pink jasmine and white gardenia to create a pleasing aroma that permeated the air.

"The flowerbeds border the entire house," she said when Michael's silence gave her the best compliment. He was too busy standing with his head back and his eyes closed, breathing in the beauty, to answer.

Her words made his head snap forward, however, to pay attention. "Davad speaks highly of you," she said, "as does Set. I love growing things too," she repeated her earlier statement, "but I know that I am destined for more important things."

"Well, of course, ma'am," Michael agreed. "You're an Angeli, one of the Five, destined to free Superi."

Nodding, she waited for him to finish and then said, "I think you are destined for more important things as well."

Diverting his eyes in shame, he replied, "I am no more than a servant, ma'am."

"As are we all," she told him. "To serve is to lead. To lead is to serve. How would you like to serve Pisces Stragulum?"

"Of course, ma'am," he hurried to comply. "In what capacity can I be of aid?"

"Davad is the Magistrate of Pisces Stragulum," she said, "but he's doing too much on his own. There's no one around him that he can trust not to act in their own interest, or to the detriment of ours, but he trusts you."

"I'm not sure if I'm qualified."

"Skills can be learned," she insisted. "Loyalty and honor cannot. You can be of great help to him, Michael, if you're willing." She added, "You're under no obligation here. You're a man free to make his own choices."

"If you think I can do it," he said, "okay." As if agreeing made it real, his excitement bubbled up and over. "Can we go and find him? I am eager to learn my new role. Thank you, Anliac. I will help grow a town into a city instead of seed into grain."

"Make time for both," she said, looping her arm through his as she started them off. "I do."

"You are not at all as I'd imaged," Michael admitted, embarrassing himself.

"I tend to hear that a lot," she chuckled.

***

"He didn't write any of that down," Davad complained as the three men exited the blacksmith's shop to return to the docks. "How is a man his age going to remember all of that?"

"I'm sure he knows what he's doing," Tristan said, smiling.

"Don't worry, brother. I'll make sure the old man gets it right. It's going to look incredible."

Spotting Lishous gaining the gangplank to Triton's ship, Davimon said, "Hey, uh, I'll catch up with you guys later." Then he shouted, "Lishous! Wait up."

"There's Anliac," Tristan said to Davad. "Michael looks happy."

Scanning until he found them approaching from the far end of the dock, Davad sighed. "I guess you'll be going now. Thanks for, you know, letting me help with the design and everything."

"Whoa," Tristan said, "hold on a moment. I sense some tension. Anything you want to talk about?"

Anliac caught the slight shake of Tristan's head, asking her to wait to join them. She stopped, feeling the slight tug on her arm with Michael's last step.

"I don't know, man," Davad told him. "I look at you and

Anliac, at Set and Shashara, and I've always thought you guys were crazy for pairing up so young, but it stinks. You know? Always being the odd man out. And it's no different being a part of 'The Five'," he said, using his hands to put emphasis on the title.

"What do you mean?" Tristan pressed.

"I understand why I'm not involved in the big fights," Davad stated, "but I'm getting sick and tired of everyone acting like I can't fight at all." Turning his neck from staring out over the oceanus, he gave Tristan a head-to-toe once-over. "Sword to sword, I could take you. The Zweihander is not a normal sword," he added as an exclusion, "and if you didn't use your abilities."

"You don't have to convince me, Davad," Tristan said. "You have your father's talent for wielding blades."

"But it's not the same as wielding an ability," Davad retorted. "Look," he said, "I've accepted my role; I've even come to enjoy parts of it, but even in this, I have no real power to produce change. The people still look to you and Anliac, and now to Set, before they look to me. Tristan, there is far too much you three don't know."

"Such as?" Tristan asked to buy himself time to come up with solutions for Davad's position.

"Do you really think Nutrine fell out of favor with the entire Fulgo Nation for doing what he's been doing for decades?" Davad asked but gave no time for answer. "Do you not question the sudden move in Imbellis from neutrality to Fulgo-controlled? Do you not wonder about the Mortalis soldiers entering through Effugere Aquam and inching their way towards Caterva Concentio? Ambassadors from Normis are saying the forces are here to aid the House of Angeli in the war with the gods, but activity in Certamen shows they're preparing for a different kind of war."

Waving Anliac forward, Tristan asked him, "Why am I just now hearing about this?"

"Because you've been too busy jumping through rifts and making fancy speeches to give two squats about what's happening around you." Davad held nothing back. "Protecting Superi from the gods and seeing the curses lifted is your job, and it's your job too," he included Anliac, nodding to acknowledge Michael before he continued. "Protecting and managing the needs of Pisces Stragulum is my job. Who, then," he asked, "is responsible for what happens to Superi in the meantime? What happens when war here distracts us from the war to come? Not even with Set's help, guys. Without the Fulgo and Mortalis coming together, we've lost before we've started."

"What is he talking about?" Anliac asked Tristan.

"Find out how fast the blacksmith can have the weapon harness ready," Tristan told Davad. "Anliac and I have a couple of kings to straighten out. And as for everything else you've said, Davad, I heard you. You'll have all the power and authority you need from now on, because without you, we wouldn't have made it this far."

"Michael," Davad said, "I hate to ask, but I could really use your help. I've a thousand things to do and only two hands."

"I'm at your service, Magistrate."

"No, man." Davad grinned. "if you're willing to help, you're my hero. I do wish," he admitted, "that we had a way of knowing who's really on our side and who's not, but everything I come up with seems too obvious."

"You speak the truth you know, my boy, but not all the truth that is." In his robe of many colors, his white hair wafting in the wind, Socmoon had returned to Pisces Stragulum. He walked towards them on the dock to offer his wisdom in a time of great need. "Gather them all and we shall see who is friend and who is an enemy."

"Socmoon," Tristan greeted with a grin. "As always, your timing is perfect."

"I wonder how that is," Anliac quipped. "It's almost like he can see the future."

XXV

Lies and Misfortune

The gathering of the gods was intense as emotions mounted. The Greek and Hindu deities were at each other's throats, spewing hateful words filled with empty threats. Others whispered in corners of blame and retribution or schemed on how best to take advantage of the more powerful, yet distracted gods. Even those of cooler temperament and wiser tongues, who sat around the circular table, could not hide their displeasure, for their places of repose had shifted in color to match their outrage.

No voice boomed louder than that of Zeus, as he dared to roar at the primordial goddess. "I demand that Kartikeya be punished, Parvati," he said. "He had no right giving aid to that Angeli."

Her waning patience was expressed in the tightening of the lines around her grey eyes as she retorted, "The Angeli was not the one suffering."

Michael, the first of the Christians to arrive, stepped from the aether and into the room. "She's right. Kartikeya merely provided the boy with the means to end it." Folding his soft white wings to cover his back, he turned towards Apollo's snicker. "You have something to add?"

Shoving off with his shoulder, from where he'd been leaning against a floating pillar, Apollo engaged. "As a matter of fact," he snapped, "I do. I told my brother that the Christians would do what they always do. They'd watch." To Zeus, he said, "The Christians are not our allies in this war."

"War?" Michael interjected. "Is that what you call a fight between a Greek god and a weaponless child?" Before Apollo could reply, Michael said, "Yes, we watched. We watched you hide atop a cloud and rain down arrows upon his head. We thought your battle with the little snake was pathetic, but your feeble attempt on the boy's life was more so, so do not lay your failure at our feet."

"The boy," Apollo sneered as hatred filled his eyes, "was far from weaponless, or could you not see the elements he wielded from where you cowered in the heavens?"

From all around the translucent wall that kept the gods from stepping unintentionally into the dark aether, deities appeared; first the Norn, though Thor was oddly absent, then the Egyptians, with Anubis to speak for them. There were lesser gods as well, such as the Native American god Ahayu-ta-Achi, yet they did not join the others as they moved forward to sit. As if alive, the table grew to accommodate the new arrivals. Short columns, conjured in their proper places, added the necessary seating for the assembly.

An orb of light heralded Raphael's entrance. Ignoring the

seat conjured by the other archangel's side, he crossed the floor to stand behind Michael to ask, "Is there a problem?"

"I hope so." Michael grinned when Tyr stormed out of thin air to point with his mace-hand at Apollo's chest.

"You lying lump of dung," Tyr growled. "Look!" He held out his arm, revealing the damage to the mace attached at the end of it. The Angeli's handprint was a clear indent in the metal. "What was it you said to me when you sought my aid?" He did not wait for reply. "You and Ares needed a little help with an infestation problem, yes? Yet," he said, approaching the far side of the table from where Apollo stood, "when we arrive, Ares is gone, and you leave me to face five while you are bested by one."

"I was not bested," Apollo countered.

With a beastly roar, Tyr came up on his toes. He brought his mace-hand around in a full arc that smashed the weapon's head into the table. "First," Tyr threatened, "I'm going to take one of your golden arrows and shove it where your precious sun cannot shine, and then…" He turned to Zeus. "Where's Ares?"

"Where is Ares?" Kali repeated, scanning the room. "He should be here."

With as straight a face as he could manage, Michael said, "Where Apollo dodged his fate by leaping to the safety of the clouds, Ares suffered a humiliating and utter defeat at the hands of the Angeli. He's probably off licking his wounds." With venom dripping from his words, he sneered and said, "So much for being a god of war."

Lightning crackled in Zeus's eyes as he stood from his seat at the head of the table. "Insult my son again, angel, and reap the consequences. Ares stood and fought. He bled to rid Earth of her trespassers. Tell me, Michael, Raphael, what has your god done besides watch? Claiming to be all powerful, yet refusing to show any power; like father, like sons, yes?"

"I would speak," Ahayuta-Achi stated, drawing Zeus's attention and his ire.

"Do so with care."

"Lesser warriors than your son suffer defeat more easily," Ahayuta-Achi said, "and yet they each heal from the blow differently. For one of Ares battle prowess, the wound may be slow to mend, but he will return a stronger warrior for the loss."

"For your sake, Ahayuta-Achi, I hope you have more to say than that," Zeus replied, his voice dropping dangerously low.

"We alone have suffered casualties," Ahayuta-Achi said. "Three of our sacred creatures have been killed in this war, but no more will die until equal blood has been spent."

Sighing, Parvati gathered the attention of the room and asked, "Is this fight worth fighting? In truth, I fail to see the gain to either side. What do they want?"

"They want Earth," Apollo stated, "and they intend to unleash chaos to obtain it. Beginning," he said, "with taking down the gods. I say we put them down first."

Twisting his torso to look to his brothers, who still stood along the room's perimeter, Tyr snarled, "Do you hear how he lies?" Locking stares with Apollo, he said to them, "Let me kill him and I'll even make it quick."

Bowing up, his arms flaring out to his sides as he clenched his fists, Apollo demanded an explanation. "How have I lied?"

"Easy on the indignation, Greek," Kali warned. "The angels did not watch the last battle alone. There are many here who know what the Superians are after."

"There are many of us here who do not." Parvati turned on her. "But we will hear it now."

"They want the curses lifted, Divine Mother," Kali replied, dipping her head in respect.

"Why did you not tell me?"

"You did not ask," Kali replied with a grin as dark as her mischief.

"That's it?" Anubis asked. "That's all they want?" Moving away from the table to pace, he stated, "What have I done? You," he said, pointing to Maat. "This is your fault. You made me believe we had no choice. You allowed this to happen."

"I gave you the facts," Maat retorted, "but you made your choices, Anubis, all on your own. You did not seek my council before acting. Therefore, do not look to me to correct your mistake."

Confused and none-too-happy about it, the other gods looked to Zeus for clarification, but he wore the same visage. Making fists and pressing the flat of his knuckles against the table, he loomed over the seated gods. "What have you done, Anubis?"

Raphael looked first to Michael, but the archangel seemed bored, and so he spoke up. "He released the Jackal from its prison beneath the Nile."

Even the Norn were taken aback by the news.

"Fear not," Raphael assured. "It is the will of Yahweh

that the beast be loosed. Should the Angeli return, let them meet in battle. Their deaths will be god-sent." Proud of his wordplay, the archangel wiggled his brows at his brother, who merely rolled his eyes in turn.

XXVI

Counterplay

"Set's going to be so excited to see you," Anliac said, looping her arm through Socmoon's. She and Tristan escorted him from the docks and back towards the town.

"Tell me," Socmoon asked, "how is his health; that of his body, of course, but that of his mind as well?"

"I'm afraid that's a question better posed to Shashara," Anliac answered. "Physically, he is whole, but he does not share much about his state of mind with any but her."

Breaching the buildings that squared off the old marketplace, they watched Set and Shashara leave his office hand-in-hand. Upon spotting them, they redirected their course.

Though happy to see his old friend, Set did not run to him in youthful exuberance, as he once would have done. Experience had taught him that Socmoon's presence meant the future would soon invade upon the present and, most likely, bring violence with it. The psyches in his mind stirred as he stepped inside of Socmoon's arms for a welcomed embrace.

Set pulled away, staring askance at Socmoon. When Socmoon diverted his eyes and dipped his head, Shashara giggled. "Why on Superi are you bowing to Set? Come here, you, and give me my hug. We're so glad you're back."

"Speaking of," Set asked, "where did you go?"

Shashara mouthed, *Be nice,* to Set on her way back to his side, then jabbed her elbow into his ribs to make sure he'd understood.

Socmoon's spine went ramrod-straight as his pale face went utterly bloodless. He swallowed hard, bobbing his Adam's apple, before he said, "Forgive my absence, I ask of you all, but the grave nature of my thoughts…"

"Not a single day passes, Socmoon," Set said, "that finds me ungrateful that your curse is not also mine. Without you, I would not have survived to become what I am. You are my friend," he told him. "I would never cast blame upon you for what it is you see, nor would I blame you for what cannot be changed. So tell me what it is you know, and let us share the burden that so terrifies you."

Socmoon's presence created a stir of its own, but gathered with four of the Five, they'd drawn uncomfortable notice from the marketgoers. "There are ears here that twitch and turn for truths they'd only wish unlearned. Let us drift where words waft not, and I'll reveal the knowledge sought."

Without waiting for their concession, Socmoon turned towards the crop fields and beckoned Shashara forward, to walk with him ahead of the others. Anliac and Tristan followed together. Their worried glances slid towards Set, time and again, to where he walked alone.

When Shashara twisted her torso to check on him, Socmoon made note of it and said, "I wish to share a secret that would have sanity calling me the fool, but trusting you to seal your lips, I do what I must do."

"I cannot keep my emotions from an epoto any easier than my thoughts from a telepath, or my future from an oracle," she said with the slightest of smiles, "but, I can promise to keep my tongue from wagging."

"Much will come to be before your part comes to play," he told her, "but believe me when I say that upon the last day, you will hold the greatest of sway." Wrapping his long arm around her shoulders, he pulled her against his side and said, "So stay safe."

"Will he?" she asked him. She didn't have to give his name.

Tristan and Anliac picked up their pace to get in on the conversation. "What's all the whispering about?" Tristan asked before Socmoon could reply to Shashara's question.

"They're talking about me," Set said, joining them.

Stepping away from Socmoon, Shashara flung her long hair behind her shoulder and said, "Actually, we were talking about me."

Passing those working the field, Socmoon witnessed them pausing in their labors to wave, smile, and bow in acknowledgment of their leaders.

"Hey," Tristan said, taking Socmoon by the shoulders and ducking his head until the old man looked up at him, "what's the reason for the tears?"

Clearing his throat, lest his voice break on emotion, Soc-

moon said, "From those you serve to lead, the Five have gar-
nered a great respect, and so it is right to interject a moment
here to contemplate what it means…" Including them all
in his retrospection, he said, "Up the gangplank scampered
youth, but for truth, it was men who stepped again upon the
deck, intent on saving two pretty necks."

Blushing, Shashara muttered, "Thanks." Anliac scowled,
rolled her eyes, and said the same.

Pivoting in a slow circle, Socmoon avoided their reason
for being there by offering knowledge that common sense
already supplied. "What bounty the House of Angeli has
provided," he praised, "and yet the rains are soon to come
and what has yet to be reaped of the harvest, by the snows,
will be undone."

"Such is the way of things." Shashara grinned. "A season
for everything, and for everything a season."

"That's not entirely accurate," Set stated. "At the breaking, twin curses were cast, and though it is the discondo
imprecatio that Superians will fight to break, it was the crux-
en clav that forced us to find a new way to survive. It's the
reason it's taken so long to arrive where we are."

"Where is the relevance to crop-growing?" Anliac asked,
bored with the conversation and annoyed by Socmoon's
avoidance.

"Ignis wielders used to heat the terra, keeping it from
freezing, so their people would have food seasons 'round,"
Set explained. "But," he said, cautiously cracking the
ground, "I think I can pull the heat at Superi's core to the
surface." As he spoke, he demonstrated, pulling a shimmering heat from the ground that wavered its way to his hand.

"This way is more effective," he said, "and it will last longer." Kneeling, he began to experiment, continuing to rattle on, though no one was listening.

Except, perhaps, Socmoon.

Seeing his concern, Shashara told him. "Set is fine."

"When he's Set," Anliac added.

With a cutting glare, Shashara countered, "He's always Set. The conversation just sparked new information, new knowledge, from one of psyches in his head. How else is he supposed to learn from them if he doesn't talk to them? And be honest," she stated. "None of you seem to care who's doing the talking when it's information you want."

Socmoon's grin was broad enough to have a distant worker smiling back and waving for good measure, but it was for Shashara. "You are the balance to his curse, and though you understand his hurt, I think, on his behalf, you feel it worse."

Afraid of the fear she read in his eyes, she attempted to lighten the moment. "Boys today are so complicated." With an exaggerated wink, she added, "I do consider trading him in, on occasion, for a more mature man."

"Wait..." Set stood and dusted his hands. "What?"

As they chuckled at Set's expense, Tristan said, "Not that I'm not enjoying the reunion, because I am, but um, wasn't there a reason you wanted to talk to us out here?"

Socmoon was hesitant to answer, and when he did, it was to Set. "Where did I go when the gods came last? It's a fair question to ask, but alas, the answer is too vast for words to easily slip past."

"I meant what I said, Socmoon," Set assured him. "You

are not to blame for what you see."

Nodding, he spoke. "Yesterday's war will be new on the morrow, and no weapon wielded, nor might, will suffice to keep from the battlefield's impending sorrow."

There was a long moment of pause as the oracle's words crashed down on them. Then Tristan snapped. "What?" His stance dared the man to repeat himself.

"Tristan, back off," Set warned. "Socmoon, are you telling us that we've already lost?" Shashara took his hand. Giving it a squeeze, he said, "Because I'm telling you now, I refuse to accept that."

"Good." Socmoon's smile was shaky, but he held it in place and said, "It is with heart and wit that we will find victory at war's end."

"I can read your emotions, Oracle, but not your thoughts," Set told him. "What does that mean?"

"Are you talking about the rumors of war breaking out between the races once the war with Earth is won?" Tristan asked him. "Davad and I have a solid plan laid out with Montilis." He gave one slow nod and said, "We know what to do."

"I know," Socmoon said, "and your plan will succeed if, by what happens next, it's not first deceived."

"Ugh," Anliac groaned. "You've got to be kidding me. We were so careful."

Eyebrows high on her brow, Shashara asked, "Did you just stamp your foot?"

"Shut up," Anliac grinned but became distracted at the cluster of people coming towards them. "I wonder which one of them craves power over peace. Do you know?" she asked Socmoon, but his smirk said he wasn't answering.

Riker was among them, wearing his traditional scowl, while Davad appeared to be trying—and failing—to calm the Senior General down. Skylar seemed in no better temperament. The way she glared at Lishous's back suggested she was none too pleased to be regulated to a secondary priority by Davimon's presence.

"It has to have something to do with the representatives," Tristan pondered. "And Donnin and Char… eesh, they don't look happy."

"I don't know." Shashara shrugged. "Vincent isn't with him."

"It's Victor," Set said.

"Are you sure?"

"No," Set chuckled, "not really."

"So," Anliac asked when the others approached, "what's going on?"

As a unit, the men turned to the women to reply. Char held up both of her hands and turned her head, as if to wash her hands of the whole situation, while Skylar stepped up.

"We need the council of the Five," she told them. "However, Oracle, you can just keep quiet."

Shashara's jaw dropped. "That was rude."

"She meant no offense," Davad was quick to defend. "We're trying to ascertain the truth when it's spoken among lies, but we each understand the need for privacy, and Socmoon sees too much."

"Not lies," Davimon corrected, "but truth cautiously given."

"Under such circumstances," Set said, "my input would

invalidate your purpose. Because I can feel your emotions, I can read them, and while it's not as accurate as what Socmoon does, it's more than enough to detect lies."

"We don't even know what that purpose is," Anliac stated.

"Okay, look," Skylar said, "I'm not a politician. I'm not the boss of anything or anyone, so maybe that's why I don't understand, but here is the situation. These idiots—" she pointed back at them with her thumb— "consider lying in the political arena a sport instead of an immorality. While engaging in this particularly wordy sport over breakfast, certain… let us say, *discoveries* were made that raised concerns. Going on the defensive, or offensive, depending on their varying positions, these idiots…"

"Call me an idiot again," Char warned, "and words will take action towards teaching you respect."

"As I was saying, before being so rudely interrupted," Skylar said, angling to keep an eye on the Fera, "they each began weaving tales to deescalate the suspicions they'd aroused. So what we need," she concluded, "is for Set to listen to their stories and call them on their lies, and for all of you to be here to deal with the truth when it's revealed."

"A word of council to mark my leave…" Socmoon grinned. "Only one, at breakfast, spoke a truth to be believed."

"See?" Davad laughed. "That's why you can't be here."

"What started all of this?" Shashara wanted to know.

"Oh, that's easy," Skylar quipped. "The Mortalis plan on putting the Fulgos' backs to a political wall with strategically placed forces." Turning to Davimon, she asked, "Did I get that right?"

Davimon spoke slowly, enunciating each word, "Post-war negotiations."

"Of course," Skylar said with an exaggerated wink. "Moving on. The Fulgos have become suspiciously silent towards their intentions after the war with Earth has ended, yet their representative is confident in the House of Angeli's support." She quirked an eyebrow at Davad, who seemed to have lost the ability to speak, though the way he licked his lips and stared at her own was nice. "Care to comment?"

Five facades of innocent ignorance met her question.

"That's what I thought," she said and then continued. "Now rumor has it, the Nox intend to take full advantage of Davimon's king's idiocy." Making a show of it, she asked Char, "It's okay for me to call Normis an idiot, right?" When Char's eyes narrowed, she shrugged and said, "Just thought I'd ask. You know, there's kind of a lot going on, so pausing for a lesson would be terribly inconvenient."

"Seriously," Davimon asked, crossing his arms, "you're going to insult my king with me standing here?"

"And how dare you, a civilian, question the word and honor of a Nox general?" Riker asked, furious, as red in the face as a Nox could turn. "You tell them, Montilis," he demanded. "The contract between the Nox and the Angeli will be honored. We have no intention to aggress against Certamen, but should we have chosen to do so, we would not sweep in behind the Mortalis. We would go through them."

Shashara dropped her shoulder in dejection and peered at them with wide, woeful eyes. "You all make me sad."

"I guess you were right after all," Davad said to Set as

they circled the tightening group from opposite directions. "Daniel is right. There's only one solution."

"Who?" Montilis asked. "What solution?"

Set winced. "It's a drastic measure."

"I know," Davad replied, "but considering what we just heard…"

"He's right." Tristan agreed. "I will not fight to defend this world only to watch its denizens tear it apart."

"So," Anliac, "then it's settled. If we cannot trust the rulers of Superi to make the right decisions, then when the war with Earth has ended, the House of Angeli will move to take control."

"Whoa," Davimon said, throwing out his hands, "let's hold on a moment and talk about this. The Mortalis have no intention of launching an attack against Certamen, nor any other Fulgo territory. We merely allowed Fulgo to think the worst, and before you ask why, I'll tell you. The last time we negotiated with the Fulgo, they'd just won a war, and we were at a disadvantage. Our intention is to see that history does not repeat itself, and that is all."

"I will say it again," Riker stated. "The Nox will honor the accord, or Superi help me, I will kill the man who gave the counterorder. General Aquam."

"Sir," Montilis began, coming to attention as Riker's rank and command distanced them from their friendship. Angering his General but earning the trust of the Five, he said, "I'm the one that started the rumor."

"Why would you do that?" Riker scowled.

Montilis glanced at Anliac and then returned his stare to Riker. "We were the first to sign with the Angeli, and the rest of Superi thinks we are little more than added bodies to their swelled cause. They believe we will not act against the Five, and the Five have declared that there will be no wars on Superi. So yes, I started a rumor that put our enemies on their heels, trusting that the Angeli would succeed in breaking the curses, and bought the Nox a measure of safety until that happened. You are my general," he said, "but this is my post. I did what leaders do. I made a choice."

Riker's reply had teeth. "It was the wrong choice."

Shashara clapped her hands together and, with a semblance of a smile, said, "Well done, Skylar, and congratulations to you all. The Mortalis, Fulgo, and Nox have the truth to guide their future decisions."

"You know the Fulgos' intention," Riker pointed out. "We do not."

"The Fulgo have no interest in conquest," Anliac assured them, "and we all stand to gain from what is now kept secret in Certamen, so leave them be. That is truth."

"What of the Fera?" Set asked, coming to stand before Donnin. "You are now the representative for your race. You are here, which means you were a part of the initiating conversation, and yet, beyond making threats, the two of you haven't spoken a word."

"The Fera have been fractured by the loss of their previous Alphas," Donnin told him with a steady stare, "and only those here, in Pisces Stragulum, are willing to call you Alpha. Though I stand here," Donnin stated, "I am one of them."

"Understood," Tristan stated without malice.

"As to the Feras' intentions following the war with the

gods, we have none," Donnin said. "We are not like the other races. We are scattered across Superi in shattered packs. Char and I will have our hands full rebuilding what has been torn down."

"We will not rule as they did," Char added. "As Alphas, we have trust to earn on every front. Knowing this, and knowing that we are newly appointed, is it not wise to keep silent? Especially," she said, "when a powerful House like the Angeli make open threats of tyrannical conquest. Or was that a part of the ploy you were playing as well?" she asked Skylar.

"No," was Skylar's terse reply. "I had no idea Set and Davad would work a confession out of them. I was just helping to set up the scenario where all of you people would have to stop lying."

"Helping who?"

The question came from so many directions, Skylar wasn't certain who to look at, but Shashara snatched all their eyes when she answered.

"Me," she confessed. "So much is changing so fast, and the House of Angeli cannot prepare for it if we cannot trust those sent to help us."

"I commend the fruitions ploy," Riker said, "and I am relieved to hear that the threat Anliac gave voice to carries with it no truth."

The shared glances amongst the Five reiterated their cause for concern, but Set's reply etched the threat in stone.

"Start a war for no greater purpose than power or glory," Set said, "and discover the truth. That was no ploy."

XXVII

Depths of Strength

Finding Skylar lying on her back on a wooden bench, basking in the suns' light on the docks of Pisces Stragulum, Anliac could not deny the woman's beauty.

Tiny, black leather boots covered her feet. Her long legs, shapely and pale, were hidden beneath a brown cotton skirt that had a split in one side, revealing a smooth, firm thigh. An expanse of ivory flesh lay bare between her hipbones and the bottom of her ribcage, where her skin danced over the defined muscles, before disappearing beneath a white, sleeveless cotton top. With each breath, silver buttons strained to keep the material stretched across her ample bosom.

The quickening pulse at the side of Skylar's neck quickened her own and carried her eyes upward to be captured by the Fulgo's knowing stare. As waves of fire fell to frame Skylar's perfect porcelain face, her full, dark-red lips turned up in a grin that stole Anliac's wit.

"Find something you like?" Skylar asked, her sweet, dulcet tone enhancing the image she made.

"Mind if I join you?" Anliac heard herself ask.

"Only if you mean it." Skylar chuckled at Anliac's wide-eyed response to her reply, then asked, "What's on your mind, beautiful?"

"You think I'm beautiful?"

Anliac had never missed her dark Nox skin quite so much as now, as her translucent, olive complexion gave her—and her blush—away.

"You are an Angeli," Skylar said from her reclined position. Her heavy-lidded eyes took a slow stroll from Anliac's neck down the simple, blue cotton blouse that hinted at the generous curves beneath. Her gaze paused at a tiny waist before sliding around flaring hips, down femininely powerful legs captured in fitted brown breeches, to a pair of black leather boots that shifted beneath her scrutiny. "You are perfect," she told her, "in both beauty and power."

Anliac's mood shifted.

"Come, sit down," Skylar offered, sitting up to make room for her.

As she did, Anliac caught sight of Lan standing with Lishous and asked, "How is your new guard working out?"

Skylar rolled her eyes. "First off, I don't see why he's necessary. He's very judgmental."

"Lishous?" Anliac asked, dubious.

Sighing, Skylar confessed. "It's not his fault." Choosing her words carefully, she added, "He has a friend who's taken a fancy to me."

Though not one to do so often, Anliac giggled. "You

mean Davad?" When Skylar merely nodded, Anliac said, "You could do worse."

"Really?" Skylar said, intrigued. "Because of the Five, you seem to like him least."

With a soft smile turning up the corners of her mouth, Anliac said, "Let me tell you a little something about Davad. He brow-beat a spoilt, selfish brat into a woman people could respect." She paused to say, "That would be me, in case you couldn't guess."

"Yeah, no." Skylar grinned. "I never would've thought it was you."

Nudging Skylar's shoulder with her own, Anliac continued. "When all of us with power found ourselves helpless, it was his strength, the kind that comes from within, that saved us. He is loyal. He's honest. Next to Shashara, he's the best of us, but do not mistake his gentle demeaner for weakness, for he's far deadlier than he seems. He is, after all, a mercenary's son."

"So then, you don't hate him," Skylar said, her smile growing into a grin when Anliac nudged her again.

"Look, Skylar," Anliac said, "I know you can take care of yourself. All I'm saying is that, well, with a guy like Davad, you wouldn't have to."

Skylar surprised them both a bit when she admitted, "I wouldn't be against it, but..." She ducked her head. "I'm kind of out of my depth when it comes to men. You, on the other hand..."

Anliac's laugh was laced with nerves, but she was quick to counter with, "I'm afraid I'm out of my depth when it comes to women."

Skylar took the diversion in stride. "Shorlynn was the same in the beginning," she teased, "so if ever you decide you want to do more than look, I promise I'll take it slow."

"If slow is what you wanted, gorgeous, all you had to do was ask."

Both women jumped, guilt dictating their expressions, off the bench and in opposite directions as Tristan made an appearance.

"Um, darling, hi," Anliac said, as she moved to stand in front of him. Trailing her fingers down his chest, petting him in nervous strokes, she asked, "How much of that did you hear?"

He gave his answer to Skylar. "You know she comes with me, right?"

"Sorry," Skylar said, a slight wrinkle to her nose, "but you're not my type."

"Because I'm a man?"

"No," Skylar chuckled, "because you're you... with all your muscles and veins and stuff."

Fighting a grin, his lips twitching as a result, Tristan said, "So, you prefer little guys."

"No." She laughed outright. "I prefer them a bit more polished, however. Ugh," she groaned as Lishous moseyed his way over. "Here's another example of base, unpolished masculinity."

"She was staring too hard not to be insulting me," Lishous stated, shaking Tristan's hand as he joined the group. "What did she say?"

Tristan grinned "She says we're base creatures beneath her notice."

"Because we're men?"

"No," Tristan told him, "because we have muscles and veins and stuff."

"Shut up," Skylar scowled, but her red cheeks ruined it. "Is there a reason you're here?"

It was Anliac's turn to blush. "Yes, actually. The um, ship. The one from yesterday. It was the first to come from Antro?"

"As far as I know," Skylar told her. "The goods on the docks right now are from Palus Regia, but most come from Regia Aquam. A ship from Effugere made port a few days back," she said as an afterthought, "but they had nothing to sell or trade."

"Then why were they here?" Tristan asked.

Skylar shrugged. "Davad put a few guards on those who were ranked, but from all reports, they spent two days walking around, asking a lot of questions, and then they left."

"What do you think, Tristan?" Anliac asked. "More spies?"

"Honestly, Anliac," Skylar said, "even if they were, nothing happened during their stay to report. Since Socmoon's return, this place is actually getting a little bit boring."

"Why the sudden interest?" Lishous asked, looking to either Tristan or Anliac to answer.

"Regia Aquam has not come to terms concerning the war," Tristan told him. "If they want equal trade rights, the Mortalis king will have to change that, or suffer the higher taxes we're going to levy against those who have not."

"And as for Antro, Pisces Stragulum will not trade with them," Anliac stated, "not until very slave has been offered freedom in their region, and Antro has yet to agree to terms as well."

"Talk to Victor…Vincent? I cannot remember that man's name," Lishous said, "but Antro is Fulgo-dominate. That puts the city under his territory of influence. In the meantime," he told them, "I'll make sure the dockmaster is aware of the restrictions on Regia Aquam and that his orders are to turn away ships from Antro."

"How can I help?" Skylar asked.

"You can go and talk to Davad," Tristan said. "Pisces Stragulum is his to manage, but I think it's a safe bet he'll agree with us."

"Yeah." Skylar grinned, starting forward. "I can do that."

"Oh!" Anliac squealed softly when Skylar pinched her bottom on the way by.

"She's as bad as a man, isn't she?" Lishous grumbled. As Tristan and Anliac laughed, he said, "Keep moving, woman. I want your pincers kept where I can see them."

Casting a wink at Anliac over her shoulder, Skylar led her glaring guardian back towards town, leaving the grinning couple behind with their own guards to torment.

"She's something else," Anliac said.

"She's hot." Sucking air between his teeth, Tristan winced. His face skewed as he peeked at Anliac's expression to judge how much trouble he was in.

Anliac made a sound in the back of her throat that brought a bead of sweet to Tristan's brow, but when she said, "Yes, she is," his visage went slack before rebounding as concern.

"Hey," she told him, brushing the back of her fingers

down his cheek, "you know you're my perfect match."

Capturing her hand in his, he kissed the back of it before intertwining their fingers. "Walk with me," he said, leading them away from the docks to follow the coast.

He was quiet, lost in introspection as he stared out over the grey oceanus. She took the moment to appreciate a different kind of beauty, one opposite of that possessed by the redheaded minx. One that she had claimed.

She missed his smooth, bald head, but the short black hair that had grown in, falling in disheveled waves and standing in stark contrast to the white of his unblemished skin, was nice too. His features had become sharper and more angular since their first meeting, but such things happened when a boy became a man. For certain, there was nothing left of the boy in his stature. Tristan had a warrior's body, a balance between raw strength and the agility to maneuver it.

"I love you," she heard herself say.

Coming to a stop, he turned to her and cupped her cheeks. "I love you too."

Her breath caught as his eyes devoured what his hands held, desperately searching for…something. Wrapping her hands around his wrists, she pulled them down to step closer and ask, "What is it, Tristan?" When he diverted his stare, she pushed. "We both know there's something you're afraid of, something you found on Earth, and something you need to talk about."

Taking a deep breath, he let it out and confessed, "I got scared."

Anliac paused for a moment, cocking her head and leaning it forward, as she anticipated what he would say. "And?" she pressed when it became apparent he didn't intend to elaborate. "If you're going to try and say you've never been afraid before, well…" She winked. "I know better. Tristan, hey," she said quickly when, instead of laughing, he winced. "Talk to me. Tell me what happened."

Taking a seat on the ground, he offered up his hand to help her sit beside him. Once she was settled, he locked his stare on the far horizon and said, "Ares is unlike any other god I've fought." Shaking his head, he continued, "It's effortless for him. He stayed moves ahead of me, Anliac. My speed kept me covered, but only barely."

"And that scares you?"

His head started shaking harder. He leaned forward to prop his forearms across his bent knees. "No," he told her, "but that's just it. I wasn't scared. I wasn't even concerned."

"Then I'm confused."

"I got distracted," Tristan told her. "One of the others had screamed. When I turned back around, it was to Ares's knee in my face. His hand came around my throat and then I was on my back. His fists I could take, but when his elbow cracked my cheekbone…" He shifted so he could see her expression. "I brought my hands up, and that's when he shoved the dagger into my side."

"That had to hurt," she admitted, "but you've suffered worse pain. Right?"

"It wasn't the pain," he insisted. "It was my involuntary response to it, or my abilities' response to it. Honestly, I'm not sure which it was. All I know," he told her, "is that it felt like the void shattered, or I did. Either way, the power it unleashed…" He nodded. "*That* scares me."

"What did you do?"

"I, uh…" Tristan shrugged with one shoulder. "I shoved him."

"That's it?"

"A hundred feet, Anliac, straight up." His words sounded impossible even to him. "I could have run from here to Caterva Concentio and back in the time it took him to fall. And that's another thing," he said. "My speed. It's getting to the point that I think my feet get in the way more than they help."

Anliac laughed. "Oh." She cleared her throat. "You're serious?"

Rolling his neck over his shoulders, he fought down his irritation to make her understand. "I've always thought that the void was there to protect me, to protect my mind from the things I have to do and from the pain this body takes to see those things done."

"Has that changed?"

He nodded again. "I think my mind created the void to protect me from the power that lies on the other side of it. We say we're the same, Anliac, but we're not. The blood that was used to change me is not the blood used to change you, and I've been what I am for far longer."

"So, you're scared of your power," she said. "Tristan, this is something you've always struggled with."

"And you still don't get it," he told her, coming to his feet. When she stood as well, he grabbed her hand and shoved her palm against his chest. "There is a hole here. I can't remember a time when it wasn't, yet the stronger I become, the deeper the hole grows. I need more power. It grows. The greater the hurt I take… the deeper it grows."

"Tristan, every ability has limitations. Trust me," she said, "not even their gods are as invincible as they think they are. Don't pout," she warned when he was clearly set to sulk. "I swear, you're the only man I know who needs weakness to be okay with his strength."

"That's not funny," he snapped.

"You're telling me? There are going to be greater gods to face than Ares, Tristan, like his father." Her inflection on the name spoke volumes. "He's bound to be stronger, and Superi help us if we face more than one with Qandisa's strength."

"Is this supposed to make me feel better?" Tristan asked.

"Look," she said, planting her fists on her hips, "the void is your problem. It's a bandage you've worn for so long that you don't even know if the wound is still under there or not. It's time to rip it off, Tristan. You cannot face the gods with half-measure."

"And how do we do that, Anliac? How can I test what I believe to be true without becoming a greater danger to Superi than Earth's gods? What are you doing?"

"There you are," she said, reaching out her hand to trouble the ground. "Do you remember when we ran to Dura Mortis?" she asked without losing her focus.

Tristan shoved his hands into front pockets and muttered, "How could I forget?"

"Ha. Good answer," she said with a grin before making her point. "We went up there so that I could learn to use my terra ability. I felt a void. It was deep, and I wasn't yet skilled enough to bring it to the surface without making a mess of things.

"How deep is this stuff?" Tristan asked. The veins in Anliac's neck and temple filled with blood and pounded under the pressure she was putting on her ability.

The ground shook harder, then a two-foot crack appeared, and from it came a misshapen ball of brown clay.

Anliac used a negative gravity force to keep it suspended between them. Without touching it, she put it on a slow rotation. "I asked Bengim about it," she explained. "He knew what I was talking about but said, so far as he knew, it had never been named. The stone is too hard to manipulate. It can't be melted. It can't be cut. He said once, he shattered a piece from a greater whole, large enough for a small dagger, but it wouldn't take an edge."

She pressed her hands together and focused on the stone. When she pulled them apart, the brown clay cracked and dropped. A shiny, blackish-grey stone the size of melon was left to float on its own. Lifting both hands, Anliac focused on crushing the stone until it felt like something would pop in her head.

Curious that it would cause her so much trouble, he asked about Bengim while she did her thing. "Speaking of," he said, "how is he adjusting to life as farmer?"

"He's adjusting," Anliac replied, the strain of her attempt showing in her voice. "The arcanite bracelets went on easily enough, and he hasn't talked about killing Nutrine. At least, not lately."

"I'm glad you talked some sense into him," Tristan said. "It doesn't seem right to release him if he's just going to go kill someone."

Giving up, she let the stone fall. As it thudded to the ground, she corrected Tristan's assumption. "Oh, no," she told him, "I fully intend to let him go after Nutrine, and I told him as much, but I also told him it wasn't going to happen until after this war with Earth is behind us."

"You're really going to let him kill a man for deeds done decades ago?" Tristan asked. "It's not right."

"If it was me decades dead," she countered, "would you leave my murderer alive? What if our children were buried beside me? Would you leave their deaths unavenged?"

His eyes crinkled around the edges. He frowned and said, "Fine, but when he's finished, he'd better hide. You know Superi is going to expect me to find him. Better yet," he said, "we need to be on the other continent. Otherwise, people will want to know how he escaped in the first place and why I didn't stop him. I can't catch him if I can't find him. That's going to be the plan."

Anliac took a step back as her jaw dropped. "Sweet Superi," she said, wide-eyed. "I just figured it out. We're fighting these battles against their gods with strength and abilities, as we must, but Socmoon said victory would be won with wit and heart. Tristan, how do we defeat the curses before their gods defeat us?"

"I'm not sure I follow." Tristan stared at her lips as they formed words, hoping they would start to make sense.

"How do you fight what you cannot see?" she asked him. "Think, Tristan. What else did Socmoon say?"

"He said the curses couldn't live without a host." His shoulders slumped. "We're the host," he said, throwing up his hands in frustration.

"No," she corrected, "we're not. Zeus is. He's the one who cast the curses. Kill him and the curses break. Maybe they know that. Maybe that's why they've sent every other god against us, while keeping Zeus swaddled in the aether somewhere."

"I think you're right," he said, "but their plan will fail. Zeus is going to die, and I'm going to be the one to kill him."

"I'm always right." She grinned. "But feel free to elaborate on what I'm right about this time."

"I think we've allowed ourselves to become distracted from our goal. It's not about defeating the gods," he said. "And trust me, I wouldn't live on Earth if Superi threatened to implode with me on it. It's about breaking the curses. Anliac…" Snatching her around the waist, he pulled her in for a kiss that set them both on fire. "You are brilliant, and you're right. We need to summon Zeus."

"Well," she said, breathless and unsteady, "that takes care of wit, I suppose, and of identifying the host, but um… whew." She struggled to maintain her thoughts while he nipped at her ear. "There is still the matter of heart."

"I have no heart to speak of," he said, pulling back to smile at her. "You have mine."

"Cute," she said, her head clearing. "Very cute, but I'm being serious. You think it is the difference in the blood used to change us that makes us different. There is truth to that, obviously, but as Socmoon would say, that is not all the truth there is. You are right in that you were changed as an infant, but are wrong when you think the difference is in the years you've spent this way."

"And you've lost me again."

She rolled her eyes. "You're different, Tristan, because you're not just the first recreated Angeli. You're the one oracles left prophesies about. Upon Malstar's success, you became the catalyst for everything. You," she said, "are the heart."

Emotions shifted, like sand caught by waves, over Tristan's face. She held his hands as he rode it out and waited for him to return to her. Once his eyes had regained focus, she told him, "You're strong enough to do this, Tristan, but remember, you're not going to do it alone."

"What if I'm wrong about the void?" he protested. "What if I'm not as powerful as I think I am, and in the moment when I need the void most, it fails to grow? What if I'm the reason we lose the war? Or worse..."

"What would be worse than that?" Anliac hated herself for asking, but the terror on his face needed addressing.

"Either I'm in control," Tristan told her, "or the power is. What if I can't come back from it?"

The thought was unsettling, but the last thing he needed from her was doubt, so she said, "That's what we have Set for."

He laughed. It bordered on hysteria, but it was a start.

"So," he asked, "what was your plan with the stone?"

"Well," she said, tucking her hair behind her ears, "originally, it was to prove that even you have limits, but now I'm kind of hoping I'm wrong." Her grin was cheeky, but his was sickly, so she hurried on to say, "Whatever that stone is made of is indestructible. Bengim, the strongest terra wielder alive, cannot work it. I'm an Angeli, and I couldn't put a dent in it."

"You want me to test my strength against it."

"Yes," she said, though it hadn't been a question. "Tristan, you have to trust your power, and if that means finding its limit, so be it."

When Anliac waved over Lynette, Daniel, refusing to be left out, followed.

"Lynette," Anliac said, "do me a favor." She levitated the stone back off the ground. "I want you to strike this stone with your sword. Don't hold back."

Lynette didn't hesitate, but when steel struck stone, it was the blade that took damage. The hilt of her sword bounced hard in her hand, and the steel blade bent to the strength of the stone, knocking her backwards.

"Mind if I try?" Tristan asked her, reaching for a sword the guard was already turning over. One swing and the blade shattered. "Not even a scratch," Tristan said, dropping the useless hilt to rub at the pain lancing through his shoulder. "Hey, uh, I'm sorry about the sword. I'll see it replaced."

"Don't worry about it," Lynette waved off his offer. "It happens to me all the time. Not all the time…" she rushed to add. "Just this…"

Tristan chuckled. "I'm definitely getting you a better sword."

"Daniel, you're a terra wielder," Anliac stated, taking note of his markings. "Why don't you and I try together?"

The two wielders took up similar stances, stretching out their arms towards the stone, wearing identical expressions of determination. Together, they worked to manipulate the stone. Its position wavered between them. In miniscule degrees, its shape shifted from spherical to oval, but their energy was depleted, and the stone remained whole.

Daniel leaned over with a bleeding nose and puked, while Anliac pulled a trickle of moisture from the air to quench her sudden thirst.

"At least we know it can be altered," Tristan said. "What do you want to do next?"

"Now let's find out if you can break it," Anliac replied.

Slipping off her shoes, she used the soles of her feet to sense what she needed. There was a slab of basaltic rock hiding on the oceanus' floor, not too far from the coast, that would serve her purpose. Dragging it above water, she levitated it to where they stood on dry ground and then dropped it.

As Tristan examined it, she explained, "With a few jewels being the exception, this type of rock is the densest I've found. I discovered it weeks ago, but when I told Triton about it, he said he wasn't interested; it's too heavy to transport. Anyway, I want you to imagine the stone is Ares's head, and let us see if we can crack it open."

Grabbing hold of the unnamed stone as Anliac released her control of it, Tristan took a step back, and without hesitation, he hurled it against the slab of rock. Besides the hole through the center of it, the slab was left in one piece, and the stone, sitting at the bottom of a crater its trajectory had created, rested without a scratch.

"Round one to Ares," Anliac stated, upping the challenge.

"Um, technically," Lynette said in a teeny voice, "that would be round…" She held up two fingers when Tristan's scowl killed her words.

"Bring it back over here," Tristan demanded, but Anliac's arched right brow suggested he add the, "please."

"Are you sure you're ready for round three?" Anliac teased. "Because if this were Ares, he'd be laughing at you right now."

Tristan waited only long enough for her to lift it into the air, then he took off at a full run. Rearing back his right fist, he slammed it into the rock without slowing his speed. As the bones gave way beneath his flesh he bellowed.

"Whoa!" Anliac shouted, snatching for the stone with her ability before it could disappear far, far, out into the oceanus. Giving it a quick once-over, she declared, "And round three goes to…"

One moment, the stone was floating in front of her face, and the next, Tristan had it pressed against his chest, trapped there by his right arm. Wrapping his left hand around his right wrist, he squeezed. It wasn't enough. Reaching for more power, he roared. His golden marks flared, but still, it wasn't enough.

Cursing, Tristan tossed it up and punched it again.

Anliac pulled up a rock wall, which the stone busted through, but she managed to stop its flight before the stone became irretrievable. Knowing full-well that Tristan had hit the stone harder the second time, yet his hand had suffered no more injury, she pushed him harder.

"Enough of that," she said, summoning it back. "It's been established that it cannot be damaged by another stone, and it's apparent your fist isn't going to do the trick either. This is about you and whether your strength alone can break that rock, or if what you need to break the rock isn't about strength at all."

By reaching for the stone, Tristan accepted what he had to do. As his fingers curled around its oval shape, he said, "I hope you know what we're doing," and then turned himself over to his power.

Accepting that there would be no turning back, he ignored the goosebumps rising on his flesh and the ice racing through his veins. Closing his eyes, he cleared his mind, and the void consumed him. It denied him the horror he should have felt at the look of terror on Anliac's face, especially as shockwaves of heated energy exuded from him. They came in even waves with his heartbeat, shoving her backwards, but knocking Daniel and Lynette into backward rolls across the ground.

A safe distance from the energy waves, the others gained their feet and watched as Tristan's golden marks deepened into an orange burn. But, as if reaching for them, the pulses of energy became tremors that troubled the ground at their feet.

Lifting his other hand to place it beside the first around the curve of the stone, his single Angeli voice sounded as many when he said, "The void is vast. There is nothing but power here." And then, with a flex of his shoulders, he turned the angle of his fists, palm to palm, and the stone folded in-half.

The explosion was tremendous when the stone gave way. Splinters of it sprayed in an outward barrage, forcing Anliac to dive towards the others and throw up a gravity shield for their protection.

"He's looking at us," Lynette whispered when Tristan's

stare illuminated their position.

"I know," Anliac said, smiling. "Isn't he magnificent?"

"And now he's coming this way," Daniel stated. "You see him, right?"

"I do," Anliac replied, but her smile was gone, along with her joy at his victory. "Leave us," she commanded. "We need to be alone."

"Are you sure it's safe?" Lynette asked, flinching when Tristan answered, "I would never hurt her," in the voice that was many.

"Go now," Anliac said, cupping his cheeks as he had her own. She waited for privacy to say, "You and your power are one and the same, Tristan. It's who you are."

"They're afraid of me."

She shook her head. "They are in awe of you." Going up on her tiptoes, she closed her eyes against his brilliant aura and kissed him. When it ended, Tristan's marks glowed no more brightly than her own, but the heat pouring from their flesh was an equal match.

XXVIII

Too Young?

Set leaned his shoulder against one of the eight poles that held erect the white, cotton bench-tent he'd set up for Shashara north of town. He'd made them a fire, protected from the surf by a moat, and placed rocking chairs before it, so they could enjoy a meal and talk without sand wiggling into places it shouldn't be. The embers still burned this morning, and so did he.

Chuckling at his failed attempt to take things beyond kisses last night, he conjured an image of Shashara. She was asleep in the interior room, on a padded straw bed upon a woven rug that matched the color of her eyes. She was so beautiful, and he counted himself fortunate that she'd agreed to let him hold her…so long as he behaved, which he'd managed to do for the most part.

The wind snapped and pulled at the cotton walls, offering a cooling breeze that roused Shashara. Stretching languorously, she sat up in bed and admired the markings on her boyfriend's naked torso. Bootless, his brown cotton pants hanging low on his hips, she watched the muscles play in his back and shoulders as he shoved his silky black hair off his forehead.

He'd come to her, shy and uncertain, last night. And though she'd never tell him, she'd wanted to say yes…to everything, but the conversation she'd had with Anliac gave her pause.

"Shashara," Anliac had said, "you and Set are so young, and as much as we hate our age playing a part in relationships, it does matter. I get that you're seventeen, but Set's not. He's barely fifteen, and I think that's simply too young to give up the last of his innocence. He has very little left in his life. Besides, you cannot tell me that you wouldn't prefer a wedding before a wedding night. It's who you are."

Looking at him now, she had her regrets, but she knew she'd made the right choice. They were young, which meant they had plenty of time. An errant thought of the war slipped in uninvited, and when she thought of the threat to the time she wanted with Set, violent images were conjured.

With a roguish grin, Set said, "I love you too." He crossed the floor to sit on the far side of the bed.

With a tilt of her head and a twinkling smile, she said, "It's customary to let the other person say it first."

Reaching for her hand, he told her, "You don't have to say it. I can feel it." With a widening grin of his own, he added, "The knowledge is all that got me through your rejection last night."

"I'm going to pretend that's one of your other voices talking," Shashara said, "because that was not rejection. That was me believing that what we have is worth waiting for." Scooting across the bed, she turned to sit in his lap. Once his arms were wrapped around her, she whispered, "We've had to rush through so much, Set. I don't want to rush us too."

"With you sitting in my lap," he teased, "the voices in my head disagree with you."

"Set!" She smacked the top his thigh and launched herself up. "You tell the voices to behave themselves," she laughed, her escape foiled by Set's capturing arms.

Whispering against the side of her neck, he said, "I will wait, because it's what you need, but I haven't been fifteen since Sole lost the gladius."

Stepping out of his embrace, she reached back for his hand and led him to the remains of the fire. Reaching out towards the oceanus with her free hand, as if to physically take hold of it, she retracted her hand, and the surf whooshed over the sand to douse the last of the coals.

"You're getting better," he said.

"Baby steps," she replied. "Anliac's giving me lessons, or at least she was, until…"

"…Tristan panicked over that stone he shattered a few days back?"

"Exactly," Shashara replied and then asked, "should we be concerned that he managed to do it?"

When he didn't respond, she glanced over her shoulder and sighed. She'd become used to Set's glazing stare when one of the psyches in his mind had something to say, and so she released his hand when he moved towards the moat.

"I think the greater concern," he replied without turning, "is that the people are concerned, but they will be grateful for Tristan's strength when it saves us."

He didn't stop at the moat, as she thought he would, but stepped over it. She shook her head as her jaw dropped. The sand was rising to ensure his steps, then falling in his wake as he left the coastline. All the while, Set was oblivious to it.

"Can you imagine what it must be like for him?" Set asked, turning again for the shore. "To have unlimited power?"

"Honestly?" she asked. "I wouldn't want it." When he spoke again, she was almost certain he hadn't heard her answer.

"You've gained one ability not your own," he said. "If you don't count the healing ability that you've had all along, and yet, it hasn't turned your world upside-down."

Sidetracked, Shashara asked, "What do you mean? I wasn't born a healer."

"You've always been a healer, Shashara," he told her. "When you were little girl, you were always bringing home wounded critters to nurse back to health, and when one of us would get sick, it was always you who sat by our side."

"That's not really healing," she said.

"You're wrong," he told her. "It's the truest form of healing, because the desire comes from your heart. There's only one difference between a woman like Char, who's renowned for her healing touch, and a woman like you. Your aquis ability allows you to speed up the natural healing process by manipulating the substance that makes up our bodies; flesh, bone, blood."

"Your mom was an aquis wielder," Shashara pointed out, "but she couldn't heal."

"That's my point," Set said. "Mom could wield aquis, but she didn't have a healer's heart. She used her ability for hurting people, not helping them. It takes both, Shashara, to become what you are."

"Huh," she mumbled, then said, "You're wrong about one thing though. Gaining an aquis ability, discovering that I have the ability to take away peoples' hurts, Set... it has changed my life in an incredible way."

"But not in the kind of way that can break a world," he said to make his point.

"True," she admitted, unable to deny it. "Then again, Tristan wasn't born with his power. It was forced on him."

"I was born with this power," he said, diverting his gaze, "but what I've become with it..." His visage turned to one of sorrow. "I chose this." Holding out his right arm, their eyes journeyed up the red lines, to the yellow arcs near his shoulder, before finding each other again.

"You did what you had to," she said.

"And yet, the result is the same," he countered.

"So that's what has you all up in your head instead of talking to me," she said, laying her palms flat on his chest. "You're concerned that eventually, your power will become as unlimited as your brother's, and that scares you?" To lighten the moment, she smiled up at him and said, "I don't think you can make yourself an Angeli." Her smile slipped at his grave expression.

"The only limitation I have is reach," Set told her, "and the Angeli are never far."

The wind whipping off the oceanus added a chilling weight to his words. "You wouldn't do that," she said, but it sounded as much a threat as a statement of fact.

"No," he assured her, leaning in to quickly kiss her lips. He moved ahead of her and added, "But I could."

"Do you know what else that means?" she pressed, refusing to be afraid of the guy she loved.

"What?" he asked over his shoulder.

"It means if the Angeli fail…" She caught his hand. "You won't."

Turning to face her, he said, "The gods of Earth are immortal, Shashara, and I'm not. I can hurt them with the abilities I wield, but I can't take their power unless I touch them."

Furrows wrinkled the delicate skin between her eyes., "But," she protested, "that's not true." She knew that he wanted to argue by the way he worked his jaw, and it made her laugh. "Do you remember the portal you conjured to Exterius Antro? The one you backed stepped through? You dropped three men," she continued when he seemed to draw a blank.

Ending his teasing before he upset her, he said, "Of course, I remember. You threatened to kill me if I ever pulled a stunt like that again. I knew I loved you then." He grinned.

Rolling her eyes, she said, "My point is, you drained three men without touching them. You didn't kill them, so you didn't keep their abilities, but…"

"You're right," he said and then fell silent. His starry gaze danced and bounced while he pulled from the knowledge locked in his head. "How did I do it? I know how to do it. Dung pile," he cursed. "Am I afraid to do it? Can I control it? I can control it. Yeah. Yeah, okay." He blinked and refocused. "Shashara, I love you! Do you know how much it would help our cause if I could master this ability?"

Caught up in his joy, she said, "I do," and laughed.

"Come on." He grabbed her hand and took off for the Fera guard standing post. "Good morning," he greeted.

"Good morning, sir." The guard nodded to Shashara. "Ma'am."

"What's your name?" Set asked, trying to pay attention to the reply coming out of the man's wolfish muzzle while checking over the white strength marks running through his thick, black fur.

"Jayson, sir, but my friends call me Jay."

"Jay… Can I call you Jay?"

"Of course, sir."

"Well, Jay," Set said, "I need to ask a favor."

"There's no need to ask, sir," Jay told him. "Just give the order and it will be done."

Beginning to get the picture, Shashara pressed her lips together and hoped Jay had the good sense to tell Set to go fly a kite. She did say, however, "Jay, you should probably hear him out before you jump in with both feet. Trust me."

"The problem is," Set began, dropping an arm across the older man's broader shoulders, "I'm not like you. I'm not big and strong and…Wow, just wow. How much would you say that sword at your hip weighs?"

"Sir?" Jay gulped.

"I could never wield a sword so heavy," Set told him. "My power is not held in my strength but in my mind, and up until a few moments ago, I thought I had to touch my enemy to drain him."

Jay reacted by sidestepping Set's arm, stumbling in his haste to back away. He stuttered, "Sir?"

Set, missing the man's fear, told him, "Shashara just had this great idea."

"Sorry." Shashara winced when Jay turned his accusatory eyes her way.

"I want to see if I can drain from people that I'm not touching," Set explained, "through the terra that I am touching. Does that make sense?"

Jay was half-turned and tensed to bolt. "Sir," he questioned, "what have I done to wrong you? Punish me if you must, but please... Please don't take my strength. Without it..."

"Oh, hey, no," Set tried to explain, moving forward with an outreached hand, "I wasn't going to... "

It was more than the Fera could take. Instinct made him draw his sword; common sense made him drop it and run.

As they stared at Jay's departing back, Shashara nudged the side of Set's shoulder with her own and asked, "What did you expect?"

"I know." Set sighed, turning back the way they'd come. "People are born with their gifts. It's a part of who they are, at least until I come along and take it."

"You're being too hard on yourself," Shashara soothed.

"Am I?" he snapped. "Sorry," he said right after. "I'm a leech, Shashara, so much so that, even with all the abilities I possess, I'm still asking others to give up theirs."

"But not," she told him, capturing his cheeks in her palms and forcing him to look at her, "for your gain."

Taking a deep breath, he held it for a moment before

releasing it.

"You good?"

"Yeah," he told her. "I'm okay."

"Good," she said, slowly backing away.

"Where are you going?" he asked, delighting in the mischief that stared back at him.

With distance between them, she grinned and said, "You can touch me all you want…from over there."

Set threw back his head and laughed. "Challenge accepted." Then the two of them began to play with the energy between them.

XXIX

A Father's Blessing

Triton stepped out of his cabin, onto the main deck, and headed towards the prow. Though the schooner hadn't lifted its anchor in over a season, he was still the captain of this ship, and his day would begin at the helm.

Davad was already there.

Glancing over, he greeted, "Good morning," as Triton joined him at the rail overlooking the bowsprit.

"Morning," Triton said. "You been here all night?" he asked, noting Davad's disheveled appearance and puffy eyes.

"I don't remember the last time I really slept," Davad shrugged, "but the sway of the ship at least calms me down. I can breathe here. I can think."

"Perhaps it's the thinking keeping you awake," Triton suggested.

"You know what they say." Davad gave a halfhearted grin. "Ignorance is bliss. Wow," he said, "just look at that."

The red suns had crested the distant horizon, setting Superi's sky on fire and turning the dark waters of the oceanus into shimmering glass. "Despite all the changes the war with Earth will bring, is it odd that I find comfort in knowing this?" With a sweeping gesture, he explained, "The suns will rise every dawn, whether I'm around to see it or not."

"Is that what has you concerned, boy?" Triton asked. "What will happen once the war has ended?"

"Aren't you?" Davad countered.

"War is always the same," Triton sighed. "Rulers plot, people die, and the victor claims the right to write history."

"And what of the conquered?" Davad asked. "What happens to us if we lose? What if we can't break the curses, or what if they curse us again, or…"

"Davad…" Triton's tone stopped his rambling. "Win or lose, this war is coming. If you face it with fear or fight it with hesitation, you are dead before you ever step onto the field. You are no coward, son. Where is this coming from?"

A delicate sneeze on a ship full of men turned them both towards the woman strutting across the deck in their direction. Her striking red hair made the suns blush in envy, and her pale, porcelain skin was perfection to behold. The long, emerald-green skirt she wore hung from a slender waist, gently caressing her flaring hips before settling around her tiny, booted feet. The white, sleeveless blouse she wore, the delicate pearl buttons straining over her bosom, was enough to drive a man to distraction.

Before she could reach them, Davad said, "It is not the fight I fear. It's dying before I ever get to live. And on that note…" He grinned. "I think I'm going to go ask that slice of life if she wants to share some breakfast."

Giving him a shove to get him moving, Triton chuckled and said, "That's the first intelligent thing you've said in days."

Wiggling his eyebrows at Triton, Davad turned to the yellow-eyed beauty and jumped from the prow to the main deck before she could reach the ladder. "Hey there, gorgeous," he greeted. "You hungry?"

"It's too early," she said, "but I could use a cup of coffee."

"Coffee it is."

Disembarking the ship, Skylar slipped her arm through Davad's and allowed herself to be escorted down the dock, towards the wide, beaten-down path that would carry them back to town.

"I see you still have your escort," Davad teased, knowing how much she hated supervision. "Lishous is a good man. You just have to give him a chance."

Her arched brow and upturned chin told him what she thought about that, but she gave it voice anyway. "He doesn't act like a guard. He acts like a big brother and it's infuriating. I've had absolutely no fun since Anliac forced him on me."

Glancing over his shoulder at Lishous, he grinned like a fool when his friend shot him a wink and mouthed, *I've got you.* Facing forward, he'd nearly walked into Anliac and her dad.

Holding out her hand to stop Davad's forward progress, she smiled at his impish expression and said, "Good morning, you two. You're both up early."

"I couldn't sleep," Davad told her.

"Nor could I," Skylar added. "Hammy snores like a pig with clogged nostrils."

"We're going for coffee," Davad said, immediately wincing and wanting to take it back.

"Would you like to join us?" Skylar invited.

Anliac might have missed it, but Montilis hadn't, so before Anliac could accept, he replied, "Thank you, but it's rare for me to find moments alone with my daughter, and I intend to take full advantage of this one."

"Suit yourself," Skylar said. She bowed her arm and waited for Davad to take it. "I believe you promised me coffee?"

Davad rolled his eyes, but he looped his arm through hers anyway. "You're so demanding."

Nudging him, Skylar teased, "You know you like it."

Davad tripped.

Anliac laughed.

Davad glared back at her, but when he looked again at Skylar, he was beaming.

"They would make a good couple," Anliac stated. "Don't you think?"

"Triton thinks so." Montilis grinned. "It's a part of his plan."

"What does that mean?" she asked.

Fighting a grin, he said, "It doesn't matter. Tell me about you. And I don't want to hear about the war with Earth, or mention of gods, or Superian politics. I want to hear about *you*."

Taking a seat on one the benches spread along the docks,

Montilis wrapped his arm around the back of her shoulders. Leaning into him, Anliac sighed. "If you take all of that away, Dad, I'm not sure what's left to talk about. We've dealt with constant conflict for so many seasons now that I cannot recall what triviality looks like."

"Triviality?"

She heard the disappointment in his tone, but that's how she felt. "Life, love, the future… What's the point, really, when we don't know if we'll survive tomorrow?"

"Tomorrow is the reason you fight today, little one," he told her, holding her for a moment without speaking. "My life has been a constant example of teaching you how to fight, but what has my life taught you of love?"

"Are you kidding me?" she exclaimed, blinking back tears. "You taught how me how to fight for love. I am who I am because of you."

Briskly rubbing the outside of her shoulder with his hand, he decided to change the subject before he was crying himself. "Tell me something. If the war was behind us and peace had settled on Superi, what would your life look like?"

She was not quick to answer. "I used to think I would follow in your footsteps and protect our city and our people, but now I think my life is here in Pisces Stragulum. I would see it grow and prosper. I would see the changes that we've begun here spread forth and sweep across our world, making it a better place for the children I'll one day leave behind."

"I've heard rumors of babies…of the Angeli variety," he teased. "Which leads me to my next question. "What about you and Tristan?"

"First off," she giggled, "I heard you started that rumor.

Though, I've yet to discover your intent." Sitting upright, she twisted on the bench to face him. "Are you trying to scare him off, or are you just dropping hints?"

"Which would you prefer it to be?"

At this, Anliac laughed outright and said, "Tristan and I are good, Dad. You don't need to worry."

"Are you sure?" he pushed.

"If you have something to say," she said, amused by her father's unusual mood, "you should say it."

Drying his palms on the sides of his trousers, he cleared his throat before forming his reply. "Okay," he said. "In truth, there are times I worry that the two of you are together out of obligation and not choice."

She turned to stare at the ships at port. "I remember the first time I saw Tristan. He was shrouded in the most brilliant light, and he had the man who'd threatened me by the neck." Twinging, she said, "I'd never seen a head pop off a body before, and the sight of him terrified me, but Dad…" She looked up at him. "I'd never felt so safe. When I thought you'd abandoned me, and Malstar was chasing me, and…"

Montilis's eyes slid closed, and his head dropped forward under the onslaught of his guilt. "I'm so sorry," he whispered.

"I forgave you a long time ago," she told him. "I've even forgiven Malstar, because I understand that, like you, he did what he thought he had to. Dad, that's all any of us can do. And—" she shrugged— "as far as Tristan is concerned, he made me his family long before we became a couple, and had I never been made an Angeli, I would choose him still."

With a slight tremble to his hand, he reached and cupped

her cheek. "I wish your mother were alive to see you, Anliac... to see all that you've overcome, to see all that you've accomplished, to see the confident, beautiful woman you've grown into."

Anliac's smile was soft. "I wish I could have known her."

"Even now, you have her beauty," Montilis said, "and there are times when you move or speak, and for a moment, I see the two of you as one. Her heart, like yours, was so pure."

"I suppose that means I get my attitude and temper from you then," she quipped, but her father's mood would not be lightened.

"It is the fear of every parent who serves... that they will leave their children behind should battle claim them," Montilis told her. "You feel it too, and your children have yet to be born. Knowing Jagarid would be there to look after you and your mother eased that fear, but then I lost them both. I lost you..." He paused to collect himself. "And when I found you again, you were surrounded by danger. I trust that Tristan can keep you alive, if anyone can, but I want you with a man who can keep your heart alive as well."

Catching the tail end of their conversation, Tristan sauntered up and said, "That's my job. Seriously, Montilis, what does a man have to do to prove he loves a woman? Propose?"

Riker chortled, "Who are you kidding?" He moseyed over, sipping his coffee from a piping tin cup. "You lack the breeding to even know where to begin."

"I don't care what his lineage is," Anliac stated, standing to join Tristan. "He's of a royal house now."

Tristan had to lock down his flight response to her approach, and his eyes grew wider by the moment.

"Breeding or not," Montilis stated, "the proposal has been made."

When Anliac's arms slid around his waist, Tristan panicked. "Wait...I wasn't... I didn't... I mean..."

"Are you withdrawing your proposal to marry my daughter?" Montilis asked, his arms crossing his chest. He stood and planted his feet like stone. "Because if that's the case, boy, I'd like to hear your reason for it."

"Of course, I want to marry her," Tristan stammered, "but..."

"You do?" A blushing glow encapsulated Anliac's visage.

"Huh..." Tristan stalled.

"Do you think it's that easy?" Riker tipped back his chin, just so he could stare down the end of his nose at Tristan. "There are protocols to follow, ceremonies to plan, announcements to be made. But why am I telling you all of this? You'll never gain her father's permission, and without it..." He shrugged it off.

"Permission?" Tristan's voice rose in pitch so fast, his voice broke.

"Oh," Montilis snapped, "now you want to ask? It's too late." He flung out one of his hands. "I've already been offended."

"Dad..." Anliac cringed into Tristan. "Leave him alone."

Montilis ignored her; he was having far too much fun to turn back now. But it was hard to hold a straight face while staring past Tristan, at the ones Riker was making behind the poor boy's back. "Do you think you are worthy of my daughter? Why? Because you're an Angeli? You may have been created into something, boy, but you come from common stock."

Seeing shadows of pain, reminiscent of that caused by the cruelty of others who'd judged him unworthy, Anliac stated. "Okay, that's enough."

"It's okay," Tristan told her as his shoulders sagged.

"No, it's not."

"I wasn't asking permission," Tristan said to Montilis, "but when the time comes—and it will—I'll be sure to check with Riker about proper protocol. And," he rushed to say before he could be cut off, "no. I am not worthy of her. I am a beast compared to her beauty, and my heart is ice compared to her warmth. Her mind marks me a fool, and I feel a coward when faced with her courage. But know this," he insisted. "I would die for her, and I will spend what life I have loving her. Now," he stated, standing taller and returning Montilis's hard stare, "if that is not enough to please a father, then I will be content with your displeasure."

Riker's burst of laughter sparked Montilis's own.

Tristan turned to see Riker laughing behind him. "Glad I could amuse you," Tristan snipped at their mockery.

"I'm sorry, son," Montilis said, "but…You should have seen your face." And then he was laughing again.

"Priceless," Riker followed up. "Good answer, though."

Montilis's visage changed from belly-rolling humor to an indignant scowl. Brows furrowed, he said, "I don't think so."

"I don't imagine you would," Riker said, his laughter building again. "It sounds a whole lot like what you told Nunbia when he thought to stop your marriage."

"Whatever," Montilis stated, grinning. "Shut up."

They all noted the portal, opening south of the dock, but thought nothing of it until the Nox soldier coming through it turned out to be the one who closed it.

"That's interesting," Riker said. "It's not often that a gate-maker puts on a soldier's uniform. Did you approve that?" he asked Montilis.

"Of course not," he replied. "We need to find the captain responsible for wasting the ability of an enlisted gate-maker and pull his rank. Someone that stupid shouldn't lead."

Spotting them, the man came at a dead run. "Sirs," he said, reaching them. Placing hand to heart, he dipped his head and waited for permission to speak further.

Riker was the one to grant it. "Speak," he said.

"Thank you, sir," the soldier said, falling into an easier stance. "I've been sent with news. There's been an uprising."

"Great," Tristan stated, "and here I thought the Nox was the one race we didn't have to worry about."

Terse, Riker responded, "You don't. This is a Nox problem." To the soldier, he said, "Give me the details."

"Sir." The man nodded and then said, "The Noble Houses of Palus Regia have freed Magistrate Rayner."

Montilis's face turned an angry red, and his hands balled into tight fists at his sides.

"They are trying to get him out of the city, and the Nobles have ordered their standing armies to kill every Regia Aquam Guard who gets in their way. Sirs," the soldier said, "with both of you here, our captains fear the repercussions of engaging the highborn. Palus Regia needs a general."

"Get another portal open, soldier," Anliac said. "We're

coming back with you."

"No, Anliac." Riker stated. "Your life is far too valuable to risk in an uprising. And Tristan…" Lines of stress appeared around his eyes and mouth. "I wouldn't presume to give you orders, but for peace's sake, do not treat this news as an act of aggression against Superi's cause, or against the House of Angeli. Trust me to handle this."

"I've no doubt you'll handle it," Tristan told him. "It's in whose interest that concerns me." When Riker nodded, Tristan said, "Send word quickly, General."

"Understood," Riker said. Gesturing for the soldier to follow, he spoke to Montilis as they made their way to the portal site, "Gather the units we have stationed here, and meet me in Palus Regia."

"If Rayner's not dead by the time I get there," Montilis said through gritted teeth, "I'm going to kill him."

"Yeah, well, it's not just Rayner we have to contend with. It's…" Riker began, but then pivoted around when Montilis yelped, appearing to fall backward. "What are you doing?"

Before the question was fully out of his mouth, the gate-maker in soldier's clothes reopened the poral and dragged Montilis through it, leaving Riker behind. Lunging for the center of the portal, as one would plunge into water, it closed too fast. Riker ate dirt instead.

"Son of a…"

Tristan and Anliac were there before Riker could gain his feet.

"What just happened?" Anliac asked as Tristan helped the other man up.

"If I didn't know any better," Riker fumed, "I'd say the

Noble Houses of Palus Regia just kidnapped your father."

"What do we do?"

"Where are you going?" Tristan asked Riker as the man stormed towards town.

"I'm gathering my men," Riker answered without turning, "and then I'm going for Montilis. Find Set," he barked.

Anliac stammered in her haste to tell him, "He's up the coast with Shashara." She was already running.

It wasn't fast enough. Tristan swept her into his arms and ran.

"Set!" She yelled a moment later when Tristan set her down again.

Scrambling from the tent with Shashara right behind him, Set exited in a panic. "What? What's happened?"

"Open a gateway to Palus Regia," Anliac told him. "Now, Set," she snapped when he didn't move fast enough.

Shashara moved to try and comfort Anliac, only to be roughly shoved aside. Set warned, "Keep your hands off her," then told Tristan, "Tell me what's going on."

Physically taking hold of Anliac to keep her from striking out against Set's threat, Tristan answered, "The Noble Houses have rebelled against the Regia Aquam Guard. They've turned their armies against them, and they've freed Rayner. Riker thinks the Noble Houses have taken him."

"Taken who?"

"Montilis."

Shashara's hand flew to her mouth as her eyes flew to Anliac.

"What makes him think that?" Set asked, his visage changing as his anger took root.

"We witnessed a gate-maker, dressed as a soldier, yank him through a gateway," Anliac told him, her voice under tight restraint.

Set angled away from them and made his way to the water's edge.

"Are you not hearing me?" Anliac screeched. "They've taken my dad. Open the blasted gateway, Set."

"I am," he said, but his voice was no longer his own.

With his arms at his sides, he spread his fingers. The terra surrounding him gave up its energy in a hot burst that turned the sand to glass. He lifted his arms, and the oceanus lapped its waves over his feet, as if in adoration, before it released its energy to his command. Beautifully, masterfully, Set manipulated the gathered energy into an expanding gateway with marveling speed.

The image beyond revealed Montilis's house. It also revealed the level of death that had visited there. Anliac was the first to move towards it, but Tristan was the first to enter. After Set was through, he closed the portal to find that Shashara had followed.

Anliac launched herself up the front porch steps and rushed into her childhood home through a busted door. Her boots clicked back and forth across the red, hardwood floor, changing to solid thuds as she hit the stairs.

"Let her go," Set told Tristan when he tried to go inside. "Tristan," he said when his brother moved to ignore him, "she will not welcome you. Leave her be."

The lilting melody of the wooden wind chimes dangling from the corners of the porch heightened their awareness of the dead bodies that lay scattered about the manicured lawn as they waited for Anliac to return.

She didn't make them wait long, however. The woman that entered was not the same one who emerged. Her eyes were glowing, as were her marks, but it was the edge to her voice that spoke of how close she was to breaking.

"They're all dead," she told them as tears she wasn't aware of shedding slid in steady streams down her cheeks. "Henry," she choked out, "his throat was slit. Selene, she… And Senome…"

Tristan's arms opened. He needed them around her, to comfort her, but he felt her use gravity to push him back.

"No!" she shouted. "Don't…Don't touch me."

"Anliac," Tristan said. "You need to listen to me. We're going to find the ones responsible for this, but you need to calm down. Right now, it's about finding your dad."

"HAVE YOU NO HONOR?"

There was a moment of pause, then Set scooped Shasha-ra into his arms, and he and Tristan chased after a daughter bent on retribution.

XXX

Betrayal

Montilis saw nothing but the gateway as he stumbled
backwards through it. Twisting his body, he turned to con-
front the soldier who'd dare to put his hands on a general.
When his mind caught up with what his eyes had seen, the
gateway was closed, and he was furious at the revealed betrayal.

With one fist reared back to knock the head off the
gate-maker, he grabbed a handful of the man's shirt with the
other and dragged him into his fist. As the gate-maker's eyes
rolled back in his head, his knees buckling, Montilis turned
to take in his surroundings.

The commotion of Montilis's entry had grabbed the
attention of the noblemen, but he was too busy counting the
dead bodies, which littered the cobblestoned street between
him and his kinsmen, to notice. The Aquam line, down to
distant cousins, had been corralled and bound. From their
condition, they'd suffered greatly for the blood they carried.

———
351

Sinpine was among them.

"How nice that you could join us, Montilis," Rayner said. "I would address you by title, but you are no longer a general of Palus Regia."

Yongur and Nunbia snickered, as did a boy about Set's age, whom Montilis had never seen.

Word of his imminent arrival had spread like wildfire through Palus Regia, and his men were ripping their way through the armies of the Ruling Houses to reach him. From beyond the two-storied buildings lining either side of the street, he heard the clash of steel on steel, the screams of the dying, and the victory cries of those who'd delivered the blow.

"I was never the General of Palus Regia," Montilis countered, his hard stare shattering Rayner's grin, "but I will always be the General of the Regia Aquam Guard."

From across the street, a man on his knees locked eyes with his general. Squaring his shoulders, his voice rang out, "HOORAH!"

A man wearing the signet of another house stepped forward with a curved, wooden bow, and blood sprayed across a woman's face when he cracked open her husband's skull. Screaming when she saw the bow rise again, she yanked their son beneath her to spare him pain. When the bow struck across her spine, the cord snapped, and her paralyzed body pinned her boy to the bloodied street.

"HAVE YOU NO HONOR?" Montilis bellowed.

"Have you?" Rayner countered. "Your malcontent for Palus Regia has evolved into a poisonous deceit that threatens everything we Nox are. You would make us subservient to the House of Angeli, and knowing that I would thwart you, you locked me up. I warned you that you would pay for it, Montilis, and the day of reckoning has come."

His men were too far away, and it would take time for Riker to gather the forces in Pisces Stragulum. He would go down fighting, but he was going to die, and so he offered his last words to his people.

"Rayner's right," he announced. "There will be a reckoning, and these traitors will find no mercy in the Angelis' avenging wrath."

Hands bound, his kin rose, prepared to die with their Patriarch. They attacked the nobles' guards and chaos ensued.

"Kill him," Nunbia shouted. "Kill them all!"

Montilis advanced, keeping his eyes on everyone… everyone except the boy.

A spear, stolen from a dead soldier's grasp, was hefted and thrown. Montilis caught the movement late, but he watched it leave the boy's hand and tracked its trajectory. Narrowly, he leaned to the side and avoided its strike. Twisting his torso mid-lean, he looked back, hoping to see the spear take the life of the gate-maker behind him. Instead, the spear disappeared into a small portal. Keeping a sideward stance, trying to make his body as small a target as possible, his head turned again towards the gathered mob, where another portal now blocked his view.

He saw the spear reemerge, and he grasped for the aquis held in the air around them to throw up a shield, but there was nothing to grab. Its wide, tear-shaped blade entered his side, between his ribs, and came out of the other in a gory burst.

"NO!"

He heard his daughter's scream, and it was beautiful. For a moment, as his body went numb and his heart slowed, he feared his final fall, but he embraced death in the arms of his little Angeli.

"Daddy…no," Anliac cried, sinking to her knees to gently lay him down. "Don't leave me," her voice shattered, "please."

"This is bad," Set said. "Really bad."

"Not yet," Anliac said, engorged with a rage-induced power brought to life by her grief.

The nobles, the soldiers on both sides, the remnants of her kin watched in horror the rise of their destruction.

"Get Shashara out of here," Tristan demanded. "Now!"

Set had never opened a gateway so fast. The influx of energy ripped a scream from his throat, but he grabbed ahold of Shashara and leapt through. They did not enter alone.

In a vain attempt to save themselves, a handful of their enemies made the mistake of following them. Though they ran right into Riker, it was Set who dropped them where they stood, mastering a new skill.

"Let's move," Riker commanded, starting his men forward.

"No," Set said, backing towards the gateway. "Anliac has it covered."

"What?"

Riker never got his answer.

Set stepped back through and shut the way behind him.

Anliac, hovered just above the terra, her hair wild, the markings on her flesh flowing like liquid gold. She pinned the gate-maker with the light exuding from her yellow eyes. Her hands never moved to give direction, but the ground opened beneath the man. His screams could be heard even after he disappeared.

Jaw dropping, Set said, "Superi help us all," as the gathered broke and ran.

She used the piercing pitch of her Angeli voice like a weapon. She screamed and so did they, yet they dared not stop, so they covered their bleeding ears and stumbled towards a safety she'd never let them find.

The ground shook until the whole of Palus Regia quaked. Buildings toppled. Houses collapsed. The swamp began to boil and the trees there caught fire. The terra split into a spiderweb of trapping fingers filled with lava. The cobblestoned streets, the granite statues, and the marble benches all gave way to the molten touch.

And then Anliac began to move.

"Tristan!" Set shouted to be heard above the noise. He pointed to Montilis's body, perched precariously on the edge of a chasm.

Running like Anliac's heart depended on it, because it did, Tristan caught Montilis just has he would have slipped into the depths of oblivion. He darted beyond the swamp, east of the city's edge, to the clearing, where he placed the body to keep it safe.

He was gone for a moment, but when he returned, Set had joined the slaughter. With Anliac floating above him and Set walking across lava and land alike with equal ease, they laid waste to the city.

While Anliac used the molten rock to spin out burning

blades that sliced her targets to shreds, cauterizing their wounds long enough for them to know she'd killed them, Set used ignis to simply aim and fire.

What structures did not fall to the rolling terra fell at the destructive whim of the wielders, and each person that fled from the collapse met a violent end. Encountering larger groups, huge spheres of boiling water were cast from Anliac's right hand, creating explosions that blew apart whatever they touched as she continued the barrage of burning blades.

The air, hot enough to blister the skin, sent Rayner scampering from his hiding place to bolt south for the coast.

Set prepared to strike him down, but Yongur's position behind them was betrayed by his emotions. The fire meant for the magistrate melted the flesh from Yongur's bones like an animal starved.

Anliac screamed.

"What?" Set gasped, willing to kill anyone she wanted if she'd silence the pain. She was beyond caring, so he tracked her stare back to Rayner.

Set's ability had to work overtime to keep his footing sure when Anliac gouged a hole from the terra, lava and all, and attempted to heave it upon Rayner's head. But even she had her limits, and Rayner was beyond her reach.

Closing his eyes, Set reached out with one hand held high and one held low. He reversed the polarity of the ground beneath Rayner's feet, effectively hold him prisoner, while activating a charge of energy in the sky. The result was a catastrophic lightning bolt that turned Rayner into pink mist.

Thankful that he could heal on the go, Tristan sucked back the pain of burns, cuts, and bruises as he hurdled the obstacles between him and the two he loved more than life. "Enough!" he yelled, his own Angeli voice carrying the weight of his command. Seeing it would take more to get through to Anliac, he focused on his brother. "Set," he said, dodging the water explosive Anliac tossed at his head for interfering, "who are you right now?"

Set fell behind as Anliac continued forward, his advance stalled by Tristan's question. "She's in so much pain," he said.

And that is when Tristan noticed the tears pouring down Set's cheeks.

"There's so much pain," Set cried out again. "The fear… it hurts, Tristan. She hurts."

Encapsulated in a dangerous void, Anliac thought she was beyond emotion, but when she heard the agony in Set's words, she lowered to the ground. The sight of him, doubled over and holding his chest, broke through the void.

"I'm sorry, but the nobles… they have to die."

"But you're not just killing the nobles, Anliac," Tristan told her while the semblance of clarity remained. "You're killing innocents."

Set came out of it first. "Oh, Anliac, what have we done?" he asked as he took in the carnage they'd wrought.

"What we had to," she replied, though her marks were fading, and the light had gone from her eyes. "Right?"

The screams of Palus Regia, the smoke, the stench of blood—Set shook his head. "We're monsters."

Anliac blinked and then she panicked. "Dad? Dad!"

Tristan tried to tell her that her father's body was safe, but it had to keep until he caught back up with her. "You're okay," he told her before she could panic over his absence. "I put him somewhere safe."

"No," another voice said. "You didn't."

"Kervan?" Set asked at the same time that Anliac hissed, "Sinpine."

Tristan noticed the general's stripe, ripped from Montilis's uniform, clenched in Sinpine's hand. "What did you do?" he asked.

"Let us go," Kervan said, "and we'll send word of where we left his charred remains."

Anliac's response was swift. She grabbed ahold of each of Kervan's limbs with a thick rope of gravity and pulled, leaving his torso and head to drop at Sinpine's feet.

"We didn't burn him," Sinpine confessed, hitting his knees, as Kervan bled out at his side. "I swear it. We only meant to escape, but the Regia Aquam Guard has regrouped in the clearing beyond the swamps. They hadn't found Montilis yet, and so when we did, we took this," he said, holding up the stripe, "to convince you to let us go."

She closed her eyes to block the image of her father's stripe in a traitor's hands. "You are the one who conspired with Inabeth to have me turned over to the tower."

Tristan stiffened at the news. He'd never been given names, but Anliac wasn't finished.

"You are the one who betrayed your patriarch with his wife," she said. "You have betrayed your general unto his death. There is no escape for you, but there will be pain."

Neither Set nor Tristan tried to stop her.

Blurring forward, she came up behind her traitorous cousin and encased him in cast of clay to hold him still. She didn't want to rush this. She cradled the base of his neck in the curve between her finger and thumb, while reaching around with her right hand to cup his forehead in her palm.

"Please," Sinpine wept, "don't kill me. I'm sorry. I'm sorry he's dead."

Whatever else he might have said was cut off when Anliac began to apply a slow and building pressure to both of her hands. When his throat came through his neck, she crumpled the clay and let him fall. Bending, she rifled through the dust to find what he had stolen. Ignoring the sound of Set vomiting, she stood in search of Tristan.

"Take me to him," she commanded. When he came to collect her, she let herself be carried.

Set met them in the clearing, where the Regia Aquam Guard stood watch over their General's body; some in tears, some in fury, but all in sorrow. Anliac sank to the ground beside her father and leaned on her hip, bracing her weight on one flattened palm. Caressing flesh that was already turning grey, she cried with them.

Seven captains made a wall of muscles and armor; as a unit, they came forward, and as a unit, they went to knee. One spoke, "We have failed, and so we submit ourselves to you for punishment."

His words broke her. "I have killed as many of our people today as the nobles. I have destroyed the city my father…" She covered her mouth with her hand. Letting it fall, she stood to face the captains. "I submit myself to you."

"Hey, now," Tristan stated, moving closer. The flare of his eyes suggested that the soldiers not go that route.

"Be at ease, Angeli," the captain said to Tristan. "She did

what we failed to do. If we lost men as a result of that failing, so be it. That is our burden. And as to the civilians…" The captain's tone was filled with disdain. "They did not rally. They cowered. Only the young will be mourned."

Anliac had said what she'd needed to say. The moment the captains had denied her submission, she'd returned to her father. "Take me home," she whispered. "Please." She looked to Set. "I want to go home."

As Set opened the gateway, she lifted her father into her arms and stood, staring beyond the opening into Riker's shattered face.

XXXI

Daddy's Girl

$\mathbf{R}$iker was a man accustomed to death, but the sight of Montilis's limp form hanging in Anliac's arms was almost more than he could take. All that held him together was the abject sorrow in the eyes of his closest friend's daughter. Her pain got his feet to moving, and as he crossed through the gateway, his men followed.

Their ranks swelling, the Regia Aquam Guard were bombarded with questions as the devastation of Palus Regia registered. Was it over? Was it the Mortalis? Did the gods of Earth attack again?"

Having no answers to give them, Riker didn't stop until he stood before Anliac. Reaching her, he didn't ask permission before he shifted the burden she carried into his own care and said, "He is home, Anliac."

Exhausted, she didn't object. "Where are you taking him?"

Surveying the destruction of his city and fighting the violence the view invoked, Riker nodded towards an apothecary that had survived. "I'll leave soldiers to guard the door until arrangements for his burial have been made," he said, "and then we need to talk."

If Anliac saw the brief flare of fury that escaped Riker's stare to hit her head-on, she hid it well. Her only reaction came when Riker turned to take her father away. Hot tears washed down her grime-coated cheeks, and her stomach churned.

Tristan's arms came around her, offering her the support she so badly needed. "You're okay," he told her as she breathed through the nausea of exhaustion mixed with sorrow.

"Ma'am," Shashara asked, approaching an elderly, white-haired woman who was fidgeting in the peripheral, "are you hurt? Do you need help?"

With her gaze drawn by Shashara's question, Anliac took Tristan's hand and led them over. "I know you," Anliac said as the old woman tottered, nearly toppling, when she attempted to bow.

"Easy." Shashara was quick to steady the other woman.

Anliac continued, "You are of my father's House."

Tugging her green linen dress to the side, the woman bared the signet branded into the front of her shoulder. "I was first brought into the House of Aquam by your mother." Worrying her hands together, she confessed, "I heard them, those men, breaking into our home. I was in the kitchen." Her wrinkled face squished in regret. "I hid in the cupboard," she said, but then, her spine stiffening, she stated, "I'm a Nox. I should have fought for those they slaughtered.

I should have died with my House…" Crumpled in tears and relying on Shashara to keep her upright, she told them, "Thank you. Thank you both for stopping those who did all of this."

"The House of Aquam is ended," Anliac said, her voice breaking, "but it was not the ruling houses that laid waste to the city we both love. It was me."

Stepping away from Shashara's touch, the woman took on a stoic visage and said, "Then you are a traitor," before she turned her back and walked away.

Anliac hit her knees.

Tristan reached for her, but Set, who'd gone with Riker to see Montilis settled, called out for him.

Shashara, concerned by the look on Set's face, nonetheless knelt in front of Anliac to console her friend. Forehead to forehead, the two women talked in whispers of pushing through the loss of a parent. It was a loss they all knew. It was the loss that bound them as family.

Turning away from Anliac, though her hearing made the action pointless, Set went up on his toes and, in a hushed tone, said, "Riker's a mess. His men can't see him like this. And Tristan, word of what she and I have done is spreading. She can't stay out in the open. She's a target now, and she's too distracted to defend herself."

"Who's targeting her?" Tristan asked as he crouched to collect her.

"The list is too long, brother," Set muttered. Shashara came to stand beside him.

Anliac came to her feet when Tristan tugged at her hand. She stepped to his body when he pulled her close to use himself as a shield, but she was numb. She didn't really care if she lived or died.

And Set knew it, so he said, "Watch her."

"I'll go with her," Shashara volunteered, but Set countered.

"No," he told her. "You're a healer now and…" He paused to rephrase his words, but seeing that Anliac wasn't tracking much, he said, "You are needed."

"Come on, Anliac," Tristan said with a gentle nudge to get her going. "Let us get you somewhere safe."

"I want to be with my father."

"Okay," he cajoled. "Let's go do that."

"Where do I go?" Shashara asked.

"I have no idea," Set confessed. "The city is in chaos and disorder reigns. We need to correct that."

"How?"

Using his aer ability to condense and amplify his words, he turned to the amassed soldiers and commanded, "Captains, report." Forward they came.

"Sir," one of the men stated, "what are our orders?"

"I don't care how you do it," Set told them, "but break these soldiers into units. I want the surviving nobles rounded up, and I want their armies brought under control. Confine both to their House grounds until Riker decides what he wants done with them. More urgently, we've got people trapped throughout the city, many of them hurt, so we need them rescued and brought to the healers."

"And I need to know where to find them," Shashara interjected.

"I'll see you to them myself, ma'am," one of the other

men spoke. "If you would follow me?"

"Take some of the soldiers with you," Set declared. "Help the healers where you can. And Captain, I hold you responsible for keeping her safe."

"Sir." He nodded, then Set was alone to direct the Guard.

"I want every terra wielder you've got," he ordered, "front and center and right now." A handful came forward, and none of them were ranked higher than a level two. To the captains, he said, "You have your orders."

"Sir," came their chorused reply. Orders were flying before they'd fully turned around.

The five wielders that stood before him were terrified, so much so that Set wasn't sure where his fear began and where theirs took over. Yet, he knew that their terror was about to get worse and braced for it.

"You know what I am and you're afraid of it," Set stated, "but I need you to get over that. I'm responsible for much of the destruction you see, and I would set some of that right, but I can't do it alone."

One of the wielder's downed his head to hide his incredulity, but Set felt it. "I'm not your general, and I'm not your captain, so I cannot rightly give you orders. I do, however, need your help."

Half-expecting them to cut and run, his relief was tremendous when their resolve firmed. One said, "What do you need us to do?"

"Follow my lead," Set replied as weight lifted from his heavy heart. "If I lift, you lift. If I level, you level." Meeting each one stare for stare, he said, "Help me repair what we can. Please."

"We can do that," Riker called out with his approach.

Extreme emotions warred within the senior general's mind, but the strongest of them was determination. Still, Set told him, "You have the wrong ability for the task, General."

Riker's face went stoic, and it reminded him so much of Montilis that his throat grew tight.

"I'm not leaving," Riker said.

"And I don't want you to," Set replied, starting them forward. "I was hoping you could help me with something else."

"What?" Riker asked, his brows pulled low.

"I need you to confirm a story this voice is spilling into my head," Set told him.

Riker stopped, closed his eyes, and pinched the bridge of his nose. He shook his head. Turning his neck to look over at the boy, he said, "You know you sound like one touched by the curse when you talk like that, right?"

Set shrugged. "It is what it is."

"What story?" Riker asked, but he was not the only one with questions.

One of the soldiers asked, "What guy?"

Another queried, "How did he get in your head?"

"Don't we have a city to repair?" Riker scowled. "Let's be about it and let the boy speak."

Their progress was slow but steady. They worked to pull together the tears in the terra, careful of the lava. They closed the chasms after filling them with buildings and homes that had been reduced to rubble. They forced the rises to level and the sinkholes to rise, and while they worked, Set shared with them a piece of their history.

The moment he began, he knew that Riker was familiar with the story by the sharp pang of remembered loss. "The Fulgo had won a great victory. They turned their eyes to coast of Palus Regia, but the city was not yet ready to defend itself. Before their ships could reach the shore, a man by the name of Felix Aquam..."

Riker cleared his throat. "Montilis's grandfather."

"Really?" Set asked. He reached out and leveled the terra between two homes, while his terra-wielding entourage kept the houses standing.

Riker nodded. "He and my father were very close. I remember him telling me about that day."

"So then it's true?" Set clarified. "He kicked off his boots and walked on water to face the battleships alone?"

"The story goes," Riker said, "that he strutted across the oceanus like he owned the whole blasted thing, and then he dropped beneath the surface. The first ship began to turn, as if in retreat, but then it made a full circle no ship could make, and its spin was increasing. Felix had formed a vortex beneath it. It disappeared and sank almost as fast as Felix had."

"Yet the ships kept coming," Set continued as he shoved a house into a chasm. Left in the wake of the lava, the wielders pushed it deeper into the planet and back where it belonged. "And, according to the voice, it's what he did next that made him a legend."

Riker nodded. "The victory made him bold. So they story says, he went to the bottom of the bay and forced another vortex to rip open the oceanus' floor, thinking to anchor it there. Yet, the first of the vortexes had become self-sustain-ing, and the second, anchored, made itself larger. They say," Riker told them, "that when Felix surfaced, they could see the fear on his face despite the distance, but a ship had managed to pass between the two vortexes."

"And so," Set said, "he went back under."

"He did," Riker replied, though it hadn't been a question.

"And he never came back up," Set finished, in case the soldiers didn't know the story.

Having reached the coast, Riker pointed to the three massive vortexes that had survived the test of time. "They ripped the Fulgo ships apart," he told them, "and never again has an enemy attacked us from the sea."

Taking a moment for the story's ending to hit home, Set said, "Bravery runs in the Aquam line. Three generations of heroes."

His smile was sad. In the silence that followed, he felt the exhaustion of those who'd conquered their fear of him to help.

"I can't thank you all enough for what you've done today," he announced. "The people are safe, the lava is gone, and the oceanus has been returned to its proper place. Rest," he said, "eat, and replenish your strength. Tomorrow, we will relevel Palus Regia, and then the true rebuilding can begin." He met them all stare for stare. "For a first pass, you did well."

"Sir!" A soldier ran up and stopped in salute. "We have a problem."

"At ease, Steven," Riker said. "What it is?"

"We didn't have to round up the nobles, sir. Nunbia did that for us, and now they're outside of the apothecary, demanding Anliac's arrest." His eyes flickered to Set. "And yours, sir."

"Tristan will kill them even if Anliac doesn't." Set knew that Riker was following, but he left him behind, hoping he wasn't too late.

Reaching the apothecary, he encountered insanity. Soldiers stood with hands gripping weapons they feared to draw. Captains stood in uncertainty as to what orders to give. And the nobles, surrounded by personal guards prepared to defend them, stood in outrage.

In comparison, those who guarded the door to the apothecary were few, but they had their orders. Still, their relief was evident on their faces when a colorful streak slowed to reveal Set. They were given a moment of reprieve when the enemy guards shifted their position to defend against his arrival.

Bootless, in nothing but the brown cotton pants he'd pulled on that morning, Set let them gawk at the markings that covered his sun-darkened skin.

"What kind of creature are you?" a noblewoman asked, stepping back. Her personal guard formed a wall in front of her.

"This is what happens when history is forgotten," Set responded. "Ignorance flourishes. Allow me to educate you," he thundered, surfing his unsettling, starburst-blue gaze over each of the nobles. "I am the last living epoto. Who here wants to arrest me?" As he spoke, he pulled energy from the terra beneath them and took a measure of theirs as well.

Nobles barked at their captains, who gave orders for their soldiers to hold their positions when many would have fallen into retreat.

"Enough of this!" Nunbia shouted, singling himself out. "Arrest him!"

No one moved.

"You are all cowards!" Nunbia fumed. "He destroyed our city!"

The door to the apothecary opened. Tristan emerged first, with Anliac following.

Riker was a thunderhead, and the rage that rolled from him opened an easy path to the Angelis' sides. His multi-colored uniform of browns, tans, and greens appeared black from Montilis's blood. Streaks of it marked his cheek and forehead. His hands were gloved in it. Pale beneath his natural coloring, his lips pressed thin and his black eyes on fire, he ordered, "Captains, form rank."

While those of the Regia Aquam Guard followed the command, those of the Houses did not. One gave voice to his refusal. "You are not my general."

Riker met Set's stare across the distance.

Set nodded and then the Captain dropped. His life was stolen, and Set hissed at the familiar burn spreading down his spine as it branded him with a new mark.

"I will say it again," Riker growled. "Captains, form rank."

And, they did.

Nunbia's outrage turned to fear when his personal guard took their place with those recruited to the Regia Aquam Guard. "You are supposed to be the protectors of Palus Regia. Arrest her! I want to see her swinging by her neck," he hissed," as my daughter swung from hers. I want her dead!"

"Anliac…"

"It's okay, Tristan," she said, tugging free of his hand to set the record straight. "I laid waste to a viper's den. You are the viper, Nunbia."

"Becoming what you are has driven you insane," Nunbia accused. "You punish the innocent because *you* are guilty. You, Angeli, are a destroyer."

"Your daughter?" Set asked the question aloud as his mind pieced it all together. "Inabeth…the one who turned Anliac over to the blood-seekers? The one who tried to have Montilis killed? The one who tried to kill us all when her plans with Sinpine failed? Your daughter…" He shook his head. "I guess the apple really doesn't fall far from the tree."

Spine stiffening, chin tilting, Nunbia said, "I am not responsible for Inabeth's actions."

"Perhaps not," Anliac countered in a disturbing monotone, "but you are the one that recommend to the council that Tristan be captured and used as a weapon."

Tristan stepped forward as if daring the man to try it.

"You are the one that recommend my death," she raged.

There was a sudden blur of forceful winds. Trained soldiers cried out in shock and disbelief when Tristan's closed fist entered Nunbia's chest and exploded out of his back. "I know you wanted his head, Anliac," he told her, using his foot to shove the impaled man off his forearm, "but I'm hoping his heart will suffice." Turning to her, he offered her what he held.

A noblewoman stumbled forward with a hand over her mouth. Going to the ground, she lifted Nunbia's head and placed it in her lap. Looking up at them, she said, "This is not how this was supposed to go. This wasn't supposed to happen. Montilis was supposed to come alone. He was supposed to die." She met Anliac's eyes. "We were going to kill you for turning against your own race." To Tristan, she said, "You are a beast that should be collared, used for a purpose, and then put down. No one is safe so long as the Angeli live. You are the reason the gods of Earth have come."

It was the captain of her own house that knelt behind her. She felt the braided wire that he looped around her neck, then she watched the Angeli give the order to end her life. It was the captain of her house that rose in rank within the Regia Aquam Guard when he said, "Take the nobles into custody until our general has time for them."

Anliac didn't wait to see the order followed but turned to reenter the apothecary. When she emerged again, she had her father in her arms. Unaware of the procession forming behind her, she ignored them all and made her way to the coast.

She laid him out on the sand. Tucking her legs beneath her, she knelt beside him. His skin was an unnatural grey, and the cold it held was one she would never forget. "I'm so sorry, Daddy," she whispered.

Piece by piece, she began to remove the uniform that had betrayed him. When the last article of clothing had been removed, she leaned forward to press a kiss to his forehead, then stood and backed away. She called for the oceanus and it answered, slowly, as if it felt her pain and sorrow.

It broke the barrier of the coastline to lift the fallen general. She bid the aquis to circle him, to wash over and under him, to remove stink of blood and death, to cleanse him for his last voyage.

In her peripheral, the Regia Aquam Guard gathered to honor his life. She knew that Riker, Tristan, Set, and Shashara were there if she called to them, but she moved forward alone.

Father and daughter made their way into the oceanus for a private goodbye. Submerged to the waist, she held her father's body with the element they shared. Broken by the sight, she swore, "Your death was not the first in the political war that has ravaged our city, nor will it be the last, but Father..." With a shaking hand, she caressed his cheek. "I will see the war ended. I will see the guilty punished. I will see this city whole again, or I swear to you, I will destroy it."

Releasing her hold and adjusting the current, Anliac's voice broke. "If the Earthlings have it right and there is life after death, tell Mom I love her. Tell Jagarid he will have to look after you both until I can get there."

The speed of his departure escalated as he was caught up by the nearest vortex. Knowing her time was short, she said, "I love you, Dad," and then the oceanus took him. It's what he would have wanted.

What she wanted was vengeance, and when she turned back to the coast with her golden marks blazing, there wasn't a single person who did not fear her intent.

XXXII

In My Way

Tristan captured Anliac's shoulders with his hands. It took far more effort than it should have to hold her in place. "Look at me," he said. "Hey. I heard what you told your dad. Anliac, you've had your vengeance. The council members are all dead, and the nobles that survived are without armies. Their power base has been shattered, and Riker now controls the city. It's done."

Her head shook back and forth in quick repetition.

"He's right, Anliac," Set said after a slow approach. "If we cause any greater harm without new provocation, we will be the monsters Palus Regia thinks we are. There may be others who deserve to be punished for what has happened to your dad, but if we kill them all, we'll be killing the innocent too. We'll be killing the ones your father came back to save."

"I can't… I'm just…" The eyes she turned to Tristan broke his heart. "I don't know what to do. Tell me what to do."

Tristan nodded to Set, who used the waves' energy to open a portal back to Pisces Stragulum. "Let me take you home."

Nodding numbly, Anliac followed when Tristan led her through the portal. Set paused to clasp Riker's forearm.

"I don't envy your road ahead," Set said, "but from what Montilis told me, there's no better man for the job. You love this city and the people know it." Clearing his throat, he added, "I hope you can forgive me for my part in the damage done here, and I am truly sorry for the loss of your friend."

Veins throbbed at his temples and on his neck, and the corners of Riker's jaw pulsated. He clenched his teeth to hold back the tide of emotion that a general had no time for. He dared not speak lest his voice betray the wire's edge he was walking, so he stared out at the oceanus, at the vortex that had claimed Montilis, and waited for Set to go away.

Set's shoulders drooped. More than the terra had been torn by his and Anliac's actions, and the healing of hearts and psyches would take time. Shashara was staying behind to lend a hand, so he entered the portal alone.

"What the... Ow..." Set rubbed his nose as his eyes focused on Tristan's solid back.

"Look," Tristan replied as he yanked his brother out from behind him and turned him northwest to face Imbellis.

"That's a rift," Set stated, seeing the storm of jagged, purple lightning, "and it's stabilizing fast. Too fast," he added.

"What does that mean?" Davad asked, catching the tail end of Set's statement. He'd rushed down the gangplank of Triton's ship with its captain, Skylar, and Shady following.

Triton took one look at Anliac's face and asked, "What happened over there?"

Tristan, ignoring both of their questions, asked one of his own. "When did it start?"

"Not long ago," Davad told him.

"It's Bealson's Grove," Tristan said, wincing. "It has to be."

Set groaned. "Curse the gods and their timing."

"I think their timing is perfect." Anliac's markings set fire across her body. Her image blurred and then she was gone.

"Crap," the two brothers swore.

Set snapped his fingers and the original portal closed, to be replaced with another. "Rally the Angeli Guard and send them through this portal."

"What happened in Palus Regia?" Davad demanded.

"Montilis is dead," Tristan told him, "and now I think his daughter is trying to join him."

"Come on, brother. Let's go," Set urged.

"I've got things here," Davad said quickly. "Go."

Once through the portal, Tristan and Set found themselves in the grove, between the Northern wall of Imbellis and the gateway site tucked inside Bealson's Grove.

"I hate it when you're right," Set said.

"We have to hurry," Tristan told him. "I want to know what we're dealing with before Anliac gets here."

The gate to the grove was closed, but the rift had stabilized. From the other side of the wall, they heard the solid thump of two sets of feet hitting the ground, then a woman's voice.

"Uh… You're right, Apollo," she said. "It's quite difficult

to walk here. I think I'll stop teasing you now."

Tristan's eyes narrowed. "Apollo."

"And they really do have two suns." The woman clapped. "How delightful. And look at all of their moons… Beautiful."

"Their suns' energy has an adverse effect on my power," Apollo told her. "And, like I told you, sister of mine, it was the gravity of this place that allowed the Angeli to best me last time."

Set's eyes were wide when he turned them on Tristan. "Did he just say 'sister'?"

"The two of you shut up," a deep male voice snapped, "and move."

There was another thud, but the terra rebelled against the shock and trembled.

"That's going to be a big boy," Set whispered. "I think you should take him."

Tristan grinned.

"Superi's gravity is three to four times that of Earth's," he said, "making this planet unsuitable for humans."

"We know that, Gurzil," Apollo scolded. "We're not here to colonize Superi with humans. We're here to kill the Angeli, to make sure that the denizens of Superi never seek out Earth again. The way in which you handled the people of Istanbul – I mean, Byzantine – was magnificent. Now we need you to teach the Superians the same lesson."

"A lesson the Greeks couldn't teach." Gurzil chortled. "Lighten up, Artemis."

"More than the Greeks have faced the Angeli," she said.

"True," Gurzil said, "yet they've never faced me."

"And yet," Artemis quipped, "they seem rather anxious to do so."

Set winced. "Busted."

"Do it now, little brother." Leaning his head from side to side, stretching the tense muscles running along the back of his shoulders, he asked, "You ready for this?"

"Why not?" Set shrugged, looking down at his dirty, bare feet. He laughed at the image of Jacob they conjured, then he and Tristan squared themselves in the center of the closed gate and shoved it wide.

Their eyes went straight to the unfamiliar god. Built like Tristan and just as tall, but with twisted locks of rope-like hair that fell around slender, single-pointed ears, to his shoulders. His chest was bare. His skin, covered in dark spots, was a strange pinkish-grey.

He was clout in black, fitted breeches concealed by lengths of grey cloth that hung from the belt at his narrow waist. An animal skull, which covered him from navel to pelvis, sat atop the buckle.

His fists and forearms were protected by leather gauntlets, and the black boots on his feet had blades at the tips and heels. But it was the way he held the shafted spear in his right hand that promised a good fight.

When Gurzil smiled, rows of short, spiked teeth appeared beneath his broad, flattened nose. His cheekbones made hollow pits for his narrowed, black eyes – eyes that watched them.

The woman, covered from neck to toe in heavy, fitted green leather, with yellow designs worked throughout, revealed her speed when she blurred to Apollo's side. The bow was her weapon of her choice, but it was her beauty that was disarming. Golden-haired with honeyed skin, heart-shaped lips, and blue eyes that pierced, she was perfection.

"Get your eyes off my sister," Apollo snarled. "I've brought someone else for you to meet." With a flourishing wave of his golden-armored hand, he grinned at Tristan. "I've asked Gurzil to introduce you to death as only an African god can: *violently*."

Though Tristan's Angeli markings stayed at a constant low-level glow, they spiked in intensity at Apollo's threat. That was the only reaction the gods received for their efforts, however, when Tristan angled himself to speak to Set.

"Yeah, I think you're right," he said. "I'll take the big guy. You deal with the woman."

"She's fast," Set said, "but I can take her."

Tristan held out his hand. "You'll be faster."

As Tristan gritted his teeth through the quick draw on his speed, Set glanced at Apollo. "What about him?" he asked, breaking his connection with Tristan's animus and giving him his hand back.

Rubbing at his forearm, more from habit than pain, Tristan replied. "Guard your back against him, but he's no threat. He's too much of coward to meet you head-on."

Gurzil chuckled.

Apollo glared.

Artemis notched an arrow.

"Hold on, blondie." Tristan surveyed the stone walls of Bealson's Grove. "If we're going to do this, we need more room."

"You Superians talk too much."

Apollo snorted at Gurzil's comment, remembering when Tristan had said the same of the gods.

"Where are they going?" Artemis asked, releasing the tension on the bow string and lowering to her side.

"They're running," Apollo sneered, "but it won't do them any good."

"That's the slowest run I've ever seen," Gurzil stated flatly. "Idiot."

Turning their backs on the gods wasn't the best plan, but while Tristan might survive being thrown into a stone wall, Set would not.

"She looked competent with that bow," Tristan said, "and we're giving her two clear targets."

"The aer shield guarding our rear flank is solid," Set assured him. "Are they following?"

"Yeah," Tristan said. "I can hear them. Crap!"

"No, no, no," Set muttered. "Not good."

They were halfway between Bealson's Grove and Imbellis, to the West of the road that led up from the city, and the soldiers of IA were on their way.

Tristan heard Gurzil say, "They were delaying our fight until their reinforcements could arrive. It will not save them."

Apollo and Artemis turned from the flare of brilliant light that burst from Tristan's markings. Before they recovered, Tristan's voice, deepened and hardened by the Angeli energy he held within, boomed.

"Stop!"

The soldiers and gods both obeyed.

"Go back!" Tristan shouted. "Shut the gates and prepare

to defend your city."

"Our plan keeps getting better and better," Set groaned.

"How many died in Imbellis during the last battle?" Tristan tilted his head. "No more, little brother. Not today."

A dozen Angeli Guards spilled through the portal from Pisces Stragulum.

"Together then," Set said. "Just the two of us."

Tristan nodded. "Close the gate."

Set reached his hand out towards the portal and then closed his fingers. The portal closed as well, and then Tristan shouted to the guards.

"Make your way to Imbellis. Protect the people."

The Angeli Guards hesitated, but they obeyed and changed course to follow orders.

"What is that?" Artemis pointed at what appeared to be a yellow lightning bolt running parallel with ground, aimed at them. It showed no sign of slowing.

"Make that the three of us," Tristan said. "Our back-up has just arrived."

"Take out the boy," Gurzil commanded. "I've got the Angeli. We'll deal with whatever *that* is when were finished."

"It's her," Apollo warned.

"Anliac!" Tristan shouted when she blew right past him. He moved to follow, but his feet slipped into the terra and became trapped.

"What are you doing, Set?" Tristan bellowed, believing his brother the traitor. He smashed his fist into the ground to break free of the terra.

"Set's not here right now," another psyche said through his brother's mouth, without looking at him.

Anliac wailed, that piercing scream that rips a person's mind apart. Not even the mighty Gurzil was immune, nor was he prepared for the gliding right-hook that slid him across the ground. His head hitting the surface like a pebble skipped across a pond.

Tristan shrugged. "I guess she will take the big one."

Grinning, Set took off towards Artemis, blurring with his brother's speed.

Artemis, bow in hand, grinned as she moved to outflank the charging youth.

Apollo's visage fell as Tristan zeroed in on him.

Knowing it would take a moment for his speed to re-generate, he taunted the sun god. "It looks like it's three on three, blondie," he said, "and everyone else has a dance partner."

Tristan started his way, falling into a jog before advancing to a trackable run. Apollo waited for the right moment to shout, "Now, Artemis!"

She let loose the arrow she had aimed at Set, then immediately notched another and turned it on Tristan. It nailed his right shoulder. She fired again and again, in quick repetition, and counted the ones that struck home. "Seven. Eight. Nine." She pin-cushioned his chest and legs, but the Superian wouldn't lay down.

Tristan, slowed by the speed he'd given Set, cursed. Knowing he couldn't dodge or outrun them all, he stood his ground and caught the arrows he could, yanking out the ones that made purchase.

The goddess was relentless. She was hurting his brother, and Set was going to kill her for it. Using every ounce of speed Tristan had offered up, the wind burned his skin as he raced to get his hands on the archer.

Apollo cut him off with a ball of light that exploded against the ground, directly in the boy's path. Throwing up his hands as chunks of rock-riddled terra flew at his face, Set changed his course but not his target. Conjuring orbs of light, one after another, Apollo launched them from both hands, like twin catapults, to hold the epoto at bay and to buy his sister time to bring down the Angeli.

Tired of being fired upon, another psyche took momentary control and launched a furious, rolling fireball at Apollo. When the god broke from his attack to defend, Set took the psyche's lead and loosed a barrage of fireballs to keep him there.

The tactic failed, and Apollo's golden bow appeared in his hand.

Remembering well Apollo's aim, Set conjured a gravity shied to protect against the arrows. Using his brother's speed, he blurred forward as if to engage. But at the last moment, just as he crossed the line of sight between Artemis and Tristan to reach Apollo, he cut a v-line instead. While Apollo watched, Set launched his attack.

Artemis's eyes went wide as the flames engulfed her, and when she stepped from it, she was orbed in a golden glow that faded as her rage increased. "You'll pay for that," she said, glaring.

"Try and collect," Set retorted. Then he was a blurred streak, headed straight for her.

Apollo launched himself into the air. From the higher vantage point, he shot an arrow at the boy's face. Tristan, freed from Artemis's focused attack, was already off the ground and reaching for him.

An arrow whizzed past the end of Set's nose. Distracted, he looked up to where Tristan had tried – and failed – to knock Apollo out of the sky. Dropping his eyes to Artemis, the goddess grinned and launched a light orb that sent him careening in the opposite direction.

Set didn't blur forward; his fury powered his speed faster than that. In a heartbeat, he'd gained the ground he wanted, but Artemis had disappeared.

Tristan's blistered skin healed before he hit the ground, but the force of the light orb had knocked him towards the front, outer wall of Bealson's grove. There wasn't a bone in his body that didn't feel the impact. He crashed through the stone wall, into the gateway site, and slid on his back twenty feet across the stone before stopping.

With Tristan down, Artemis and Apollo turned their full attention to Set. Between them, Set was losing. He'd given up on forming offensive attacks. It was all he could do to keep the gravity shield in place while the voices in his head argued until he couldn't hear himself think.

"Make up your minds," Set growled aloud, then diverted the energy he was using for the shield into his speed. Dodging, rolling, jumping, he danced between their attacks to lay hands on one of them, but the siblings' attacks balanced each other with beautiful perfection. He couldn't find his way through.

The roar that sounded from the grove paled Apollo's face. "He's coming," he said to himself, then raised his voice to shout, "Artemis! If we face them both, we lose. Kill him.

Now!"

Artemis stopped cold. "I do not take orders from men," she snarled, but her brother got his way. Her fury triggered, an aura of power radiated out from her like heatwaves across a prairie. From within it, the goddess grew to thirteen feet tall, and her weapon grew with her. The bow was enormous, and the arrows, eight feet long and a fist wide, were fired one after another.

Panic quieted the voices in Set's head, or maybe it was simply that their fear was all the same. So, in silence, they waited for the one that would kill them all.

"No!" Tristan bellowed. Three heads turned in the direction his voice had come from, but he was no longer there. There was no blurred streak to track his progression. He disappeared to reappear, and it happened in a blink.

The arrows fired from Artemis's bow were plucked from their flight. Gathering them together, Tristan threw them, all at once, into Apollo's unsuspecting chest.

"Apollo!" Artemis cried, seeing her brother go down.

CRACK!

She screamed as her right knee was crushed beneath Tristan's left hook. His fist punched its way through the bone and cartilage, destroying it. Dropping to the ground, shrinking in size, she grabbed hold of her leg above the injury and formed a tourniquet by squeezing with her hands. The flow of golden blood, marbled with red, was stemmed, but she wasn't healing. Looking up at the twin red suns of Superi, over the shoulder of an avenging Angeli, she understood what Apollo had meant. Their suns were a curse.

"Hold onto this one," Tristan told Set, "while I finish

things with her brother." With a hundred feet separating him from his target, the ground exploded where his feet shoved off. A heartbeat later, he was in the god's face. He got in one solid punch before the coward disappeared.

Stars flashed in his eyes when a large stone *thunked* into the side of his head, spinning him around. Dazed, his path wasn't a direct one, but he took off for Apollo again.

BOOM.

Another rock clocked him in the back of his skull. Cursing because he hadn't seen the god move, he turned around to find him and dropped to one knee when his left thigh muscle took a straight hit.

Artemis screamed, and the sound sent chills sweeping up Apollo's spine, for only death could pull forth that level of agony. Her protective aura had failed, and her healing ability was compromised. Liquid gold spilled from her ruined limb.

The boy had both hands wrapped around her throat, and they were doing far worse than straggling the life from her. He was draining her power, and he was reveling in it.

Pushed beyond the line of sanity, where rationality might have lent a hand, Apollo pushed his power outward. A hundred orbs of light fired from him as he charged down on the boy to free his sister.

It was Tristan's turn to fire a stone. Striking Apollo in the center of his back, he took advantage of Apollo's stumble and positioned himself in the god's path.

Catching his step, he didn't care about the Angeli standing his way. He barely noticed him. What he saw was the boy's kaleidoscopic markings giving up their color for one of gold as Artemis's power was absorbed. Her eyes, desperate, cut to the side and found him. She was dying.

"Let...her...*go!*" With every word bellowed, Apollo fired balls of fire that were hot enough to be called suns.

Out of options, Tristan took his stand and used his bare hands to block them all. His skin burned, and his hands shattered with each deflection. He had enough time to heal before the next reached him, but just barely.

"Set," he groaned, "you feel like lending a brother a hand?"

"I will kill you!" Apollo shouted and fired again.

"Look at me," Set whispered, letting Artemis's unconscious body fall. He admired the markings that now flowed through his flesh like the blood of a god. "I am..."

Taking a step back, Tristan turned sideways and backhanded his brother, hard, before turning to punch Apollo's last fireball right back at him. When Apollo went down, Tristan swayed under the pain, but was in Set's face before his hand could heal.

"An idiot," Tristan finished for him. "Do you really want to be one of them? Do you truly want her in your head for the rest of your life?"

"If you could only taste her power," Set said, and his voice was wrong.

Tristan stepped back. "Set...no." His brother's eyes were a milky, illuminated white, while his voice was dark, ominous, and hollow. "Let her go, brother."

"Watch your back," Set warned, but there was no concern carried in that eerie tone.

Tristan was afraid to turn his back. Apollo was a secondary threat compared to what he faced, yet he turned anyway.

Apollo had his hands in the air and was approaching at a slow, measured pace. "Please," he said, "no more. Not her. Take me. Look at me, you damned parasite!" Ignored, he shouted, "I'll lift the curses. I'll lift them, just… Don't touch her!"

There's was a shift in the aether. Set felt it. He didn't have to turn to know that a portal had been opened. In his heightened state, he felt the synchronized advance of soldiers' feet through the ground beneath his own.

"It would seem even the gods have a weakness," Set taunted in that voice, shrouded in malice. "They can bleed…" He reached down and grabbed a handful of Artemis's hair, pulling her torso from the ground. "And they love."

XXXIII

Run, Little God...

Shashara was the first through the portal from Pisces Stragulum to the field of battle between Imbellis and Bealson's Grove. "There," she said, pointing towards Set and Tristan. "Thank Superi," she sighed. "They're okay."

"Let's move out." Davad shouted the order, and dozens of the Angeli Guard answered. As they poured through the portal and moved past him, he stated, "All reports say there are three gods. Find Anliac and you'll find the third. Daniel, hold up."

"Sir." Tristan's personal guard grimaced at the delay. "I should be with him."

"I know," Davad told him, and gestured forward a Fera burdened down by the weight of Tristan's monstrous sword. "Tell him the thing does him no good if he doesn't carry it."

"It's too beautiful a blade to bloody," Daniel protested. His eyes traced over the sword's two-foot, red handle with an even flow of encircling, silver vines; over the cruel, defensive guard with its fourteen-inch, flowing blade; down four feet of thick steel to its double-edged end.

"And too heavy to wield," the Fera grumbled. "Even the Angeli would feel the weight of this beast on his back."

"Nah," Daniel said, grinning as he got them moving, "Tristan would just grow a stronger back."

Davad glanced at his sister. Seeing her grin, he laughed. "Come on, Shashara. Let's get you to Set."

"I'm going to give whichever fool psyche convinced him to leave me behind a piece of my mind, I'll tell you that much," Shashara warned. Then, arms pumping, she took off to do just that.

Davad kept apace. "Anliac's all right, right? Tristan wouldn't just be standing there if Anliac were in trouble, right?"

"Right," Shashara concurred, but they both picked up their paces.

Set had Artemis on her knees. He held her there with one hand pressed down on her shoulder as Tristan confronted Apollo.

"If you're lying..."

"I'm not lying," Apollo insisted. For the first time since his sister's capture, he looked away from her and saw the Superians' approach. "I am a god," he said. "Of course I have the power to lift the curses." Searching through the far-off faces, he found the one of importance and said, "Let her go."

"Not until you've lifted the curses," Tristan told him, noting the subtle shift in Apollo's stance. "Free us," he said, thinking the coward intended to run, "and I'll have Set open a rift and send you both home. Just tell me what you need."

Surprise registered on Apollo's face. He looked at Set and said, "So *you're* the rift-maker."

"I am so much more than that," Set replied, his dark voice echoing on shadows of itself as he pulled a little more power from what Artemis had to offer. The power that coursed through him transitioned the color in his markings to a brilliant, solid gold.

"Did you know, Superian, that there are those who call me a god of love?" Apollo asked. "I'm good at discerning matters of the heart. I can tell whom a person will love, or who they're in love with." Looking down at his sister, he told her, "If he kills you, he will never die, for I will see to it that he suffers for eternity."

When Apollo's stare rose to meet Set's, the epoto knew true fear. Twisting, yanking Artemis around with him, he found Shashara walking beside Davad and screamed. "SHA-SHARA, RUN!"

Tristan was right on Apollo's heels. Putting more energy behind his speed, he shot in front of the god to cut back with a right hook that rolled the god. Apollo came up like it had never happened and took off for Shashara again.

Tristan angled his path to intercept. Coming up at his side, he lowered his shoulder to ram him. With a grin, Apollo waited until he could see the victory dancing in the Angeli's illuminated, yellow eyes and then blasted him with an orb of light energy.

It exploded. The concussion of it tossed him backward, and the light felt as if it had burned away his eyes to fry his brain. The pain made his breathing labored, but he healed.

His eyes cleared quickly, but Apollo had gained considerable ground.

Davad heard Set bellowing, but the distance was too great to make out his words. Tristan's expression, however, appearing between blurs of speed, said enough. He stepped in front of his sister and called for the nearest guards.

"Get her back through the portal," he ordered them. "Now."

"What?" Shashara squawked when she was lifted from the ground and tossed over a Mortalis man's shoulder. "Why?" She pounded ineffectual fists against his armored back. "Put me down!"

"You two," Davad said to the others, "make sure they make it."

On the verge of throwing an epic fit, Shashara made eye contact with the golden-haired god and changed her mind. "Sweet Superi," she muttered. "He's after me."

Her guard ran faster.

Beating a path back to the portal, Davad shouted. "Fall back! Protect the portal! Form a line!" He heard a familiar clicking and pivoted in a full circle before he found the man known for making it. "Rupert!" he shouted, waving his hands in the air to gain his attention. With the Fera's speed, it didn't take long.

"It looks like you're in trouble again, little packmate," Rupert stated, his perpetually sad face appearing grim.

"Tristan needs his sword," Davad rushed to tell him. He pointed in the direction Daniel and the Fera had gone with it when the race between the gods had forced them to double back. "They're not going to make it back here in time."

Rupert was already running. Reaching the two men in heartbeats, he yanked the sword away from them by its handle. The tip hit the ground as his eyes went wide. Growling as if the sword had laid down a challenge, Rupert's neck thrust forward from his shoulders. He took off running again, dragging the sword behind him.

"Help him," Daniel barked at the other Fera after trying and failing to snatch up the other end of the sword himself. Then they ran.

"Tristan!" Davad shouted. He ran as fast as he could; curse their gods, he was trying.

Tristan launched himself at Apollo's back, crashing through the Angeli Guards, and wrapped his hand around the god's neck on their way down.

Apollo, however, had caught his prey as well. As his hand curved around her delicate shoulder, he squeezed and was rewarded with her scream.

"Let her go, or I'll take your head." Tristan warned, tightening his hold until Apollo's eyes bulged in their sockets.

Refusing to give up his prize, Apollo maintained his grip on the girl, groping for Tristan's forearm with his the other. Making contact, his hand turned into a fingered rod of white power, and the heat of it began melting through the Angeli's skin.

When her lungs had emptied with her scream, Shashara couldn't draw a full breath for the weight of the two men pressing down on her. It was all she could do to fight through the pain to stay conscious. The sickly-sweet scent of burning flesh assaulted her, gagging her.

She saw her brother and a dozen guards running towards

them. Rupert… Was that Rupert? He had Tristan's sword. He and Daniel and another man she didn't know were running towards them too. There was a ringing in her ears that wouldn't stop.

No. Tristan was screaming.

There was a pop as a tendon in Tristan's forearm snapped. His arm went lax.

Apollo scrambled to his feet, dragging Shashara with him. With a flash of lightning, he conjured and opened a rift at his back. Gripping Shashara tighter, he jumped through, taking her with him.

Tristan roared and went in after her.

Davad, pulling free his dracon blade, was hot on their heels.

"Hurry," Daniel shouted, "before it closes."

Rupert stumbled when the other Fera dropped his end, but he didn't stop.

"What are you doing?" Daniel asked. "He needs his sword."

"I'm not going through that," the Fera said, backing away.

"Go," Rupert told Daniel with the rift fast approaching. "I'm right behind you."

Lan stepped through the portal from Pisces Stragulum in time to see Davad, and then Daniel, follow Tristan through a rift without hesitation. He witnessed Rupert's struggle to lift the sword high enough to cross the bottom edge of the rift, but lacking sufficient strength, he used his speed and began turning in a circle. Edging his way towards the rift, he launched himself sideways and hoped for the best.

"No!"

Lan reached out as if he could stop the rift from closing, but it was too late. Tristan had his sword, but Rupert had been severed, his legs left twitching on the field of battle while his eyes closed somewhere on another world.

***

"Come on, war god," Anliac taunted when a rift opened and the god turned to run. "Don't leave it like this."

That's when she heard Tristan's roar. She heard his pain and everything changed.

She gained on the god as he limped a pathetic retreat, his body battered by their battle. She could see through the hole in his right arm, a hole she'd put there with his own weapon after she'd taken it away from him. Bits of his intestine seeped through the rip in his right side, put there by a conjured blade of her own making.

It wasn't that she'd taken no injuries during their fight. She had. She was bloodied and bruised, but her rage had taken her to a place beyond pain, while the god was being crushed by it.

Hearing Tristan scream again, she snarled, "Game over." She reached out and tangled her hands in the long, rope-like strands of the god's black hair. Simultaneously, she trapped his feet in the terra and planted one of her own between his shoulder blades. Her marks mimicking the sun of Earth, she burst his ear drums with her cry, then she pulled.

Gurzil's neck bent until his spine couldn't withstand the pressure.

Anliac landed hard on her backside as his head snapped free of his shoulders. Black blood gurgled and oozed from around the severed, white column, to course over drooping shoulders and sagging knees. Still, she waited to see if he would regenerate. Could a god could heal from this? Could they live without a head? The question was given answer when Gurzil's body burst into flames and disintegrated into grey ash.

"Good enough," she said aloud, then ran for where she'd left Tristan and Set.

The scene she came up on made no sense. There was a wall of soldiers guarding the Imbellis gate, but she wasn't sure from what. The portal to Pisces Stragulum had been doubled in size, and the Angeli Guard were not alone in rushing through it. At first glance, she thought the pulsating glow of golden markings from across the field was Tristan, but it was not.

Blurring to Set, she asked, "What's happened? Where's Tristan and Apollo?"

Standing beside Set, Lan answered, "Apollo's taken Sha-shara."

"Set…" Anliac glared. "Start talking. Where are they?"

"I don't know," Set barked, shaking to such a degree that the goddess on her knees trembled.

His flesh was slicked with sweat, and his eyes appeared as rifts themselves as he struggled to hold the goddess's power without taking it. The psyches in his head were drooling over it, but he did not want to become what she was… Did he?

Knowing better than to touch him, Anliac placed herself squarely in front of him and said, "As long as they are there and we are here, our hearts are lost. We are monsters without them, Set, so we have to find them."

The goddess showed no fear as Set took her throat in his free hand and forced her to look up at him. Slowly, he fed a portion of her power back into her animus. As his golden marks faded into a multitude of colors and his voice lost its rending edge, he said, "Tell me where to find my family, or Superi help me, I'll turn you over to her."

***

Throwing back his head, Apollo shouted towards the sky, "Father! Brother! The Superians are here!" Immediately, the earth quaked, and the towering trees shook until their leaves gave up their hold to rain down like autumn out of season. "Earth is under attack!"

Tristan took in his surroundings in a sweeping glance. A single sun stood in a blue sky that was quickly turning grey with clouds. They stood upon a large, grass-covered hill with two primary clearings, divided by trees that rivaled those of Turris in all but girth.

With no other enemy in his path, Tristan started forward, but hesitated when Apollo yanked Shashara in front of himself and clamped down on her decimated shoulder. The sound of her scream was worse than any blade.

"Let her go."

Davad, coming up from behind, sounded so much like his father that Tristan turned, half-expecting to see Jacob's face. What he saw instead made him scamper back towards the rift.

"Rupert…"

From his hip bones down, the Fera didn't exist.

At the sight of Tristan's face, a soft clicking started off

in the back of his throat, then he squeezed the sword handle he had no hope of lifting. "Take it." His teeth and lips were stained in blood. "Kill…their gods," he gasped on his last breath.

"Or what?" Apollo chortled at Davad's threat. "You're little more than human. Weak. Pathetic."

"Sir," Daniel said, dropping into Tristan's view, "take up your sword."

Tristan did, and when he turned on Apollo, the god stared death in the face.

"Father!" Apollo's voice cracked as he called out for salvation.

His father answered with a booming roar of thunder. As the sky became a cauldron of churning, dark clouds, brought to life by streaks of violent, white lightning, Apollo's fear receded and his arrogance returned.

"And so it begins…"

XXXIV

War of Worlds

Meeting her brother's stare with a steady one of her own, Shashara pleaded, "Kill him."

Apollo chuckled. "He can't."

Davad rolled his right arm and threw his sword. His marksmanship was dead-on. Surprised, Apollo shifted to avoid the blade, but exposed his chest in the process.

Tristan moved so fast that no one saw it coming, least of all Apollo. His leverage was snatched from his grasp before the Angeli's open palm nailed him center-chest, nearly folding him in half, as he was sent flying backwards.

Tristan, knowing Apollo wouldn't take long to recover, tossed Shashara to her brother. Davad, brought to his knees by the unexpected weight, passed her off to Daniel, who looked her over for serious injury before helping her to stand.

"Are you okay?" Davad asked her.

"I'm fine," Shashara groaned through gritted teeth, fuming that she'd been captured. She was afraid to look at her shoulder, which pulsed with every heartbeat. "But Tristan can't stand alone. You have to help him."

"Daniel," Davad said, "I don't care what you have to do. You make sure she survives. And if she doesn't..." He pointed down the side of hill, away from Apollo, towards large, wood-framed human houses that stood in the distance, and said, "Take it out on them."

"It looks like you're just in time," Tristan said, sword in hand, as Davad took his place beside him. "Here he comes."

Together, they watched as Apollo emerged from the tree line that separated the two clearings atop the hill.

"I wouldn't miss it," Davad said. But before Tristan could decide to bolt and leave him to catch up, he added, "I'm not my father."

"Okay?"

"I'm not my father," Davad repeated. "I'm not too proud to admit that I need your help, but Tristan, that god's life belongs to me."

With cold clarity, Tristan replied, "Understood." Then they were moving.

Thunder roared their only warning as twin bolts of lightning crossed to block their path. Striking the trees to either side of them, they exploded into a barrage of splintered projectiles.

Tristan barely noticed the licks of pain, but Davad screamed with each new hit. Blinded by the flash, he ignored the fire sweeping across the grass, charring it black, as he searched for Davad. Shielding him as best he could until the onslaught was over, Tristan asked, "How bad are you hurt?"

"Does it really matter?" Davad asked, taking Tristan's hand to get up. Then he shouted, "Are you kidding me?" when a terrible wind, bending and snapping trees in its path, threatened to blow him off his feet.

Tristan's weight kept him planted, but it was all Davad could do to hold his ground. Apollo seemed invulnerable to the wind, and it motivated him to reengage, but they lost track of him when the debris forced them to protect their eyes.

The wind died as suddenly as it had stirred, but in the wake of the chaos was a god of gods, surrounded in a brilliant, white aura of undeniable power. His white hair, long and flowing, like the pointed beard that covered his lineless face, was the only evidence of age. Ten feet tall, his entire frame was hung with thick, bulging muscle. He towered over them in a white toga that reeked of authority like the scarlet cloaks of IA lawyers, while his shoulders, forearms, hips, and shins were shielded by golden armor, imbued with lightning that raced through the metal.

"Who are you?" Davad asked.

"Silence, mortal." The aether rippled with the deep bass of the god's order, reverberating outward to rattle their ribcages. "I was merciful when last our worlds collided. Now you will feel my wrath, for I will destroy Superi."

Tristan's expression turned stoic. "Davad," he muttered without looking over, "go back to Shashara."

"I'm not leaving you."

Light exploded from Tristan's yellow eyes as the golden, sinuous lines tracing his pale flesh broadened into thick bands. His neck, veins protruding, punched out from his broad shoulders as his blood pumped, engorging his muscles until they looked to split his flesh. He bellowed, "I said… *go!*"

Davad stumbled in his scramble to put distance between himself and whatever had taken over Tristan. "Okay then," he conceded. "You've got this. I'll just be…" When Tristan's golden markings flared again, he warned, "You two should be running," as he took his own advice.

"I am Zeus! You pathetic…"

An animalistic snarl ripped out of Tristan's throat. He flexed uncontrollably, and his muscles doubled in size as the well of energy within him reacted to Zeus's power. He roared again as his bones broke, stretching and spreading, until his frame could hold the new weight. His collar tightened, strangling him, as his tunic became a vice that trapped his lungs. He tore himself free from it, rending cloth and flesh alike. His trousers split at his outer thighs and ripped down the back his calves. His breathing was labored as he suffered the pain of yet another physical change. His bottom jaw stretched, thickened, and hardened.

Tristan locked stares with Zeus. In a voice that carried a power second-to-none, vibrating the chest of the god, he thundered, "I've been looking for you. You did this."

The ground exploded as Tristan's image all but disappeared.

Zeus saw it coming and threw up a lightning shield to deflect Tristan's right hook. Tristan bounced off the shield. When he hit the ground, he rolled towards Apollo and came up swinging. The uppercut connected with Apollo's chin with a boom to rival a bolt thrown by Zeus himself.

Sailing through the air, headed towards punishing trees, Apollo watched his father turn to track his flight path. Tristan was coming up from behind. He shouted warning, but he knew his voice wouldn't carry that far. There was nothing he could do.

Zeus winced when his son hit the trees. A shadow fell, giving away the Angeli's position. Turning, he added power to his shoulder thrust, and the two collided in a concussion of energy that punished their surroundings.

Zeus reached up with one hand and pulled down lightning.

Tristan stepped sideways with his left foot and, bracing himself, crushed Zeus's kneecap beneath his right boot heel.

Zeus snarled through clenched teeth.

As the god was brought to his knees, Tristan said, "You should get used to that view, earthling."

The conjured lightning struck, exploding around Zeus. It ripped apart and scorched the ground, felling trees, but missed its target.

"There are two sides to every story," Tristan said, giving away his location as he walked towards the center of the downed trees. "And for that reason, had you agreed to lift the curses, I would have let you live. Yet, by your words and actions, you've chosen to repeat history. Now," he said, adjusting his grip on his sword, "instead of offering peace, I will make an example of you."

Before Zeus could recover from the Angeli's audacity, Tristan closed the distance between them. His speed was phenomenal, but Zeus drew his Earthen-forged sword in time to counter Superian steel and blocked the strike meant for his chest.

Sparks flew. Their feet dragged trenches into the ground as they slid twenty feet before coming to a stop. Zeus took pause to reassess his opponent.

"We Greek have a special place for creatures like you," Zeus snarled. "It's called Tarturas. Know, Superian, that my brother awaits you, and he's eager to hear your screams."

Tristan saw the muscles in Zeus's thighs bunch just prior to his attack, and he braced for it. The god was slower than he was, but the distance was closed in an instant, and Zeus's strength was greater.

A solid kick sent Tristan crashing into a standing tree at his back. It cracked and toppled backwards as Tristan shoved off it to go after the god again.

Zeus advanced and met his attack.

Blow for blow, block and parry, blood of red and gold flowed as the two fought for dominance and victory.

Trepidation crept up Tristan's spine as he struggled to keep the gods' blade at bay. Of superior height, Zeus pounded him with over-the-head with downward strikes, causing him to doubt not only his sword's ability to hold up under the onslaught but his own strength to take the beating as well.

His knees buckled, panic struck, and the void was awoken again. A wash of power rushed over him, turning his golden marking to pure white. When he came off the ground, countering Zeus's last strike, the battle turned.

Needing only one hand to hold his sword, Tristan used his left to backhand the god, hard, across the left side of his face. Stunned by the insult, Zeus dropped his guard. Tristan front-kicked the god, propelling him into a line of trees destroyed by his passing.

The white aura of power enveloping him condensed, folding inward on itself, and further hardened his massive muscles. There was no pain, unlike all the times before. In its absence, he felt the well of energy inside of him. It was endless, and with that revelation came both fear and exhilaration as he finally understood. There was no limit to what he could become.

His introspection was cut short when he heard the crackling of a rift. He turned to see a path back to Superi, twenty feet wide and ten feet tall. Set, dragging Artemis by the arm, came through it first.

"Where is she?"

Set's voice was hollow, and the sound of it chilled Tristan's blood like the whisper of death. Hoping it was his brother's hold on the goddess causing it, he answered. "She's with Davad and Daniel. There," he said, pointing behind them to beyond the rift, but was distracted when Anliac came through.

She was not alone. Superians were pouring through in a hodgepodge of Nox, Fulgo, Fera, and even Mortalis. They wore colors that no longer applied as they followed the lead of those in Angeli Guard uniforms. They, of course, answered to their general, and Anliac was quick to give commands.

"Set, where is she?" Anliac asked after, but it was Tristan's finger she followed back to Shashara's location.

Halfway down the South side of the hill, between the rift and the human houses, Daniel fussed over Davad and

Shashara, who sat huddled next to a cluster of trees. Davad, spotting them, stood and waved before helping Shashara to her feet.

As the next wave of defenders came through the rift, a gruff voice asked over her shoulder, "Where do you want me?"

"Bengim," Anliac sighed, "your timing is perfect." Pointing towards Daniel and Davad, who had Shashara tucked between them and were making slow progress up the hill, she said, "They're hurt and they're vulnerable here. Go to them," she ordered, "and kill anything that comes near them."

"I came to fight," Bengim objected.

"Protect her for me," Set promised as he and Tristan reached Anliac, "and I will personally be in your debt."

Bengim grinned. "Now *that's* worth sitting on the sidelines for." He started down the hill to reach his charges.

"Where are the gods?" Set asked.

"Trust me," Artemis sneered from under his grip, "they're coming."

"I found the one responsible for casting the curses," Tristan told Anliac and Set, growing tense as time pressed in on them. "If I kill him…"

Artemis chuckled, winced, and then settled for a smirk. "You don't have the power to kill an immortal."

Set covered her face with an open palm and drew from her animus until she was back on her knees. "Tell me, goddess, would your power suffice to kill a god?"

"Stop," Tristan cautioned when Set's voice drew deeper from some inner well of darkness. "I'm all for seeing what happens to you if you take her power, but I'd rather find out after the fight. Right now, I need you to stay *you*."

Groaning, Set severed her from consciousness and let her body drop. "You have no idea how hard it is to deny myself what she has," he admitted. "The psyches are salivating over it."

"You heard Artemis," Tristan said to Anliac as he scowled at Set. "We don't have long before the gods converge. So get over here, woman, and kiss me."

Several inches taller and broader than when she'd left him to his fight with Apollo, his shirtless state revealed all the changes to his body, but she went to him without hesitation.

Hiding her concern, she smiled and went up on her toes to capture his cheeks. "You're determined to make me the little woman, aren't you?" she teased, making sure he saw her smile before she gave him what he wanted and kissed him.

When it had ended, Tristan brushed the end of his nose against her own and then pulled her close. He held her there, keeping her close for as long as he could. Then he peered over her head at his brother. "I was afraid you weren't coming."

The ground began to shake. Anliac pulled away as she and Tristan sought the source of the vibrations. Then, seeing Set's eyes were focused, they saw what he did: a white-haired god marching towards them, each heavy step troubling the ground.

"It takes time to open connecting portals and gateways to every major city on Superi," Set said, "and longer still to connect them to a rift anchored to another planet."

Tristan whistled. "Impressive."

"So is that," Set said, nodding towards Zeus. "But know this, brother," Set continued. "If ever you need me and I'm not here, it's because I'm dead."

Making eye contact from a hundred yards away, Zeus paused in his stride to roar, and with it, lightning fell. Trees exploded, and the ground was churned as the very terra looked for an escape.

Squatting, Set looked up at Tristan to say, "Let's finish this, you and me." Then he placed his hand upon the goddess. Pulling from her power until his marks began to glow, he managed to stop before he killed her, but only because he heard Tristan say, "We're out of time."

"This fight can't happen here," Tristan continued. He glanced over Anliac's shoulder, towards the rift, as more and more Superians came through it.

"I'll protect the rift," Anliac assured him. "Take the fight to him, but Tristan…" She caught his hand when he nodded and moved away. "Come back to me, or I swear on Superi, I'll rip Earth in half."

Dragging her close, he nipped the end of her nose with teeth that weren't sharp before. He felt her stiffen in his arms and knew that the change hadn't been lost on her, but then she kissed him, long and hard.

"Go," she said, pushing him away to get him moving. "Set…" her eyes flared in a defensive response to the power radiating from him.

"I've got him," Set assured, then the brothers were gone.

Anliac didn't waste a moment. "Okay, people, let's

move! I want a dozen guards on them." She pointed at Shashara and Davad, as Bengim stood still and used the terra
like a rolling board to reach his charges. "I want that rift
covered on all sides. No god passes into Superi. Do you hear
me? They die here. The rest of you, form ranks."

"What are we fighting?" a soldier shouted.

"HAVE YOU LOST YOUR MINDS!"

"That," Anliac answered as Ares appeared between the
rift and a tree line.

"YOU WOULD DARE ATTACK EARTH?"

Conjured armor of black plate, forged for an immortal,
encased the god as he called forth his dead minions from
their graves. "Rise…and destroy them."

The ground trembled as fissures snaked across it, cracking it in all directions, releasing hundreds of undead. Some
still had flesh stretched across their bones, while most were
no more than skeletons that moved. Draped in the reminiscent rags of the uniforms they'd died in, they clawed their
way free of the earth to fight for the god who'd summoned
them.

Twig-loose bones rattling their decayed ribcages, they
scattered within the larger force of two hundred Superians,
on unsteady feet, as the holes marking their graves closed.
Their confusion upon their reawakening lasted until Ares,
positioned half-way down one side of the hill, gave his order.

"Kill them all!"

Interspersed amongst the Superian forces, an undead
aimed a metal stick and pulled a lever with his finger. Fire
shot from the end of it, and a Superian went down. A mo-

ment later, the skeleton became a scattered pile of bones when a vortex of aer ripped him apart.

"Attack!" Anliac shouted into the stunned lull that held both sides.

Opening trenches beneath the feet of the undead, intent on putting them back, Anliac unearthed as many as she buried. She tried to use spikes to build a battle line for her soldiers, but there were simply too many. They were too close. Armor smashed against armor, blade against blade, fist against flesh, in a battle of strength and will.

Ares and Anliac, god and goddess of war, stood as generals and commanded their legions as they gauged each other from across the field.

Anliac saw his arrogant smirk turn to one of disbelief. It had taken the Superians a moment—not all had seen the undead at the Battle of Imbellis—to wrap their minds around the reality of what they were facing, and only in that moment had Ares held the upper hand.

As the Superians struggled to adjust to the lighter gravity of Earth, which caused them to move at uncontrolled speeds, tripping them on their own feet, blowing them passed targets, they'd been vulnerable. However, they didn't stay that way long. Once they discovered Earth's effect on their abilities, the balance had tipped in their favor.

A Mortalis captain, his spear held at his waist, charged three of the skeletal beings. He speared the first before pivoting left and, with a swooping blow, cut the second in half. Changing his grip, he used the butt of his spear to block the sword strike of the third, while shoving through the undead's soft torso with his free hand to rip out its spine.

Anliac's glowing eyes encouraged her people to fight each time the light of them swept passed. The captain was no different as he shouted up to her, "Hoorah!" reveling in the fervor of battle before moving towards his next target.

What her eyes fell to next was not Superian. There were four of them crawling out of the earth. Their heads were beastlike and horned, snouted and fanged. Their bodies, though built like enormous men, were covered in fur, and they walked on hooved feet. One held a staff as thick as his thigh; another, a hammer that rivaled Tristan's sword for size. The other two seemed content to fight with their claws or abilities not yet revealed, but it was the arrival of a new Earthling that held Anliac's attention.

In silver armor, with glorious, widespread, white wings, he was distractingly beautiful. She didn't see when the beasts attacked the front line of Superians guarding the rift, but she witnessed the cluster of Nox, focused on defending against the undead, fall by their hand.

"HOLD THAT LINE!" Anliac shouted. "IGNEIS WIELDERS, ATTACK!"

As Superians dove out the line of fire, the four beasts went up in an inferno of flames that stole their screams before reducing them to ash. The winged man grew in physical size as his rage was magnified. Locking eyes with Anliac, he pointed at her heart and advanced.

Positioned as the last defender of the rift, she held her place but was forced to witness the slaughter of her kinsmen. She hated him for it, but there was no denying the beauty of his movements. Each turn was fluid, each twist was made with purpose, and each forward step left death behind.

He'd come as close to the rift as she dared to let him, so she took her first step to meet him.

"Anliac."

The familiar sound of Triton's voice blurred her vision with tears.

"Where do you need them?" Triton asked, referring to those who'd come with him.

Ten men and two women, dressed in dark grey uniforms overlaid with black armor, awaited orders. Though they were of differing races, three or four black-painted lines, running diagonally from temple to chin, marked them as mercenaries. They served but one purpose.

"Stop him." There was no need to say who. The winged man was on the warpath.

Triton, coming to stand at her right, growled in a guttural language she didn't understand. The mercenaries seemed to understand it well enough. They broke into quads and came at their enemy from three different directions.

Razoran found his place on her left, nudging the unconscious goddess with the toe of his boot. "Who's she?"

"Where is everybody?" Triton asked, surveying the battlefield. "It looks like we're holding our own, but—"

Urgent new shouts from their flank spun them around. A new god, wearing bronze armor and standing fifteen feet tall, had ten cyclopes under his command, but they were not the concern.

"Um, what are those?" Razoran asked, scratching behind his triangular ear.

Made of bronze and covered in spiked armor, the monsters hovered beside the god on wings that grew from their bellies.

"Triton," Anliac began.

"Don't do it," he cut her off. "Your place is here, defending this rift."

Her voice, piercing in its violent beauty, flowed with as much power as the markings that had shifted from gold to burnt amber when she said, "My people need me. My place is with them."

"I'll hold the gate," Razoran rushed to offer.

"Not alone, you won't," Triton countered. Turning to Anliac, he said, "You're right. Go, but use the mercenaries. You paid for them, after all."

As if they'd heard and were determined to prove their worth, the kill squad closed in on the winged man, but it took only two to bring him down. The first, a Mortalis with white scars of battle decorating honeyed skin that stretched a frame as large as Tristan's, used speed to reach the man's rear flank. Grabbing hold of a wing, the Mortalis shoved his foot into the side of the man's knee, snapping it sideways.

The second was a woman, a Fera who reminded Anliac of Luce, especially when she leapt into the air and caught his neck with her claws to slow her descent. Using the gained momentum as the Mortalis stepped out of her way, she slung herself around the winged man, slicing through the muscle into bone. Gold blood, marbled with red, spewed like a geyser until the body hit the ground.

The sky began to darken as the clouds churned. A trumpet sounded in the West, and for a moment, the fighting ceased. The golden armor of a thousand angels fell through the high, grey clouds like a river of light. They landed, on

one hand and one knee, upon Earth in a beautifully choreo-
graphed rotation that radiated power and authority. Without
expression, they came to their feet, rising as one glorified
unit with their weapons—shortswords and shields, spears
and pikes, broadswords and staves—at the ready.

The cyclopes, their bronzed god leading the way, approached the rift from the South, and they brought the flying,
metal beasts with them. To the North, the direction in which
Tristan and Set had disappeared, Ares stood in firm command of his undead legions.

When, from east of the rift, a horn sounded in five short
blasts, Anliac cursed. "They're boxing us in," she warned,
then watched as five oozing, black ulcers infected the
ground.

Razoran groaned. "That can't be good. Whoa! Not good!
Not good!" He shouted in a hurry when sickly, webbed-
winged monsters with slick, black skin and twisted bodies
slithered from them. "I think I'm going to puke."

An eight-armed goddess appeared amongst the slick,
black creatures, a weapon in each hand. When Anliac saw
her, she grabbed ahold of Artemis and yanked her from the
ground.

Superians and Earthlings alike were affected when Anliac
called out the goddess by name. "Kali!"

Seeing Artemis bloodied and near death Kali warned,
"Let...her go," but her voice needed no amplification, for
the battle had stalled.

Ares, seeing Artemis for the first time, bellowed, "Release her, or by the gods, I will unleash hell."

"Hold your tongue, Greek," Kali ordered. "Your dominion does not reach so far."

"She will not be released until the curses are lifted," Anliac told the gods, "and we're assured that no Earthling will step foot on Superi again."

"I don't care what promise I made to Parvati," Kali hissed. "You do not make demands." A warped grin twisted her lips as she stepped forward. "You can leave, or you can die," she said, "and my children will feast on your bloody corpses."

In her peripheral vision, Anliac watched a new line of thirty Nox soldiers coming through the rift, and right behind them was a file of Fulgo wielders. Taking a deep breath, she let it out and said, "Seriously, Triton, you and Razoran had better both be dead before this rift is taken."

"What's it to be, Angeli?" Kali shouted. "Will history repeat itself? Will Superi run?"

"What are you going to do?" Triton asked, unanswered, as Anliac reversed the gravity beneath her feet and lifted herself into the air.

Her position gained her a vantage site of the bigger picture, and the image she beheld flared her golden markings until they mimicked Earth's sun. Her voice, piercing, gave command. "Nox, look east. Take out those monsters. Ignis wielders, move south! If it's made of flesh or metal and not on our side, ash it. The rest of you…keep these rotten corpses at bay!"

"KILL THEM!" Kali bellowed. "KILL THEM ALL!"

Ares called out to his minions, but by turning north, he revealed his intent.

"Oh, no, you don't," Anliac growled, and the ground

shifted according her to will. It rolled into a lapping wave with a cavernous underbelly that froze mid-fall. It wouldn't stop a god, but it would stop everything else.

Ares threw back his head and screamed in frustration.

Having created a three-sided battle to protect Tristan and Set, she gave one last thought to her love, and then she set about winning the war. "Mortalis," she shouted, "rip the wings from those golden, armored backs. I want them grounded. Fera," she barked, "I want bodies between the rift and the gods. Move through the lines. Rip them apart. Mercenaries," she shouted, "kill for Superi. FULL ADVANCE!"

XXXV

Does Anyone Really Win...

A full-sized pine tree, rotating like a horizontal disc, made Set's speed work against him as he tried to avoid it. His body leaned back, but his feet kept going, and he ended up head-height with the tree. Tristan saved him with a right hook that sent the tree careening and crashing into those farther out, shattering their trunks into a right-sided spray of fractured pieces.

"Whew...thanks," Set said, dusting himself off. "Hey, look at that."

"It would appear Earth suffers from the touch of its gods," Tristan noticed. The destructive path through the tree line, where the ground was gouged and overturned, would take them to Zeus and Apollo.

Finding them, Set cast a crooked grin at his brother and asked, "So, uh, how much stronger is the big one from Apollo?"

It was Tristan's turn to grin. "He's not as strong as he

thinks he is, but I'll take the golden one. You deal with the one who started this war."

"Done," Set said. Then he was blur that streaked off to the right, bait for Apollo to take. He wasn't disappointed.

Sword in one hand, held level and leading the way, Tristan advanced at a slow but building gait.

Zeus, thinking to limit the use of Tristan's sword, turned for the tree line at his back.

The moment the god turned, Tristan used his speed to get around him. Zeus was met with a horizontal slash of Tristan's blade as it reached for his chest.

Zeus deflected the strike with his sword, and a whirlwind storm of swords began. Earth was their battlefield, but the terra could not hold them. Their speed and agility carried them up the trunks of trees, felling some, to fight in the boughs of others before they, too, were topped and toppled by swinging blades. On solid ground, their speed made them all but invisible as they squared off to match strength for strength.

Zeus, confident that his superior skill and knowledge would gain him the advantage, put both to use. After every few combinations, he changed tactics. He tried new stances, cycling through fighting styles that the Superian would never have faced, yet he was losing. His stamina was waning, but the speed of the Angeli was showing no signing of slowing. By the gods, he would swear the boy was getting stronger.

Pulling back his sword arm, Zeus threw his fist in a left hook.

Tristan caught it.

Shocked that a mortal had done the impossible, it was

the pain of his hand being crushed that snapped Zeus back into the fight. Conjuring a lightning bolt the length of a short blade, he buried it into Tristan's thigh.

It was not meant to be a fatal wound, but it should have backed the boy off. Instead, with a sickening roll in his gut, he watched the wound heal. His head whipped to the side, wrenching his neck, as the back of Tristan's fist struck him in the mouth.

The taste of his own golden blood enraged him. Forgoing skill, he dropped his sword and dumped his power into his strength as he goaded, "Come, boy. Let us end this."

Without a word, with his sword in hand, Tristan was all focus as he advanced.

Zeus waited for Tristan's right shoulder to tense as it lifted that monstrous sword and then he stepped inside of the swing to push down on Tristan's wrist. He rolled the handle outward and out of Tristan's grip. Disarmed and forced to face him in hand-to-hand combat, Zeus's grin returned, confident that his strength would prove superior.

Tristan saw how Zeus had done it, but it was too late to do anything about it when Zeus popped his sword from his hand. He watched it flip, blade over hilt, and shook his head in disbelief. He grinned at the skills he was learning—skills, he was certain, no one on Superi could match. As the tip of the blade stuck in the ground, leaving its length and hilt to waver back and forth, Tristan realized the god's mistake, and his muscles swelled with excitement.

Tristan grabbed hold of Zeus's left wrist, his claws sinking through the skin, opening veins that would drain the god's blood. Then he wrapped his empty right hand around his throat and squeezed.

Zeus felt his throat collapse and conjured a lightning bolt to sever the hand from his neck, but it struck empty space. The Angeli had swept behind him, popping his left shoulder out of its socket. He took his arm with him, locking it in place for an instant, before the Angeli severed it at the elbow with his claws and a swift yank. A bloody gurgle was his scream.

A white orb fell from the sky and blasted them apart.

Tristan flew backwards, into the newly defined perimeter of the tree line, as Zeus disappeared into the crater made by the orb's arrival.

The dark clouds parted, and a beam of light landed upon the burning orb as it unfurled into the likeness of a man. Eight feet tall and in golden, silver-lined armor, he stretched his white wings before folding them down his back.

"You foolish Greek. Look," he commanded, "at what you've done. You claim to be head of your pantheon, the strongest of your kind, yet here you are, groveling for salvation as you struggle just to breathe."

Tristan, back on his feet, saw the man and paused in wonder. His straight hair was black as pitch, and his skin was as pale as his own, but it was the man's piercing blue eyes that reminded him of the depictions of Angeli discovered beneath Collibus Dolor. He approached the edge of the crater with more questions than aggression and asked, "Who are you?" while there was still distance between them.

The man turned to face him. "I'll deal with Zeus. You will take your people and go home."

"I thought the ancient Superians were all long dead,"

Tristan replied, his curiosity unsatisfied.

"You think I'm an Angeli," the man stated, his eyes narrowing as his nostrils flared at the offense. "I am Michael, an archangel and faithful servant of Jehovah. Those who call themselves Angeli are usurpers of a holy name. Leave," he all but snarled, "before I forget that my god is under orders to let you live."

"I am my own god," Tristan challenged, "and I'm under no such orders."

Michael never saw him move, but the weight of the Superian slamming into his left shoulder sent him into a spin. Unfurling his wings, he caught an updraft and used it to gracefully find his bearings – and his opponent.

Landing with a smile, he taunted, "Oh, this is going to be fun." Power pulsating from him in an aura of white, he asked, "Will you fight me as you are, or should I retrieve your sword?"

Tristan barely heard as the blood rushed into his head, and his heart pounded in his ears. His focus was on the strength and energy emanating from Michael. It was intoxicating. He felt it; the void felt it and wanted all of it. Yet, even as the void reached across the chasm to claim it, Tristan feared the well of his own power overflowing and tried to pull it back. Clinging to sanity, hoping to keep leashed the raw, animalistic impulses surging through his body, his heart pounding in his chest, he looked away.

From his position close to Zeus, who was on his knees with a hand clasped around his throat, Michael looked at Tristan and shook his head. "Pathetic."

That, Tristan heard. As his head snapped up, he pinned the

archangel with glowing eyes.

"Now we're getting somewhere," Michael stated as he watched the Superian turn feral.

His double-pointed ears flattened to the sides of his head as the lines of his jaw sharpened, jutting his chin. His legs, having busted through his trousers, leaving them as tattered rags held up by a stretched leather belt, thickened, but it was the claws that ripped through the toes of his boots that grabbed his attention.

"Impressive," Michael said, "if you intend to fight with your feet," but then said, "Oh, never mind," when the claws on Tristan's hands elongated as well. "Come, monster. Let us fight. The victor will claim the title of Angel."

Tristan saw the attack coming, but his mind was at war with his body, and his reaction time was too slow. Michael landed a solid left hook to Tristan's face, then followed it with a heavy right uppercut that snapped the Superian's head back on his spine. One, two, three body hooks went unchallenged before a reverse ridge-hand caught Tristan square in his throat.

Tristan's chin, dropping at an angle towards his collar bone, trapped Michael's left hand.

Michael's grin slipped into a scowl as he dumped an overload of power into a right-uppercut that cracked into Tristan's ribs. Air whooshed from his lungs, and the blow sent him sliding sideways several feet. All at once, his body and mind reconciled. As the fight came into focus, he countered with a right hook of his own.

Pain exploded in Michael's right side as his armor dented, and his ribs broke under the blow. His wings, folded forward like sidewalls, were spared, but when his back hit the trunk of an oak, he hit the ground at a run and exploded towards Tristan with his sword drawn.

Tristan ducked the first slash of the blade. He came up inside the swing to slice four perfect lines through Michael's golden armor. Michael felt the warm wash of his blood as it soaked into the white cloth beneath his gear across his ribs. Using a wing, he swept Tristan off his feet.

He was down for less than a heartbeat, but when Tristan stood, he faced a fully healed angel in heavy, plated armor, bearing a broadsword in one hand and a shield in the other.

Michael tracked Tristan's eyes back to his lost sword. Before the Angeli could make a move for it, he slammed his sword and shield together. The concussion of it kicked up a dust storm that blasted into Tristan's face, blinding him long enough for Michael to block his path to the weapon.

Tristan, however, didn't need his eyes to find his target. He had other senses for that. Using the dust cloud for cover, he added a burst of speed and came at the angel from his rear flank.

Michael, smirking at the predictability of youth, knew the attack was coming. At the last moment, just as those slashing claws would be reaching for his back, he launched himself into a backflip that carried him over Tristan's head. He brought down his shield and cracked it against the back of the Angeli's skull.

Stumbling forward, Tristan lost his balance entirely and reached out with his hands as the ground rushed up to meet him. Yet, instead of falling, Tristan felt fire erupt in his left shoulder and then he was sailing, face-first, towards a tree.

Twisting to protect his nearly-severed arm, he took the hit to his right side and crumpled to the grass.

Stunned and in incredible pain, Tristan was slow in coming to his feet. Leaning against the tree trunk, watching Michael as intently as Michael was watching him, he gritted his teeth to trap his scream and realigned his mangled arm to his ruined shoulder.

Michael, right brow arched, watched the Superian's flesh knit itself back together. "They said you were a fast healer, but I underestimated their word. Next time," he vowed, "I'll just take your head."

Tristan's neck punched forward from his shoulders as a savage snarl tore its way from his throat.

Pulling a four-inch dagger from the inside of his boot, Michael let it fly.

Tristan, tracking the blade, sidestepped, but Michael had outpaced his own throw and, with a solid, backhanded swing, knocked him back into the weapon's path. The dagger buried itself in the side of his neck and cut off his ability to breathe.

Refusing him the opportunity to yank out the dagger and heal, Michael delivered shield-strike after shield-strike, forcing Tristan to stay on his heels. Eyes bulging from lack of air, forearms blackened from blocking the shield, he was forced back. Pain lanced through his upper thigh, but the dagger prevented him from looking down.

Michael was relentless. When the dagger he'd thrust into Tristan's thigh failed to bring the Angeli down, he conjured another and went for his throat.

Tristan let himself fall backward, dropping below the

strike. Pulling the dagger from the side of his neck, gasping for air, he stabbed it upward into Michael's side. The blade hit the angel's armor and snapped at the hilt.

Michael yanked the blade from Tristan's thigh. In a furious down-strike, he thought to end it but hit dirt instead when Tristan rolled from beneath the attack and disappeared.

The Superian moved at an untraceable speed, but he could hear him. The leaves he ruffled, the twigs he snapped underfoot, they offered clues. When a running wind whipped by his left side, he slashed out with his sword and then, pivoting, swung out his shield to the right.

Tristan, thinking to throw Michael off with his first pass, was caught by the angel's countermove. He'd meant only to block the shield, but his claws went straight through it. With a violent, wrenching pull, the shield was ripped from Michael's hand and tossed to the side.

Taking his sword in both hands, Michael turned a full circle and plunged the blade towards Tristan's heart. It entered through the front of Tristan's left ribcage and came out the back. Tugging to free his weapon, his attempt was thwarted.

Tristan grabbed Michael's wrist and, though it drove the sword in deeper, pulled the angel close to grab hold of the nearest wing peeking above the man's shoulder.

When the delicate bones crafting his wing gave way to Tristan's crushing grip, Michael panicked. Tristan let him struggle. He let him pull for all he was worth, then he let him go. As Michael half-fell, half-twisted to run, he screamed when the Superian took his wing.

Zeus, recovered but weaker than he'd been in eons, found his resolve and came up at Michael's side. "Either we fight together," he said, "or this will end badly."

"I do not need you," Michael stated, pain pulling at his voice. He screamed, "I am in command of LEGIONS!"

His last word was a battle cry, and the angels harkened to his call, spilling from the sky and emerging from the forest around them. Arrayed in gold and silver armor, with a myriad of weapons drawn, they surrounded Tristan with clear intent.

A colorful streak, cutting a direct path towards them, made Zeus call out, "It's the other one!" But his warning came too late.

Set appeared behind Michael, kicking his leg out from under him to bring him down to size. "Thanks for yelling so loud," he said. "I almost didn't find my brother." Then he grabbed hold of the one wing the guy had left, to connect to the angel's power, and moaned. "Oh…" Set's eyes rolled back in his head and his neck lulled on his shoulders as the physical connection allowed him easy access to the angel's energy. "Incredible," he whispered as Michael began to scream uncontrollably.

Zeus turned to bat Set off, but Tristan caught him with two open palms, square in the chest. Digging his claws through armor and flesh alike, Tristan clenched his fingers into fists and grabbed hold. Taking control of the god's fall, Tristan slammed his back into the ground, again and again, until Zeus's eyes went blank. Dragging the limp god in one hand, Tristan swooped to retrieve his sword with the other before dumping Zeus at Set's feet.

"It, uh, looks like you've ticked off some angels, little brother," he said.

It wasn't Set's markings but Set himself that glowed golden. His eyes were twin suns that rolled like orbs of fire, and the sound of his voice gave even the angels pause. "I don't think I can let him go. It feels…so good. Let me kill him, Tristan. I want his power."

Tristan's gaze swept from the dozens of angels waiting to kill them to a brother who'd changed as much as he had. Finally, he said, "If you kill him, you'll probably lose what little of you is still in there." He looked again at those surrounding them. "I have an idea, but if I should fail—" he kicked Zeus— "drain them both and kill them all."

Set reached down and took Zeus by the wrist. Together, god and angel screamed as the others advanced.

Coming to terms with the unfavorable odds, Tristan cursed, taking faint comfort that the approaching angels did not glow as Michael had. He held his sword, but Davad was the weapon wielder of the Five; like father, like son, and he felt more confident using his bare hands. Still, as the angels closed in, it was Jacob's voice in his head. As old battle lessons echoed in his mind, he followed orders.

Their number is not greater than your stamina, and they cannot all come against you at once, Tristan. Breathe. Make your way through them…one kill at a time.

Letting his sword fall, Tristan sidestepped a slashing blade and came in close to grab the angel's head in both hands. Turning towards another, his eyes flaring at the large war hammer in the angel's hands, he flattened the head of the first, bursting it like a ripe berry. As the angel dropped, Tristan snatched his weapon from his hand and struck up with the sword to block the downward strike of the hammer.

The weapon rebounded against Tristan's sword to cave in the angel's face. Its dead body flipped feet over head before smacking the ground.

Three others thought to attack from his rear flank, but Tristan's hearing made it a fool's plan. He dropped the angel's sword as he pivoted to grab his own from off the ground. In a single turn, with one fluid swipe of his monstrous sword, he severed them into pieces.

Set watched the next angel take his broadsword in both hands, running full out towards Tristan's turned back, with the blade held high over his head, and he simply couldn't resist.

With a speed that made lightning seem motionless, Set dropped his captives and intercepted the angel mid-run. His fist and forearm became a white-hot rod of destruction that exploded against the angel's oncoming chest, leaving a melon-sized hole behind. He was back at his position before the angel realized he was dead. Snatching up his captives, he grinned down at them, bathing them in the beam his eyes now gave off.

"That was… exhilarating." Then he pulled from them again. Only this time, the sound of his crazed laughter was louder than their agony.

"Who's next?" Tristan shouted after turning to see not only his brother's save but the angels' hesitation.

"Tristan, get over here," Set called.

"What is it?" Tristan asked, at his brother's side before the request had been fully given. "Why aren't they attacking?"

"Angels can see the shifts in aether like an epoto," Set

told him.

"So?"

Set pointed. Not ten feet from where they stood, a ripple in the air opened into a portal with an endless black backdrop, and Munsin stepped through.

"Please," he begged Set, his hands held open in front of himself, "you don't understand what you're doing. You don't know what it will cause."

***

Kali watched as another of her demonic children went down. Furious, she grabbed hold of a dark-skinned Superian with one of her eight hands and lifted him off the ground, swinging and kicking, by his black hair. Then she cut him to pieces with the weapons she held in the others. His head dropped last.

Walking a battlefield littered with one-on-one conflicts, there were six Superians who stood out from the rest. Five men and one woman, who ripped through her children as if they were gods themselves. They fought as a unit with flawless skill, and with a fluid action that left nothing but blood and death in their wake. They had to die.

Kaprali, a demon that stood fifteen feet tall on four legs that resembled arms and hands and had a webbed wingspan of six feet, formed from the earth at Kali's bidding. It lowered its burnished-brown, featherless but bird-like head for her to stroke. Laying a finger alongside its razor-sharp beak, Kali turned its long, sinuous neck towards the six Superians.

"Stop them," she ordered.

Kaprali cooed to its mistress before folding its wings behind itself and charging, trampling a squad of Fera soldiers that got in its way. One, a female, was flattened underfoot by its massive weight and carried three paces before falling off.

The red markings in the Fulgo's flesh peeked from beneath the black armor at his wrists as he scooped down to retrieve his sword; he'd taken his last kill with his bare hands. The three vertical lines running down his pale face marked him one of the twelve hand-chosen by Triton to fight for the House of Angeli.

It was the monster's squawk that turned his head, flinging his long, thin, black braids about his face and shoulders. "Scopum!" he shouted, and a massive Mortalis looked up and grinned.

Wiggling his blond eyebrows at the redheaded vixen fighting at his side, the Mortalis waited. She cupped her hands around her full lips and bellowed, "Scopum! Scopum!" The last three members of their side of the kill squad heard the call and came at a run.

"Let's go kill us a bird."

The back-up wasn't needed. Kaprali was at a full gallop, but so was the redhead. "This is going to be so gross," she shouted on her way passed the Fulgo, who laughed.

"No," the Mortalis said to himself, waiting for the Fulgo to give the signal, "but it's going to hurt like…"

A glimmer sliced in front of the monster's front arms. The moment it missed a step, he popped a portal directly in its path, putting his weight behind an uppercut that slung back its neck, then bounced like a boulder against the side of a mountain to crash into the ground. The position, however, afforded him a beautiful view of the redhead diving for the monster's throat.

As the Mortalis went down and the redhead made her leaping dive with twin daggers leading the way, the Fulgo gave a quick twist of wrist, and she began to spin in mid-air. As the monster's neck slung back from the Mortalis's blow, she entered at its neck. She slung blood, hide, and gore as she exited between the wings on its back. Releasing his hold on the aether around her, she landed lithely on the balls of her feet as the beast fell.

Wiping the gunk from her eyes, she slung out her hands to dislodge the ick. "I say we find the god conjuring these nasties and take them out," she suggested as the kill squad came together.

Seeing how easily Kaprali went down, Kali was of a similar mind, but then a fresh wave of tall, pale-faced Superians came through the gate. Sighing, she said aloud, "That rift needs closed." But as she scanned the hill, looking for who to send, she found desperation instead.

Ares's undead were locked in conflict with the Superians, and they were losing. Most of her demonic children were already dead. The tide of battle had turned. War had entered its final hour, and desperation was the only option left.

"I can't believe that I have to do this," she groaned, but then said, "AZAZEL!"

The ground did not tremble; it quaked, blurring Anliac's vision of it from her lofted position. She watched the familiar black ulcers form in a six-point pattern on the ground, but she hesitated to send men because Kali was close. It was a mistake and it cost them.

The ulcers burst and pooled into a massive, bubbling, black ooze that coalesced into a dark demon that stood on hooves at nine feet tall. His legs, thick with muscle, were covered in course, black fur, but when he unwrapped his cloak-like wings from around his upper torso, smooth, chiseled perfection was revealed. Twisted horns protruded from above both temples, and four sharp fangs shot past his thin lips. His nostrils flared, emitting puffs of grey smoke. Fire shot from his eyes like burning torches as he surveyed the battle before turning to Kali.

"Ah," Azazel chuckled. "I see now why you broke your word." Reaching out, he stroked a curved, black claw down her check, drawing a tendril of blood.

Kali's upper lip furled. Her purple-cast skin darkened to near black as her blood heated, and her hands trembled to wrap themselves around the demon's throat.

"What's wrong?" he taunted. "Can the goddess of destruction not contend with one little battle?"

"You owe me, Azazel," she said, her glare its own warning, "and I'm calling in the debt."

An angel, tossed off the end of a Superian spike, flew straight towards the demon like a gift from his god. As fast as thought, in Azazel's right hand, a seven- foot scythe grew. With it, he split the angel in half.

"The Superians offer me angels to slaughter. Why should I help you?" Azazel asked, waiting until the two pieces had landed before turning back to her for his answer. "You know unleashing me will draw his attention. Tsk, tsk, Kali," he said, shaking his head. "No one wants that."

"I'm aware of the consequences, Azazel," she snarled, "which is why you're going to keep your word and honor our bargain. You're going to close that rift and win this war for me. I will not stand before Him defeated."

"Stand?" Azazel laughed, showing rows of sharp teeth. "We all kneel before Him," he said. With a flourishing bow, he added, "For the last time, your wish is my command."

Anliac saw the monster revert into ooze and then it disappeared. Frantic, she searched for it, then panicked altogether when its reformation began before the gateway. "Triton! Watch out!" She wasn't as fast in the air as she was on the ground, and now she was going to be too late...

Triton turned to see the demon grow a short blade in his left hand. He saw the thrust that would shove the sword through Razoran's back and into his heart. "NO!" he shouted, leaping between them. He grabbed ahold of the blade with his bare hands and pulled it into his own chest. As his life's blood poured from the wound, he gathered it into a conjured dagger and buried it through the front of beast's throat.

The blood dagger turned black and was absorbed into Azazel without inflicting injury.

Pushed forward, Razoran turned to see the cause and caught Triton as he died. The snarl that ripped from Razoran was raw agony and unhinged rage. He let his captain fall to draw his sword. Beyond reason, he attacked, slicing and hacking with blade and claws, lunging with his gaping maw in the hope of eating the demon alive.

It was the wolf's commitment to the battle that made Azazel prolong it. Ducking and dodging the inferior assault, he played with the pup until its strength waned, then turned the tip of one wing into a stake and pinned him through the left shoulder. Creating a twisted blade that promised a swift death, he aimed for his heart, and…

He looked down at a three-foot sword, with a white dracon climbing its silver length, emerging from his gut. In a fast spin that slung Razoran, who'd been attached to his wing, off to the side, he turned to face his attacker.

As the sword turned black, consumed by his flesh, Azazel said, "No weapon conjured against me will prevail, for I am them, and they are me. But I do love a good try." He grew from his hand a six-foot broadsword. "Tell me, boy," he taunted, waving the weapon around, "is it cowardice that makes you attack from behind?"

Triton was dead and Razoran was broken, so though Davad swallowed hard and his heart raced, he did more than hold his ground. He brought the image of his father to the forefront of his mind, then he lit both hands on fire and launched himself, weaponless, at the monster. Wrapping his legs around the demon's waist to hold on, he caught its head between his hands and set it on fire.

His hand absorbed the broadsword, and he replaced it with a dagger that he shoved into the boy's right thigh, "I see it wasn't cowardice," he stated, his amusement real. He slung his head back and forth to dislodge him.

Davad screamed through gritted teeth, but the fire in his hands burned hotter as his grip increased.

Anliac dove head-long from the sky with ice swords in hand to save Davad and kill the demon. She was almost within reach when the whole world went wrong.

From below the apex of the hill, on the side where the fighting was at its worst, a concussive BOOM spread in an outward wave of force that encased the whole of it. It knocked Anliac and angels from the sky, as those on the ground became like tossed stones. People disappeared as if plucked up by invisible hands, only to be replaced by ones not there a moment before.

The fighting was ended not by defeat, nor by victory, but by what came next.

XXXVI

Truths and Pains

Tristan and Set, who maintained his grip on Zeus and Michael, found themselves translocated to the center of the battlefield. They faced Munsin and a god they'd never seen, with blue-black hair and blue bird markings over his bare chest. His youthful appearance belied his age, but his eyes held ages of knowledge.

"Now, Shed," Munsin stated. A shield shimmered to encase them then became an invisible cage that trapped them inside.

There were too many gods and warriors in this war, and separating them had drained more than Munsin's power; it had drained his essence, but he was not finished yet. With his hands held before him, palms pressed together, he muttered, "May Earth forgive me," and through five shimmering doors, they came.

Anubis was of perfect masculine form, but with a jackal's head.

Kuan Yin was an image of feminine beauty and grace, but her black eyes held the promise of destruction if provoked.

Rongo, with flesh like tree bark, was strong and steadfast.

Utu, covered head to toe in red, plated armor, was shorter than the other gods, but twin swords stuck up from over his shoulders,

And Set, the god that should have never been released, arrived last.

Tristan and Set were surrounded.

Anubis, his onyx gaze slipping to Zeus and Michael, jerked up his head to demand, "You, filth. Release them."

Set's eyes were white orbs, and his body glowed golden with the engorgement of power he'd siphoned from the gods on their knees. With an arched brow and crooked grin, he met Anubis's stare and said, "I'd love to get my hands on you."

One step forward, and then the boy's hopeful expression stopped Anubis from going further. Instead, he pointed at Tristan and told him, "This is over. You will leave this planet, or we will make what the Greeks and Christians have done to you seem but a dream, for we will be your nightmare."

Set laughed, and the chill of it swept over the massive gathering, atop the hill, to spread fear even unto the dead and demons' hearts. "If this is a nightmare, I hope never to wake, for you have made my brother all but a god, and you've fed me more power than I thought existed. Your threats hold no weight with us."

When Set released his hold on Zeus and Michael to move

towards Tristan, the two immortals dropped through holes in the ground, through egresses conjured by Munsin, to re-emerge behind the circle of gods. Apollo and Ares dropped from overhead to come to their feet beside Zeus, who could do no more than stay upright on his knees. Confused by his wretched state, they bellowed in rage, "What did you do to him?" as they turned and attacked.

Shed threw up a separate shield, one that solidified long enough to thwart the gods' move. Munsin shouted, "Silence! You Greeks have done enough to advocate war. We are here to end this."

"Speak for yourself," Set said, stepping forward from the other gods, "I was released for the sole purpose of creating chaos. I love to stir the pot." He grinned. "And I'm not Greek." Vanishing, he appeared before Superi's Set.

With a single backhand that came so fast, the Set of Egypt had no chance to counter, a concussive boom knocked the god past his starting point. He bounced off the inside of the shield hard enough to bury him in the ground, unmoving.

With his head falling back on his shoulders, Set's white eyes rolled back in his head as he took in a relaxing breath. "Who's next?"

Stretching out a limb-like arm, Rongo held out his creviced hand. "Peace, Superians…Please…" His words having gained their attention, he continued, "Rumors have long existed of the transgressions committed against you, and we understand your desire to extract vengeance upon the guilty. Revenge is a game the gods know well, but we ask that you hear us out before taking further action."

"The time for words has passed," Tristan stated.

"Then allow me to put action behind our words," Shed countered.

Those not wounded unto death began to heal, and as they did, they found their way to the summit, where the gods stood with the brothers, deciding their fate.

Tristan shook his head as his anger mounted. "You heal a handful and expect gratitude? Either you don't know why we're here, or your arrogance knows no bounds. Which is it?"

"He's right," Utu spoke. "We know nothing of this war or how long it has been fought. As Rongo has said, we know only rumor."

"Then let us discover the truth," Kuan Yin replied. Then her voice, like the force of rushing water, pushed its way into the minds of them all. *Who began this conflict?* The answers were not what she was expecting, but her compassion compelled her to look upon the Superian brothers to say, "It is no wonder you hate us all."

Shaking his head to clear it, a contorted grin spread across Set's animalistic features as the god of Egypt stood in the crater his body had created and found the one who'd put him in it. "You..." he growled, but then became distracted. "Well, well, what have we here?"

"Anliac!" Tristan called out when she hit the shield hard from the outside and rebounded. Flying to her feet, Anliac slammed her fists into the shield, again and again, as hot, angry tears coursed down her cheeks.

"Does she belong to you?" Set asked. "Because that beauty could up the stakes."

"Touch her," Tristan snarled, baring his claws like blades

and teeth like daggers, "and I'll rip you to shreds.

"Promises, promises," the god chuckled.

Hearing their general's screams, seeing her pounding against the translucent shield to reach their champion, the warriors of Superi rallied at her back and fell into formation.

"Anliac… Anliac, stop," Shashara pleaded. She made her way through the amassing armies to the edge of the shield, her progress slowed by Davad, who walked with a limp.

Breathing hard, she pressed her palms against the barrier between Tristan and herself. Anliac was overwhelmed by the changes in Tristan, but no more so than Shashara when her blue gaze found Set in time to hear the Egyptian state, "I was told I would get to kill you."

"You're welcome to try."

Shashara gasped and jerked a hand over her mouth to hide it. That cold, hollow voice did not belong to him.

"Enough, Set," Tristan warned.

"I don't take orders from you, boy," the god of Egypt growled.

"I wasn't talking to you." Tristan sneered. "I was talking to my brother, but trust me, you don't want the conflict you think you desire. I'm far from spent, and you are not my brother's equal."

Set turned his stare to the younger brother. "Your name is Set?"

"What of it?" Set asked.

Set ignored the question to grin sideways at Anubis. "You would have had me kill one who shares my name. That's low," he stated, "even for you."

Uncertain as to who held the power, Tristan encompassed

them all in his demand. "I want the barrier keeping her out dropped now," he told them, "or this little bubble is going to feel real tight, real fast."

The gods tensed as Munsin hesitated. "Do you vow to hold the peace?"

Tristan's temper sparked. Set felt his increased intensity, and it increased his own, until the two brothers were illuminated in matching golden auras, like two Superian suns burning amidst Earth's gods.

His patience at its end, Tristan bellowed, "I didn't start this!" His body responded to his mounting fury, his muscles engorging as his blood heated.

"Tristan, no!" Anliac cried from beyond the shield. "They've changed you enough."

Pivoting to face her, he said, "We didn't want any of this."

"I know," she replied sadly.

Rongo interrupted, "What is it you do want?"

"We want these damning curses lifted," Tristan shouted. Beams of yellow light poured from his eyes to pin the nature god in his place. "That is all we have wanted for two thousand years."

Kuan Yin nodded at Utu, who, in turn, slipped into the minds of the gods. But where Kuan Yin had held her tongue, he would not, for now he knew the Superians' pain.

"Apollo began the war," he said, "and the Egyptians played their part, but it is Zeus who holds the binding to the curses cast. The Superians discovered this, and they came to kill Zeus, believing his death would free them."

"They call them the twin curses," Kuan Yin interjected, "the Cruxen Clav and the Discindo Pestis. One traps the mind and drives it to insanity before it can comprehend evolution, and in so doing, damns them to a life without advancement. Compared to Earth," she explained, "Superi has been prisoner to a very dark age. And, the second..." Her lips pressed thin as she shook her head, looking to Utu to finish.

"The second," he told the other gods, "the Discindo Pestis, genetically and physically ripped them apart, forever destroying their true form, and leaving them as fractured pieces of a ruined whole."

Kuan Yin's delicate features twisted into fury as Utu's sorrowful regret for the dastardly deeds done to Superi's denizens hit her hard, and she turned that rage on the deserving. Apollo hit his knees beside his father, and together, they screamed.

Ares drew his sword and raised it against Kuan Yin, but Shed stepped in between them. "Foolish Greek, let not the thought cross twice, or see your skull cracked and your mind removed."

The Five stood as one, despite the shield, and bore witness to the gods turning on one another.

"Release them from the curses," Kuan Yin commanded Zeus over his pleas for mercy, "or your agony will find no end."

"I can't," Zeus gasped. "I haven't the power."

"Explain," Kuan Yin stated, easing up enough that he could.

Panting from the pain, he said between breaths, "He took my strength. Return it," he vowed to Set, "and I'll lift the curses."

"For what my word is worth to you," Munsin said, "he's telling the truth. Gods feed off the worship of their followers, and most of the modern world thinks him a myth. He cannot lift the curses if he lacks the power it took to create them. It is much to ask…"

"Not here," Set stated. "You will leave your armies on Earth, and you will all step through the rift. If I am to give back his power, it will be on Superi, where we can see the fulfillment of his vow…"

"…Or," Tristan continued, "if the curses go unbroken, we can offer you up to our people for their vengeance."

Munsin waited for the other gods to concede, then asked Shed to drop the shield around them. When he did, Anliac, who'd never taken her hands off the barrier, stumbled forward and then blurred in her run to be at Tristan's side. Shashara, desperate to reach Set, was about to ask Davad to wait for her when Azazel, with Kali by his side, stopped them.

"I am a demon," he said, "without conscience, and yet I hold great value in courageous acts of passion. You fought well, Superian. You honored the man who fell, and for that reason, I regret that your wound will never heal." With those parting words, they moved on.

"Who fell?" Shashara asked. "What was he talking about?"

Before Davad could answer, the living and the dead, the Superians and the gods they'd warred against, stood upon Superian soil.

XXXVII

Dievas

The field between Bealson's Grove and the city of Imbellis filled up with those conjured back from Earth. Shed, the one who'd translocated them, hit his knees. The gods found themselves surrounded not merely by those brought back from Earth but by the wave of Superian forces waiting to invade it.

"Idiot," Munsin snapped as realization hit him. Snapping his fingers, he created a black egress beneath Shed that he fell through and disappeared. At the looks given him, he shook his head and sighed. "There was no reason for him to do that. For one, I'm better at it than he is, and for another, we were all capable of walking through that rift," he said, pointing at the one behind the gods of Earth to further his point.

"We are not all here," Anliac stated. With exception of Michael, the angels and demons had been left behind, and Artemis was nowhere to be seen.

"Those that matter are present," Anubis retorted. Narrowing his gaze at Superi's Set, he pointed at Zeus and said, "He cannot do what you've demanded until he is released."

Set's hesitation was not born of fear; he did not relish relinquishing the power he'd obtained, but in moving forward, he made his decision. His multitude of markings produced an incredible golden light that brightened with his approach. When he laid hands upon the Greek, Set made the transfer feel like liquid fire.

Zeus screamed again…

When it was finished, Zeus gained his feet without a tremble. He was content that the light of power had resettled in its rightful place within his animus.

And yet, though they no longer held their illumination, when the golden marking remained on Set's skin, Michael, still on his knees amongst the other gods, asked, "Aren't you forgetting someone?"

Returning to his brother without so much as a glance towards the angel, Set replied, "No, I am not."

A masculine chuckle made Anubis glare at the Egyptian. "Shut it, Father." he warned.

Ignoring Anubis, the god grinned at his namesake and said, "I am not actually of Earth. You should find me when this is over. We could be friends, you and I. Hey, watch him," he warned, and all eyes went to Zeus.

With Zeus's power returned, Utu decided to take no chances. Throwing back his head, his body awash in an aura of power, he bellowed, "Forseti!"

It was a rift that opened, but it expanded as fast as a portal to show a redheaded, bearded, barrel-chested warrior. His visage was confounded by the sight of the battlefield.

"Hold!" Kuan exclaimed as thousands of Superian came to attention. The Five fanned out into a formation that promised violence of epic proportions.

Stepping through the rift, his voice like hardened steel, he captured Kuan's stare and said, "Show me truth and I will give you justice."

The goddess held nothing back. She revealed all into his mind, and in so doing, she released Forseti's rage.

The onslaught of information did not hinder his steps as he marched for Zeus while the images yet flowed. By the time Kuan had retreated from his mind, Zeus was backing away.

"You damned, Greek," Forseti thundered, reaching for the god.

"No!" Zeus shouted, crossing his forearms like a shield across his face.

Forseti grabbed hold his wrist with his meaty hand. "You will be tried, Zeus, but first, you will release them, or on my honor, I will call Odin down upon thee and demand the wrath of a thousand deaths be heaped upon your head."

Attempting to face the Five, Zeus resisted, and so Forseti wrenched him around, against his will, to face them as well. When he spoke, it was to the Greek. "Release them, Zeus. I will not tell you again."

His jaw clenching, Zeus replied, "I need my son."

Apollo waited to see if there would be objections before he took the few necessary steps to join his father. "I don't think you want to be touching him when the curses are released," Apollo sneered at Foresti, "but if you'd rather take your chances…" He shrugged and let the threat loom.

Once given space, the father leaned in towards the son and whispered words that Tristan alone could hear. He had no issues with the exchange, for Zeus had told Apollo to lift the curses from those who could hear so that Earth and Superi would never collide again.

He shrugged a shoulder and shook off Anliac's concern when she peered up at him. "It's all good," he reassured her.

"Let us hope so," she said, refocusing on the gods.

The two deities stood shoulder to shoulder, arms held before themselves, with their elbows locked and their palms facing the ground. Like the calm before a storm, the denizens of Superi braced themselves for the unknown.

And with a single word, their world was changed.

"EXSOLVO!"

A flash of light, like an expanding disk, cut through the gathered Superians. Not by one or two, not by dozens or hundreds, but by the thousands a collective gasp. With the inward breath came clarity of mind that was like new birth. Pockets of shocked and terrified shouts bounced from the surrounding fields and groves, but it was not long before the Five saw the cause for themselves.

"What's going on?"

Turning towards the question, the men were both Superian, yet their faces were unfamiliar. One was a Nox with fire markings running up his left forearm. The other was a Fulgo. His markings, those wrapped around his neck like a collar, marked him an aer wielder. However, with the curses removed, their markings were lifting from their flesh like water rising.

"What's happening?" the men called out.

It was Shashara's sweet, awed response that sent the two men running in opposite directions, their speed bolstered by sheer terror.

In awe and disbelief, she said, "You're merging…"

Rumors run fast, but the truth flies. As her words wafted through Superian ranks, some gave in to their fear and fled the crowd. Others lost focus of the gods to seek out who might merge with them. The brilliant beam that shot from the rift grabbed the attention of everyone, even those fleeing.

To blink would have been to miss it, but the light unfolded from itself, dimming as it did, until there stood a god, fourteen feet tall, appearing none too pleased. His hair was white and flowing. His toga, simple in design, shimmered with all the colors of the spectrum in a chaotic display that came in waves. Power radiated from him as his focus found first Apollo, then Zeus.

"My God!" Zeus cried out as Apollo pleaded, "Have mercy."

But the god replied, "I think not." Then, screaming, father and son dropped into the black abyss that formed under their knees.

The Five held their ground, their armies restrained by Davad's raised hand. Michael and the gods took to their knees and hid their faces until the god's attention turned from them.

"Who are you?" Tristan asked, breaking the silence.

"Better question," Set interjected, subconsciously rubbing his hands together, "what ability lets you do that?"

"Set Mattewson!" Shashara smacked his hands down and

then, realizing what she'd done, smiled abashedly and said, "Sorry." Then she some kind of curtsy that embarrassed her even more.

The god's smile was indulgent, and when he spoke, his voice carried with it a current of peace that washed over the people. "I am called Dievas the Almighty, and I govern the galaxy that is home to us all."

"You are not our god," Anliac stated with a challenging tilt to her chin.

Dievas's grin stretched wide his beatific face and then he began to shift his form, changing with a perfect rhythm that gave a clear view of each face he wore. He was a man, a woman, a child, an ancient. He was an Earthling, a Superian, an Asgardian. He was every race, even a few they didn't recognize. He was everyone and no one, until at last, he was Dievas the Almighty once again.

"Perhaps not," he said, "but those who have wronged you serve me, and for that, they will be punished."

"We don't care what you do with them," Davad told him. "We only wanted the curses lifted."

"And that is why I've come," Dievas replied. "My Greek children have plagued your planet for long enough, and yet, when given the opportunity to make right their wrongs, they chose deception."

"What are you talking about? "Tristan asked. "I heard Zeus tell Apollo to free everyone who could hear from the curses. What deception have they wrought now?"

"Exactly," Dievas told him. "Zeus and Apollo only freed those within the sound of their voice."

Fingers twitching, Set said, having seen through the word

play faster than his brother, "We've been betrayed."

"Hear me," Dievas stated, "and feel the truth I speak. I release you all." The wind that stirred was not born of violence, but of healing. Like the sweet scent of spring, it swept over the whole of Superi in an instant. He decreed, "I've repaired the damage this war has caused to your world, and never again will a rift open upon Superi for one who holds ill intent in their heart. Munsin."

"Yes, my lord," he replied, quick to step forward and bow again.

"Take my children home," Dievas said, "and see a trial set for Zeus and Apollo. Be assured," he stated for the benefit of the others, "more trials will follow."

"As you command," Munsin said, bowing deeper at the waist. Then he opened doors that swept them into a common egress and through the rift.

Opening his arms, Dievas gestured for Set and Shashara. The two found themselves standing, suddenly, before the Almighty, with his open palms pressed upon their heads.

Set's eyes were fury when he lifted his stare, but the visage of peace that Dievas wore stole his anger and compelled him to say with true gratitude, "Thank you, Dievas, for ending it."

Shashara's head was bowed, her shoulders trembling with the silent shedding of relieved tears. "You've given us hope," she whispered, her mind unraveling as it wrapped its way around its newfound freedom.

"You are wrong," Dievas told her, though his gentle smile and tender tone removed the hard edge from his words. "It is the hope held between you both that drew you to me. I will use that hope to house a new seed, one that will bring about your golden age."

His hands lit up upon their heads. There was no pain, only marvel and awe, and it widened their eyes and dropped their jaws. It shook their whole bodies with laughter, until joy and excitement pulled them together in a rush that collided in a kiss.

Dievas's laughter was a contagious rumble that tickled the heart and caused those who could hear to join him. "Live well, Superians. Live in peace. Let the seed of technology spread forth from hopeful minds to cultivate a world full of possibilities." To Set and Shashara, he said, "Do not covet the fruit it bears, as do my children, but feed the masses. Help your people grow and evolve, for with the knowledge I've given you, you've the power to be your own gods..."

Moving to the gateway, he paused. Winking at Tristan from over his shoulder, Dievas added, "...Some of you, anyway," before he became a beam of light that vanished through it.

And then the way was closed.

XXXVIII

Merger

With the last god gone, more than joyous exaltations resounded from the fields and grove, as grief for the dead rang out to mock their victory.

Anliac moved to Tristan, laid her head on his chest as he pulled her close, and asked, "Do you think it's really over?"

"The war? Yes," Tristan told her, "but the cost…"

From within Set's embrace, Shashara tipped back her head to look at him. Running the flat of her palm up his chest, her fingertips came to rest in the hollow of his throat, where she could feel the deep vibration of his new voice.

"We left Exterius Antro to save the girl…" Grinning, Set squeezed Shashara's waist. "And we ended up saving the world. The dead are heroes and the living are free."

"Davad, thank Superi," Skylar gasped. Her pale face was flushed, and her red hear was running as wild as her frantic yellow eyes. "I can't find Triton."

Hot tears filled the stare he gave back to her, coursing

---

down his cheeks to leave streaks in the grime coating them. "Triton is among the heroes. Come," he said to Set, "let the living and the free bear witness to the cost."

He heard their questions, their demands for an explanation, but he couldn't speak around the burning knot in his throat. Instead, grateful when Skylar took his hand, he followed the sound of a familiar cry. Limping, he led them to Razoran.

Tristan's marks burst to life, and his fists clenched as tightly as his jaw. When Davad, going awkwardly to his knees before falling to lean on one hip, propped up by a hand, he said, "I feel my father's death more keenly with Triton's passing."

"Oh, Davad," Shashara whispered, leaving Set to wrap her arms around her little brother. "I'm so sorry."

Davad broke. Clinging to her like a child caught in the grip of a nightmare, he cried. "I keep losing fathers."

Razoran, unaware of the low growl he was producing as he crouched over the dead and bloodied body of his savior and friend, snarled and snapped at Skylar when she reached for him. "The demon was coming for me," Razoran confessed. With Triton laying between them, Razoran peered at Davad and asked, "Why didn't you let him kill me?"

"I could not lose you too," was Davad's reply, and the fight left them both.

Lan came up behind Tristan and Anliac and touched them on the shoulder to get their attention. When they'd turned, he said, "Forgive my intrusion, but your Generals are awaiting instruction. And, um…" He hesitated. "There's something you should both see."

"Okay," Tristan said, "let's go."

They turned and Anliac gasped.

Lan and Tristan were stopped in their tracks.

"Guys," Anliac croaked, "we might have a problem."

While others turned to look, Set and Shashara were on their feet, standing front and center before the guards that had protected them since the Five had claimed Pisces Stragulum.

"Jonas," Shashara cried, one hand flying to her mouth as the other flattened over her stomach. "Oh, sweet Superi. How can I help?"

"It doesn't hurt," he rushed to assure her. "Right, Travain?" he asked Set's guard. "It doesn't hurt?"

"You need to move away from each other now," Shashara warned, "or the two of you will merge. Set," she urged, "tell them."

"They know that," he told her, "and they also know that they belong as one. You can't feel it, Shashara, but they can. I can too." To Jonas and Travain, he said, "You were born into a cursed world, but with this merging, you will be the beginning of a new age."

With more and more gathering round to watch the spectacle, the two men turned to face each other. In unison, they said, "Brother," before they clasped forearms.

Their flesh and bones did not burn; it became like a melding metal that moved as slow lava, until two arms were one. Connected, the merge began, and the aether drew them together. Shoulder to shoulder, neck to neck, and all the while, a force of light gained in strength. Yet, when heart met heart, the light became a brilliant burst that turned heads away.

When they looked again, a man there stood, but he was

neither Jonas nor Travain. He was no taller than a Mortalis, though of a leaner build, and while his ears held the single tip of the Fulgo, his blue-black hair hinted at Nox blood. It was, however, the vertical pupils in his emerald green eyes, like that of a reptilian Fera, that proved he was truly whole.

The members of two family lines pushed their way forward, each calling out the name of the one they felt they'd lost, but the man answered to only one.

"Can you speak?" Set asked. "Do you know who you are?"

"I am Jonas," he said and then his legs gave out.

"What of Travain?" Set pressed. "Is he gone?"

Laying a blanket over his shoulders because his clothes had not survived, Michael answered for him. "Travain is as much a part of Jonas as Jonas is a part of him," he said. "I can hear both psyches talking in his mind. They are learning about each other, sharing their histories, their secrets, their hopes and dreams." Swiping at tears he hadn't been aware of shedding, he stated, "It's quite beautiful, and yes," he said in answer to Set's unspoken question, "I believe this is happening all over Superi."

"Then the denizens need to be warned," Set said, coming to his feet. "As our minds come awake, there will be confusion, and I would not add panic to it."

"What are you thinking?" Anliac asked him.

"Find me some runners," he replied, "and I'll set the portals."

"I'm on it," Lan said.

Set pointed at a cleared area to the left of where they stood. He closed his eyes, focused, said, "Antro," and a portal appeared. His hand moved to the right. "Regia Aquam," he said, and another portal crackled open. Point, name, and conjure—the process continued until every port city had a connection on the field.

Lan stood prepared with runners for them all. Char and Donnin were among them, as were Davimon and Lishous, whose white fur was stained and matted red.

Stepping forward, Davimon moved to face the Five, then took to knee before laying his sword at their feet. "My doubts were many, and my mind was closed," he told them, "but the prophecy spoke true, and children led Superi into war." A quick peek at Anliac's scowl forced him to look down to hide his grin before he continued. "Your actions have removed my doubt, and victory has cleared my mind. So it is as a free man I kneel. Long live the Five, and long may they reign."

"Long live the Five," Char said, as Donnin followed with, "Long may they reign." Together they took their place beside Donnin.

"Long live the Five! Long may they reign!" The words took root and grew into a chant, which became a roar as the people bowed to the House of Angeli.

Tristan, no longer the boy that favored the shadows, produced his own light as he amplified his voice to address his people. "Rise! Denizens of Superi! Stand as equals, for that is the freedom you bled for! That is the freedom the dead at our feet gave their lives for! Rise!" he called. "Go, see the world as it was meant to be seen, and together, we will usher in an age to make history!"

"Hoorah! Hoorah!"

"Lan," Tristan turned to him and said, "have Set indicate which portal leads to where, then let's work at getting our people home. They deserve to give their dead a proper farewell, and they need rest."

"Yes, sir," Lan said. His beak opened to give the orders, but Anliac stopped him.

"Lan, you said there was something we needed to see?"

"I'll start organizing the exodus," Donnin offered. "I don't need to see that again."

Lan nodded and said, "Follow me."

Tristan laid a restraining hand against his brother's chest. "Not you, Set. You're the only one who can keep the portals straight."

"I'm going to stay with Jonas," Shashara said, "and Davad's not leaving…Razoran," she finished, unable to say Triton's name.

"We've got this," Anliac said, then gestured that Lan should show them the way.

It was deep in the grove, far away from where she'd left them. As impossible as it seemed, all twelve mercenaries were not merely dead, but had been torn apart.

"Curse the gods," Tristan snarled.

"This wasn't the gods' doing," Anliac told him. "Lan, I want an accounting of every ruler of every house that did not lose blood in this war. We made a promise," she said to Tristan, "and it is one I fully intend to keep."

XXXIX

This is Not Goodbye

The city of Imbellis was packed to bursting, and the tower had never held so many. All awaited the answers they hoped to find in the gathering of the Five, who stood upon a dais, placed in the center of the largest assembly room.

Healed of their wounds and rested with time, they made an imposing sight. Dressed in black fitted pants, with silver capes hanging from their shoulders over matching black tunics, the V signet of their House was laid squarely against their chests.

Davad had earned the sword at his hip by the wound he'd taken in his thigh, so it was fitting that both the blade and cane that helped him stand had belonged to Triton.

Set stood with more power and knowledge than Superi had ever seen, yet the cost was one he would not pay twice, for he'd lost most of himself in the trade. If not for Shashara—brave, beautiful Shashara, who bore more outward scars than them all—he would have disappeared, but as always, she stood by his side.

Anliac, shoulder-to-shoulder with Tristan and a step forward from the others, was truly the one who'd been changed the most by the war. The loss of her father had nearly broken her, but the secret she carried in her belly tempered her grief with joy. Turning to catch a glimpse of his strong profile, her eyes fell on the hilt of his sword, and she smirked.

Enormous by anyone's measure, the sword was carried with ease upon Tristan's back, but while impressive, the blade was the least intimidating thing about him. To win the war, his body had become a weapon. His height put him a head taller than all but the Fulgo, and his muscles were enlarged and engorged with a power that negated the need for iron or steel. And though the war was ended, the physique would serve him well in his elevated position.

Yet, despite leading them to victory, the Five felt like they were facing a firing squad under the onslaught of questions and complaints from those they were said to rule.

Riker, Donnin, Nutrine, and Davimon stood with them, each representing a major city, but it was not from them that the people wished to hear.

"What are we supposed to do?" a man called out. "How are we supposed to lose our loved ones to the merge and see them as anything other than dead?"

"I can assure you," Shashara replied, "your loved ones are not dead. They are not all gone. They are simply whole, and we must all remember that to merge with another is a choice."

"Tell that to my boy," cried a mother, "when my daughter woke up with his marks on her hands and his mind in her thoughts. Twins, they were, and now…"

"Or what about my wife?" a man shouted. "She didn't choose. She stumbled, and a stranger reached out to her, and then she was gone."

A woman from Antro shouted above the noise. "On two separate occasions, I have witnessed for myself the merging of slaves and masters. Imagine the chaos when the servants were the ones to remain."

"Slavery is prohibited," Anliac stated, her eyes flaring as she pinned the woman in her place. "We will visit your city soon."

When the woman fell silent, Davad spoke. "People," he said, "change brings with it challenges. Right now, because the changes are fresh and new, even frightening, and in some cases…heartbreaking, it is easy to fight against them. However, if there is one thing that Set and Shashara have taught us over the past few weeks, it is that change, once it has begun, takes on a life of its own."

The questions did not slow. If the Five were getting through to any of them, they were lost in the crowd.

Hours later, the Five, with their entourage of rulers, guardians, and friends, made their way through the back gate of the tower and into the fragrant night provided by the grove.

"You did well," Nutrine told them, offering a slight bow to show his respect. "I would have lost my temper far sooner."

"Can you believe that guy?" Tristan asked. "To wish for the curses to be returned? To say we were the cause of a true curse? I wanted to punch his face in."

"There is nothing you can do to change willful igno-rance," Anliac told him. "Nor can one do much with willful tenacity," she said, shooting a loving glare at Shashara.

Davad, leaning heavily on the engraved, silver staff Ra-zoran had pulled from Triton's cabin wall, paced a few steps before forcing himself to stop. Clearing his throat, he spoke to those not of the Five. "We cannot begin to express our gratitude for your support, and we will work diligently to repay that support with equal loyalty. But for now, we would ask for a moment alone. We have one more ending before we can embrace our new beginnings."

"I have heard of your plans to divide and conquer," Nu-trine said, smiling. "Remember, Certamen lies at a crossroad to all your paths, and we are already known as the city of angels."

Tristan chuckled. "You'd better hope the archangel nev-er hears you say that," he said, clasping Nutrine's forearm before nodding at the members of the Pero.

"Riker," Set told him, "Anliac and I have not forgotten our vow to see Paulus Regia returned whole, but..." He shook his head. "I'm no good to anyone the way I am. The psyches in my head were dangerous before, but with the power I now possess, I must deny them access until I can control it myself."

"Palus Regia will be fine," Riker assured him. Then, bowing to Anliac, he said, "And the House of Aquam will always be waiting for its master."

Davimon placed his hands on his hips and shook his head. "A man kneels and offers his sword in service to a new king," he said with his crooked grin, "and the king offers him a crown to a destroyed city..."

Tristan stretched out his hand, and the two men clasped forearms before tugging each other into a backslapping embrace. "Will Lishous be returning to Regia Aquam with you? Well," he interjected, with a glance at Anliac, who only grinned, "to what's left of it, I mean?"

"No," Davimon told him, "and I was as shocked as that look on your face says you are, but he said there are more important things than personal vengeance to attend to." When Anliac winced, he said, "I did not mean..."

She cut him off. "You asked us not to kill Normis, but I'm not yet as evolved as Lishous. Those twelve were more than mercenaries. They were Triton's friends, most of our parents' friends, and they died as our protectors. I couldn't let him live, Davimon," she said. "We know what he did for you. We know that he saved your life, but it would have been an injustice for his crimes against so many to go un-punished."

"Though I am made a King—" Davimon took up her hand and placed a kiss to the back of it— "I am and will remain a faithful servant to the Five." His shoulders sagged a moment under the weight of a heavy heart, but to ease the weight he saw in Anliac's furrowed brow, he said, "It had to be done, Anliac. I do understand. Although," he teased to make her smile, "you could have left me the fortress." At the turn of her lips, he added, "I'm just saying." He shrugged his shoulders and grinned.

With handshakes or hugs exchanged, Riker and Nutrine took leave. Donnin said, "I'll wait inside for when you're ready," and then he, too, was gone.

For a time, left alone, the Five stood as silent sentinels in the night as the magnitude of their journey struck home. At last, the silence was broken by the sound of Shashara's tears.

"So this is it," she whispered. "This is where we say goodbye?"

"You and Set can always join us in Imbellis," Anliac told her. "Davad is right. Pisces Stragulum is not large enough to be the seat of power in Superi."

"No," Shashara declined with a sad smile. "Devias did not gift us with all this knowledge to play politics. We will build an institution for higher learning and for experimentation towards technological evolutions." Her visage was ethereal in her excitement. Giving Set the shy smile she saved only for him, she said, "We will make Satio Mapalia the cornerstone of knowledge and learning. Beginning with," she told them, "finding answers to our questions about Superi's gravity."

"Why start there?" Davad asked.

Shashara shrugged. With a grin, she said, "That way, if we make things go boom, there's less people getting blown up."

"Set…" Davad shot him a look that brooked no argument. "You will not blow up my sister." Mischief added sparkle to Set's starburst eyes when he grinned back at her brother. "I'll put all my minds to work on it."

"Yes," Shashara said, reaching up to run her fingers through his hair before letting her hand cup his cheek. "We are."

"This does not make me feel better." Davad scowled.

Set laughed. "I still can't believe you turned down Triton's ship." He captured Shashara's hand to lace his fingers with her own.

Davad's hand fell to the wound in his thigh, the one that would never heal, and rubbed at the dull ache. "A man needs both legs to work a ship and 'Captain' is not a title I've earned. I don't know what Triton had been thinking, but that schooner belongs to Razoran. Now him passing it over... *That* I can't believe.""

"Triton was the only tie to the oceanus that Razoran had ," Set explained. "I know," he said, "because Razoran showed me the coin Triton left to see him safely back to Dura Mortis, along with a letter that delivered his last order."

"What was it?" Davad asked.

Set's voice broke, but he answered, "That he would live for them both."

"Skylar sure rose through the ranks at lightning speed," Shashara said to lessen the sting of Triton's memory. "I think the men will like having a woman running roughshod over them."

"They'd better not," Davad barked a little too fast, and they laughed. Knowing they would all soon leave, he shrugged his shoulders and confessed, "She's the most beautiful creature I've ever seen, and Pisces Stragulum is the city she calls home. I will stay and make it strong for her."

"Oh, little brother..." Shashara smiled. "It is not Pisces Stragulum that she calls home. You are."

"Even better, sis," he said, "because I want what you and Set have, what Anliac and Tristan have found in each other. I never care to find the one I could merge with, because I have found my other half in her."

"The hour grows late," Anliac said, "but I hate not knowing when we might see each other again."

"And for that..." A tall man in multicolored robes came bustling up from the tower door, his wild white hair and bushy beard misplaced by the wind of his rush. "I have a solution."

"Socmoon," many voices said at once as smiles replaced their somber mood.

"Yes, yes," he said, "I have come to offer my services to the new rulers of Superi. It matters not if you stay as one house, or if you choose to spread out and span the world. I will keep you united in mind. I offer you my foresight so that none will ever seek to undermine the will of the Five. What?" he asked when they stared, slack-jawed and unresponsive.

Anliac grinned. "I understood every word you said."

"What's changed?" Davad wanted to know.

"Haven't you heard?" Socmoon asked. "The curses have been lifted, and with it, the curse of colorful words." He laughed. "Wretched thing," he said, "poetry."

"That is good to know," Tristan said, "considering we leave here for Dura Mortis."

"You will not go alone," Razoran said, exiting the same door from the tower that Socmoon had used. He approached with a pack slung over his shoulder. "Here or across the world, I serve the Five. It's what my captain would have wanted."

"How long have you been standing there?" Set asked.

"Not long," he replied. "Socmoon caught up to me in the city. After telling me to prepare for travel, he told me where to find my companions. Donnin is…" He glanced at the door. "He's here now."

Set took a centering breath and three portals, showing the reluctance of their conjurer, crackled in complaint as they opened. "We were reborn on the night this began," he said. "Determined, we vowed that what had been taken from us would be reclaimed. To keep that vow, we started a revolution that reignited a war, then we delivered a retribution that will never be forgotten. So now, though we take different paths into our future, our journey has forged us as one."

"Long live the Five," Socmoon vowed, "and long may you reign."

Superi World Series

Clint Thurmon & Christina R. Williams

Reborn

Book 1

Reclaimed

Book 2

Revolution

Book 3

Reignited

Book 4

Be sure to check out books 1 through 4 of the Superi Series!!

Clint Thurmon

Author and Creator of The Superi Series

Clint Thurmon is a native Texan. He lives in Southeast Texas with his wife Crystal, and has an adopted daughter, four sons, and a baby girl. Clint works as the director of projects of high voltage construction. He enjoys an active lifestyle involving several forms of martial arts, as well as physical training and weight lifting. Highly ambitious, and extremely motivated, Clint has proven that one can have it all; a loving family, a great job, and the world of Superi placed between the covers of a book; making his dream a reality.

Christina R. Williams

Author of Twisted and Armour
Co-Author of The Superi Series

Christina Ranae Williams was born in Claremore, Oklahoma. She currently resides in Southeast Texas with her husband and three children; where she's spent the last thirteen years focusing on her family. At thirty five, she's made the decision to turn to the next chapter of her life, by embracing her passion for writing; reaching for her dream with the help of Superi's creator Clint Thurmon.

www.ingramcontent.com/pod-product-compliance
Lightning Source LLC
Chambersburg PA
CBHW030644120726
47905CB00001B/50